BURNING MAN

BURNING MAN

ALAN RUSSELL

THOMAS & MERCER

Published by Thomas & Mercer
P.O. Box 400818
Las Vegas, NV 89140

ISBN-13: 9781612186092
ISBN-10: 1612186092

To Cynthia,
Who never gives up.

PROLOGUE:

HELLFIRE AND DOGS OF WAR

Even before I pressed down hard on the gas, Sirius was aware that something was up. The dog knew me better than I knew myself. The dividing window between us was open, and he pushed me with his muzzle. Sometimes he begs treats off me that way, but he wasn't looking for a handout this time.

"Whaduya want?" I asked in a Brooklyn accent three thousand miles removed from my own.

He rested his muzzle on my shoulder and I felt his hot breath on my neck. "Doggy breath," I told him, but he wasn't shamed at all.

"All right," I said. "It could be a big call, a *really* big call. This might be your chance to make Rin Tin Tin look like a pussy."

I moved my head to get a look at him, and he took that as an invitation to give me a lick.

"Cops don't kiss other cops," I told him, wiping away his slobber.

1

His eyes were sparkling. That's what Jenny noticed when I first brought him home. "Look at his sparkling eyes," she said. "They look like little stars."

"Twinkle, twinkle," I had said to her.

"What's his name?" she asked.

The dog had kept his reserve with me for most of our first day together, but from the moment he and Jenny met they acted as if they were twins separated at birth.

"His name is Serle," I said, curling my lip and using my most authoritarian German accent.

"What's that mean?"

"Armed," I said, "as in armed and dangerous."

The way he was already cuddled up in Jenny's arms didn't make him look very dangerous. "That won't do," she said. "His name is Sirius."

"You can't be *serious*?"

Jenny ignored me. The dog's ears had perked up when she dubbed him Sirius, no doubt because it sounded like Serle. "Just look at your sparkling eyes, Sirius," Jenny had said.

She named him after the Dog Star, the brightest star in the night sky. It wasn't a name exactly in keeping with LA's furry finest. His peers had names like Duke, Jake, Rico, Bravo, Tango, and, of course, Joe Friday.

The dog nudged me again. The traffic was beginning to slow us down and Sirius was anticipating my next move. "All right," I said and flipped on the siren. Sirius added to the sound effects with a few high notes of his own. One of the occupational hazards of being a K-9 cop is loss of hearing because of your partner's barking and howling.

I probably should have given him the German command of *Nein* or *Pfui*, but instead I said, "Shut up, Elvis." Sirius had been born and raised in Germany, but three years in California had him well on his way to becoming a surfer dude. He knew my slang well enough and stopped his howling.

The siren had its Moses-like parting effect, and once we were able to navigate through the blockage of traffic I flipped off the horn. Most of LA's K-9 units work out of Metropolitan Division, which means on any given shift we can be called out to handle situations over an area of 470 square miles. No one puts more miles on its cars than a K-9 unit does. When the call had come in, we were dispatched because we were the closest to Benedict Canyon.

The city of Los Angeles is rife with canyons, with neighborhoods built up and around them. Benedict Canyon is an affluent area, and its residents usually feel far removed from urban LA. The ravine starts in the Hollywood Hills and drops down in a north-to-south direction, ending in Beverly Hills. Even small homes in the BC area usually command seven figures. Residents are enthusiastic about their special enclave, but occasionally snakes slither into paradise. Decades earlier, the Manson Family visited a house in Benedict Canyon on a fateful August night and when they left, five people were dead, including the actress Sharon Tate, who was eight months pregnant.

As if on cue to that bad history, the wind began to whistle and wail. To my right I caught a glimpse of a huge shadow moving past a streetlamp, and turned to see a body-sized palm frond drop from the sky. As the branch struck the street, I could hear its impact even through the squad car's closed windows. The Santa Ana winds were blowing again, and it was a good thing LA was living up to its stereotype of not being a pedestrian town. No one was out walking, and those in their cars looked as if they just wanted to get home safe and sound. It was on nights like this that it was easy to imagine being back in the Old West. LA is the largest city in the country, but during Santa Ana conditions dust devils do their spinning, and tumbleweed can often be seen rolling on its streets. I had seen neither tumbleweed nor devils yet, but the night was young.

In that morning's *LA Times* there had been an article on the Santa Ana winds, which had been blowing for much of the week. The article had quoted from Raymond Chandler's story "Red Wind," describing those hot "winds that curl your hair and make your nerves jump and your skin itch." Chandler had said that when the Santa Ana winds blew through, anything can happen.

My partner was ready; he wagged his tail.

It was too dark to see much of the dusty movement of the hot air being funneled down through the canyons, but I could feel its surge. Every so often my squad car rocked back and forth as if it was being shaken by the draft of some big rig. The blow was pushing everything in its path, an unseen big, bad wolf huffing and puffing. Down the street I could see traffic lights throwing their colors around. It was like looking at the light show of a kaleidoscopic lighthouse. Nobody I knew liked Santa Anas—except for the serial murderer the media called the Santa Ana Strangler.

The Santa Ana winds blow hardest between November and March, and over the last two windy seasons the Strangler had strangled eleven women, each taken during a Santa Ana condition. Some of the tabloids were calling his murders "Gone with the Wind." Only minutes earlier there had been a hot call. A woman in Benedict Canyon had fought off an attack by a masked man with a garrote. Neighbors had heard her screams, and their pounding at the door had driven off the woman's assailant. Her attacker had been spotted fleeing into the darkness of the canyon.

In the distance a fire truck's siren called out, and then a few moments later another joined in, and then there came the sounds of a third. Sirius's ears were up and at the ready. I could tell he was considering joining the chorus, so I said, "Don't even think about it."

One of his two ears wilted.

I lowered the window and sniffed. A hairy muzzle joined me in that pursuit. Somewhere not too far away a fire was burning. Santa Ana winds and fire are a fearsome combination. As a patrolman, I had worked evacuations of neighborhoods during a few bad burns and been a reluctant witness to the winds whipping up the fires. It wasn't a detail I had ever liked. Up close you could see why Santa Anas are called the "devil winds." The Spanish word for Satan is *Satanás*; some believe "Santa Ana" is just the anglicized *Satanás*. The hot winds don't come from the desert, it is whispered, but from hell.

Sirius offered a throaty growl to all the unseen demons. If the demons had any sense, they fled the scene. Jenny had always been convinced the dog was privy to a world lost on us poor humans, and not just because some of his senses are so much more keen than those of any of us *Homo sapiens*. Jen and I used to laugh when Sirius tilted his head and cocked his ears, as if listening to a voice. Sometimes he'd even carry on conversations with that voice, making pleased and excited sounds. "Sirius is talking to God," Jenny would say; her tone was always playful, but I could never tell if she was kidding or not. Jenny thought Sirius was special.

The sirens were all converging on one spot: the same place where I was going. I was waved through several checkpoints; a cordon had been set up around the area. Even from two blocks away the smoke was bad, and where I was going it was worse. As I turned a corner I saw a house in flames.

Firefighters were running around, positioning their hoses. Winds were driving the flames high into the air, pushing the fire perilously close to neighboring houses. Fire trucks took up most of the street, and their played-out hoses made for hard speed bumps. An orange glow covered the area, and the shooting flames looked contagious enough to make me position my squad car for a quick getaway. Maglite in hand, I ran forward, scanning house numbers. Sirius stayed closer to my side than my own shadow.

There was shouting all around us. Some of the residents were grabbing hoses and filling buckets of water, ready to make a stand, while others were scrambling for prized possessions and in the process of evacuating. Everyone was looking for guidance, even the cops on the scene. Officers were being besieged for answers they didn't have. The night showed a lot of white eyeballs. Fire gets everyone's attention like nothing else.

Only one house on the street was on fire—so far. It was torching up like a bonfire, the flames licking high above the roof. The attack on the woman had taken place a few doors down from the house on fire, so I hurried past it. Squad cars and unmarked sedans were parked in front of the house I was looking for, and two officers were posted on the walkway outside. Their attention was more on the nearby fire than guard duty, but at our approach both of the uniforms stopped their eyeballing of the flames. One of them pointed to the front door and said, "The detectives are waiting for you inside."

As we passed by, both men inched away from Sirius, allowing us a wide berth. Fellow officer or not, my partner was a close relative of the wolf, and he did have big, bad teeth.

At the entryway I told Sirius, "*Setz!*" His body language showed me his unhappiness with the command. Every week, handlers practiced exercises called long sits and long downs, training designed to try our charge's patience. It was the dog's job to assume the designated position and wait for hours if necessary. Sirius would stay put even if he didn't like it. Inside, I could see that evidence techs were already working the scene, and from past experience I knew they preferred dog hair to not be a part of their trace evidence.

"*Bleib!*" I told Sirius, the German command to stay. He deflated and made a sound somewhere between an exasperated sigh and a moan that voiced doubts about my decision-making ability. The sound was familiar to me. I was known to make similar noises when given orders by superiors that didn't know their asses from a hole in the ground. I liked to think I could make that distinction. My partner's eyes tracked me, hoping for a reprieve, until I disappeared inside.

Crime scenes are normally handled in very deliberate fashion, but the nearby flames had everybody jumping. Two detectives from Homicide Special, along with a crime scene unit, were working the family room. Anything that might have a connection to the Santa Ana Strangler had the highest priority in town.

One of the suits recognized me and came over. I seemed to remember his last name was the same as some Ivy League school. Brown, I thought, or Yale.

"Cornell," he said.

On a multiple-choice test I would have gotten it. "Gideon," I said.

As he wrote down my name, Cornell said, "Where's the mutt?"

At another time I might have told him it wasn't my responsibility to know where his wife was, but not now. The room was already tense enough.

"Front door," I said.

He gave a quick, preoccupied nod. "We've gathered some clothing and other items the suspect came in contact with. We want your dog to get a nose full of eau de bad guy and see if he can pick up on his scent. We're pretty sure he's still in the canyon. The SOB must have known we'd try to seal off the area. I'll bet you dollars to cents he snuck out of the brush and set that house fire as a diversion."

The family room had a view out to the canyon, but at night it was like looking at a sea of black. The nearby fire hinted at the expanse of foliage in the ravine, but the light from the flames didn't penetrate far into the brush. A sudden flare of light in the darkness caught my eye; moments later there was a torching of undergrowth and shrubbery.

"I'll pass on that bet," I said. "Apparently one diversion wasn't enough."

Cornell turned to see what I was pointing at and then cursed. We watched the wind begin to whip up the flames. Both of us knew we were looking at a tinderbox. Under these conditions it was likely that dozens of homes would soon be in jeopardy.

"He must have brought some kind of accelerant with him," I said.

In a wishful voice Cornell said, "Maybe, if we're lucky, he'll burn up in his own hell."

From what I knew of the Santa Ana Strangler, his crime scenes were very organized. If this was the Strangler, he would have planned for an escape route even under extreme conditions.

"He would have expected a call to go out for dog teams," I said. "He set the fire to discourage pursuit and eliminate the possibility of being tracked."

"That's probably not the only escape plan in his bag of tricks," Cornell said. "At one of his other crime scenes a fire was also set and a witness described a fireman that was never accounted for."

It would be easy for a sooty firefighter to make his escape with all the chaos going on. Only seconds had passed since the canyon fire had been lit, but I could already see the orange glow spreading. The tracking conditions were already poor and would only get worse.

LA's K-9 units have weekly field exercises where officers take turns wearing padded bite suits and acting out the role of bad guy. Whenever the chief trainer for Metropolitan Division puts on his bite suit and calls for a dog to be unleashed, he always shouts one particular line from Shakespeare's *Julius Caesar*.

I voiced the same line: "Cry 'Havoc!'" I said, "And let slip the dogs of war."

Cornell gave me a look. "Huh?"

"If my partner is going to have any chance of picking up the scent, we have to act now."

Sirius was on a thirty-foot lead. His nose was to the ground and his body language told me that he had the scent. Handlers like to describe the way a dog tracks in missile terms: Sirius had the target on his radar. Whether he'd be able to close on that target and stay on the scent was another matter. The air was smoky. A wet cloth covered my face, but Sirius didn't have that luxury. He needed his nose fully functional, which meant he'd have to endure the smoky conditions without any buffers.

We entered the brush, following a trail into the canyon. The fire was about a hundred yards away, but it felt closer than that. The swirling winds were hotter now. I could hear the hunger of the fire as it feasted on the undergrowth. The snapping and crackling of the dry chaparral, and the gusting of the wind, filled the natural amphitheater with whistling and howling. Anyone sensible would have retreated from the chorus of hell. It's not natural to walk toward fire, but that was where my partner was leading me, and he was doing that because I asked it of him.

The fire was unchecked; firefighters weren't yet ready to take on the canyon's blaze. With every step I remembered why I had never wanted to be a fireman. My wet mask wasn't stopping my throat and nose from hurting, and the smoke was making my eyes tear. Most of the time I walked with my eyes shut, trusting to the senses of my partner. I was used to playing blindman's bluff with Sirius. Part of our K-9 exercises involved blindfolding handlers and then ordering our dogs to track. The training gave the dog the confidence to lead and the handler to follow. We were a team forged over thousands of hours of working together, and the death of the woman we both loved.

I made encouraging sounds. Sirius was no bloodhound, but his sense of smell was still about a million times better than mine. LA police dogs do a lot of cross-training, and tracking was a frequent exercise.

"*Such!*" I encouraged, using the German pronunciation, *tsuuk*, and telling Sirius to track or find, but even more often than that I said "Good dog" or the German words of praise "*So ist brav.*"

In stops and starts, we continued into the canyon, the elusive scent drawing us forward. We traveled on anything but a straight line. Sirius tugged me one way and then the other. Most of the time his nose was to the ground, but sometimes he raised it up and sniffed the breeze, doing his best to pick up the scent over the smoke that filled the air. He seemed oblivious of the nearby fire; I was anything but.

We navigated our way through patches of laurel sumac, lemonade berry, and sagebrush. With the Maglite I tried to sweep the area to avoid yucca and patches of cactus and jumping cholla. Sirius forged his way through thick patches of chamisa, and I followed him through the obstacle course.

The wind was driving an ever-more-muscular fire. Embers and sparks were being lifted and sent sailing. I raised my head and watched as hundreds of cinders came parachuting down around us. Most of the fiery offshoots were burning out before hitting ground, but I could see a few were getting footholds. Soon I'd have more than one fire to worry about.

No one would fault me for calling off the search. It was possible, maybe even likely, that if we kept going the fire would outflank us and cut off our escape route. And yet I was sure if we didn't continue the Strangler would get away, and once free he would kill again and keep killing. The Strangler was twisted, evil, and smart; in short, law enforcement's worst nightmare. There had been few breaks to come out of his cases; this was our chance to nail him.

Sirius sneezed, and without thinking I said, "God bless you." My partner acknowledged my words with a little wag of the tail and then he put his nose back to the ground and started sniffing. He wasn't thinking about quitting. Judging by the bounce in his step and his vigorous pulls on the line, he was locked on his target.

I took the leash in one hand, and with the other I pulled my Glock G28 from my holster. The glow from the fire allowed some limited visibility, but it was still difficult to see because of the curtain of smoke hanging over the canyon.

Sirius started tugging harder and making excited sounds that indicated he had the suspect on target lock. I was tempted to release the missile, but that would have violated protocols. Sirius wasn't the only one that had been trained. The department had pounded it into our heads to announce our presence and the imminent threat we presented. Opposing lawyers always argue that police dogs are just as much of a weapon as a firearm. Most of LA's canyons have squatters, transients, and undocumented workers that throw their bedrolls down in the midst of the brush. It was possible, with the smoke and bad conditions, that Sirius had mixed up the Strangler's scent with some other human's. As unlikely as that was, I couldn't take a chance.

I reined Sirius in and huddled with him in the darkness, making us as small a target as possible.

"K-9 unit!" I shouted. "Come out with your hands up or I'll send the dog!"

Over the crackling fire, I tried to hear or see any signs of flight. There was no answer to my summons. I called out again, this time in Spanish. My bilingual attempt also met with silence.

My right hand rested atop the crest of my partner's neck. Sirius's hundred-pound frame was tensed and ready to go. I never liked sending him into the unknown, but that was sometimes part of the job.

"*Still*," I whispered, telling him to be quiet in German.

As silently as we could, we closed in on a formidable stand of chamisa. The thicket was a perfect spot in which to hole up, offering up a barrier to anyone seeking entrance. As we crawled closer, Sirius began doing his pointer imitation. He knew where his prey was. We moved another five feet forward. I wanted to be as close to my partner as possible when I sent him in. You never let your partner hang out to dry.

We stopped and listened. Growing ever closer was the raging fire. It was difficult hearing anything over its roars. I raised myself from a crouch and gave the command that Sirius had been waiting for: "*Geh voraus!*" Go ahead!

Sirius charged into the undergrowth. I saw a blur of black and tan, and then out of the darkness it looked as if there was a rapid blinking of red eyes. I threw myself to the ground; someone was shooting at us.

"*Fass!*" I screamed. "*Fass!*"

People are always surprised to hear that police dogs need to be taught to bite. Thousands of years of domestication and breeding have taken the bite out of Bowser, but by using bite suits and training, and essentially making the biting into a game, K-9 handlers can reverse a dog's inhibition to biting humans. I was calling for Sirius to bite. If there'd been a command to tear off the Strangler's head, I would have been shouting for that. My partner heard the urgency in my voice and tore through the chamisa.

More shots rang out, at least a half dozen in rapid succession, and then I heard a man screaming "Call him off! Call him off!"

By the panicked quavering of his screams, I knew he was being shaken around like a rag doll. I had been on the receiving end of attacking police dogs dozens of times, and I was always glad that the padding of the bite suit was between their teeth and me. It was a humbling—and frightening—experience to be in the grip of those jaws.

The shaky screams grew even louder. The man was afraid he was going to be eaten alive.

"*Pass auf!*" I shouted; Sirius was now being told to guard.

The screaming stopped but not the whimpering. Sirius would stay clamped down on the suspect and not let him move.

I patted around for the dropped Maglite and found it. Only after starting to rise did I realize that blood was flowing down my leg. "Shit," I said. I was hit. The adrenaline that was still pumping had masked the pain. That wouldn't last, I knew. I was afraid of what the light would reveal and started sucking down air. What I saw made me breathe a little easier. The bullet had struck my upper thigh but missed my femoral artery. There was plenty of blood, but I didn't appear to be in any danger of bleeding out. I took a few measured breaths, fighting off light-headedness. My partner didn't need me fainting.

With an effort I got to my feet and then started limping forward. I shone the light into the brush and caught the glint of Sirius's eyes. Further maneuvering of the light showed that Sirius's jaws were clamped down on a wrist. His captive's face was so white as to appear spectral. Even the thick smoke couldn't cover the man's stink. Sirius had scared the shit out of him.

I moved the light back to Sirius's eyes. There was something wrong. His eyes weren't sparkling.

"T-tell your dog to let me go," the man said. "There's been some kind of mistake here. I'm a firefighter."

He moved his shoulders to show off his fireman's slicker. I said, "Shut up."

I fought through the brush, ignoring the inconvenience of my leg. Branches grabbed and clawed at me; I took them on in a frenzy of panic, and what I couldn't push through I snapped away, finally making it to Sirius's side.

My praise sounded so inadequate: "Good boy."

He was hit in several places but responded to my words with a wag of his tail. I tucked my flashlight under my arm and kept my gun up and ready. I scratched Sirius behind his ear where he liked it best and my fingers came back bloody.

"Your dog broke my arm I think. It hurts like hell."

I didn't reply other than to put the light on the suspect and then scope out the area around him. Sirius's attack had knocked his gun out of his hand, but not before it had done its damage. I pushed aside some brush and pocketed the weapon.

"This is all a misunderstanding," he said. "I came out here to set a backfire. I thought you were the arsonist."

"If you say another word without my leave to speak I will shoot you dead."

He could hear that I meant what I said. All my attention was on Sirius. "What a good dog," I told him, and he wagged his tail once more, but this time the motion was weaker.

"*Aus*," I said, telling him to let go.

Sirius released his hold on the hand, and then let his head drop to the ground. His body language told me he was pleased he had done his job. It also told me what I didn't want to see.

"No," I said to him. "You are not going to die!"

Sirius didn't understand my words but heard their urgency. He tried raising himself up but couldn't do it.

"You're going to help me carry him out," I told the Strangler. "If you try to escape, I will shoot you. If you stumble, I will shoot you. If he dies before we make it out of here..." My voice caught a little, but I managed to finish the sentence: "I will empty my gun into you. Do you understand what I'm saying?"

It wasn't Miranda, and I didn't give a damn. He nodded.

The fire was closing in all around us. I didn't give a damn about that either. My partner was dying.

We lifted Sirius up and started moving in what I thought was the direction of the houses. It was a guess, though; the smoke was that thick. I didn't even notice my bleeding leg. Time was precious. With every step my partner was losing more and more blood. The smoke was a thick, stinging curtain. We were walking in a blinding fog that allowed no clue as to where we were, or which way to go. It was possible we were walking around in circles, wasting time we couldn't afford to lose. Sirius was making sounds I'd never heard before—scary sounds that came from a body failing him—and then he had a seizure or a series of seizures, and we had to stop walking to put him down. He fought through his spasms and I felt his chest; it was still rising and falling. The seizure wasn't a death rattle. My partner was still with me.

"It's all right," I told him. "I'm here. You hold on, you hear me? We're going to get you help."

Just behind us, a stand of pampas grass torched up in flames. The Strangler screamed, "We have to leave the dog!"

He started to move away, and I raised my Glock and aimed at where his heart was supposed to be. "No!" he yelled, just in time.

The murderer spared me from murder.

We picked up Sirius once more. His breathing sounded like an overheating radiator. Blood was filling his lungs. I motioned the way to the Strangler with my gun. There was no path to go but through fire. We stumbled forward, and it was so hot our flesh began burning, but I wasn't about to leave my partner. The Strangler screamed as his clothes and skin smoked and burned, but he knew I would shoot him if he dropped Sirius.

We avoided fire as best we could, but there was no getting away from it. The inferno was everywhere. "Trailblazing" took on a whole new meaning. I tried to see through the flames, but my eyes had been pummeled by the smoke and were puffy to the point of closing up on me. The Strangler began coughing violently, but even over his paroxysms I could hear the horrible wheezing of my partner. Show me the way, I thought. Maybe I croaked the words aloud. There was a part of me that recognized my flesh was on fire, but that didn't stop me. I couldn't let my partner down. I looked around, trying to see anything. The smoke had blotted out the heavens save for two stars.

"We'll go past the second star and straight on till morning," I said, and the Strangler didn't object.

It was the route to Neverland, at least according to Peter Pan. The Strangler followed my lead, which was better than staying and burning in hell. As we made our way through fire, more of our clothing burned away. There was no escaping the heat; it burned from all sides. Peter Pan hadn't mentioned that. Still, it seemed to me that Neverland was getting closer and closer.

We pushed through some burning chaparral and into a clearing. Water splashed over us and our bodies smoldered, the smoke rising from our rags and fur. The helping hands of surprised firefighters reached for us, and I had enough presence of mind to announce that I was a police officer.

As paramedics rushed over to us, I hurriedly cuffed the Strangler. "We're okay," I told them. "It's my partner you need to help!"

That didn't stop them from trying to help us. "My partner," I said again.

Crazy people carrying guns tend to get your attention. The EMTs ran a few lines into my unmoving partner. Only after Sirius received medical treatment did I allow myself the luxury of passing out.

CHAPTER 1:

NOBODY EXPECTS THE SPANISH INQUISITION

Returning from Neverland was harder than getting there. Some days I wondered if I'd ever get back.

The limo chauffeuring us pulled up to the curb of the Westin Bonaventure. I hadn't wanted a limo, but the department had insisted. Sirius had liked the ride. The limo had a sunroof that opened, and my partner had enjoyed periscoping his muzzle out the car to catch the breeze. Still, he probably would have been just as happy sticking his head out the window of a MINI Cooper.

The driver ran around and opened our door. I had Sirius on a leash, and Sergeant Maureen Kinsman had me on one, or thought she did. Maureen works out of LAPD Media Relations. She is young and wears more makeup than any cop I have ever seen, including those that work John Patrol. Maureen was perfect for her job. She liked to talk nonstop, which made it easy for me to keep our conversation going with only an occasional nod.

"Once we get to the banquet room, I'm going to introduce you to Kent McCord," she said. "He told me he wanted to meet you before the presentation."

The door opened, and I started as some flashes went off. Three photographers were there to meet us. Hotel guests turned and rubbernecked, assuming that the paparazzi had a star in their sights. What they saw was a slack-jawed man with a scarred face and a scruffy-looking dog.

"The press is all over this," Maureen said, apparently delighted. I did my best to approximate her good cheer.

Somewhere in my therapy I had heard the phrase "Fake it until you can make it." I don't know whether a fellow burn patient said it or a therapist, but for the last six months, faking had become a way of life for me. Because I wanted nothing more than to get back on the force, I was doing everything I could to avoid a forced disability retirement. After Jen's death I didn't really have a life; I only had a job. Getting severely burned had put that job in jeopardy, which terrified me. That was one of the reasons I had agreed to this luncheon. I wanted to show the brass that I was still part of the team.

Sirius and I followed Maureen. She kept up the conversation for all three of us. All I had to do was offer up my best Bobby McFerrin "Don't Worry, Be Happy" face, which wasn't so easy with my scarring. Lots of eyes took notice of us as we walked through the hotel. I told myself that Sirius was drawing their attention, not my face.

I had been brought in with burns on over half of my body surface area, and a good many of those were third-degree burns, or what medical professionals call full-thickness burns. That meant there were patches of my body where all my layers of skin had been burned away. It also meant six months and counting of skin grafts, operations, and physical therapy.

When I look at my naked body in a mirror, the patchwork designs from all the skin grafts make it appear as if I am wearing a harlequin suit. I am told that with time and more therapy the scarring will fade, but that for the rest of my life I'll be tending to what the burn people refer to as my "scar management."

I am not the only one dealing with scars and physical issues. Love me, love my scruffy dog. All during my rehabilitation my partner has been doing his own physical therapy alongside of me. I do my stretches and then help him with his. He thinks it's a great game; I wish I did. Both of us are working on achieving our optimal range of motion, or ROM, as our therapists call it. Sirius and I have both come far, but the fire and being shot took a lot out of us. Sometimes I think we're the Humpty Dumpty twins, and that neither of us can ever quite be put back together again. This is an opinion I keep to myself, and it's not something Sirius talks about either. Everyone thinks that Sirius is the perfect patient, and that I'm not far behind. He's the real thing; I'm the fake.

The mantra of my burn therapist, whom I call the Iron Maiden, is "rehabilitation, reconstruction, and reintegration." Those are apparently her code words for torture. Whenever I see the Iron Maiden I do my best Monty Python imitation and yell "Nobody expects the Spanish Inquisition!" She thinks I'm kidding, but I'm not. Every time I see my inquisitor, my heart races and I get cold sweats on those parts of my body that still sweat, which are those places where I didn't receive skin grafts. You don't sweat where you've received grafts, which is why burn patients are always mindful of overheating.

The Iron Maiden and I both share a laugh when I call her "my torturer." Around her I'm upbeat and put on my happy face. I know she's worked me as hard as she has for my own good. Her torture is necessary so that my tendons don't shorten, and my ligaments and joints will have the best possible function. Her therapy has worked for me; I now have full range of motion in my legs, arms, and hands. I can flip someone the bird as good as I ever could.

I let Maureen lead me through the hotel gauntlet. She chattered the whole time, and rarely needed me to join in the conversation. "That's a great suit," she said. "Where did you get it?"

Jen had bought the suit for me years before, but I'd only worn it a few times. The last time I'd worn it, I remembered, had been at her funeral.

"It was a gift," I said.

Maureen took up her monologue again. Under the suit she had complimented was a not-so-sharp-looking compression garment; what I called my hair shirt. I usually wear my compression garment twenty-four hours a day. It is a skintight layer of clothing that extends from my feet to my neck that's supposed to help improve my hypertrophic scarring. The Iron Maiden describes hypertrophic scarring as skin that exhibits the three Rs of being red, raised, and rigid. In my case there's a fourth R—the right side of my face. It's that which shows my trial by fire more than anything else. There's an angry red patch of elevated skin that extends from my cheekbone almost to my chin. When I catch people staring at the scar I say, "You should see the other guy."

Fake it.

My surgeons and doctors seem annoyed by this particular patch of scarring, perhaps because it's so visible. Nowadays, after more than a few operations, there's nowhere else on my body with as much hypertrophic scarring. Around my facial scar there are even a few nasty keloids. One cosmetic surgeon wants to try lipofilling my face, while another thinks I might be a good candidate for laser surgery. Those potential treatments will have to wait.

Still, someone up high must have decided my face was good enough to be seen in public. Or maybe my facial disfigurement, he or she decided, would better serve the department. It didn't take a genius to figure out that Sirius and I were being used to combat a recent spate of bad press suffered by the LAPD. Months earlier the governor had announced that the two of us would be receiving California's Public Safety Officer Medal of Valor, the state's highest award for heroism. Not long afterward, the LAPD announced it was awarding me its departmental Medal of Valor. When I asked about my partner being similarly honored, higher-ups told me that a recipient of a Medal of Valor had to perform an act displaying extreme courage while *consciously* facing imminent peril. Apparently they didn't think a dog could be conscious of peril. I did and threatened to skip the ceremony. When word of my potential boycott surfaced in the media, the department did a one-eighty better than Kobe Bryant and announced that Sirius would also be receiving a commendation. He was going to get a Liberty Award, the canine version of the departmental Medal of Valor.

Getting medals isn't so bad; getting them in public is. There was a reason for the pomp and circumstance, though. One commander had confided to me that heroes were always good for getting extra departmental funding.

"Here we are!" Maureen said.

I had never seen a meeting room so large. It was like one of those aircraft hangars designed to house jumbo jets. What made it even worse was that as cavernous as the space was, it was filled with people. My heart pounded and my chest and throat tightened, making it difficult to breathe.

"I need to make a pit stop," I said. "Is there a bathroom nearby?"

"There's one just down the hall," she said. "Why don't you meet me back here in five?"

"Five," I said and then took off with Sirius.

The bathroom had urinals on one side, stalls on the other. The stall side appeared to be empty. Sirius and I went into an oversized stall that was designated for the disabled. I qualified, even though I didn't want to. I sat down and fought off the shakes.

The week before I'd met with the departmental shrink, a small man with a big, bald head named Dr. Lockhart. Cops forced to see him call him Doc Rock Hard. Rock told me he just wanted to have "a little chat."

"How are you feeling?"

"I'm really encouraged. Every day I'm getting that much better."

"Many people that sustain injuries such as yours suffer depression."

"Not me," I said smiling. *"I'm grateful to be alive. All that physical therapy must be keeping my endorphins up."*

"Do you have any fears of what the future might bring?"

A shake of my head; an Alfred E. Neuman look of "What? Me worry?" "I guess I'm luckier than most. I have a very supportive girlfriend."

That helpful and imaginary girlfriend was the same one that I had invented for the mental health professionals at the hospital. Her name was Patty Norville and she was an elementary school teacher. Patty helped me with my exercises. The only drawback in our relationship, I said, was that Patty was a cat person. I always laughed when I said that. Patty was supposed to be coming to the next burn patient get-together. I had this feeling that poor Patty would be coming down with a bad cold just prior to the party.

"How are you sleeping?" Dr. Lockhart asked.

"Like a baby," I said.

"No insomnia or recurring disturbing dreams?"

For once, I was glad of the skin grafts on my face. There were no beads of sweat to give me away. If I'd been a pinball machine, I would have been going tilt, tilt, tilt, tilt.

"Not that I can recall."

Fake it until you can make it.

My deception fooled Rock Hard, as it had fooled everyone else. They had all bought into my clown act. Smokey Robinson's "The Tears of a Clown" had become my song.

I had investigated my condition on the Internet. According to the medical literature, I was a textbook case for posttraumatic stress disorder. During the day I can control my symptoms, at least to a degree, but not at night. That's when all hell breaks loose in my dreams. During any given week, I have the same dream three or four times. That doesn't sound so bad. The reality is that several nights a week I find myself burning to death.

The dreams feel real. Nothing in my mind tells me that I'm dreaming. I relive what happened. I smell the smoke and feel the fire. All my despair comes back; all my pain returns. My flesh manifests what I feel. When I wake up, my skin isn't just hot, it's burning.

When I was a kid I remember my friend Craig Steinberg asked me, "You want to see a match burn twice?" I told him I'd like to see that, so Craig struck a match, blew it out and then pressed the hot tip into my flesh. It hurt, but it didn't quite burn the flesh. That's how a match burns twice.

That's how it is with me. I keep burning. I am the burning man.

In my research I had found one doctor who had written about this phenomenon. He called the dream sequences "mental metabolization," and according to his research certain patients relived their burning again and again, "often very realistically."

His conclusion was an understatement. On a few occasions I awakened from my dreams of fire and pulled back my compression garments only to find my skin red and blistered. No dream should be so vivid. It doesn't help matters that I can't talk about my dreams to anyone but Sirius. I know the LAPD wouldn't give me my job back if there was any hint of lingering PTSD. It makes sense to err on the side of caution if your employee is carrying a gun.

That's why I was working so hard pretending all was well. That's why I had agreed to this public luncheon and ceremony. The truth is that most of the time I feel like the Martin Sheen character in *Apocalypse Now*. I am Captain Willard waiting for a mission in my hotel room in Saigon.

I took a few deep breaths. By this time Maureen would be looking for me. I reached out and scratched Sirius behind an ear, and he responded by leaning his head into my hand. His presence made the impending ordeal a little more bearable. We exited the booth, and I paused at a sink to splash down my face. As I patted myself dry, I avoided looking at my reflection.

We made our way out to the hallway. In the distance I could see Maureen standing in the midst of a circle of people. She was nervously wringing her hands and didn't seem to be talking quite as much as usual. Her head turned in our direction, and when she caught sight of us her relief was visible.

Pointing our way she said, "There they are!"

Several photographers broke from the pack. I didn't smile—with my scarred face, the result looks like a grimace—but I did my best to look affable.

One of the photographers directed me with his hands: "Can you turn this way, Officer Gideon?"

I did as he asked. Judging from the angle, he preferred my bad side over my good. I guess scars make for more compelling photographs.

"We need the dog in the shot," another photographer said.

"Give the lady what she wants," I told Sirius, and signaled him in his pose. My partner doesn't think he has a bad side.

Maureen introduced me to Kent McCord, who was emceeing the event. For a time McCord had been the face of the LAPD, playing the role of Officer Jim Reed on the TV show *Adam-12*. We posed for a few obligatory shots and then chatted for a minute.

McCord wanted my opinion on a few cop jokes that he was planning to use on the crowd. "Shoot," I said.

"How many cops does it take to screw in a light bulb?" he asked.

"How many?"

"Just one, but he's never around when you need him."

I gave it a thumbs-up, so he tried another. "So this man has to work late, and when he's driving home he gets pulled over for speeding. Now the cop notices the driver has these tired-looking eyes, so he says to him, 'Sir, I can't help but notice that your eyes are bloodshot. Have you been drinking?' The driver isn't happy with the insinuation, so he says to the cop, 'Officer, I can't help but notice that your eyes are glazed. Have you been eating doughnuts?'"

It got a laugh out of me, which seemed to please McCord. I decided it was my turn to tell a cop joke. "So," I said, "how many cops does it take to throw a suspect down the stairs?"

He asked, "How many?"

"None," I said, "he fell."

"I might use that," he said, pulling out a pen and scribbling it down.

McCord struck me as a good sort. He didn't put on airs like other actors I'd met. It was unusual that Hollywood had actually selected someone right for a cop role. I had heard about one actor who put up a stink over having to wear a Kevlar vest during a shoot because he thought it made him look fat, but I didn't have a chance to tell the story to McCord.

"I'm afraid I have to break this up," Maureen said. "We're already running behind schedule."

The meeting room hadn't shrunk any in the ten minutes since I'd last seen it. There were probably a thousand people in the room, some of whom I actually knew. Friends and colleagues came over to pat me on the back and say a few words. It took Maureen a long time to get me to our table, which not coincidentally was in the center of the banquet room. There was a place for Sirius at the table as well, which gave me a little breathing room. He sat to my right, and I offered him a water glass from which he drank.

"I took the liberty of ordering Sirius a steak," Maureen said.

"I hope you ordered it extra rare."

Most of those at my table were LAPD brass, which required me to make small talk, but luckily all the well-wishers that kept converging on our table spared me from having to manufacture much in the way of conversation. I was shaking more hands than a politician on the stump.

Finally, the show began. In the front of the room the assistant chief was offering up the LAPD Media Relations version of what had occurred on the night of the fire. His description of events wasn't like what happened or like my dreams. The police officer he described didn't suffer from fear and panic, nor did he lose his mind for a time. It was a good war story, but not the one that I lived. I tried to ignore the stares directed my way, just as I tried not listening to what was being said. It was easier to think they were talking about some real hero rather than me.

Kent McCord was the next speaker. After his jokes, he talked about bravery, heroism, and duty. The more I pretended to be having a good time, the hotter the room seemed. I felt on the verge of spontaneous human combustion. That wouldn't be the kind of PR the department wanted, but I knew it would clear the room fast. I recalled Richard Pryor's line about racing out of his house when he'd been on fire: "When you're running down the street on fire, people get out of your way."

The loud sound of applause interrupted my musing. All around the conference room people were standing and cheering. Suddenly the space wasn't cavernous anymore; it felt small and stifling.

I motioned for Sirius to come with me, and as he struggled to his feet the applause redoubled. The old show business rule still applied: never follow a dog act.

Gene Ehrlich was the new chief of police. He had inherited a department rocked by scandals. Ehrlich came into town with more than a white hat: he was a cop with an MBA from Harvard. The top cop knew a good photo opportunity when he saw one and stood waiting for us in the front of the room. I tried not to limp but wasn't successful. Sitting sometimes does that to me; the fire had forever taken some of the elasticity out of my ligaments. Flashes kept going off, and I was afraid that Sirius and I would be the new poster boys for an updated Spirit of '76 picture. I walked slowly so that Sirius could keep up with me. He was still dragging his left back leg. Television shows to the contrary, you don't get shot and recover overnight. His vet was confident his leg would come around in time. Sirius's fur had mostly grown back, but he was bald in a few places where the scar tissue had prevented his hair from coming back in. I was thinking about getting him several toupees. Like me, Sirius had lost a lot of weight. One of the things about severe burns is that you almost always lose weight.

We finally made it to the front of the room, but my torture didn't end there. I had to stand while the chief offered up more platitudes. Finally, at his signal, I lowered my head and he placed the medal around my neck. Chief Ehrlich didn't dub me with a sword, but the ceremony still felt knightlike. I found one more use for skin grafts. No one could see me blush. As the medal was draped over me, applause filled the big room.

After the chief was finished with me, he dropped to a knee and draped a similar medal around Sirius's neck. The crowd went crazy over that and then went even crazier when Sirius extended a forepaw for the chief to shake. I didn't tell him to do it. Sirius acted on his own volition, but the chief must have thought I directed him. As the moment was captured by the media, the chief was smart enough to know that the picture of top cop and hero dog was going to land him on the front page of every newspaper in the country. He could also count on the spot getting him two minutes on local television, and thirty seconds on national.

In the glow of that coup and while basking in the applause, the chief put his arm around my shoulder and whispered to me, "When you come back, Gideon, whatever position you want, you've got."

CHAPTER 2:

HAIL TO THE CHIEF

The goddamn fire kept reaching for us. The blast furnace was every-fucking-where. A frustrated tear escaped my eye; the droplet siz-zled on my cheek. I tried to hold my panic in check; my partner was bleeding out and I didn't know where to go. The fire seemed to be chasing us. We moved away from the worst of the flames but couldn't escape the smoke. It billowed, writhed and constricted; the black snake squeezed my lungs. Seeing anything was next to impos-sible. My eyes felt as if they'd been punched out. I struggled for air and it seemed as if I was only swallowing fire. My insides burned; my flesh was burning. In my arms my partner wasn't moving. With one hand I slapped at Sirius's fur, trying to put out a fire fueled by his coat. With my other hand I held him tight, along with my gun. If the Strangler made a run for it, even hell wouldn't stop me from shooting him. And then, from all sides of us, a wall of fire rose up and dared us to pay the price of passage.

My partner's muzzle pushed at my face, and my first thought was that he was still alive, thank God. And then I realized that Sirius was there at my side to deliver me from my after-fire. The jolt of awareness that came with knowing I was in the here and now made me feel as I had just jumped into ice water. My flesh stopped sizzling and I gasped, taking in air.

And then there came to mind the image of me standing in front of Chief Ehrlich. What I saw and felt didn't make me feel any better.

I looked at the clock. It was 3:07. In less than seven hours I had an appointment with the chief. I patted Sirius to show him that I was all right. Because of my dreams, he always slept on the floor next to my bed. Drained from my fire walk, I tried to go back to sleep. I never dreamed of fire more than once a night, or at least I hadn't so far, and maybe because of that I slept again.

At half past seven I was up for good. Physically, I was almost back to where I'd been before the fire. For more than a year I had never missed a physical therapy session, and I worked just as hard on my own. To a casual observer, the scarring on my face was the only telltale clue of my injuries.

I had thought that my physical recovery would put an end to my burning dreams, but my dreams hadn't cooperated. There were times when I didn't wake up burning for two or three nights in a row, but every time I began to hope that my fires were behind me my dreams always returned with a vengeance.

Perchance to dream, perchance to burn.

I kept my condition a secret because I knew bringing in a shrink would derail, or at a minimum delay, my getting back on the force. The way to stop my dreams, I thought, was by getting back to who I was before the fire.

Jen had been the photographer in the family, and she'd turned the video camera on me a number of times during our five-year marriage. I used those tapes as reference material, reliving birthday parties and Christmas gatherings, and even watching home improvement videos of me building a deck and painting our new house. The guy I studied was confident, even with paint on his face. He had a one-liner for everything. He was a man who spoke his mind, usually managing to do it with a wisecrack. The person on the tapes came across as a tough guy, but he softened whenever he was around his wife or dog. It hurt a little—you could even say it burned—reviewing these tapes, but I did it to try to remember who I was and how I should act. In looking back at the tapes, I realized that I had been an innocent, unprepared for life without my wife and the firestorm that was coming at me.

I learned from the tapes and did my best to play the former me. My imitation was good enough to fool almost everyone, but it didn't stop my fire walking. I burned, and I burned again and again. Because of the frequency of my fiery dreams, I kept expecting that over time I would build up a tolerance to them, but that still hadn't happened. My night terrors continued to plague me. Maybe there are some things you can't, or shouldn't, get used to.

Still, there was one strange benefit from my burning dreams that I thought of as the "moment after." When I realized my flesh wasn't really afire, my heart would stop its thundering and relief would rush over me. It was then that I had my moment of clarity; or sometimes, like this latest episode, it was more like a moment of ambiguity.

Maybe the sudden reprieve my body experienced after my fire dream made it relax in such a way that a kind of window opened. Maybe I had to pay a high price for gaining insight of any kind. It's not like the moment after was a gift from the gods, or that it made me Confucius or anything, but it often gave me a perspective that I wouldn't otherwise have had. Earlier in the week I had gotten this image of the Iron Maiden reacting to one of my pranks. The Iron Maiden is big on Norman Vincent Peale–type messages and loves posting rah-rah words up on the walls. Her pearls of wisdom for the week had been "Hard work pays off in the future," and "The early bird gets the worm!" When no one was around, I had used a Sharpie to add my own editorials below hers: "Laziness pays off now," and "The second mouse gets the cheese!" At the time I was pleased with my handiwork; everyone laughed when they saw what I wrote, including the Iron Maiden. But in my moment-after insight I could hear the false notes in her laughter and see the disguised hurt on her face. The Iron Maiden's cheerleading routine might not have been sophisticated but it was heartfelt, and in my moment of clarity I could see that I had pissed on her efforts. Sometimes what you see in the mirror isn't always pretty.

It was easy to imagine how and why the Iron Maiden had come to mind. My subconscious—probably tired from working overtime on my own pyre—had cued me into my inappropriate behavior. But my latest middle-of-the-night vision of Chief Ehrlich wasn't as easy to interpret.

In some ways my conjuring up the chief shouldn't have come as any surprise to me. The doctors had finally approved my going back to work, and today was the day I planned on cashing in his marker. I wanted Robbery-Homicide Division, what LAPD cops called Homicide Special. That was what I was going to ask him to deliver. I had thought I was sure about that, but my moment after was making me have second thoughts about my game plan.

In my postdream awakening I had this sense that the chief was offering me a job in Robbery-Homicide. That's what I was expecting from him. What I didn't expect was my coming to the job interview naked. What was worse was that my unclothed body revealed the extent of my burns. My vision had distorted the picture of my body, making my skin grafts red and raw and all my flesh rigid. Somehow, my year of healing and all my gains looked to have been reversed. My body showed all the ravages of the fire and more. Instead of going forward, I had this sense that I was going backward.

It wasn't exactly Marley's ghost rattling his chains and talking to me, but the image of my body degenerating spoke to my doubts. Could it be possible that Homicide Special wasn't right for me? My subconscious, or whatever it was, seemed to be telling me that. It must be nerves, I tried to tell myself. Homicide Special was what any LA cop wanted. It was the top of the detective food chain. Besides, lots of people had dreams where they were naked, and even though my moment after wasn't quite a dream, it was close enough.

I tried to tell myself that there might have been some other reason I was naked in my vision, but the more I tried to convince myself of that, the more strongly I began to feel that taking the position in Homicide Special wouldn't be good for me. Doubting Thomas had seen his own wounds and they weren't pretty. Still, it was too late to be reconsidering the job. I had made my appointment with the chief to press him for this placement. That's why Sirius and I were now waiting in the antechamber of the chief's office. There was no fallback position I had in mind, no other job in the department that interested me. When you are prepared to ask for a boon, you better know what it is you want.

I ran my hand along my partner's head and neck. He was no longer part of the equation. Sirius's injuries precluded him from returning to K-9 work. That added to the emptiness I felt, but I hadn't brought him along just to feel nostalgic. Sirius was there as a reminder to the chief of what we had both given and what we were both owed. Besides, it was likely the chief remembered my partner more than he did me. The two of them had made the cover of *Time* magazine with their memorable handshake. There had also been a shot of me on the inside of the magazine, but the picture they'd selected made me look as if I should have been wearing the white mask of the Phantom.

Sirius and I sat waiting outside of the tenth floor suites at the Office of the Chief of Police (OCP). Two large desks manned by officers barred entry into that space. This wasn't my first time in LA's Police Administration Building (PAB), but I'd never been to the OCP. The new ten-floor limestone building had cost the citizens of LA almost half a billion dollars. The architectural firm designing the building had tried to construct it in such a way as to allow a sense of openness between PAB and the city hall building. Spatially at least, that seemed to have been achieved. PAB was part of the new LA skyline; city hall was to the south, the *LA*

Times building to the west, the Caltrans edifice to the east, and the Cathedral of Saint Vibiana to the southeast. The view from the tenth floor was so impressive you didn't even notice the smog.

After a twenty-minute wait a smiling administrative assistant, definitely a civilian, came out from the inner sanctum.

"Good morning, *Officers*," she said, showing a lot of white teeth beautifully set off by her mocha skin. "I'm Gwen and I'll be showing you to Chief Ehrlich's office."

"Don't blow it," I whispered to Sirius, but I was really talking to myself. My dog doesn't need a muzzle; my tongue does.

As we walked behind her, I reminded myself to be the old Michael Gideon, the one I'd studied on videotapes. I had practiced for this role; in another lifetime I'd even lived it.

The LAPD is the fifth largest law enforcement agency in the country. To put that in perspective, the FBI is the fourth largest. There are almost ten thousand officers serving the city of Los Angeles, not to mention three thousand civilians, including Gwen. You don't just walk in off the street to see the chief. Most LA cops retire never having had a personal audience with the chief.

Gwen motioned us into an office, and Chief Ehrlich came out from behind his desk to greet us. "Officer Gideon," he said, shaking my hand. "And my four-legged friend Sirius," he added, bending down and offering his hand. This time Sirius only sniffed at it, and a bit suspiciously at that. It was probably the "four-legged friend" comment.

"Please sit," Ehrlich said.

The chair I planted myself in would have been acceptable to royalty. Ehrlich took a seat behind his desk, crossed his hands and smiled for us. He was good about making eye contact and didn't seem distracted by the scarring on my face.

"I am glad to see you are both doing so well," he said.

"Thank you, sir."

He knew why I was there, but was still going to make me ask. No one doubted the chief's smarts, but he was only eighteen months into his job and the rank and file hadn't yet made up their minds about him. Ehrlich had come from outside the ranks of the LAPD. Because he had a number of eclectic interests and degrees in subjects other than law enforcement, the media liked to refer to him as a Renaissance man. His nickname was "the Professor." His proponents said the nickname referred to his time teaching at Columbia University; his critics said it reflected Ehrlich's tendency to lecture and be pedantic.

"The last time we talked was last April at the Westin Bonaventure Hotel, sir," I said. "On that occasion you said that when I was ready to come back to the force, you would see to a placement of my choosing."

The chief offered the barest nod. If I hadn't been looking for it, I might not have even seen it.

"The doctors have cleared me to come back," I said. "Unfortunately for Sirius, his injuries are such that he is no longer fit for K-9 duty, and he is now officially retired. Without him as a partner, I don't want to return to Metropolitan K-9."

I took a deep breath and tried to forget the view into myself that I'd experienced that morning. The vision that came after my fire dream wasn't infallible, or at least I didn't want to think so.

"What I'd like to be is a detective," I said, "with a placement in Robbery-Homicide Division. I want Homicide Special."

Ehrlich twisted his fingers into steeples and took a few moments before answering. "If you get your wish, have you con-sidered the ramifications?"

Only seventy-six detectives are attached to Homicide Special. Because those detectives work on all the high-profile cases, it's a job everyone wants. "I know it will ruffle feathers."

"It will do more than that. There's going to be a lot of talk about how the fix was in. Experienced detectives that have been waiting for placement on Homicide Special are sure to raise a stink. It's unlikely anyone at RHD will greet you with open arms."

"I can live without the hugs," I said. "I paid for the position with my pound of flesh."

"I won't argue with that, but walking into a hornet's nest doesn't sound like the best way to start off in a job."

"Is that your way of telling me it's not going to happen?"

"If you're set on Homicide Special, then I'll start the ball rolling. I think there is a better option for you, though, a position that I believe is suited to your skills, needs, and desires."

"Vice?" I asked. My self-imposed muzzle hadn't lasted very long.

Ehrlich chuckled, or at least made the attempt, and then asked, "Why did you go into K-9?"

"I like dogs."

"From what I understand you like autonomy even more than you like dogs."

If he thought I was going to argue, I didn't. I couldn't.

"Before taking this meeting, I put in some calls to people that know you."

I tried to look surprised, but the truth is that I had heard from several people the chief had talked with. The chief had told them to keep it on the QT. I knew that because that same phrase was used by a few of my sources, even if I wasn't exactly sure what the QT was.

"Everyone said you were bright," Ehrlich said, "perhaps to a fault. They said you were impatient, and that you use caustic humor as a defense mechanism. Is that about right?"

"Sometimes the humor is more puerile than caustic."

The chief didn't slap his knee, but he didn't appear to take offense either. "How is it that you became a cop?" he asked.

"I was a sixth-year senior at Cal Northridge and was being forced to reluctantly graduate. There was a job fair on campus and I started talking to some cops manning the booth. My first question was about the department's retirement package, and they told me right then and there that I was LAPD material."

"What was your major?"

"For five and a half years it was undeclared, which seemed to suit me, but then the Northridge administrators said they were sick of me and that I better get my sheepskin in something. Since I had taken so many courses in so many subjects, I discovered that I qualified for the trifecta in anthropology, history, and humanities. If they'd let me stay another year, I could have had the pick six with political science, religious studies, and psychology, but I ended up with minors in those."

"It sounds as if you enjoyed school."

"It seemed like a good alternative to growing up."

"You're single I understand."

"You understand right. As you undoubtedly know, my wife died."

He nodded. "How did that affect you?"

"For a long time it was like starting and ending my day with a kick in the balls."

"What about now?"

"It's more like a kick in the ribs."

"Do you have any family?"

"A mother," I said, and then after a moment's hesitation I gestured with my head to Sirius and added, "And my friend with the mange here."

Sirius looked at me with his big, brown eyes. His mouth was open and it appeared as if he was laughing. I'm glad my partner appreciates my sense of humor.

"Your encounter with Ellis Haines made you famous," said Ehrlich.

Haines was the real name of the Santa Ana Strangler, who was now also known as the Weatherman. When you're considered the worst of the worst, I guess you're entitled to two nicknames.

"As I understand it," said Ehrlich, "you could have cashed in but didn't. There were all sorts of movie and book deals offered to you, but as far as I know you turned down all those offers. Why is that?"

"I wanted creative control and ten percent of the gross. They might have accepted my demands, but unfortunately Sirius was holding out for a lot more. When I told him they were considering a female poodle for his role, he went ballistic and there was no reasoning with him."

"You're right," the chief said. "Your humor is probably more puerile than caustic." At least he said it with a smile. "But let's call it what it really is: a wonderful defensive mechanism. And when you use it, most people probably forget the question they asked. I am still curious, though, as to why you didn't sell the story of you and the Strangler."

"Not everything's for sale," I said, "even in Los Angeles."

He nodded. I don't know if it was my answer, but the chief's mind seemed to be made up. "Your notoriety from that case has put you in a unique position. Like it or not, the city of Los Angeles looks upon you and Sirius as heroes. To the public, that's a designation that far exceeds rank. It's no secret that the department would like some of your luster rubbing off on it."

I was already shaking my head. "We did the required appearances. I am not going to be used as a glorified PR tool. I did the dog act. I won't do the dog-and-pony act."

The chief gestured with his hands for me to calm down. "I'm not talking about putting you onstage. Yes, your name would be associated with this office, and you might be required to serve on some committees and do some public outreach, but what I have in mind isn't some PR flak position, because frankly I don't think you're qualified for that."

"You got that one right."

"There's no name for the position I'd like to offer you, but what I need is much the equivalent of a devil's advocate."

I looked to see if the chief was smiling. He wasn't. I spoke to my doubts, and maybe my vision: "Are vestments optional?"

"In the Catholic church the official title of the devil's advocate was Promoter of the Faith. It was the job of the *advocatus diaboli* to present any and all facts unfavorable to the candidate proposed for beatification or canonization."

"I don't know how to break this to you, Chief, but I don't think you have to worry about anyone in the LAPD being nominated for sainthood."

"I think I'm aware of that, Officer Gideon," Ehrlich said. "What I'm trying to tell you is that every organization needs its professional skeptic."

I remembered my moment after, and how I'd had to confront my own festering wounds. I had even attributed a name to how I was feeling, a name I used again. "You're looking for a Doubting Thomas?"

"I am looking for a point man that can both think and work outside the box. Los Angeles is like no other police department in the world. Our citizenry call this place La La Land, and Hollyweird. We have a unique caseload, and periodically our department is forced to confront situations that are anything but run-of-the-mill. I am looking for someone who can deal with the unusual, the peculiar, the curious, and perhaps even the enigmatic."

"So you're talking about me working Elvis sightings and crop circles?"

"I doubt those would even raise eyebrows in Los Angeles. What I was broaching was the possibility of you working special cases."

"Where I would be your devil's advocate?"

"That position no longer exists in the Catholic church," he said. "I believe the church erred when they discontinued that post. Saints need exacting scrutiny."

"Sinners need it even more."

"Does such a position interest you?"

"What would I tell people? That I work in the Defense against the Dark Arts Division?"

"I have another name in mind: Special Cases Unit."

"And would you be the one deciding what a special case is and what's not?"

"That would be my prerogative, but I'd also expect you to be keeping an ear to the ground and working up cases on your own. With your injuries you could have retired on disability. It's clear that you're here because you want to be."

"There are some cases that fall between the cracks," I said. "They're low-priority and they shouldn't be."

"You would have carte blanche to work such cases, as long as they didn't interfere with your special cases."

"What's your definition of a special case?"

"Justice Potter Stewart said he couldn't necessarily define pornography, but said, 'I know it when I see it.' We'll know it when we see it."

"Would I be reporting to you?"

"You would."

"I am not the person you're looking for if what you want is a departmental snitch or a personal lapdog."

"Those are not positions I had in mind for you."

"You already have an Internal Affairs Division. I am not going to be playing your devil's advocate to other cops, am I?"

He shook his head and said, "Only if the case is deemed special."

"When do you want my decision?"

"How long do you need?"

"By week's end."

"That works for me."

I stood up and we shook hands. Sirius bounced up, but we weren't able to make our escape without the chief offering some more parting words.

"You should know," Ehrlich said, "that this wasn't a spur-of-the-moment offer on my part. I have been mulling over the idea of a Special Cases Unit for some months now, and when you arranged for this meeting, I started considering you for the position.

"I expected that you would come in asking for placement in Robbery-Homicide, and I hoped to be able to convince you to give the other position a chance. To that end, I was willing to sweeten the deal."

From what he was saying, he still was. "Sugar works for me."

"Upon your acceptance," he said, "you would be getting your detective's shield and with it almost total autonomy."

I wasn't overwhelmed and my face showed it.

"From day one of the job," Ehrlich said, "I'd have you on the transfer list to RHD. That way, if things don't work out, you can ultimately make your move to happier hunting grounds. You might have to wait a year or two to get placed, but by going that route there wouldn't be nearly as much acrimony."

That would be a better way of doing it, I knew, but it certainly wasn't a deal maker.

"And finally," Ehrlich said, "there is the designation of Special Cases Unit. The word 'unit' suggests more than one individual, and that means you would need a partner in special cases. Because you already have a partner, I see no need in breaking up that team."

Sirius's ears perked up, almost like he knew what the chief was saying. It was likely he was responding to his tone of voice. This was the sugar.

"Sirius will have office privileges with me?"

"He'll even have his own desk if he wants one."

"Where do we sign up?"

CHAPTER 3:

A ROSE BY ANY OTHER NAME

Rather than work out of the Police Administration Building, Sirius and I had set up shop at the Central Community Police Station. For almost a year Central had been our home. We were less than a mile from the PAB; close enough that its shadows could almost touch us.

As we approached Central I took notice of the looming presence of the PAB. "If it weren't for you, we'd be at the new headquarters," I said. "The chief must have heard stories about your fleas."

The truth of the matter was that I had opted out of an office at PAB. The high-rise wasn't a good fit for Sirius and me. I was well served by not being near all the big suits, and I hadn't wanted to have to take a long ride in an elevator every time Sirius needed to water.

One of the best things about my job is that I rarely have to report in to a supervisor. Central's captain might not be of like mind. Because we aren't directly under her command, Captain Becker probably wishes the chief had found a different home for us, even though she has never come out and said that.

"We'll be lucky if Captain Becker doesn't evict us," I said. "She's a cat person."

Sirius wagged his tail and waited for me to open the door. Cat person or not, the captain was a lot more affectionate with my partner than with me. She is the only one in the station that calls me "Detective." Everyone else has nicknames for me, all dog related. I am Hound Dog, Horn Dog, Junkyard Dog, Watchdog, Underdog, Bowser, Barker, and Fido. Dog food names and flea medicines are also popular. If the paw fits, you wear it.

As I walked in the door, the watch commander flagged me down. Sergeant Perez has a line of service stripes on his left sleeve, what other cops call hash marks. The hash marks bespeak his years on the job; his wrinkles do the same. "Hey, Alpo," he said, "I got one that's right up your alley."

The watch commander tends to forget that I'm not officially assigned to Central. He knows I work Special Cases Unit—what he calls "Strange Cases Unit"—and that I report to "the brass," but he likes to treat me as his extra uniform, or in his non-PC terminology, "my spare bitch."

"It's another abandoned newborn," he said, handing me the call sheet, "but this one's no Moses."

Moses had been one of my first special cases. His mother had set the newborn adrift in a basket in the LA Aqueduct. Unlike baby Moses on the Nile, the LA Moses didn't survive his journey. At the onset of the case, there had been the suspicion that the death of Moses was ritualistic in nature because of strange writing on the newborn's clothes and his basket. As it turned out, though, Moses's mother was mentally ill and had interpreted a one-day downpour as the start of the next great flood. She had thought she could save her son by putting him in an ark.

"If you don't want it, Sherlock Bones," Perez said, "just pass the case to Juvie and let ACU take over the investigation."

"You can count on me and my Hound of the Baskervilles," I said.

Perez passed over what information he had. Throwaway babies don't qualify as high-priority cases, because unfortunately they occur all too often. The baby had been abandoned on South Hill Street, which was nearby.

Sirius and I did an about-face and returned to the sedan. The traffic over to Hill Street was stop and go. It was that time of day when commuters were arriving to roost in their office buildings that make up the skyscraper skyline of downtown LA. Over the last quarter of a century, the downtown area has become trendy and expensive, home to concert halls, museums, and water gardens. Expensive lofts and upscale security condominiums have sprung up everywhere. I am not sure which has undergone more cosmetic surgery in LA—its residents or its residences.

As we drew near to the crime scene, Sirius started nervously pacing the backseat. Police dogs and fire dogs never really retire. "Relax," I told him. "You know how tech people get cranky about dogs shedding at crime scenes. But I'll make sure you have a seat on the fifty-yard line, all right?"

Sirius stopped his pacing. I flashed my badge to a uniform standing near the curb, pointed to where I wanted to park, and he lifted up some crime scene tape for me to get by. The forensic field unit was already at the scene, and Sirius and I watched a photographer leaning over a railing, clicking away. I opened all the windows halfway, and Sirius stuck his nose out the window and took a few sniffs. My guess was with those sniffs Sirius probably knew more about what had occurred than anyone working the scene for hours. Sometimes I don't envy his sense of smell.

When the sergeant gave me the call information, he hadn't mentioned that the baby had been abandoned at the foot of Angels Flight. I wondered if the baby had been dumped there on purpose, or if the station's name had inspired someone to leave her there. Angels Flight has long been touted as the shortest railway in the world. The cable railway connects Third and Fourth Streets. It was built at the turn of the twentieth century, serving the well-to-do in their large Victorian houses. Even when the neighborhood went south and flophouses replaced the Victorians, the railway managed to endure for more than half a century. Downtown redevelopment had brought back Angels Flight a half block from its original location, but a fatal accident in 2001 had shut it down for six years. The railway was finally running again, but it wouldn't be running today.

I offered greetings and nods but didn't engage those at work. Before doing anything else, I always take a long, last look at the dead. I bent over like a catcher, getting close to the ground, and tried to filter out my emotions and personal feelings; I was supposed to be the dispassionate cop. This time that didn't work.

At least, I thought, the baby hadn't been left in a Dumpster. She had been put in a cardboard box and placed behind a railing at the bottom of the stairway that connected the two streets. Pigeons flocked the area looking for their morning handouts, but the usual habitués that used the concrete embankment as a bench weren't being allowed in to feed the scavengers.

Looking up, I saw the face of what many called the new downtown. Imposing glass edifices filled the skyline, leaving the old downtown in its shadows. Angels Flight was supposed to be the bridge to those two worlds. Maybe there was no bridge to those two worlds.

It appeared some thought had been given as to where to abandon the baby. The cardboard box had been left in a protected spot above street level. During the day there was a steady stream of pedestrians that passed by the spot. Whoever had abandoned the baby had wanted it to be found. I continued to hunch down, thinking my cop thoughts. The area was fairly well lit at night, but it would have been easy to stay in the shadows and anonymously drop off a baby. It was unlikely that anyone would have trekked down the stairway from above; I had walked the steps a few times and knew the incline was both steep and long. No, someone would have pulled up to the curb and quickly dropped off the baby and box behind the railing.

I stared up at the empty tracks of Angels Flight. When it was in operation, one railway car went up while the other came down. The cars were named after famous biblical mountains, the one Sinai and the other Olivet. In Catholic school I had been told that Mount Sinai was where God spoke to Moses and where he waited to receive the Ten Commandments. Mount Olivet's history was no less storied—it was where Jesus retreated on the night he was betrayed, and where he said his farewell to the Apostles. I tilted my head back and scanned Bunker Hill. As far as I knew, no miracles had ever happened there.

Rising, I drew nearer to the cardboard box. Because of the incline, the box was tilted at an angle. I looked inside, and if I hadn't known better I would have thought some girl had abandoned her doll. The body was impossibly small. She was facedown in the box and draped in a blanket. Her face was planted deep into a small pillow.

The baby had olive-colored skin, but I couldn't really determine her race. The skin pigment of newborns often changes dramatically over the course of a few days. There were no visible signs of any trauma, but the blanket swaddled most of the body.

I swore under my breath, unable to hide my anger at the senseless death. In 2001, California passed the Safely Surrendered Baby Law, which allows a mother to anonymously surrender her newborn within three days of birth at any emergency hospital and most fire stations. The law was designed to prevent unsafe newborn abandonment. Nowadays, mothers no longer need fear arrest or prosecution for giving up their babies. Mothers that have somehow managed to keep their pregnancy secret for nine months can keep their secret forever and not be punished. It is a good and needed law, but another expectant mother had apparently not heard about it.

The uniformed officer posted just beyond the crime scene tape took my obvious anger as an invitation to comment. "You ask me, people should have to get a license to have children."

My grunt of acknowledgment was interpreted as encouragement to speak further. "I got a newborn of my own," he said. "As soon as I saw the kid, I knew the mother was felony stupid and didn't know jack about babies."

The officer knew a lot more about newborns than I did and my eyes dropped south to his tag. "What told you that, Officer Alvarez?" I asked.

"The damn box wasn't level, and the baby was just left face-down in it," he said. "That's an invitation for disaster. My wife would kill me if I put our newborn to sleep on her stomach. And the pediatrician must have told us a dozen times that you never wrap a newborn in a blanket, and you especially don't put a pillow in the crib."

His comments made me look harder at the angle of the box, and at what was left inside it. You don't usually think of a pillow and blanket as being instruments of death.

"The mother must have been worried about the baby getting cold," I said.

Alvarez did his imitation of Dr. Spock: "That's what sleepers are for." Then he added with cop disdain, "Of course the mother's probably a wasted teenage tweaker who didn't even know she was pregnant."

He knew his newborns but not his profiling. From working the last dumped baby, I'd learned that women who abandon their newborns don't fall into any neat category: they can be any race, creed, or color. College students are as likely to offend as high school dropouts.

"You were the first on the scene?" I asked.

Alvarez nodded. "After determining the baby was dead, I cleared the area and made sure nothing was disturbed."

"You want to name her?" I asked.

The officer rubbed his hands on his thighs, leaning one way and then the other, clearly uncomfortable with my question. "It doesn't seem right, naming the dead."

"No, it doesn't, but the baby's going to need a name before she's buried."

"I'll pass, if you don't mind."

"No problem," I said and then thanked the officer before returning my attention to the baby in the box.

My adoptive parents were churchgoers with an abiding faith in God. One of my father's favorite quotations was from the Sermon on the Mount, and he would often repeat Christ's words to me: "Not a sparrow falls to the ground without His care." I looked at the fallen sparrow; by naming the baby I would provide her with an identity. The memory of my last trip to a unique and troubling graveyard made me remember roses.

Rose, I decided, and my victim had a name.

I checked with the crime scene unit, making sure it was okay for me to do a close-up study of Rose. The blue blanket surrounding her was a polyester blend. A woman's white cotton T-shirt, size medium, swam over the baby. As I lifted the shirt, I was surprised to see that Rose was wearing knit pink bootees. Rose wasn't wearing a diaper, and her pink-streaked body made it appear as if she had been hurriedly washed before being clothed and deposited in the box.

There was some food residue on the blanket, crumbs of some sort. Forensics was probably already on it, but I'd double-check to make sure they bagged it. I removed the pillow, rested Rose on it and then made sure there was nothing else in the box.

The coroner's office would decide how Rose had died, but I was betting they would rule her death as an accidental homicide. Dumped babies aren't usually clothed or blanketed, and this was the first time I'd ever heard of an abandoned baby wearing pink bootees. My gaze lingered on her tiny feet. Someone should have been playing with the little toes and spouting nonsensical words about a piggy going to market.

"The mother hedged her bet."

I turned around and saw Della Tomkins, a veteran of the Forensic Field Unit. We had met at several crime scenes. On those other occasions, Della had been bright and cheery, but this time she couldn't even force a smile.

"We found a pair of blue bootees on the steps," Della said. "Mom must not have known the sex of the baby she was going to be abandoning."

I had heard that Della and her life partner, Abby, had been going to fertility clinics for the past year in the hopes of Abby's conceiving. They were doing all that they could to have a baby.

"Find anything else?" I asked.

"A few steps away from the box we found some crumpled cellophane wrapping with the remains of some partially eaten bread. We think the crumbs in the box match the bread. At first I thought it was banana bread, but judging from its aroma I'm now leaning toward pumpkin bread."

Halloween had come and gone a few months back. I thought of pumpkin bread as a seasonal offering, but maybe it was a popular item in the trendy bakeries or bistros that I never patronized.

Della stood next to me and the two of us contemplated the newborn. "I'm identifying her as Rose in the book," I said, referring to the casebook.

"I thought Lisbet named the newborns."

"She encourages the detectives to come up with a name. It's her way of getting us emotionally involved."

"Does it work?"

I didn't say, but Della already knew the answer. It's easy to depersonalize a baby Jane Doe, but not as easy to forget a forsaken newborn that you've given a name.

"Has anyone called the Saint?" I asked.

I offered up Lisbet Keane's nickname for what it was, a term of respect. An outsider had earned the begrudging high opinion of the coroner's office and the LAPD.

"I just finished talking with her," Della said. "She'll pick up Rose after the coroner releases her."

Before Lisbet had come on the scene, newborns had been cremated and placed in a mass grave in East LA. A decade earlier, Lisbet had seen a news spot on an abandoned newborn and felt called upon to attend to the baby's burial. While she was negotiating for a plot, two other dead newborns turned up. Though only a college student at the time, Lisbet had decided she would somehow find the money to bury all three. In the years since she had gathered up every abandoned newborn and seen to their burials. Lisbet's caring didn't stop with the dead—she had been the driving force behind establishing California's Safely Surrendered Baby Law. In only a few years, most of the country had followed California's example, and as a result nationwide there are now fewer throwaway newborns.

"I'll call her later," I said.

Even saints need to make a living. Lisbet was a freelance graphic artist, a job that allowed flexibility for her unusual calling. As far as I was concerned, she was too young and too attractive to be a saint.

I looked at Rose and said in a voice kinder than my own, "Don't worry, your adopted mom will soon be picking you up."

"Amen," Della said.

My eyes turned to the rail of Angels Flight spanning the heights. The railway didn't operate in the evening, but I hoped that sometime during the night it had made a special ascent.

CHAPTER 4:

THE CRY IN THE WILDERNESS

From inside the rectory office, I heard a familiar and comforting voice announce loudly enough for me to hear, "Well, we can't keep one of LA's finest waiting, can we?"

Father Patrick Garrity, known by everyone as Father Pat, was the pastor at the Church of the Blessed Sacrament on Sunset Boulevard. When people think of the Sunset Strip, they don't usually envision a church, but for more than a century the church has been a part of a neighborhood better known for its sinners than its saints.

"Get in here, Michael," Father Pat shouted. "I'd like to embarrass you in front of a few people."

I have never visited Father Pat without him telling the story of our first meeting to at least one person. As I entered the rectory, he stood up from his chair and opened his arms to the prodigal son. His hair was completely gray now, but the blue eyes behind his thick glasses were still young. There had been a time when I was sure Father Pat was ten feet tall. The physical reality was that he was half of that and resembled in build a well-fed friar. As he squeezed me tight, my holster pressed hard into him; for a moment his face wrinkled in distaste at his recognition of the weapon, but then he patted my shoulder and his smile returned.

He turned and made eye contact with a young Hispanic man wearing vestments who I guessed was the latest fresh-faced pastoral intern. "This is *the* Michael Gideon," he said. "You might have heard me mention his name a time or two."

Barbara, the church secretary, had followed me into Father Pat's office and stood there beaming and nodding, but the young priest didn't know me from Adam. Or Eve.

"This is 'baby Michael,' " Father Pat said, "the gift left on our doorstep."

"Oh, that Michael," the intern said.

"Yes," Father Pat said. He turned his eyes on me and said, "Your reputation precedes you."

"There's a reason I've never invited you to my workplace."

"I met Michael more than thirty years ago," he said, "back when I was svelte, handsome, and quite full of myself."

"It's hard to believe the svelte and handsome part."

Father Pat motioned for Barbara and me to sit down. He never let anything get in the way of his telling a good story, even if everyone had heard it before.

"In my early years at Blessed Sacrament," he said, "I was the low man on the totem pole. Part of my duties included giving the eight o'clock Monday mass, which always seemed a bit of an anticlimax after the weekend services, at least to this wet-behind-his-ears priest. On Monday I knew that only a small number of regulars attended mass, and it was always a rare Monday when I didn't think that my talents could be put to better use.

"As I was getting myself ready in the sacristy, I suddenly took notice of a strange sound, but because this has always been a neighborhood of strange sounds I decided to pay it no mind. The plaintive cry only lasted for a few seconds, and I was glad of that. I tried to convince myself that it was a stray cat, but I still couldn't shake this uneasy feeling.

"I told myself that I had no time for any wild goose chase, what with a mass to prepare for, but the truth of the matter is that I didn't want to be bothered. Still, I suppose I continued to listen out of one ear, for it was only a minute or two later that I again became aware of some faint crying. The sounds were weaker this time around and were gone so quickly I wondered if I had imagined them.

"Because the homeless and transients have long been a part of this neighborhood, I suspected the cries were human, but that wasn't enough to make me act. 'It's probably a maudlin drunk,' I told myself, 'grieving because he's run out of liquor.' On that self-righteous note, I tried to convince myself to not be bothered, but there was something oppressive about the silence. I didn't hear the quiet so much as I sensed this void. When I think back to that time, I am sure I was being given a test, and had I turned my back, I believe I would have failed it to the detriment of my soul. That is why, when I tell this story from the pulpit, I suggest that all of us need to listen to what we don't hear as well as that which we do, and cocksure priests most of all."

Father Pat gave a side glance to the intern and winked. "It was a cold January morning, much like the mornings we've been having this week, and I remember as I hurried outside my breath produced a vapor trail. I started in the direction I thought the sound had come from, making my way to the back lot, but I was stopped by a metal chain that was strung up to keep cars out. I was wearing my robes, and as I stepped over the chain I tripped on it. My fall was almost deterrent enough to send me back. As I lay sprawled on the ground, I remember bemoaning the state of my vestments and thinking how it wouldn't do for me to officiate mass with a tear in the left knee of my pants, and how I needed to go back right away so that I would have time enough to hurriedly change into other clothing. I knew full well that the regulars would not like it if the service started late, and that these particular parishioners would be sure to give me an earful if mass did not begin on time. Just as I convinced myself that I had to turn back, I heard a sound. It wasn't loud enough to be a wail but was more like a fading whistle. I turned my head and scanned the entire back lot but saw nothing.

"With a few very unholy words and an aggrieved limp, I decided that I couldn't leave without at least a cursory look of the area. It's probably a bird, I told myself, and I am just a bird-brain on a fool's errand, but my recriminations didn't stop me from inspecting the blacktop. I scanned the area and was just about to give up when I saw a movement out of the corner of my eye. The breeze was blowing along some leaves, pushing them to a spot in the corner where other leaves and trash were piled high by the wind. Back then my eyes were sharp, but I did not want to believe what I was seeing. I found myself staring at a small, still hand.

"Without thinking—perhaps afraid to think—I sprinted to the little one's side. I swept away the leaves and debris, and feared I was too late. The baby wasn't moving, and his skin had a bluish hue. I lifted the babe up and felt how cold his body was, but even as I despaired that I had come too late, my prayers were answered, for I saw him take the slightest of breaths.

"I tucked the naked baby into the folds of my robes and took off running as fast as I dared. On that morn it felt as if I sprouted wings, for the ground seemed to fly by under me. I rubbed the baby's arms and legs as I ran, but he did not respond and made no sounds.

"I raced in through the side entrance of the church, and when I appeared to the congregation I am sure that I looked every inch a madman, what with my bulging eyes, heaving chest, and torn clothing. I hurried through the sanctuary, pausing only for a moment to genuflect, and then ran through the nave. The organist stifled a scream and stopped her playing, and the congregation stood up to get a look at what I was carrying, but I didn't take notice of any of that.

"I made it to the front of the church and tried to remember what to do. I had only assisted in baptisms, and for a moment I froze before gathering my wits. I could not have this baby die before receiving the First Sacrament, and I was sure his young life hung in the balance.

"I reached into the baptismal font, and my hands were trembling so much that I spilled more holy water on the ground than I did the baby's head. Three times did I make the sign of the cross, giving unto the newborn both name and blessing: 'I christen thee Michael in the name of the Father, in the name of the Son, and in the name of the Holy Spirit.'

"Around me I heard a chorus of 'Amen' and only then noticed that the entire congregation had followed me to the baptismal font. Their presence and encouragement reassured me, and the words of the First Sacrament came a little easier: 'I christen you that you may know the pure and holy spirit of God, your eternal source of faith.'

"I felt a weight lifted off of me then, for I could see that the baby was still breathing. It also seemed to me that he did not look quite as blue. Because I had rushed through the administration of the First Sacrament, I decided to offer a Whispered Verse of Assurance, and for Michael's ears alone did I murmur a verse from the Bible.

"When I finished, I glanced around at all the curious faces. Everyone was looking at this baby with wonder and awe. I thought to conclude the baptism with an economy of words so that we could get Michael medical care as soon as possible, and so I raised him up with both my hands and offered him to God, saying, 'We pray for the care and protection of Michael in body and soul. We surrender him to your hands. Please, Dear Heavenly Father, bind your angels to bless and attend him always. This we pray in the name of our Lord and Savior Jesus Christ. Amen.'

"I am not sure if Michael responded to the holy water dripping down his face, or the way the audience was enthusiastically calling out 'Amen.' Maybe he was just warming up, or maybe Michael was reacting to being lifted into the air. It's even possible Michael was offering his own commentary on my baptismal efforts. All I know is that he was not the only one sprinkled that day. Suddenly, a stream fell down upon my head; with devastating aim Michael relieved himself upon me.

"There might have been one or two that tried to refrain from laughing, but their good intentions were quickly lost. All of us broke down laughing, and I laughed the loudest of all. I took that little boy's flow as a sign from God. Michael was going to live."

I had heard the story a hundred times but would never tire of it. Judging by the laughter around me, I wasn't alone.

"For years Father Pat has been threatening to immortalize that moment with a statue," Barbara said.

"Not a statue," the priest said. "I was thinking more of a tasteful stained-glass window."

"Remind me not to give to your building fund this year," I said.

"Michael is the only baby that I ever baptized twice," he said. "His parents wanted to have a more official baptism the second time around."

"But before Father Pat committed to a redo," I said, "he wanted written assurance that I would be wearing a waterproof baptismal gown."

"It was either that or me going to the bishop and asking if I could conduct the service in a bathing suit."

The church had used its influence to make sure I was adopted into a Catholic family. My parents had worshipped at Blessed Sacrament until we moved to the San Fernando Valley, but even then Father Pat had stayed in touch with me. Over the years our paths had frequently crossed. After my encounter with the Strangler, Father Pat had visited me often at the hospital. He knew me well enough to recognize that this time my visit wasn't just a social call. After the others excused themselves, Father Pat looked at me expectantly. We weren't in the confessional booth, but it felt like it. He took a read of my tired eyes, but I wasn't there to talk about my hellish dreams.

"I caught a case this morning," I said. "A newborn girl was abandoned."

I didn't have to tell him there was no happy ending. He nodded his head and closed his eyes in silent prayer. My eyes stayed open. I was a throwaway kid investigating another throwaway kid. My biological mother was never found; I would find Rose's mother.

CHAPTER 5:

CROSS-IMAGING

The door opened a crack, and a solitary brown eye peered at me suspiciously from behind the safety of a door chain. Even law-abiding citizens, those without so much as a parking ticket, are wary of talking to cops. When you have a face that's scarred like mine, people tend to be that much more suspicious. After being burned in the fire, I kept trying on friendly faces for size in the mirror, but what looked back at me were distorted grimaces and leers. It's been easier to not smile.

"I'm Detective Gideon," I said, showing my badge wallet.

The night before, I'd canvassed apartments in the area, and I had started knocking on doors again early that morning. If you want to catch people, you need to seek them out at odd hours.

I explained the purpose of my visit to the brown eye. When I finished, the chain came down and the door opened a little wider revealing a midthirties white male. "No," he said in answer to my questions, "I didn't see any baby or anyone carrying a box." He yawned and shook his head. "Isn't it early for you guys to be coming around like this?"

"I'm sorry to have disturbed you," I said.

I did my closing speech, the one where I handed over my card and asked to be called if something came up that might be useful to the case. Sirius and I were already walking away when the man called out, "Wait a sec. Aren't you the cop that took down the Weatherman?"

With my back turned to him, I offered a noncommittal wave. If he'd known anything about baby Rose, I would have lingered, but I could do without another conversation about Ellis Haines. That was a trip down memory lane I didn't need this morning.

The sound of music called to me from my cell, the opening notes to "Hail to the Chief." The chief is the only person in my cell phone's contact list to whom I've assigned a ringtone.

"Gideon," I said.

"This is Gwen from Chief Ehrlich's office calling, Detective. Are you available to talk to the chief?"

"I'm all ears."

"Thank you," Gwen said. "Please hold for a moment."

For some reason the chief never calls me directly. I don't know if it's an LA thing or if it's standard practice among the ruling class to have someone else do the dialing for them. I do know this is the town that invented the phrase "I'll have my person call your person."

As I waited for the chief I asked Sirius, "Are you my person?"

I heard the wind tunnel effect that accompanies speaker phones and then Ehrlich's voice: "Good morning, Detective."

I resisted the urge to put my cell on speaker phone to return the effect. "Morning, Chief."

"I have a new case for you, one that I'll want you to run point on, even though for media purposes it will be handled through Robbery-Homicide. A young man's body was found in Runyon Canyon Park. I want you to get over there before the story breaks and the media shit storm hits."

Most of the city's homicides involve young men, and usually such deaths aren't considered very newsworthy. The chief hadn't yet told me what was special about this case.

"What is it that will be attracting the vultures?"

"The young man was crucified."

I had seen too many forms of death on display, but this would be my first crucifixion. Ancient Rome suddenly didn't seem so ancient. Given a choice, I could have done without this history lesson.

"I'm on the way."

"Captain Brown will coordinate with you on this. He'll be contacting you shortly."

Brown was the chief's liaison. Behind his back he was called Radar, after the character made famous from *M*A*S*H**. He resembled the corporal and his weapon of choice was a clipboard. His other nickname was Captain Nose, short for "brownnose."

"Let's hit it," I told Sirius.

The two of us jogged back to the car. For now, the baby Rose case would have to be put on the back burner. Police work is nothing if not a series of interruptions.

The morning commute had already started; it was a good thing I had a cherry topper. I flashed my light and siren and surprised commuters as I passed by on the shoulder. A lot of conversations were interrupted as cell phones were tossed aside and drivers suddenly became law abiding. I was two minutes from the park when Radar called.

"Are you there yet?" he asked.

"Golgotha is almost within sight."

"That's the kind of comment the media better never hear."

"Afraid it might upset the money changers?"

Radar decided to ignore me. "A Parks and Recreation worker discovered the body, and the park was immediately secured and closed. The media has not yet caught on to what occurred."

I knew that wouldn't last more than an hour or two. Word always leaks out.

"The chief wants you to keep him up to date on this one. He expects there will be lots of scrutiny."

"You think?"

Crucifixions aren't everyday events, even in Los Angeles.

"I'm at the scene," I announced.

I clicked off in the middle of him saying "Call me when…"

A uniform was standing at the park's palm tree–lined southern entrance at Vista Street and Fuller Avenue. Sirius was pacing back and forth in the backseat, his tail wagging furiously. Runyon Canyon was a favorite park of his. Usually it was full of gamboling dogs.

I offered up my ID to the uniform, and after looking at it he said, "You'll want to park up the hill as far as you can, but even then you'll have a walk."

He looked around to make sure no one was listening in and said, "The body is way up the trail at a place called Clouds Rest. You'll see signs along the path directing you there."

"Thanks, I know where it is."

There were half a dozen cars parked in a ragged line near the trailhead, including the forensics van and the coroner's wagon. The parking lot wasn't far away, but something in most cops' DNA compels them to do almost anything to avoid walking any farther than necessary. I passed by the parked cars, but not out of nobility. Most visitors to the park enter through the southern entrance at the bottom of the canyon, and from there they choose one of two walking trails. The clockwise route is the shorter and less strenuous route to the back of the canyon and the eastern ridge, which is Clouds Rest. The counterclockwise trail is longer and harder, with more ups and downs.

What the other cops didn't know was that there was a third and shorter route to Clouds Rest that started from the lower fire road. Their way would have taken them half an hour of walking; my route would cut that time in half. I parked along the bend in the lower fire road, and Sirius and I began our hike. The 130-acre park is designated as "urban wilderness." It might not be Yosemite, but you don't have to venture far into the canyon before you feel as if you've escaped from LA. The park's southern entrance is just two blocks from Hollywood Boulevard, making it a popular getaway for Angelenos.

We followed an upward path that went along a dry riverbed. Before bulldozers and development, LA was chaparral country and the park is a natural museum to LA's former terrain. We made our way through sagebrush, flattop buckwheat, and laurel sumac. The muted greenery was typical of most drought-resistant plants, although occasionally we passed by some red-berried toyon, which all the locals call California holly.

The last part of the hike was the hardest, a steep rise that had me using my hands in a few spots to steady myself. All the climbs throughout Runyon Park are worth it. Depending on your vantage point and the smog, you can see everything from Catalina Island to Griffith Observatory to the Capitol Records building, but today I didn't stop to take in the view. I was thinking about what awaited me at Clouds Rest.

"Why would you pick this spot to crucify someone?" I asked.

It was out of the way but not that out of the way. Lots of people walked the trails every day. For some, it was part of a regular exercise regimen. The murderer wouldn't have been able to get in or out easily. And if you dragged a cross up a hill, someone was likely to notice. No, it wasn't the first spot I would pick for crucifying someone.

Sirius's ears perked up and his body went on the alert. He sniffed the air and got a preview of what was ahead. It was another half a minute before I saw the activity. A handful of people—forensics techs and the coroner's people—were clustered around a coast live oak. The tree was typical of its kind: it had a gnarled trunk and contorted branches and was rather compact, at least as oaks went, but it was large enough to be supporting a body.

The young man's arms were spread out along two branches, and his torso was backed up by the trunk. As I came closer, I could see the odd angle of the victim's toes. Because his ankles had been nailed into the tree, he looked as if he was pigeon-toed and walking on air. The victim wasn't wearing the loincloth associated with every crucifixion tableau I had ever seen. He had on running clothes, with lightweight Speedo shorts and a tank top that said BHHS.

I kept enough distance from the tree to not impact the lighting. Techs from Scientific Investigation Division were busy using digital and video cameras to record the scene. Everyone working the crime scene offered some form of acknowledgment to Sirius and me except for the two detectives from Robbery-Homicide. The detectives continued talking to each other and studiously avoided me. Normally it was RHD that took over any high-profile cases from other detectives, something known as "bigfooting." They were used to having the shoe on the other foot—or bigfoot. In this instance, I was the perceived bigfoot.

I knew one of the detectives, a longtime veteran named Worsley that everyone called Gump. The nickname didn't come from *Forrest Gump* but from an NHL goalie named Gump Worsley whose main claim to fame was that he was the last NHL goalie to play without a mask.

Gump finally acknowledged my presence. He had big ears, deep wrinkles, and a protruding lower lip. His nickname fit him; he looked like a Gump. "We're saved," he said. "The cavalry has arrived."

I nodded and then turned my eyes back to the victim. I had been viewing him from the side before, but now I was looking straight ahead. Two supports had been nailed into the tree, a foot rest and a seat rest. Because the victim was only elevated a few feet off the ground, we were almost eye to eye, or should have been. There was a gaping hole where his right eye was missing.

Gump noticed my reaction. "You didn't know he was shot?"

I shook my head.

"It was close range," he said, "probably a nine millimeter. It looks as if it happened right over there."

Two techs were working the area where he pointed, and lots of evidence bags were already filled. The ground was wet; in places you could see the russet stains of blood. There was a swath of wild mustard that had been crushed, showing the path along which the body had been dragged over to the tree. I was glad the victim was already dead before being crucified, or at least it appeared that was the case. He hadn't suffered slow torture. If the victim was already dead, though, why had the murderer gone to the trouble of staging the man's death?

"Got anything on the victim?" I asked.

"Everything's already been tagged and bagged," Gump said. "He was wearing one of those runner's belts with compartments where we found a driver's license. Meet Paul Klein."

I looked at the victim, studied the shirt, and said, "BHHS?"

"As in Beverly Hills 90210," Gump said. "According to his ASB card, which was also in the belt, he was a senior at Beverly Hills High School."

"What else do we know about him?"

"He drives a late model BMW. It was ticketed yesterday for being left in the park after it closed. The Parks and Recreation worker that found him said that Klein is a regular in these parts. Apparently, he runs up here most days."

"Running might not have been the only thing he was doing," the other detective said.

"Martinez," he added, tilting his head slightly by way of introduction.

"Gideon," I said. "And what else might he have been doing?"

"Dealing or using or both," Martinez said. "We found a stash of pills in his belt. He was holding a baggie filled with X and OC."

"X" was Ecstasy; in this instance, "OC" was OxyContin and not Orange County.

"He also had a gold money clip with almost four hundred dollars, and an American Express Card. In case you're wondering, it was only a Platinum card, not a Centurion."

"Times are tough even in Beverly Hills," Gump said.

Sirius decided to get into the conversation. His staccato bark sounded like "Rough!"

Gump and Martinez thought that was funny, but I knew Sirius was trying to tell me something. I followed his gaze. He was staring out over the Sunset Strip off into the distance. I couldn't see anything, but became aware of a noise, a whop, whop, whop that was drawing closer.

"Shit," I said. "It's a helicopter."

I grabbed some of the plastic wrapping covering the ground and ran over to the crucifixion tree. For just a moment I hesitated, staring into the bloodied face of Paul Klein. Then I threw the plastic wrap over him before adding my sports coat as a covering. The plastic wrapping would help prevent any contamination to the crime scene.

Martinez and Gump came up behind me, while overhead the helicopter circled the area trying to get the best footage possible. Before long I knew that the sky would be filled with other prying birds.

"I'll call in and get us some tarps ASAP," I said.

When the media becomes too invasive, sometimes it's necessary to work behind curtains.

"Forget the tarps," Gump said, "just get me an RPG."

CHAPTER 6:

THE AGENCY AND THE ECSTASY

All morning and into the afternoon I worked the scene. It's often the small details that make or break a homicide case, so it is a painstakingly slow process. The homicide scene was curtained off, but that didn't stop the helicopters from hovering. Occasionally the wind blew open the curtain, and the voyeurs did their peeping. Klein's body had also been shrouded, but the outline of what was there was only too visible.

Gump and Martinez were still working the scene when I left to go interview Michelle Klein. It was the one part of the investigation they were happy to hand off to me. They would just as soon not be the ones looking into the eyes of a mother who had just lost her son.

The name of the victim had not yet been released to the press, which meant I wouldn't have to fight through a media gauntlet to talk to the mother. The Klein house was located north of Sunset Boulevard, in the hills that were Beverly Hills. Despite its name, most of Beverly Hills is actually flat, but the northern part of town is hilly and more exclusive.

I knew the media was lined up and waiting on Fuller Avenue, so I avoided it by driving the long way out and exiting the park on Mulholland. I didn't want to advertise my connection to the Klein case; the investigation was already enough of a three-ring circus without bringing in the spectacle of my history with Ellis Haines, the serial killer who had somehow obtained cult status since Sirius and I had captured him.

The January sun was already on the run, even though it was only three thirty. My stomach had been complaining for hours, so I stopped for subs. I went with an Italian on wheat with all the veggies; Sirius had turkey breast and roast beef on whole grain. When we're not on a case, he gets kibble with chicken breast and steamed broccoli, which is probably why he likes eating out more than I do. In the backseat he made quick work of his sub.

I chewed a little more thoughtfully and also chewed over the questions that needed asking. There was a lot I wanted to know about Paul Klein. Given the chance, I like to rehearse field interviews in my mind, but whenever I thought about Klein I kept seeing him nailed to a tree. The more I tried to will that image from my mind, the more it stuck. Sometimes things should stick, so I reached for the right music to be pensive by. Billie Holiday was perfect for that, and I found the CD track I was looking for. There have been plenty of protest songs written, but none as powerful as "Strange Fruit."

I listened to Miss Holiday's lament about the strange, bloody fruit that southern trees bear. My coat's lining was spotted with Paul Klein's blood, so I would have to leave it in the car before interviewing his mother. Holiday's song was about a lynching in the south. Klein hadn't been lynched, but he had been crucified. Someone had nailed him to a tree after he was dead.

Strange fruit indeed, I thought. I listened while Holiday emoted about bulging eyes. One of Klein's eyes was missing from having been shot. It was that hollow that had kept drawing my stares. I would have to travel through that dark cave to find answers. The song and the case were bitter fruit to contemplate.

Another of Holiday's classics, "God Bless the Child," began to play. She seemed to be summing up my cases and my thoughts. I had started the day with baby Rose, and I'd probably end it in fire.

Into the hills of Beverly I drove. There weren't any gated communities, but it was a community of high and imposing gates, and you couldn't even see most of the houses from the road. Good fences might make for good neighbors, but they make for bad rubbernecking. A lot of the houses I passed by were known by fanciful names that predated the current owners, many of them associated with old-time Hollywood. Every day, tour buses make the rounds of the area, pointing out the past and present homes of stars, and recounting scandals and murders that happened in this domain of the wealthy. For a small city, Beverly Hills has had more than its share of notorious murders: Bugsy Siegel was gunned down in an alleged mob hit; Johnny Stompanato was stabbed to death by Lana Turner's daughter when he was allegedly assaulting the actress. Ron Levin was shot in his Beverly Hills apartment, an apparent victim of the Billionaire Boys Club, and Jose and Kitty Menendez were victims of their own two sons, who used a twelve-gauge shotgun on their parents in an attempt to get an early $35 million inheritance. The thick hedges and high fences that surrounded the pricey Beverly Hills homes hadn't managed to keep away trouble.

I pulled up the drive of the Kleins' house and extended an index finger to the call box. An accented voice spoke from the intercom: "Yes?"

"I am Detective Gideon, here to speak with Mrs. Klein."

The wrought-iron gate opened, and I drove up a flagstone driveway. I parked in front of a house that had been built in the style of mission revival, even though I imagined it was bigger than any of the original California missions. There were long corridors with arches; white paint had been applied over the stucco finish. The front yard had a parklike feel, with tiered fountains and well-tended gardens.

After opening the car windows for Sirius and telling him to be good, I walked up the path. The door opened before I reached it. A small Hispanic woman started at the sight of my scarred face, but she recovered quickly and said in the same voice I'd heard over the intercom, "I take you to Miss Klein."

I followed her down a long hallway. We passed by a showcase living room that was about the size of my house, and an equally imposing dining room. The domestic stopped at a door and lightly knocked.

"The policeman is here, Miss Klein," she said.

A muffled voice answered, and the maid opened the door and gestured for me to pass. Once I was inside the study, the door closed behind me. It took me a moment to get used to the dim lighting. Michelle Klein was holed up in the darkness. There was just enough light for me to see her red eyes and blotchy face. She was seated behind a desk. It seemed it was all she could do to raise her chin up from her chest to look at me.

"Thank you for seeing me," I said. "I can't imagine how difficult this must be for you. I am terribly sorry about the death of your son."

She didn't respond with words or body language. I extended my business card her way, but she didn't take it, so I put it down on her desk.

"I am Detective Gideon. Is it all right if I sit, Mrs. Klein? I am afraid there are questions I need to ask."

She tilted her head slightly, and as I was taking a seat in a chair she asked in a raspy voice, "How did he die? They never told me how Paul died."

"He was shot."

She sighed, swallowed hard, and her head dropped back down to her chest.

"But I am afraid there was more to it than that," I added. "The circumstances of his death were very peculiar. After Paul was shot, he was nailed to a tree."

It took a few moments for my words to penetrate her grief. She stared at me in disbelief. "What?"

"His limbs were nailed to a tree."

My words shocked her when few other things could. "He was crucified?"

I nodded.

"What sick fuck would do that?"

I didn't answer.

"What kind of crazy fucking asshole would desecrate my baby?"

She slapped the sides of her face with both hands, and the sound of the impact was loud in the small space we were sharing. Her dark eyes searched mine, looking for answers.

"We have every resource available committed to finding your son's murderer."

My rote words brought her no comfort. "Where did he die?" she asked.

"From the evidence we've uncovered, it looks as if he was shot in Runyon Park. He was wearing running clothes. Was that a place where he frequently went running?"

"He ran there two or three days a week," she said, clearly distracted by the news of the defilement of her son. "That's where you found him? That's where he was…" The word caught in her throat.

"Yes. He was found on a remote trail, nailed to an oak tree."

After a few moments of silence she said, "Ask your questions."

"Did your son have any enemies?"

She shook her head.

"Did he have a rivalry going on with anyone?"

"What do you mean?"

"For example, maybe he and another boy were interested in the same girl?"

Another head shake. "The girls were the ones always calling Paul."

"Did he have a girlfriend?"

"He only had what he referred to as his girlfriends de jour."

"When was the last time you saw your son?"

"Yesterday morning."

"You weren't concerned that he didn't come home last night?"

"Paul was eighteen," she said, offering up the figure as if to challenge me, or to assuage her own doubts. "He was an adult. He had his group. Everyone was always crashing at one house or the other. I assumed he was at a friend's house. Paul called me yesterday afternoon while I was working and told me he'd be going out later. That's why I wasn't worried when he didn't come home."

"Was he often out late on school nights?"

"I wasn't a fucking negligent parent, if that's what you're implying. Paul was an honor student. He was an athlete. And he had already been accepted early decision to Cornell University. He had earned some freedom to do as he wanted."

"Do you know if your son used drugs?"

"He tried pot a few times and he sometimes drank at parties, but Paul was always responsible. He would never drink and drive."

"Is it possible Paul was dealing drugs?"

Her denial was quick and certain. "Of course not."

"Then do you have any explanation as to why he was carrying a baggie full of OxyContin and Ecstasy in his running belt?"

"I don't know why, but I do know Paul would never do anything stupid like deal drugs."

"Did he go to raves?"

"No."

"You don't think he ever took OxyContin or Ecstasy?"

"I never saw any sign of that."

"Could he have been supplying his friends?"

"Why would he do that? He had plenty of his own money. His father—my ex—has been trying to buy the affection of Paul and his sister ever since we divorced eight years ago."

"Does your daughter live in the house?"

Michelle shook her head. "Sandra is a sophomore at Williams."

"What does your ex do?"

"Adam Klein?" she said, as if I should know the name.

I shook my head.

"He's a producer."

It still didn't ring a bell, but then I don't spend my spare time reading *Variety*. "What kind of a relationship did Paul have with his father?"

"The kind of relationship you'd expect from a schmuck with a new family. I was the first wife; Adam's on his third."

"Does your ex have other children?"

"He and the latest Mrs. Klein have two children, both under five."

"What did Paul think of that?"

"Paul had anger issues since the day Adam walked out on us. It's hard for a boy to understand why his father is an asshole."

"Did Paul see a therapist?"

"A long time ago. And for the most part he put his abandonment issues behind him."

"You said your former husband tried to buy Paul's love."

"He gave him money. And he bought Paul his BMW."

"How often did they see one another?"

"They got together maybe once a month. Adam would take Paul to a Lakers game or out to dinner."

"You said that Paul called you at work yesterday. What do you do?"

"I have my own real estate agency."

"I imagine that's a lot of work."

She didn't answer at first but then said, "I took a client out to dinner last night and didn't get home until late. I just assumed Paul was spending the night at a friend's house. He was always with his group, what he called his entourage."

For a moment she showed a fleeting smile, but it quickly turned into a flinch; it hurt too much for her to remember.

"Tell me about his group."

"They were boys from his high school. When they went out, there were always four or five of them."

"Did he have a best friend?"

I got a small nod. "He's known Jason Davis since sandbox days."

"I'll need Jason's personal information, along with the names, telephone numbers, and addresses of Paul's entourage."

She reached for a black address book on the desk and extended it to me. "I know most of them by their first names, so I had Paul enter their names that way."

Michelle closed her eyes for a moment and in a tired voice she said, "Look for Alec, David, Cody, Sam, and Jason. They were his mainstays."

She leaned back in her chair. Because she was no longer hunched forward, I could now see the rips in her blouse. There were tears in at least half a dozen spots. My scrutinizing didn't go unnoticed.

"When I was a girl, I watched as my grandmother ripped apart her clothing when she learned her sister had died. I remember how she looked so crazy. Her face was all contorted, and she attacked her clothes in this violent, terrible way. Back then I couldn't understand why she would do such a thing. Now I do. But I didn't stop at just ripping my blouse. That wasn't enough. So I started tearing my hair out. And the only reason I stopped doing it was because the pain began making me feel better, and that was wrong."

"Can I call someone to be with you?"

"My daughter is flying home. She'll be here tonight."

While I filled out my field interview cards with the phone numbers and addresses of Paul's friends, Michelle Klein stared into space. Every so often a tear made its way down her cheek. When I was finished, I stood up and once more offered my condolences. She said nothing until I began closing the door behind me.

"Get the bastard," she said.

* * *

After I left the Klein house, I called Jason Davis. Judging from his reaction, he didn't yet know of Paul's death and couldn't understand why an LAPD detective was asking to meet with him.

"What's this concerning?" he asked.

"Paul Klein," I said and didn't elaborate further.

Although Jason was eighteen, I offered him the option of either speaking to him at his house in the presence of his parents or meeting him somewhere. Jason decided he didn't want a cop questioning him in front of his parents and suggested we meet at a coffee house on North Beverly.

"I'll be easy to spot," I said. From experience I knew it was better to get the matter of my appearance out of the way early. "Just look for a guy with an ugly scar on his mug."

When I arrived at the coffee shop, I found all the outside tables deserted, which was as I hoped. Southern Californians aren't known for braving the elements, and with the thermometer hovering around sixty degrees, they had retreated indoors. I told Sirius to park himself and then went inside. There wasn't much in the way of food still available, but I found an egg salad sandwich that didn't look too mushy.

The sandwich went well with the hot coffee, or at least what I ate of it did. Sirius got the lion's share. While waiting for Jason, I called Gump. He and Martinez were still working the crime scene at the park and would probably be there most of the night. According to Gump, LAPD Media Relations was in the process of releasing a statement to the press detailing the circumstances of Paul Klein's death.

"The shit's just about to hit the fan," Gump said. "The media air force has been trying to get footage all day. They know there's a body in the tree, and they know there's something *muy* hinky about this one."

As if to emphasize what Gump was saying, I could hear the sounds of a helicopter flying low over the crime scene.

"I guess the kid's father is some bigwig, right?" Gump asked.

"He's a producer."

"That figures. Media Relations tells me he's got a press conference scheduled right after their announcement. Supposedly, he's going to offer a million-dollar reward for information leading to the arrest of his son's killer."

"That's all we need," I said, knowing that kind of money would bring every crackpot with supposed information to the party. "We'll have to pull some uniforms to handle the calls."

"Yeah, we might as well just open our own psychic hotline."

A preppy-looking kid, hands in his designer jeans, made a slow approach to where I was sitting. He acted wary, looking from me to Sirius and then back to me again.

"I'll get back to you," I told Gump.

I pocketed my phone and motioned for the kid to sit, saying, "The dog's friendly."

Before sitting he asked, "Can I see some ID?"

I pulled out my badge wallet and showed him my detective shield. When he finished looking at it, Jason Davis sat down in a chair opposite me.

"Michelle Klein told me you've known Paul for a long time."

"My whole life," he said.

"If you haven't heard then, I am afraid Paul is dead."

Jason's mouth opened and he stared at me in disbelief.

"He was murdered yesterday," I said.

I continued to watch him. Jason's surprise and shock looked real.

"Do you know anyone that might have wanted to harm Paul?"

He shook his head and said, "I can't believe it."

"Are you aware of anyone that threatened Paul?"

"No. This is crazy."

"Paul's body was purposely put on display. He was nailed to a tree, which suggests to me that this killing was personal. Can you think of anything Paul might have done that might have made anyone want to do that to him?"

Jason shook his head again.

"When was the last time you saw Paul?"

He thought for a moment and said, "Yesterday at school. He was supposed to meet up with us last night but he was a no-show. We called him a few times, but he never picked up."

"Where was he going to meet you?"

"At the Music Hall."

Laemmle's Music Hall 3 is a movie theater on Wilshire Boulevard.

"Who else was there with you?"

"Sam Drexler, David Popkin, and me."

I already had the other boys' names; they were part of Paul's group.

"Were you surprised when Paul didn't make it?"

"We just figured something came up."

"So you saw the film without him?"

He nodded.

"Michelle Klein said your group is close and that Paul called you his entourage."

"That's what he sometimes called us," Jason said, "but we usually call our group the Agency."

"Like the CIA?"

"More like CAA."

Creative Artists Agency is one of Hollywood's biggest talent agencies. These kids had grown up in Tinseltown. It made sense that they'd wrap themselves in its glittery fabric.

"So the Agency is sort of a club?"

"That sounds like something with rules. We're just a group of guys that hang out together."

"That's what gangbangers always say."

"It isn't like that. We don't break laws or wear certain colors. We don't even have a secret handshake. What we are is more like a team. The six of us have been playing lacrosse together all through high school."

"Was Paul a good player?"

"He's been one of the best the last few years. That's why he was picked as captain his junior and senior years."

"Was he bossy?"

"He liked to be in charge."

"Did Paul use drugs?"

Jason's answer was immediate: "No."

"He didn't drink?"

"Well, yeah."

"What about weed?"

"Hardly ever," Jason said. "Paul was a runner and didn't want his lungs to get messed up."

"Can you think of a reason why Paul was carrying a baggie full of OC and Ecstasy?"

A head shake. "Not even one."

"And you don't know of anyone that would have wanted to hurt Paul?"

"Not really."

"Not really?"

"Most people liked Paul."

"Who didn't?"

He shrugged. "I don't know. It's possible some losers were jealous of him."

"Such as?"

"I really couldn't say. Paul sometimes acted cocky, though, and there might have been one or two kids that weren't from old Beverly Hills that he rubbed the wrong way."

"What do you mean by old Beverly Hills?"

"People from around here."

"I'm still not following."

"There are a lot of kids at our school that go around speaking different languages, like Farsi."

"And Paul didn't like that?"

"Lots of people in Beverly Hills don't like it. A few years back there was this big fight when election ballots came out in Farsi. And the people of Beverly Hills got so sick of houses being torn down and Persian Palaces being put up that the zoning laws were changed."

"Persian Palaces?"

"Everyone calls them that."

"So Paul didn't like these newcomers?"

"What he didn't like was when they acted like they were still in Tehran. When he heard kids speaking in Farsi, he'd start talking real loud in pig Latin."

"He targeted Iranian students?"

Jason shook his head. "It was more like a joke."

"But others might not have found it funny?"

"I don't know. You wanted to know if anyone could have disliked Paul; that's all I could think of. But I don't think his speaking pig Latin is the kind of thing that could have gotten him killed, do you?"

I almost said, "There are some people you'd be advised to not say 'Uckfay Ouyay' to," but instead I just asked him another question.

CHAPTER 7:

TOWER OF BABEL, TOWER OF HOPE

Gump and Martinez were still working the case at two a.m. when I took my leave of them. None of us had turned up any real suspects. Paul's friends—I had talked to all five members of the Agency—couldn't think of anyone that would have wanted him dead. The only person that had offered a motive for Paul's death was his father. Adam Klein said he believed his son's death and crucifixion were payback from organized crime.

"This is the Mob's way of getting back at me for making *Traffic King*," he told me over the phone.

"I am not familiar with *Traffic King*," I said.

"That's because its release date is two weeks from tomorrow. The story is about human trafficking, about the modern slave trade."

"Your film is about present-day slavery?"

"That's right. The Traffic King is a modern-day slave lord. He collects and sells human beings. He ravages lives."

"What does that have to do with your son's death?"

"It's organized crime retaliating for my putting the spotlight on their activities."

"Is *Traffic King* based on a true story?"

"I would call it more of a composite story. In sheer numbers, there is more human trafficking going on today than ever before."

"But your movie is fictional?"

"That doesn't take away from its inherent truth."

By that point in our conversation, I had stopped taking notes. Before reaching him by phone, I had heard Klein selling this same revenge theory to the media. It had sounded out there, but at the time I thought grief was coloring his thinking. Now I wasn't so sure, but I hoped he believed in his theory. If he didn't, that meant he was using the death of his own son to promote a movie.

"I think it's a stretch that your son would have been targeted because of this movie."

"That's because you don't know how despicable and violent the modern slave trade is. It would be just like them to exact revenge for my having exposed their methods. When you see the movie, Detective, you'll understand what I'm talking about. They are afraid of their house of cards toppling. That's what happens in the film, and as a result their slave trade is severely disrupted."

"And how does all of that come about?"

"A woman whose girl is abducted by slave traders gets vengeance against the human traffickers. Getting her daughter back isn't enough; she goes after the Traffic King."

I held the phone away from me and just looked at it. When I could talk, I thanked Mr. Klein for his time and hung up on him.

During the drive home I thought about the producer's conspiracy theory. "Hard to believe," I said to Sirius. My partner didn't answer. He was already asleep in the backseat.

The good thing about driving so late was that there was little traffic. Casa Gideon is in Sherman Oaks, the so-called gateway to the San Fernando Valley. Being that gateway is a dubious distinction, and I'm not sure whether the title is a compliment or a ding. Jenny and I had chosen to live in Sherman Oaks because of its proximity to our workplaces, and because when we bought our home it was somewhat affordable. Officially, Sherman Oaks isn't a city but a neighborhood in the city of Los Angeles. When you think of neighborhoods, most don't have sixty thousand people like mine does. One of Sherman Oaks' claims to fame is that it is the acknowledged birthplace of Valley Girls. In the 1980s, the Sherman Oaks Galleria, the megamall of its time, was the big meet-up spot for the high school crowds. Frank Zappa had to endure listening to the unique lingo of his daughter and her friends, and decided to immortalize the way they talked in song. After that, movies followed and the whole country became familiar with Valspeak. Unfortunately, the speech patterns continue to this day.

Like, gag me with a spoon.

Jenny had told me that although the TV series *The Brady Bunch* was filmed on a set, the writers always imagined that the household existed in the suburbs of Sherman Oaks. Our plan had been to have our own nest with children, and we picked a house that a family was supposed to fill, but it never worked out that way. Jenny had even insisted that we put up a white picket fence in the front yard. As I pulled into the driveway, the night couldn't mask the fact that the fence needed a new coat of paint. The whole house needed TLC that I was no longer inspired to put into it.

Sirius stayed at my side as we walked up the pathway to the front door and then waited for me to enter the house first. When the two of us worked together in K-9, there had been clear divisions of rank, with frequent classes and exercises to reinforce that pecking order. The dogs are taught their handlers are generals and that they are grunts that have to obey no matter how insane the orders are. Sirius always went along with this game so as to not make me look bad, and still does.

I made Sirius what was either a late dinner or an early breakfast. He eats on the patio and was waiting outside for his catered affair to be served. I sat down while he ate. It was cool but not uncomfortably so. Our backyard is full of mature fruit trees, and at different times of the year it's awash in nectarines, apples, apricots, lemons, plums, figs, avocadoes, oranges, limes, and tangelos. It was a good thing the trees were so well established when their care fell to me; so far I'd managed not to kill them. Jen had been the gardener and the cook. The breeze brought with it the bouquet of citrus, and I remembered her tangy lemon meringue pies.

Sirius made short work of his food. I thought about making myself a late snack but decided sleep sounded better than food. I had a six-thirty appointment with the assistant principal at Beverly Hills High, so I'd be lucky to get three hours sleep. My hope was that I would be too tired to dream, especially with my early meeting. When my head hit the pillow, I dropped off. The next thing I knew I was in hellfire.

* * *

Both of us were staggering under the weight and heat. The smoke was pummeling us, hitting us in our throats and lungs. The Strangler collapsed to a knee, and Sirius's legs slipped through his hands and hit the ground. I held on to my partner's head and legs, but just barely.

"We're going to die," the Strangler said.

His lips were blistered and it was tough making out his words. Soot covered his face. His eyes stared out, red coals among the blackness.

"We have to leave the dog if we're going to have a chance."

Sirius was still breathing; blood was no longer pouring out of him, but I was afraid that was because he'd bled so much already. Without answering the Strangler directly, I shifted the direction of my gun. It wasn't easy holding up my partner, with the gun in my right hand, but I'd managed. In a few moments, I could holster the gun and then carry my friend by myself.

The Strangler read my intentions and all but jumped to his feet. I reluctantly eased the pressure on my trigger finger. In the fire my morality had burned away.

My partner was a dead, unwieldy weight in our arms, but I couldn't let him go. As he struggled for air and continued to fight for life, his sounds made me press on.

Holding Sirius between us, the Strangler and I resumed our death march.

In the limbo of past and present, the crippling forces of grief and despair made my chest feel as if it was being staved in. That pain hurt even more than the burning fire.

And then I was gasping in the now, the dream behind me, as my partner's licks awakened me and cooled my burning flesh.

In the calm of the moment after, I found myself focused on the crazed red orbs of Ellis Haines. As we had walked through hell, his eyes had always been on me, but now, in my vision, I watched as he plucked out his right eye and offered it to me.

And then I heard the words—or maybe I thought them—"An eye for an eye."

I fully awakened then, and I thought of Paul Klein and the gap of his missing orb. I wondered whether the bullet was a statement. If I could believe what my vision was telling me, the shooting had been carried out by someone who believed in an eye for an eye. If that was the case, the killer had acted upon what he or she perceived to be a grievous wrong.

Sirius offered up another lick.

"I am awake," I said, reaching for his head with both of my hands. "Anyone ever tell you that you're the best nightmare cure in the world?"

He leaned into the bed, gladly accepting my praise and scratches. The love fest was cut short when my alarm went off.

"We need to hurry," I told him, "or we'll be late for school."

I had driven by Beverly Hills High School many times but never had reason to go on its campus. The school is located in the southern part of Beverly Hills and borders on Century City. Contrary to what television might have you believe, the high school's zip code is 90212. Pictures taken from the school's playing fields invariably include the background of high-rise hotels and buildings on Avenue of the Stars and little Santa Monica Boulevard. I turned on Moreno Drive and followed the signs. Along the way I saw media vans lining the street. Signs directed me to student and faculty parking, but a security guard was barring entry and apparently doing his best to keep the media at bay. When I showed him my wallet badge, he waved Sirius and me through.

After parking the car I told my partner, "You'll have to wait for me."

Sirius didn't even try to pretend he was disappointed but instead just curled up on the backseat.

"I was at least hoping for an argument," I said.

He raised one eye and then closed it.

The BHHS campus is sprawled out over a lot of acreage, and it took me a few stops and starts to orient myself. Anyone expecting a prep school for the rich would have been disappointed. The school was mostly nondescript, with little to distinguish it. The producers of the original *Beverly Hills 90210* must have decided the same thing: they used the exterior of Torrance High School, which was some twenty miles away, for their shots.

As I made my way to the administrative offices, I encountered more security guards. There was a lot of talking going on over walkie-talkies. The guards were intent on keeping the media away from the campus, which was more than all right by me. Even though it was early, teachers and students were already arriving on campus, drawn by news of Paul Klein's death. Judging by its brightly lit offices, the school's administration had arrived early to deal with the crisis.

When I announced myself to a receptionist, she said, "The assistant principal is expecting you."

Even though I am closing in on the age of forty, the receptionist's words took me back twenty-five years. They had been scary back then; there was a part of me that thought they still were. The only thing that had changed was the title: it was now assistant principal instead of vice principal.

Most adults offer their first names when being introduced. Assistant Principal Durand did not. "I am Mrs. Durand," she said.

She was about my age, with short, dark hair set off by pale skin. The assistant principal might have been attractive if she smiled, but she didn't. Maybe frowning was one of her job requirements. Maybe her night had been as long as mine. I keep hoping that one day I will arise reborn from my phoenix dreams instead of feeling like day-after barbecue.

"I am here investigating the homicide of Paul Klein," I said. "I'm going to need to talk to those individuals that might have known Paul best, including counselors, teachers, administrators, and of course students."

Durand folded and unfolded her hands several times before she responded with carefully measured words: "I will do what I can to help you, Detective, but I wouldn't feel comfortable having you talk with students without first getting the permission of their parents."

I wasn't surprised by her response. The first rule of school administrators is to avoid any possibility of a lawsuit.

"Paul was an adult. Confidentiality laws shouldn't factor in here."

"His eighteenth birthday was less than three months ago. Most of the students at this school are under the age of eighteen, and some of our Beverly parents might not like you talking to their children. School records are much like juvenile criminal records: they're supposed to remain sealed."

"One of your own was murdered. Doesn't that mean something to you?"

"Of course it does. I will try and work with you, Detective, but I must be mindful of that slippery slope."

"Did you know Paul Klein?"

She nodded but didn't elaborate.

"When I was in high school, the vice principal was the disciplinarian of the school. Is that your role?"

"That is just one of my duties."

"But if students are written up, or if there is trouble, you're the sheriff?"

"I would likely be involved in the process, yes."

"Did you ever call Paul into your office?"

She hesitated and then said, "Not officially."

"But unofficially you did?"

Weighing her words she said, "There was an instance where a student complained about his behavior."

"What were the circumstances?"

"I was told that Paul was acting inappropriately toward one of our students."

"I'll need you to be more specific."

"Paul and some of his friends were heard teasing a student. The complaint was secondhand, mind you. It didn't come from the party being teased."

"But you talked to the student that was teased?"

"I did. And it was that student's wishes to not proceed with an investigation into the incident."

"In that case, you wouldn't mind me talking with this student?"

"I'll have to consult with someone in administration and get back to you."

I sighed, hoping my dramatic posturing would get me somewhere. When it didn't I said, "I assume you also talked to Paul about this incident?"

She nodded. "It was his belief it was no big thing."

"Was the student being teased foreign born?"

"Why do you ask?"

I pretended to flip through some old notes, looking for something. "Here it is," I said. "One of Paul's friends mentioned the incident. The young woman was Iranian, right?"

"She was *Persian*, yes," Durand said, emphasizing to me what must be the more politically correct term.

"Are many of your students native to other lands?" I asked.

"Almost a third," Durand said. "At Beverly we pride ourselves on our diversity."

"You haven't found any racial or monetary divide among your students?"

"Beverly is a public school, and in real life it is nothing like how it's portrayed in television and film. There are many apartments in Beverly Hills, and quite a few of our students come from families that are anything but affluent."

I pretended to look through my notes again. "I didn't get the name of the girl Paul was accused of teasing. What is it?"

"I prefer withholding her name until I get some directive from above."

I thought about sighing again but didn't. Every day, the assistant principal probably dealt with much more talented actors than me. "Over the years did you have any other dealings with Paul?"

Durand hesitated before speaking and then carefully said, "Last spring we talked after an incident in a lacrosse game. There was a formal complaint from another high school saying that one of our players head-butted a member of its team. The opposing coach suspected that Paul was the one that committed the offense, because earlier in the match he'd had a run-in with that player."

"Was Paul guilty of the head butt?"

"He said he wasn't involved, and that it was likely the other player was accidentally hit with a stick."

"What happened with the complaint?"

"Our athletic director dealt with it, but as far as I know nothing came of it, since the victim couldn't identify who hit him."

"Were Paul's teammates questioned?"

Durand nodded. "They all said the same thing, that it must have been an accidental stick."

"Sticks and stones," I mused aloud.

I didn't continue with the rest of the nursery rhyme, because it's bullshit and every kid knows it. Only a sociopath can declare, "Words will never hurt me." Words do hurt, sometimes more than anything, which meant I would have to investigate the stick incident and the hurting words.

* * *

I met with Frank Rivera in his homeroom. The room didn't have a chalkboard and I wondered if they were no longer fixtures in high schools. There was a whiteboard and on it were class reminders. At least I didn't have to worry about tomorrow's quiz. There was a large map of the world on one wall. Next to it was another map that was labeled: The Black Death Project. The poster detailed the spread of the bubonic plague.

Rivera was a history teacher and the lacrosse coach. He was a small, intense Hispanic male who liked to punctuate his points with an emphatic index finger. His favorite word was "heckuva." According to him, Paul Klein was a heckuva leader, heckuva kid, heckuva player, and heckuva teammate. By the end of our talk, I was getting a heckuva headache.

"I heard there was a complaint registered against Paul by another team last year," I said.

"It was dismissed," Rivera said.

"Tell me what happened."

"The whole thing was a case of sour grapes. Their team lost."

"Did Paul head-butt their player?"

Instead of answering, Rivera said, "Earlier in the game their kid basically coldcocked Paul. That's what happened."

"And Paul avenged that?"

Rivera avoided my eyes. "I am not saying that. I am just saying the bad blood started with them."

I left with the name of the other player, and the certainty that Klein had hit him when no one else was looking.

* * *

There was a special assembly scheduled to start the school day at Beverly—the name everyone seemed to call BHHS. The assembly was only open to Beverly students, teachers, staff, and the special counselors that had been brought in. Because I wasn't being allowed to attend, Mrs. Durand promised to post my name and number as the LAPD contact.

With time before the assembly, I walked around Beverly's grounds trying to spot Jason Davis. Emotional groups of students were clustered around the campus. One group was standing outside of the swim gym. Looming over it was a sign saying HOME OF THE NORMANS, with a painting of a knight atop a charger. I was tempted to take a look inside the swim gym to see if its interior had changed much since Frank Capra immortalized it in his movie *It's a Wonderful Life*, but I didn't want real life impinging on one of my favorite make-believe scenes. Jenny had loved that film, which now made it bittersweet for me to watch, but over the holidays I had found myself sitting down to it again. The scene filmed at Beverly Hills High School is where Jimmy Stewart and Donna Reed are dancing the Charleston. The two are so intent on each other that they don't even notice when the floor opens up underneath them. The couple fall in the drink, and then they fall in love. And that was how the swim gym was forever immortalized. I wished I was investigating the movie and not a murder.

For the students of Beverly, there was only one topic of the day and that was the murder of Klein. Among the girls there was lots of sobbing, hugging, and comforting going on. The guys mostly shuffled their feet and looked grim. The outpouring of grief and expressions of shock were to be expected, given the circumstances. For many of these kids, Klein's murder was their first encounter with death, let alone a crucifixion.

Amid the more than two thousand students, I wasn't able to spot Jason Davis, so I ended up calling his cell number. When he answered I could tell by the background noise that he was also on campus. "This is Gideon. I am at Beverly. Do you want to talk in person or over the phone?"

"Phone," he said, and then I heard him putting some distance between himself and others.

"I need a name," I said. "Who's the Persian girl that Paul and your group were caught hassling and got him brought before the assistant principal?"

Jason didn't answer right away, and when he did he played dumb: "What Persian girl?"

"Wrong answer," I said. "Try again."

Jason's memory improved. "Bugs."

"Her name is Bugs?"

"It's her nickname."

"What's her real name?"

"I am not really sure. I think her first name might be Dana."

"You know her well enough to harass her, but you don't even know her name?"

Jason didn't offer a denial. He didn't say anything.

"Go get her name for me. And I also want you to take her picture and send it to me at this number. Do it surreptitiously, and by that I mean…"

He interrupted. "I know what surreptitious means."

Of course he did. It had probably been one of his SAT prep words.

"Do you know what expeditious means?"

When he said, "Yeah," I hung up.

Two minutes later I heard the doorbell sound that accompanies my text messages. I hit Receive and saw that Davis had sent me a picture/text message. That was something I still hadn't figured out how to do with my phone. He had written "Her name is dinah hazimi, or something close to that."

I studied Dinah's picture. The girl hadn't known she was in a camera's crosshairs. Jason's face shot wasn't great, but it was enough for me to identify her. Dinah's lips were pointedly pursed, but they didn't hide what was under them.

"Malocclusion," I whispered aloud, wondering if Jason also knew that word.

Dinah, known by the Agency boys as Bugs, had buck teeth.

A steady stream of students had been going to and from a fenced-off site on Olympic Boulevard that was adjacent to the school. Their pilgrimage spot was a tower, but with the commencement of the school's special assembly, the migration had stopped. Without any more students to film, and with their morning news segments concluded, the media and news vans drifted away. When I was sure there were no more cameras monitoring the site, I made my way toward the Tower of Hope.

Hidden behind the tiled 150-foot tower was an active oil derrick. Over the years there had been a number of feature stories written about the well. The LA Basin is home to vast oil deposits, and Beverly Hills High School happens to be located on one of them. The derrick produces around five hundred barrels of oil each day, and BHHS is a beneficiary of the oil, receiving about $300,000 in royalties a year.

In 2001, the formerly drab, gray structure hiding the derrick was transformed into what was called the Tower of Hope. The tower's floral facelift came after thousands of teal-colored tiles— called Portraits of Hope—were affixed to the structure. Each of those tiles was hand-painted by terminally ill children being treated in Los Angeles hospitals. The tiles were a symbol of hope, and each of the four sides of the tiled tower represented one of four seasons of the year.

That was the feel-good story. A few years later there was a different story, and the Tower of Hope became known as the Tower of You Better Hope You Don't Get Cancer. Litigants sued the oil company, among them a number of former Beverly students, claiming that benzene and other chemicals released during drilling had resulted in a cancer cluster. The last I had heard, most of the lawsuits had disappeared. Throughout it all the derrick had continued pumping.

The Tower of Hope was near to the track and baseball field. Paul Klein would undoubtedly have passed by it many times while running around the track. As I approached the tower, the handiwork of the students became visible. All morning they had been making a memorial for their fallen classmate. Laid out against the fence were flowers, stuffed animals, candles, drawings, cards, and pictures of Paul. The memorial stretched around two sides of the tower.

Many of the candles were lit. I didn't know if that was a good idea so near to an active oil well, but I didn't extinguish them. There were hundreds of notes, cards, and drawings. The messages of sorrow, of words like "We will miss you," and "We love you," and "God bless you," were everywhere. I walked by teddy bears, helium balloons, a few Stars of David, and some white lacrosse balls. There were also several piles of stones, and I wondered why those would have been left until I remembered that it was a Jewish tradition to leave stones at grave sites.

I pulled out my digital camera and began snapping pictures of the makeshift memorial and afterward put on gloves and began sifting through the items. I had almost finished going through the items on one side of the tower when I picked up a large, handmade card on which an artistic hand had colored in the words "Gone but not forgotten." As I opened the card, I expected to see more platitudes on the inside but instead found the scripted words "You made my life HELL, and now you've gone to hell. There is a God."

After returning the card to where I had found it, I took pictures from all angles. Someone had made sure their offering didn't look out of place, but they hadn't forgiven Klein even in death. I didn't expect to find another needle in the haystack, but a few minutes later I turned over a blown-up picture that showed Paul running and saw that someone had written in block letters "What goes around, comes around." The block letters suggested to me that either the writer was male or someone trying to disguise her writing, whereas the handwriting on the card looked distinctly feminine. Amid all the adoration of Klein were two dissenting writers.

I hadn't brought any evidence bags, so I slipped the card and picture inside my coat. My timing was good; less than a minute later a squad car pulled up to the curb. Yes, Virginia, there really is a Beverly Hills Police Department, even though the entire city is less than six square miles in area and has a population of only thirty-five thousand people.

An unmarked car pulled in behind the squad car and a suit emerged. The detective scowled at me for longer than necessary and then said, "Can I help you?"

What he really meant was "What the hell are you doing here?"

"Nope," I said, making an entry in my notepad.

The suit continued to stare at me, and I continued to ignore him. Because the homicide had occurred in LAPD's jurisdiction, we had the case, but that didn't mean BHPD had to be happy about it. In fact, it was likely the suit eyeballing me was doing his own parallel investigation into Klein's homicide.

"I hope I don't have to tell you that nothing is to be removed from this area."

"You don't have to tell me," I said, hoping the items under my coat weren't visible.

I pretended to be inordinately interested in one particular section of the memorial and clicked away with my camera. Later, when I vacated the area, the detective would probably drive himself crazy figuring out what I had been so focused on. As I took my leave of the tower and started back toward the campus, I nodded to the two Beverly Hills cops.

The assembly was over and classes had convened by the time I returned to BHHS. I went to the administrative offices again, and after a five-minute wait was once again able to see Assistant Principal Durand.

"Dinah Hazimi," I said.

Durand didn't act surprised but did correct my pronunciation of Dinah's last name, which was Hakimi. Then she said, "Dinah is a minor."

"Then call her parents and ask them if they've heard about the murder of one of your students. Tell them the police are here conducting an investigation, and that you're asking parents if it's all right if their child talks to the authorities."

Durand thought about that and then reluctantly nodded. She asked me to leave her office while she made the call. I sat in the waiting area, which offered a vantage point into her office, and watched her talking on the phone. I couldn't hear what she was saying and wasn't able to read her expression. The call was brief, lasting no more than two minutes, and then she motioned for me to return to her office.

"Mrs. Hakimi said you could talk to her daughter. Before that happens, though, I am going to talk to Dinah, and I will tell her that she doesn't need to sit down with you if she doesn't want to."

* * *

Whatever the assistant principal told Dinah didn't scare her off. Durand accompanied her to a small conference room where I was waiting. After making introductions, Durand left the room and I motioned for Dinah to take a seat across the table from me. She was shy, avoiding direct eye contact. The girl was five foot and a little change, and no more than a hundred pounds. Dinah was fine boned, with high cheekbones, glistening hair, pretty dark eyes with long lashes, and almond skin. If not for her pronounced front teeth, she would have been considered very attractive.

At the start of our talk her hand self-consciously covered her mouth, but before long she seemed more at ease in my company and her hand dropped to the table. I think it was my scars that put her at ease. Misery loves company. Or it might have been that I started with softball questions.

"How well did you know Paul Klein?" I asked.

"Not very well," she said.

"What year in school are you?"

"I am a junior."

"Did you have any classes with Paul?"

She shook her head.

"I understand you had a problem with Paul and his friends last year."

Dinah stiffened a little and then said, "Not really."

"Someone saw him teasing you. It must have been pretty bad. Kids don't usually report things."

She shrugged, pretending indifference, but she had to blink away tears from coming to her eyes.

"What was he saying to you?"

"I don't remember."

"I think you do. And I think that wasn't the only instance where he was bullying you, which explains why you left this at the oil well memorial."

I placed the handmade card on the table. Dinah's hand covered her mouth, but she would have been better served to cover her eyes. The fright and dismay at her being discovered were clearly on display.

"Tell me about the hell he put you through, Dinah."

In a small voice she said, "I don't want to talk about it."

"You seem like a smart girl. Why did you let yourself be a victim?"

Her eyes sparked. "What was I supposed to do? He was popular. And if I had complained to the school, his pack of friends would have vouched for him."

"How long has the bullying gone on?"

"Since my family moved to Beverly Hills in the ninth grade. Up until that time, I had never even heard the name Bugs Bunny."

My hand reached out to her card and gently traced the lettering where she'd written "You made my life HELL."

"It started during my first week at school," she said. "I was trying my best to fit in. I was sitting in the cafeteria by myself, and that's when this boy sat down right across from me. He was holding a carrot in his hand, and standing behind him were five or six other boys. 'Eh, what's up, Doc?' he said to me. I didn't understand what he was saying, so I said, 'Excuse me?' And then he said, even louder this time, 'Eh, what's up, Doc?' And that got not only his group laughing, but what seemed like the whole cafeteria."

"Welcome to Beverly."

"He knew where I was the most self-conscious."

"How bad did it get?"

"Bad. It was ongoing torture. I remember one day he and all his friends wore these Billy Bob teeth. And whenever he saw me, he'd open his mouth and show off his terrible teeth, and he'd shout so everyone could hear, 'I want to marry you, Bugs, but you're not my first cousin.'"

"I am sorry."

"The more others laughed, the more it hurt. Last Halloween he came to school dressed as Elmer Fudd. He had this brown hat and baggy suit, and he kept coming up to me asking me if I'd seen any wascally wabbits."

"How often did he bully you?"

"It varied. Sometimes a week or two would go by and he and his group wouldn't bother me, and I would hope and pray that he was finally done with me, but it never lasted. He always came back."

"No one ever intervened?"

She shook her head. "Everyone was afraid if they did he would go after them. And he was smart about the way he did it, making it look like a big joke."

"Were you his only target?"

Another head shake. "There were others. Sometimes I'd see him going after them. I probably should have said something, but I never did. I was just happy that he was leaving me alone."

"I need the names of the others being bullied."

"There's a ninth-grade boy named Sam Nahai that he liked to bother."

"Did Paul only target Persians?"

She thought about it and said, "Mostly, but not all. He liked to give an overweight boy named Steven a hard time. Paul and his friends called him Chinny Chin Chin."

"Chin?"

"He said Steven had more chins than there were in a Chinese phone book."

"So Paul was an equal opportunity bully?"

"No, I wouldn't say that. Persians were his favorite targets. He liked to speak with an accent and say he lived in Tehrangeles. And when he talked about Brownies, he always made sure you knew he wasn't referring to Girl Scouts."

"What are Brownies?"

"Brown Jews," she said.

It was clear I still didn't understand, so she said, "The Persian community in Beverly Hills are Sephardic Jews. There are many Ashkenazim—European Jews—that look down upon us."

Klein, a Jew, was apparently an anti-Semite. I wondered if his bigotry had anything to do with his death.

"What did you think when you heard Paul was crucified?"

Dinah looked me in the eye and said, "I was glad."

"What else?"

"I was relieved. It was a weight off my shoulders. From now on I'll be able to look at a razor blade and see a razor blade."

"What do you mean?"

"He made me so miserable there were times I thought of killing myself."

"What stopped you?"

"I made a friend at the Community Crisis Line, a good man who made me think beyond the moment and look to the future. And now I have saved almost three thousand dollars. Soon I will be able to pay for my braces."

Dinah smiled and almost showed her teeth.

CHAPTER 8:

HIS PERSONALIZED LICENSE PLATE SAYS "SHAMAN"

I worked the high school until midafternoon, trying to learn more about Klein. I also tried to get a lead on the identity of the second dissenting note writer. The assistant principal arranged it so that I could talk to Steven (Chinny Chin Chin) Needleman and Sam Nahai. Neither of the boys pretended to have any love lost for Klein, but neither struck me as the poison-pen note writer or the murderer. The boys hadn't been bullied to the extent Dinah had, and both were passive sorts. Even while he was being harassed, Nahai said he had been able to put his situation into perspective. "I just remembered the words of my grandfather, who always said, 'I was sad because I had no shoes, until I met a man who had no feet.'"

Klein's Jekyll/Hyde persona wasn't something his teachers recognized. As far as they were concerned, he was an excellent student and a good citizen, albeit one who sometimes engaged in what one called "good-humored mischief." Paul was apparently adept at masking his bullying and dark side.

Neither Paul's friends nor his enemies were aware of his dealing or using drugs. No one could explain why he was carrying OC or X. Planting drugs on a corpse made no sense, but then neither did crucifying a dead man.

It was three o'clock when I met up with Gump and Martinez in downtown LA at the Eastside Market Italian Deli. Both detectives were going incognito to avoid the press and were wearing dark glasses, baseball caps, and windbreakers instead of their usual sports coats. Because we had missed the deli's lunch hour rush, we were able to get a table by ourselves.

Martinez and Gump both went with the DA Special, a sandwich with sausage, meatballs, roast beef, and pastrami. I had a sandwich for each fist—a tuna fish, and a chicken breast. That's one of the good things about having a partner that likes just about everything. Half of each sandwich would go to Sirius.

The two detectives hadn't slept—not even a catnap—and it showed. When they removed their sunglasses, the deep bags under their eyes were only too apparent.

Gump said, "Things were already fucked up enough before Hollywood and his press conference fucked us over that much more."

"Hollywood" was Adam Klein.

"Because of Hollywood and his reward offer," Gump said, "the phones are ringing off the hook, and the brain-dead media is more than happy to play along. The only thing that beats a Mob hit is a Mob hit with a crucifixion to boot."

"It's a Roman thing," Martinez said.

"If anyone thinks Paul Klein was a martyr," I said, "they're barking up the wrong tree."

It was an inadvertent pun, but Gump and Martinez didn't know that and they laughed. I told them what I had found out about Klein and produced the two poison-pen letters left at the oil derrick.

"Klein might have bullied the wrong guy," Gump said, "and gotten payback."

"That doesn't explain the crucifixion," I said. "Why would someone go to that kind of effort? That speaks to vengeance."

"The Mob wouldn't have gone to that effort," Martinez said. "The most they would have done was whack off his johnson and stick it in his mouth."

"Someone wanted to put Klein on display," I said.

To do that had required a lot of planning. Supplies had to have been brought into the park.

"Those planks that were nailed into the tree were new," I said. "The killer brought lumber up the trail. He would also have needed to bring nails, spikes, and probably a small sledgehammer. You don't carry around those kinds of things without being noticed."

"He could have just said he was hunting vampires," Gump said. "In this town, that would be considered a reasonable explanation."

"We already talked to a lot of the park regulars," Martinez said. "No one remembers seeing anything out of the ordinary. But if our guy was wearing a backpack, it probably would have gone unnoticed."

"Did the ME tag anything unusual about the body?"

"You ask me," Martinez said, "I think we should put Hadji on the suspect list."

Hadji was the politically incorrect name of Dr. Rupert Singh, the chief medical examiner of Los Angeles County. The name came from the cartoon *Jonny Quest* and referred to Jonny's Indian friend.

"Truth," Gump said. "That man sure knows his crucifixions."

"Years ago the Haj wrote a paper for some medical journal," Martinez explained. "He assisted in an autopsy of this two-thousand-year-old crucified corpse, and ever since he's been hooked."

"More like nailed," Gump said. "You know how he usually leaves all the cutting to others? This time he was waiting for us with open arms and an open scalpel. When I dealt with him in the past, he was about as talkative as his corpses, but this time we couldn't shut him up."

"Yeah," Martinez said, "Hadji said that whoever did the crucifying knew what they were doing."

"How the hell do you learn how to perform a crucifixion?"

"Don't know," Gump said, "but it helps to have the right equipment. Doc says the killer used spikes that matched up pretty closely with the size and shape of what was used in the old days. We might have caught a break with that. The killer did his nailing with six- and eight-inch-spikes, and those aren't the kinds of things you find at your average Home Depot. Spikes like that are used in heavy construction for driving through planking and timber."

"Or flesh and bone," Martinez said.

"It wasn't only that he got the right spikes," Gump said, "but he knew what to do with them. Hadji said the killer had to have studied crucifixions, because he drove in the spikes like he was some kind of expert. According to the Doc, if you don't do your nailing right, you don't support the body."

I had tried not to think about the surreal image of Paul Klein's body. That was probably human nature, but I was an investigator. Klein had been so securely nailed into the tree everyone had wondered if they would need to cut down the oak in order to get his body.

"He put the spikes between the carpals and the radius in the hands," Martinez said, reading from his notes, "and then went in through the second intermetatarsal space in the feet."

Gump said, "Thank you, Dr. Martinez."

"Any time, Nurse Worsley."

I did a rim shot on the creamer with my pen. "At the crime scene we were wondering if it was possible for the killer to have acted alone. Did Doc weigh in on that?"

"There were lots of ligature marks found on the victim," Gump said. "Haj was pretty sure it was a one-man operation. He said the victim was hoisted up onto the tree and then strung up on the limbs and supports before any nailing took place."

"That would explain those rubbing marks we saw in the upper branches," I said. "That would also be about the only way one person could hoist up that much dead weight. Klein probably weighed a buck seventy."

"You could get a job guessing people's weight in a carnival, Gideon," Gump said. "The vic was one-six-eight."

"Maybe that was the reason the killer went to the trouble of putting up the footrest and the seat rest. He wanted to have them to support the victim's weight."

"You mean the suppedaneum and the sedile?" Martinez asked, again reading from his notes.

"You might be Latin," Gump said, "but you can't even read Doc's words right."

"Latin's a dead language. Who's going to tell me whether I'm saying them right or not?"

"It's not a dead language. It's the official language of Vatican City."

"You must be almost fluent in it then, all those years you served *under* priests as an altar boy."

Gump blew Martinez a kiss and said, "Carpe denim—seize my jeans."

"Eat my shorts."

"I'd be afraid of crappy diem."

I'd had enough of the comedic stylings of Homicide Special and stood up to leave. "How many LAPD detectives does it take to nail a crucifixion case?" I asked.

"Is there a punch line?" Gump asked.

"Not yet," I said.

* * *

The three of us worked into the evening. Martinez spent most of his time putting the book together, while Gump and I pursued leads. If there was progress, it was the kind of which none of us was aware.

The Crucifixion Killing, as it was being called, had the media doing cartwheels. The news of Paul Klein being found with drugs had somehow leaked out. The early reports that had portrayed him as the best and the brightest, as an athlete-scholar, suddenly changed. Reporters were now saying Klein was suspected of being a drug dealer.

It was almost ten o'clock when I made it home. There were no clouds in the sky, but that only made it that much darker and colder. For a few moments, I sat in my driveway. I didn't want to go into an empty house, and I was afraid of what my dreams might bring.

January, I thought. The month was a black hole, and I didn't have the gravity to resist its pull. Staying active wasn't helping. Much as I didn't want to admit it, the darkness was sucking me in.

Sirius made a whining sound, and I reached my hand back to his muzzle. He was focused on something, and that's when I noticed the lights coming from my next-door neighbor's house. On a dark street there was one point of light. My neighbor's living room curtains were open and the glow from inside his house dispelled the shadows. There was only the one car in the driveway, a Jaguar with the personalized license plate of SHAMAN.

There was a reason my partner was fixated on the house. One of his favorite humans in the world lived there. As if on cue, my neighbor's front door opened and he stepped out on the porch.

"Let's go see our favorite fakir," I told Sirius.

My partner didn't need to be told twice and raced off for Seth Mann's door.

When Seth first moved in, I remember asking him what he did. "I'm a shaman," he told me.

Wondering if I'd heard correctly, I said, "So, on your mortgage application, that's what you wrote down as your occupation? Shaman?"

"Of course," he said.

Maybe shamanism is a growth industry. Although his job isn't run-of-the-mill, Seth has always been a great neighbor and friend. After Jennifer died he did all the organizing I couldn't bring myself to do, and when Sirius and I were being treated in the burn unit, Seth helped us in every way imaginable. He even supplied the two of us with a homemade balm that he said would bring us relief. His potion smelled rank, but it did seem to have some healing properties, or maybe it was the beer that Seth invariably snuck in with his potion. Because Seth and Sirius are thick as thieves, whenever I leave town my partner vacations next door.

Before I even got a chance to enter into his house, Seth extended a bottle of Sam Adams my way. My shaman only drinks premium beer.

"Did you divine the kind of day I had?"

"No," he said, "but there was divine intervention of a sort. Father Pat was worried about you. Apparently, you didn't return his calls. I found him waiting for you on your front porch."

"Shit," I said.

"Not to worry," Seth said. "I invited him inside. We had a nice talk and toddy. I promised Father Pat that I would see to your spiritual needs tonight."

"I'd rather you saw to my toddy needs."

Father Pat and Seth didn't exactly practice the same religion, but each enjoyed the other's company. On several occasions I had been party to their wide-ranging discussions. As strange as it seemed, each had great respect for the other. On very different paths they had found God.

Seth's house reflects his travels. He's been all over the world spending time with medicine men, witch doctors, healers, and sages. During Seth's journey to become a shaman, he was even adopted by a tribe deep in the Amazon rain forest. By the sounds of his initiation ceremony, it's not a tribe I'll be joining any time soon. I was pleased to see my two shrunken heads now on display, gifts I'd presented Seth at his recent birthday party. After he told me he'd spent time working with a Shuar medicine man and then mentioning in passing that not too long ago the Shuar were infamous for shrinking the heads of their enemies, the shrunken heads seemed like an obvious present. The two heads look the real thing; one of them even bears a miniature resemblance to Seth's round face, fan ears, flat nose, and hooded eyes. What it doesn't show is his big smile and even bigger stomach. Imagine a cross between a koala and the happy Buddha, and that's Seth.

By now I was used to the figurines, masks, rattles, drums, and effigy figures displayed on the wall shelving throughout the house. There was also no shortage of native pottery, vases, and baskets. Tobacco leaves and other pungent herbs filled bowls and containers and contributed to a beguiling aroma that filled the house. I have always made a point of never looking too closely at what kind of herbs are in the house.

Seth does workshops and has a loyal clientele. He says that his work requires him to be a combination of psychotherapist, healer, and social worker. Before becoming a shaman, Seth was a financial manager at an insurance company. One day he was wearing a suit, he told me, and the next he found himself being "liberated" in the Amazon rain forest. At least once a year, Seth returns to the jungle for what he calls a "refresher course." Invariably, Seth says, he drinks ayahuasca, a brew made from a plant known as the visionary vine, and the vine of the dead. Evidently, what doesn't destroy you makes you a better shaman.

I plopped down in an easy chair while Sirius sprawled out in his hemp dog bed, filled with organic millet hulls that Seth had bought for him. A drug-sniffing dog probably wouldn't have looked as comfortable as Sirius did. Seth brought over a water bowl for him before taking a seat on the sofa.

"Father Pat didn't offer particulars," he said, "probably a confessional thing, but he did say you were working a difficult case."

"He only got the first part of my day," I said. "It got worse. I'm working two cases now. One you probably haven't heard anything about; the other you've probably heard too much."

I told him about baby Rose and Paul Klein. Seth is a good listener, and I surprised myself by talking at length. He took my empty and brought me another beer while I talked about the cases.

"They're both so quirky," I finally said.

Seth asked, "How so?"

"Rose was found with pink bootees. I have never heard of an abandoned baby wearing bootees. And they weren't just any bootees. They were knit by hand. In fact, someone knit a blue pair as well. We found those at the crime scene. I'm thinking the mother didn't know if she was carrying a boy or a girl, so she had both colors. But why did she go to the effort of getting bootees if she was going to throw away her own kid?"

"She cared about her child," Seth said. "She wanted her to be warm."

"She didn't care about her enough."

I looked into my bottle. There were no answers there, but I brought it up to my lips anyway and tilted it.

"If I find the time tomorrow, I'll be doing bootee calls," I said. "Assuming the mom didn't knit the bootees, she must have bought them someplace."

"I hope you find what you are looking for."

As usual, Seth's words were ambiguous. "What aren't you saying?"

"Father Pat wouldn't have come seeking you out if he wasn't worried about how you might react to this case."

"This case isn't about me. It's about an abandoned baby that died."

"Then you shouldn't mind that we're concerned about the abandoned baby that lived."

"That baby is fine, thank you. But he could use insights into this case."

Seth took a sip from his beer, thought a moment, and then recited:

"God appears and God is light, to those poor souls who dwell in night, but does a human form display, to those who dwell in realms of day."

"What the hell is that supposed to mean?"

"Those are the last four lines of William Blake's 'Auguries of Innocence.' I think Blake was commenting on perception. He understood that things appear different in daytime and night-time, even though they are the same. When I...journey, I understand this."

"You're talking about your soul flights?"

He heard my skepticism and said, "If the sun and moon should doubt, they would immediately go out." And then he smiled and said, "More Blake."

Seth talked about soul flights the way someone else might talk about going to Italy. As I understand it, even though his body stays grounded, his awareness—his soul—goes places. During his flights, Seth says he has an "awakened" vision and is able to see things he wouldn't be able to otherwise. I guess what he was saying to me was that in my unenlightened state I probably didn't know my ass from a hole in the ground.

"Why don't you do a soul flight for me and find Rose's mother?"

"It doesn't work that way. And besides, it was a journey meant for you. Perhaps it will be part of your healing."

"Speaking of healing," I said, tilting my empty beer.

"Would you like another?"

"If you ever hear me say no, then I misheard the question."

Even though it was more than two years since the fire, Seth was convinced I hadn't yet healed. I had convinced doctors and police administrators of my fitness, but not Seth. Maybe I was one of Blake's poor souls that dwelled in night; maybe my shaman had seen that on one of his spirit flights.

Seth returned with a tray filled with bread, some cheese, and the beer. I was willing to bet beer tasted a lot better than ayahuasca. He also brought a dog biscuit for Sirius. My partner enthusiastically inhaled it.

"So what did your Mr. Blake have to say about crucifixions?" I asked.

"I can't recall any verse of his, but I do seem to remember that he drew several disturbing crucifixion scenes."

"Is there any other kind?"

"Was it bad?"

"It was bad. It was strange fruit."

Seth knew my shorthand and nodded.

"The boy was shot in the eye."

"I heard."

"Something tells me that wasn't coincidental. My gut feeling is that the kid was killed for revenge, as in an eye for an eye."

"Are you talking Hammurabi?"

"I am. The boy was a bit of a prick. He was a bully."

"You think one of his victims struck back?"

"Maybe," I said. "I'm not sure." More definitively I added, "Someone wanted an eye for an eye."

"How do you know that?"

"Gut feeling."

"Wouldn't murder have been revenge enough? It seems to me that crucifixion would be…overkill."

"Paul Klein was put on display. His sins were exposed for all to see."

"As I understand it, the boy had a drug problem."

I shook my head. "The drugs were planted."

"Any idea why?"

"Not yet."

"Crucifixion isn't an easy process. I remember reading Sebastian Horsley's account of it."

"Who is he?"

"He was an English artist. Horsley was quite the eccentric. He liked to wear top hats and velvet coats. And he collected human skulls."

"Everybody has to have a hobby."

"Horsley decided to go to the Philippines to be crucified."

"That doesn't sound like a pleasure trip. Why the hell would someone go and get crucified?"

"It was supposed to be an art project. Every year, devotional crucifixions take place in the Philippines over Easter. It's not a full crucifixion in that there's a platform to stand on, but nails are driven through the hands of the penitents. Horsley's crucifixion didn't go as planned, though. His foot support broke."

"That had to have hurt."

"The pain was so terrible he blacked out. There is no good form of capital punishment, but crucifixion is among the worst killing methods ever conceived. It wasn't just a means to kill someone, but was meant as a punishment to inflict terrible pain and to humiliate."

"That's what the killer wanted," I said. "He felt the need to humiliate Klein, the young man who had everything."

My burning vision had told me that.

"With your two cases I don't imagine you will be traveling," Seth said, sounding hopeful.

I had made arrangements for Seth to take Sirius later in the week. Shaking my head, I said, "I haven't canceled the meeting yet."

Seth paused a moment before saying, "Oh."

His restive note made me ask, "Is there a problem?"

"Not with my taking Sirius. But I worry about how your meetings with Ellis Haines touch you. They're not healthy."

Every month I went and visited the Weatherman at San Quentin. The trips were bankrolled by the FBI. Ostensibly, I went to gather information for their Behavioral Sciences Unit. Haines wouldn't talk with the Feds—he'd only talk to me. That's how I rationalized my visits, but the truth is I felt my own need to see him. I journeyed to my own shadow side.

"It's just talk."

Seth shook his head. "No, it's not."

He chewed on his upper lip a moment before continuing. "I know you doubt the worth of what I do."

I opened my mouth to offer some objection, but he waved it off. "It is who you are, and I don't take it personally. That said, I will tell you that part of my work involves helping those that are sick in body and spirit. In order to assist them, I need to understand the nature of their illness, and that requires me to do special journeys so as to find what ails them.

"Some of those I help are afflicted with what I call soul loss, which is what happens when the soul gets fragmented and a part of it does not know how to return to the body, or realizes it's not safe to return. A moment ago I spoke of your own healing. Your wife's death, and your near-death experience at the fire, marked you. I am convinced that part of your soul escaped and has not been able to find its way back."

I started shifting in my chair, the same way I start shifting at my front door whenever I experience a home invasion by the likes of Jehovah's Witnesses or Mormons. The difference was that Seth wasn't selling anything but revealing something.

"You mask everything well," Seth said, "but I know you no longer feel the control you once had."

"That's why there's Viagra."

Seth smiled, but he wasn't diverted. "These monthly visits drain you. It is like going to a vampire. The only difference is that he is sucking what remains of your soul instead of draining your blood. You are playing with fire."

"Playing with fire is what first brought the two of us together."

"Haven't you had enough of the burning?"

His question was too close to home. "I'm trying to douse it," I said, draining my beer, "but it's a stubborn fire."

"I am glad you have a guardian spirit," Seth said, looking at Sirius.

Seth was convinced that ever since the fire Sirius had been transformed into Canis Major or something like that. My shaman was certain that Sirius was looking out for me.

"Do all guardian spirits have as much gas as this one?" I asked.

The shaman found that funny, and that effectively stopped him from shaking his rattles anymore in my direction. I hadn't told him about my burning dreams, but I had this feeling he already knew about them. Maybe he'd heard me crying out in the middle of the night; maybe he really was a witch doctor. One thing I knew for sure was he was a friend, and that's a rare commodity.

We'd had enough heavy topics for the night, so we turned to the usual topics of sports, sex, and politics, frequently interspersed by laughter. It was typical guy talk, but yeah, it felt good for my soul.

CHAPTER 9:

A LITTLE HELP FROM MY FRIENDS

When I went to bed I said, "Not tonight." I am sure Father Pat wouldn't have thought that much of a prayer, but it was about as good as I could muster. It wasn't good enough, though. Once again the flames came, and I burned.

Like all my other burning nightmares, the fire was real to me. You would think after reliving the horror so many times that I would have some clue I'm just dreaming, but that's not the way it works. As always I was thrust back into the fiery pit.

* * *

Even in hell some smells are worse than others. The reek of burning rubber assaulted my nostrils.

It was probably a burning tire, which had been dumped in the canyon. Or maybe, just maybe, the fire had spread to the street and one of the cars was going up in flames. My pulse quickened. Hope made me breathe faster. By following the stench we might find our way out. It was a straw to grasp before it burned into a husk.

The smoke was thick. It pushed and pummeled. For the sake of my partner, I stopped running from it. Sirius had been too still for too long. The Strangler was gasping as loudly as I was. He looked at me, hoping I would give him permission to drop his burden. While I lived—and he lived—that wouldn't happen.

I leaned closer to Sirius. "We're almost there, boy," I lied. "We're almost there. Just hold on."

Through the smoke, Sirius's eyes opened. They were glazed. He was almost no longer there.

I swiveled my head, trying to get a bead on the burning rubber. It was coming from somewhere nearby. I had to find its source. And then it became all too apparent what was burning: the bottoms of my shoes were smoldering. I was fire walking.

"Shit!" I yelled. "Shit!"

I jumped up and down, stamping my feet. Tears came with my dance moves, the pain traveling up and down my body. There was a reason I'd been dragging my feet around: when you've been shot in the leg, you tend to do that. My hot foot gyrations were the equivalent of driving a hot poker into my wound. Adding insult to injury was the fact that my dance wasn't helping to put the fire out on my soles. The ground was too damn hot. The fire in my shoes wasn't going out.

I awoke to all the sheets kicked off the bed. It felt as if the soles of my feet had been pressed by a hot iron. My heart was racing, my flight instinct in overdrive. Sirius kept nudging me, making sure I was all right. I took a few heaving breaths, and he licked my sweaty brow, vanquishing the demons for another night.

When you escape hell, you are not supposed to look back. Orpheus made that mistake. Whenever I escape the fire I try to not dwell on the pain, preferring to float away on a cloud of relief, but before that happens I experience my moment after.

Dinah Hakimi was looking at me. In the background of my vision I could hear a familiar tune, the Beatles singing "With a Little Help from My Friends." Dinah was exaggeratedly mouthing the words that she got by with a little help from her friends. As she lip-synched she was smiling and not trying to hide her protruding front teeth. Behind her teeth, though, something else was hidden, and reluctantly she reached behind them to reveal a razor blade.

And then Dinah reached for a piece of paper, and I could see it was the card she had left at the tower of hope. She took the razor blade and cut into where she had written "You made my life HELL," and blood started flowing from the page.

The image was surreal and disturbing, and I doubt whether I would have been able to fall back to sleep save for another image that came to mind. Lisbet Keane was smiling at me and imparted a peace that had long escaped me. I inhaled the aroma of something nice, something that reminded me of Thanksgiving, and then I slept.

When I awakened a few hours later, I stayed in bed thinking about the moment after I had experienced. I was fairly certain the razor blade symbolized Dinah's contemplation of suicide. The young woman had sought out help, I remembered. Too many desperate young people never do that, thinking they can get by on their own. Dinah had gotten by with a little help from one of the suicide hotline counselors. She had said he was a good man.

I decided it was worth seeing if she was right about that.

I called Dinah's cell phone, but when she didn't pick up I left a voice message. A few minutes later I received a text from her. The message said, "I'll call u in half an hour." It was likely that she didn't want to talk to me with her family around and wouldn't call until she reached school.

When she phoned back I could hear the background noise of youthful chatter. Dinah talked as she walked and said, "I only have a few minutes before class begins."

"This shouldn't take long. I need the name and number of the man at the Community Crisis Line that counseled you."

"Why do you want to bother him?"

"It's necessary background."

"Our talks were confidential."

"I am not going to ask him about what you talked about."

"It still feels like an invasion of privacy."

"What do you think a police investigation is? Is there a reason you don't want me to talk to him?"

"I don't want him to get into any trouble."

"Why would he get in trouble?"

"He went out of his way to help me."

"And how did he do that?"

"We talked on the phone a few times when he wasn't working at the help line. And he met with me once or twice."

"And I'm assuming personal calls and meetings aren't allowed?"

"He only did those things because he was afraid I might do something drastic and wanted to make sure I was all right."

"Where did the meetings take place?"

"We talked in his car."

"You met with him in his car?"

"That's where I asked to meet. I didn't want anyone seeing us."

"Was there any physical contact between the two of you?"

Dinah's answer was shrill: "Of course not! All he did was try and help me. See, I was right. I knew you'd make it look like he did something wrong."

"It seems to me he would have helped you a lot more by reporting the bullying to the school administration."

"He wanted to, but I convinced him not to."

"I need his name, Dinah."

"He never gave it to me. The help lines are anonymous."

Her voice tailed off. Even she knew her lie sounded lame. "You know, with one phone call I can get his name, but do you want me to do that? It would mean involving other people, including your family."

"Can't you understand that I don't want to betray a confidence?"

"If you call him now and explain the situation, he'll understand you don't have a choice. And after you do that I want you to have him call me back at this number."

Dinah sighed and then clicked off.

Two minutes later my phone rang. A male voice asked me if he was speaking with Detective Gideon, and when I told him he was, the man said, "This is Dave Miller. Dinah Hakimi said you wanted to talk with me."

"You're her counselor?"

"I am not a licensed counselor. I am a volunteer at the Community Crisis Line."

"How long have you been advising Dinah?"

"We first started talking about a year ago."

"Dinah didn't want to give me your name. She was afraid of getting you into trouble."

"I've already reassured her about that. I told her that I brought any trouble on myself by breaking the rules."

"So why is it that you thought you were above the rules?"

"That's not what I thought or think. I understand the reasoning behind the rules. I know counselors need to maintain boundaries between themselves and those they are trying to help. And in the eighteen months I've worked at the Community Crisis Line, I never violated those rules. In Dinah's case, though, I felt the need to intervene. I tried to refer her to specialists, but she refused to talk to anyone but me. When she threatened to kill herself, I agreed to meet with her in person."

"Was she crying wolf?"

"I don't think so. But I still should have found a better way to help her other than by meeting with her."

"I'd like a face-to-face with you—today, if possible."

"Since today is my volunteer day, I am going to be in the LA area anyway. I can talk with you in the early afternoon, but I am scheduled to be on the phones beginning at three."

"Where are the offices of the Community Crisis Line?"

"Culver City."

"And where are you driving from?"

"I live just above Temecula."

Temecula is in the south of Riverside County and nowhere near Culver City. "That's a long commute."

"I only do it one or two days a week. When I first started volunteering at the Community Crisis Line, I lived in West LA and then last year moved to De Luz. It's a bit of a drive, but I didn't want to quit the help line."

"Let's meet in Culver City at two then. Do you know a good spot to talk?"

He thought a moment and then said, "Are you familiar with the lobby bar in the Culver Hotel?"

I almost said something about following the yellow brick road but refrained. I had frequented the Tiny Town retreat a few times and told him I would be there at two.

* * *

Over a cup of coffee and a piece of burned toast, I googled "bullying causes teen suicide." I was sorry to see there were so many hits and so many sad stories. According to what I gleaned, there are about five thousand teen suicides in the United States every year, but in some ways that's only the tip of the iceberg; for every successful suicide, there are many, many attempts. There is even a word for a suicide caused by bullying: "bullycide."

Among teens, suicide is the third leading cause of death, and sensitive children are especially vulnerable to bullies. I wondered if the bullying pack sensed that, and if they targeted the vulnerable just like animals of prey did. Even the mental health professionals aren't sure of which comes first: the depression that worsens from the teasing, or the teasing that causes depression. What isn't in question is that the bullying makes it worse for the suffering victim. Even someone strong like Dinah Hakimi had been beaten down by her tormentors.

Unfortunately, home is no longer a place to be safe from the bullies. Cyberbullying can be just as bad, if not worse, than being physically bullied. Electronic character assassinations are all too commonplace. Young people don't have the coping mechanisms that come with age, and I read about suicides that had resulted from poison-pen websites and devastating instant messages and anonymous posts. One mother had gotten involved in her daughter's fight and posed as a sixteen-year-old boy to lure in her daughter's rival. After pretending friendship, the mother had written devastating comments about the girl, who ultimately committed suicide.

Those stories and others dominated my thoughts during my drive to the Police Administration Building. Gump and Martinez were holed up on the fifth floor, the home for Robbery-Homicide. We met in a conference room and went over where we were with the case.

I found a spare desk and used my laptop to continue delving into the world of cyberbullying. I wondered if Klein and company had gone that route, and added it to my list of things to check out.

Of course Klein hadn't been averse to the old-fashioned kind of bullying either. I made a call to Troy Vincent, the lacrosse player Klein had allegedly coldcocked. When I identified myself and the purpose for my call, Vincent sounded distinctly uncomfortable.

"You're not supposed to say bad things about dead people, are you?" he said.

"That's a saying," I said, "but not a reality."

Reluctantly, Vincent agreed to meet with me the following morning at his high school.

I thought about the need for people to speak ill of the dead. If not for Dinah Hakimi's card, I might not have gotten a lead on Paul Klein's bullying. These days, when people die their obituaries are available online, and friends and acquaintances are encouraged to leave testimonials. I had this feeling that sometimes it's not only friends that feel the urge to write something. I looked up Paul Klein's obit online and then went to the guest book where I could read the entries that had been left. Almost eight hundred people had written notes for Paul, the kind of figure that's usually only generated by professional athletes and actors. Klein's unusual death had struck a nerve not only in LA but also in the country.

After looking through a few hundred entries, I began to suspect something wasn't right. Each of the notes expressed sorrow. As far as I could determine, there were no undercurrents and not even a hint of discord. That didn't seem possible to me. Even saints have their detractors. I was certain a censor's hand was at work.

My suspicions were confirmed when I contacted the Dearly Departed website and was able to talk to its obituary editor, Mary Ann Wiggins. "About a third of our staff spends its days vetting comments on the guest book," she said. "Nothing gets posted until we have checked through it carefully."

Cyberbullying apparently didn't only extend to the living. "People like to speak ill of the dead?"

"You wouldn't believe what comes through here. It's nastier than you could imagine."

"I'm a cop."

That meant I had seen and heard everything, but that didn't stop Wiggins from telling me a few stories. I heard about sons and daughters trying to "set the record straight." It was *Mommie Dearest* multiplied tenfold. She also told me about outsiders with axes to grind who weren't placated by death; people wanted to expose supposed pillars of the community as drunks, pedophiles, adulterers, and whoremongers.

"Of course our readers don't get to see those comments," Wiggins said.

"Those are exactly the comments I want to see," I said.

"I don't know if that would be possible."

"I am hoping you can make it possible. It's important. Your assistance might help us nail a murderer."

I second-guessed myself for using the word "nail," but Wiggins didn't seem to notice. She promised to see what she could do, and said she would get back to me. Wiggins sounded sincere.

Tom Sawyer got to watch his own funeral and hear what everyone had to say about him. Public bereavement is one thing, private thoughts are another. Someone had taken speaking ill of the dead to a new level by crucifying Paul Klein and putting him on display. If I was lucky, maybe even that kind of revenge wasn't enough for the killer, and even now he was intent on inflicting more damage on his victim.

* * *

Before meeting with Dave Miller, I did a cursory background check on him. Miller was fifty years old and had been a successful jeweler, the owner of two mall jewelry stores in the Los Angeles area. He'd been divorced for ten years. Miller had never been arrested; he didn't even have a recent moving violation. There were no court actions other than the divorce attached to his name. Many jewelers are registered handgun owners; Miller had never registered a gun in his name.

I arrived a few minutes early for our meet-up and parked in a parking lot a block from the hotel. The Culver Hotel has been around since before the Great Depression, and has managed to survive earthquakes, economic downturns, and redevelopment. When it was built in the Roaring Twenties, the six-story building had been described as a skyscraper. These days it's a national historical landmark. Its main claim to fame, though, is that it housed the Munchkins.

When *The Wizard of Oz* was being filmed in 1938, 124 little people stayed at the Culver Hotel. If Judy Garland is to be believed, the occupants of the Culver Hotel were into nonstop partying. The hotel guests might have been little, but they partied big—there were stories of drunken escapades and wild sex parties. All of those supposed Munchkin antics inspired the 1981 movie *Under the Rainbow*.

Dorothy left a black-and-white Kansas for the color of Munchkinville and Oz. When I stepped into the lobby, it wasn't exactly like stepping into another world, but I did appreciate the high ceilings of the hotel as well as its old world charm.

There were only a few people in the lobby bar, and only one of them was sizing me up. I walked toward the man's table, and he got to his feet. He was middle-aged, with droopy brown eyes, frown lines, and salt-and-pepper hair. Because I've worked with dogs for much of my adult life, I often categorize people as breeds. Happy, animated sorts are golden retrievers. Those that are nervous and hyper are Jack Russell terriers. Beautiful people are poodles. Those with OCD are border collies. Solid citizens are Airedales. Class clowns are Labradors. Sensitive sorts are basset hounds. Independent types are cairn terriers, a breed that came to mind because of my being in Munchkinville. Toto was a cairn terrier, but Dave Miller was no Toto. The man reminded me of a basset hound, probably because of his eyes.

We shook hands and confirmed our identities. A server came over. I ordered an iced tea; Miller went with a tonic water.

"So what made you flee LA?" I asked.

The question appeared to surprise him. "Flee?"

"Why did you move to Temecula?"

"I like to describe it as a *Field of Dreams* thing, but without the voices. I had this Kevin Costner midlife crisis I suppose. After twenty-five years of being a jeweler and having responsibility over two stores, I cashed in my chips and bought a forty-acre avocado farm."

"So now you're a farmer?"

"No, I'm a landowner pretending to be a farmer."

"It's just a hobby?"

"If it is, it's an all-consuming hobby. Last year my avocado crop brought in more than sixty thousand dollars, but that doesn't take into account all of my expenses. I figure with all the hours I put in I didn't even make minimum wage."

"It sounds as if you've embarked upon quite an adventure."

"Is that a polite way of saying I'm crazy?"

"Maybe you just like guacamole more than most."

"You're right about that."

"Was this ranch a lifetime dream of yours?"

Miller shook his head. "An opportunity presented itself and I acted."

"It sounds like a big change. Most people would be scared to start a new life like that. Wasn't it hard leaving behind friends and family in LA?"

"I don't have any family in LA. I'm divorced. And now that I have a place in the country, all my LA friends have a good reason to come and visit me. It almost feels like I've opened a bed and breakfast."

"How is it that you started volunteering at the help line?"

"My best friend committed suicide," Miller said. "Afterward I wondered what I could have said or done that might have made a difference. It bothered me that I never really picked up on all the signs I should have seen. And then one day I heard a public service announcement asking for volunteers for the Community Crisis Line."

"Are most of the help lines manned by volunteers?"

"Some are and some aren't. Community Mental Health operates one help line, and the LA County Department of Mental Health has another. Cedars Sinai operates a line that has teens helping other teens. And then there are the national help numbers as well."

"What kind of formal training did you have?"

"I went to classes for a month. There were sixty hours of lectures and a few tests I had to pass. Before doing the training, I had to make a four-hour-a-week commitment for a minimum of one year. More than anything, though, I think I needed to demonstrate that I had a sympathetic ear. That's what I am there for—to listen."

"But with Dinah Hakimi you did more than listen?"

Miller nodded. "I don't offer this as an excuse, Detective, but more as an explanation. I didn't want another death on my conscience. I never helped my friend like I should have, and I wasn't about to make that mistake with Dinah. I must admit to being somewhat surprised, though."

"Surprised about what?"

"That you sought me out for this talk. I know I shouldn't have met with Dinah privately, but we didn't do anything against the law, and I'm willing to take a polygraph to that effect."

"I am not here about your private sessions with Dinah. I am here because the bully that was plaguing Dinah was murdered."

"Oh," Miller said. He nodded several times while taking in the news. His face didn't reveal his take on the information.

I waited for him to break the silence. When he did, Miller said, "If Dinah is a suspect in any form or fashion, she shouldn't be."

"And why is that?"

"She could never commit murder. She is a gentle soul. She would hurt herself sooner than hurt someone else. That was the problem, you see. She turned her anger inward. Even though she was without blame, she started blaming herself, and that began a vicious cycle."

"How do you feel knowing that her tormentor is dead?"

Miller didn't answer right away. When he did he said, "For Dinah's sake, I'm relieved."

"Some mental health therapists go into the profession because they like to think of themselves as saviors."

"I am not a mental health therapist."

"But you're a voice in the darkness."

"I hope I am."

"I think I became a cop to help others. It must have been hard to listen to the anguish of a young lady and yet not be able to do anything about it."

"It was difficult, but I was doing something about it. I listened to Dinah, and I tried to make sure she didn't fixate on the present but instead looked to the future."

"Do you have any children?"

Miller shook his head.

"Did you begin to feel paternal with Dinah? When we talked on the phone, you said you broke the rules because you felt responsible for her."

"I care about Dinah, but I have never thought of her as a daughter."

"Did you ever consider confronting the bullies? It must have been hard just sitting back and having to hear about all their mind games."

"I am sure everyone has fantasies about being a knight in shining armor, but I know it does no good in the long run to fight someone else's battles. What I did was to try and teach Dinah coping mechanisms."

"How did your friend kill himself?"

Miller took a deep breath, sighed, and said, "He shot himself."

"Why did he do it?"

"I think the pain became too great for him to endure it any longer."

I nodded. As much as I didn't want to admit it, I had been there. "I can understand why you wanted to help Dinah," I said, "but I am still going to have to contact the director of the help line and tell him what transpired."

Miller nodded. "I figured as much. That's why I set up a meeting with him this afternoon. I don't anticipate a good outcome."

"For what it's worth, Dinah thinks you saved her life."

"It's worth a lot."

Miller dropped a Hamilton on the table, took a last sip of his tonic water, and said, "If you don't have any more questions for me, it's time for me to go and face the music."

We both stood up and shook hands. And then I took a seat again, and watched him leave. Even now I thought of Miller as a basset hound. He carried his sensitivity—and sadness—with him.

I sipped my iced tea and looked around the open space. Years ago there had been a reunion of the Munchkins. They had returned to the Culver Hotel and reminisced about their time making the movie. The little people had said tales of their debauchery were exaggerated, and that they were too tired from working fourteen-hour days to party to excess.

Still, there were persistent stories of many of the Munchkins getting drunk night after night and belting out the tune "Ding-Dong! The Witch Is Dead." According to the stories, though, the little people preferred substituting the word "bitch."

Right now my cases had me feeling like the Scarecrow. I wasn't ready for my close-up, but I was ready for the refrain, "If I only had a brain."

The witch wasn't dead, but Paul Klein and baby Rose were.

Maybe Munchkinville wasn't the idyllic place it was made out to be. There had been a Munchkin coroner in *The Wizard of Oz*, I remembered. His lines had always made me laugh, and I tried to remember them.

Finally they came to me and I said, "As coroner, I must aver, I thoroughly examined her. And she's not only merely dead, she's really most sincerely dead."

I finished the iced tea. It was time to get back to the sincerely dead and those that had made them that way. That was a job that fell to cops, or maybe the Lollipop Guild.

"Refill?" the server asked.

"No thanks."

Toto was waiting, I thought. Outside I watched palm trees bending to a strong gust of wind. At least I didn't see any flying monkeys.

CHAPTER 10:

LA SAINTS AND LA AIN'TS

You know you're leading a strange life when you find yourself looking forward to a visit to the morgue. In the morning I had fallen back to sleep after my burning, lulled by the image of Lisbet Keane and the aroma of pumpkin bread. Somewhere in my subconscious I had remembered my three-thirty meeting with the coroner, Lisbet, and Rose.

When you are working multiple cases, one invariably takes precedence. Because the Klein crucifixion was high-profile, I'd been forced to put the investigation of baby Rose on the backburner, but her death had continued to play on my mind.

As far as I know there isn't any official name for the spot where I was cooling my heels, but everybody calls it the body pickup zone. It's a spot where you usually find mortuary employees or cemetery drivers waiting for bodies to be released by the Los Angeles County Department of Coroner, so it's not somewhere that most people want to linger. I tried not to breathe through my nose while pacing around the outer room that served as a waiting area, but even the open-mouth trick wasn't helping.

It would have been worse had I been inside watching the autopsy. That's what I should have been doing, but I had convinced myself that my being a witness wasn't important to the case. The truth of the matter is that I just couldn't stomach the thought of watching another baby being cut open. I had been there for baby Moses; once was enough.

In LA, the coroner's department is charged with looking into and determining the cause of all violent, sudden, or unusual deaths occurring within the county. On average, they investigate about twenty thousand deaths a year, with 10 percent of those deemed potential homicides. That results in around twenty autopsies every day; today baby Rose had been among that number. The pathologist had told me he would have the results by three o'clock, but I knew that I wasn't the only one in on the death loop.

Lisbet Keane—aka the Saint—entered the body pickup zone, and when I saw her I forgot about the escaping odors of death that were causing my stomach to do loop-the-loops. Lisbet's pale complexion set off her dark hair and wide-spaced eyes. She carried a smile a little fuller than Mona Lisa's, but not that much fuller. When Lisbet saw me, her enigmatic smile deepened. Hours earlier, in the aftermath of my burning, I'd seen her appear looking just the same as she did now. All day I'd been looking forward to seeing her.

"Detective Gideon," she said.

I was glad she remembered my name, but her memory might have been helped because we had talked on the phone earlier in the week about Rose.

"It's nice to see you, Ms. Keane."

As far as I can determine, Lisbet isn't judgmental. I have never heard her condemn the mothers that abandoned their babies to such tragic circumstances; her emphasis is always on the babies themselves. Still, she seems to understand that LAPD has a job to do.

"I was afraid I was going to be late," she said.

I refrained from telling her that Rose wasn't going anywhere and instead said, "Dr. Chen's running a little behind today."

I positioned my head so that my left side was facing her. That's my good side that doesn't show the scarring. I rarely bother to do that, but then usually I'm not trying to impress anyone.

"How is Sirius?" she asked.

This proud father smiled. Most people shy away from police dogs, but that wasn't the case with Lisbet. We had met during my investigation of baby Moses, the newborn that had drowned in the LA Aqueduct. Lisbet had invited me to attend Moses's memorial service, and to my surprise I had agreed to do so. It had been a hot day, and the cemetery where Lisbet's charges are buried is more than an hour's drive outside of LA in the desert community of Calimesa. Because it was an outdoor ceremony, I positioned the car so that Sirius could see what was going on. Lisbet noticed him pacing in the backseat and told me it would be all right if I freed him to attend the service. Afterward Lisbet had praised his behavior, and Sirius had almost turned into a lapdog in his efforts to please her further.

"He's out in the car getting some shut-eye. Most of his hair has grown back since the last time you saw him, so he's getting to be his old, vain self again. He was a little more humble when he had all of those bald patches."

She smiled at my words, and I had to remind myself that trying to make time with a woman there to attend to a dead baby might not be the best of ideas.

"He's a sweetie," she said.

"Yeah, he's a sheep in wolf's clothing."

"I grew up with dogs. I wish I could have one, but my apartment doesn't allow animals. I was considering moving into this complex that allows dogs, but then I learned they have to weigh less than ten pounds. That doesn't sound like a dog to me."

"I saw one of those miniature things last week. A woman was walking down Rodeo Drive carrying this designer dog in her designer bag. The thing looked like a rat with a bouffant."

"I think I saw that same rat."

We shared a little laugh, but it must have sounded as wrong to her ears as it did to mine for we both stopped abruptly. Being there for Rose made any laughter out of place. The silence between us grew until Lisbet bridged it with a question.

"How is your investigation going, Detective?"

I shook my head, not telling her that Paul Klein was taking up most of my time. "The race is not always to the swift."

"Nor the battle to the strong."

I shrugged. "I'm afraid I don't remember the next line."

"I don't either, but I seem to recall that it concludes by saying that time and chance happen to us all."

"That's what every investigation counts upon," I said, "time and chance."

The door opened, and Dr. John Chen and a clerk emerged. The clerk was carrying a clipboard and a small plastic bundle, and after Lisbet signed several forms he somberly passed over the package. The plastic masked but did not conceal the small, naked figure within.

"Hello, Rose," Lisbet said, her tone gentle and caring.

Even though I expected Lisbet to respond as she did, I still felt uncomfortable. Most people don't deal with the dead in the way that she does, and I was relieved when she excused herself to go outside to carry on her one-way conversation with Rose. I knew that Lisbet always spent an hour or two at the coroner's office giving the babies that were released to her the kind of welcome to the world they never received in life. Through a window I watched as she took a seat on a nearby bench and cradled Rose in her arms. If I hadn't known better, I would have thought that a mother had stopped to nurse her baby. I tried not to stare but couldn't seem to avert my eyes. As I watched, I felt myself growing more and more conflicted. Lisbet was too young and vital to be spending all her attention on the dead. There was a part of me that wished I was the one nestled at her chest instead of a baby that would never respond to her.

I turned my eyes to Dr. Chen and saw he was also caught up in the viewing. I had always considered Chen as hard as nails, but I could see that behind his glasses his eyes were misting. Everyone at the coroner's knows Lisbet; she has won over the entire building. On one occasion when Lisbet gathered one of her dead charges, a dozen workers had come out and sang "Amazing Grace."

Chen abruptly turned away from Lisbet and looked down to the paperwork he was holding. He did his best to assume a cut-and-dried voice and said, "Cause of death appears to be positional asphyxiation."

"Which means what exactly?"

"It means that respiratory compromise occurred and the baby suffocated."

"Was it accidental or was she smothered?"

Coroners aren't different from anyone else—they like to hedge their bets—but Chen didn't see the need this time. "All signs point to it being accidental. Usually we see positional asphyxiation when a baby gets wedged in a space, most often between a mattress and a wall, but it can also happen when a baby gets entangled in bedding, which is what appears to have occurred."

"Was the baby alive when she was abandoned?"

Chen nodded. "We found no evidence of trauma. The baby's respiration was compromised because of the soft bedding she was placed in. With the box angled like it was, she was not strong enough to fight gravity and was smothered in the blanket wrapped around her."

Gravity, I thought. "Would we were talking about an apple."

Chen chose not to comment.

* * *

The late afternoon traffic was the usual stop and go, and with the time getting short I started nervously drumming my fingers on the steering wheel. After my burning dream I'd awakened to the aroma of pumpkin bread, and had decided my subconscious was telling me how to proceed. This particular gift shop was supposed to stay open until five, which left me twenty minutes to travel about a mile. In LA that's no sure bet. As I continued to tap away at the steering wheel, Sirius got up and started pacing around.

I stopped my rapping. "All right, I'll cease and desist with the drum rolls."

My partner seemed glad to hear my voice. I had been silent since taking leave of the coroner's office.

"When clues dry up, some detectives grasp at straws," I said, "but not me. I grasp at crumbs and follow their trail."

Judging by the thump-thump of his tail, Sirius seemed to think that was a pretty good thing.

"I suppose you think you're going to extort some treats out of this visit. Think again, flea head. If you don't watch out, people will start thinking you're a doughnut-shop cop."

Earlier, I had googled "pumpkin bread in Los Angeles," and it had led me to an unlikely source: the Monastery of the Angels. There were a number of articles and websites that glowingly described the pumpkin bread made by the order of cloistered Dominican nuns just two blocks off of Hollywood Boulevard. The bread was made fresh every day and was sold out of the monastery's gift shop.

I knew of the monastery's existence but had only driven by it. The nuns had picked about as worldly a spot as there was to lead their cloistered lives. The monastery is only a stone's throw from the 101 freeway; the traffic noise has to be a constant reminder of the world outside their walls. Many locals don't even know about the monastery in the midst of the city. Its appearance is no give-away: to the casual eye, its stucco walls and steel gates look more industrial than ecclesiastical.

Nearing the monastery, I found myself staring at a familiar sign propped up in the Beachwood Canyon foothills: HOLLYWOOD. The white lettering stood out in the growing dusk. I wondered if the nuns ever took notice of that same sign. I looked at my watch again. Like Cinderella, I had a pumpkin deadline.

It was five of five by the time I parked. I left Sirius behind and jogged through the parking lot, cutting over to the pathway that took me past the public chapel to the front reception area. There was an OPEN sign on the entrance door, which gave me hope, but that same door was closed and the reception area had a deserted look that appeared to contradict the invitation to come inside. I tried the door, found it locked, and then knocked. A muffled voice called out from somewhere inside the building, and then I heard footfalls. From inside the door a woman with a Jersey accent asked, "Is there something I can help you with?"

"I'm Detective Michael Gideon."

A curtain opened and I held up my wallet shield.

"Are you here to buy something?"

"I am here to ask some questions."

"Just a sec."

Clicking locks turned and the door opened to reveal a middle-aged woman with big hair and lots of makeup who was wearing a sequined sweater that shimmered with various cat designs. It was a good thing Sirius was in the car.

"I was just closing up," she said, doing a lot of talking with hands that also gestured for me to enter.

"If you don't mind, I need to take a quick look inside the shop."

My request surprised the woman, but she shrugged and then did another operatic sweep of her arms. The space I entered was barely boutique-size, and my eyeball inventory didn't take long. Most of the wares had a religious bent, but not all. There were several boxes of chocolates on display, as well as two loaves of pumpkin bread, but what most captured my attention was a shelf of knitted goods. I went for a closer look and pushed aside the hats and mittens in favor of a pair of pink bootees. The image of Rose in her bootees came to mind, even though I wished it hadn't.

The cat woman offered up some history regarding the bootees I was holding. "Sister Mary Ruth does most of the knitting. She's almost ninety, but she's a terror with her knitting needles."

"I'll try not to get on her bad side then," I said, returning the bootees and looking at the speaker. "Do you work here?"

"Dottie Antonelli," she said, extending her hand. "I'm a volunteer, but I'm here two or three days a week."

"Is there a gift shop manager?"

Dottie shook her head. "There's a committee of volunteers that helps the nuns. Somehow everything works."

I handed Dottie my card; her eyelids, heavy with makeup, managed to widen some. "I guess you're not here about parking tickets."

"Guilty conscience?"

"Always," she said, wagging a good-natured finger at me.

"I'm hoping I can talk with whoever might have waited on a woman that I believe was shopping here one day last week."

"You're talking about seven or eight volunteers that might have been working," Dottie said, "and that doesn't include the nuns."

"Nuns work in the gift shop?"

"Why do you ask? Guilty conscience?"

"You know anyone with a Catholic upbringing who doesn't have one?"

I got a smile and another finger wagging, but her fire-engine red nails sort of vitiated the tsk-tsk effect. "When we're busy, one or two of the sisters sometimes come out to help."

"Is there any way you can round up some of those sisters that might have been working in here last week?"

"You mean now?" she asked and then shook her head. "This isn't a good time. The sisters are at Vespers. What you need to do is make an appointment with the prioress to talk with them."

"Is she here?"

"She's almost always here. This is a cloistered monastery. That means the nuns pretty much stay put behind these walls."

"So, can I talk with her?"

"You'd be interrupting her. She's working."

"Working?"

"Don't sound surprised. Nuns don't like to be distracted from their work."

"Making the pumpkin bread?"

Dottie laughed. "That's more of a sideline. Their full-time work is praying."

"They pray full-time?"

My incredulity got me a Jersey girl retort. "I find it hard enough to do it part-time. What about you?"

"You have a point."

"It's almost twenty-four/seven for the nuns," she said. "They live a life of enclosure so that they can dedicate themselves completely to prayer. You'd think if you withdrew from the world you wouldn't give two hoots about it, but they spend all their time praying for it."

"They've taken on a big job."

"You're telling me. I don't let anything get in the way of me and my eight hours, but the nuns even give up their sleep for prayer. They take turns getting up during the night to do their adoration and keep vigil with Jesus."

"I am sure he appreciates their company."

Dottie regarded me suspiciously, but I must have passed muster because she chose not to upbraid me.

I asked, "How many nuns are there here?"

"Fewer and fewer," she said. "Nowadays there are around twenty, and most of them are as old as the hills. There certainly aren't enough for all the praying that's needed."

I remembered a line I had once heard: "Too many sneezers, and not enough *Gesundheiters*."

"You can say that again."

I started thinking aloud. "I need to find out if anyone worked in the last week and waited on a woman that bought some pumpkin bread, as well as two pairs of bootees, one pink and the other blue. I suspect this woman was pregnant, but it's possible she wasn't showing."

"Some women are like that, but not me. My three pregnancies I was out to here"—Dottie gestured to a spot beyond where her fingers could reach—"and that was after only a few months. I always looked like I was carrying a litter."

Dottie provided me with a Sharpie, a stapler, and running commentary while I wrote up the details on my wanted poster and attached my card. When I finished up, I took an appreciative sniff of the air.

"That pumpkin bread smells great."

"It tastes better than it smells," Dottie said. "Usually it's all sold out by noon."

"I'll take a loaf then."

"You'll want some of the hand-dipped chocolates as well," she said, reaching for a box and not giving me any choice in the matter. "There's never any left over. Today's your lucky day."

"You sure you don't work on commission?"

"Bring the chocolates home to your wife and see if I'm not telling it like it is."

"I'm not married."

Deadpan she said, "With all your charm?"

She bagged up the chocolates. "A box of chocolates can make a woman forgive a lot of flaws. If you want to catch a mouse, you need the cheese."

"I'm a cop, not an exterminator."

"These chocolates are so good some woman will even put up with your bad jokes."

"Thanks for your help and the million calories."

"The nuns made them. How can it be bad for you?"

I gathered up my goodies. The bag she handed me was surprisingly heavy. By the feel of it, the nuns must have put the Great

Pumpkin into my loaf of pumpkin bread. We said our good-byes, but I stopped short of walking out the door. My subconscious was still mulling over why Rose's mother had come to this spot. Sinners look to repent in different ways. Maybe the pregnant woman hadn't known where to turn other than God. She might have been so ashamed of her condition that she had considered the need for penance in a big way. I wondered if she had come to the monastery to ask how to go about becoming a nun.

"Is it possible that our mystery woman could have talked to one of the nuns before she came into the gift shop?"

Dottie shrugged her shoulders. "Why not? The nuns might be cloistered, but they're not invisible."

"Let's say she came to the monastery and asked how to become a nun here. Would she have to talk to anyone in particular?"

"I suppose the prioress. That would be the Reverend Mother Frances."

"And you're sure she's too busy to talk to me now?"

"If you're here about an investigation, I would be more comfortable getting you an appointment with her tomorrow. If you're here about your own spiritual issues, I am sure she will see you now."

"Late afternoon tomorrow would work best for me."

Dottie promised to call me in the morning to confirm the time. I thanked her for all her help, but again I couldn't quite bring myself to leave. Something was still nagging at me.

"The reverend mother's name is Frances?"

I said it as if the name was familiar to me, even though I was pretty sure I didn't know a single person in the world named Frances.

"You might have read about her," Dottie said, looking rather pleased.

"What? Was she awarded Mother Superior of the Year?"

"No, the reverend mother experienced a miracle."

"How can I top that?"

"You can't."

CHAPTER 11:

TOTALLY FUBAR

For dinner I had the pumpkin bread and most of the chocolates. Both were as tasty as Dottie had promised. I told myself it was a balanced diet, and that I was getting my fruit and vegetables in the pumpkin bread. As it turned out, it was a good night. These days my definition of a good night is when I don't burn. In the morning my alarm sounded and I got out of bed actually feeling refreshed. That was lucky for me, because today was my day for going back to high school.

I drove to the coast, making my way to a peninsula known collectively as Palos Verdes, which the locals refer to as PV. Although PV doesn't have the reputation of Beverly Hills, the beach community is every bit as affluent.

Palos Verdes High School is only half a block from the beach and sits on some of the most expensive high school real estate in the country. I arrived early enough to take Sirius for a walk along the coast. There was a no-dogs rule on most of the area's beaches, so my partner and I had to be content to do our walking within sight and sound of the surf.

After the walk, I picked up a coffee and went to the agreed-upon meet-up spot near the front of the high school. While waiting, I drank my coffee and took in the view. Even over the noise of arriving students, I could hear the sounds of the ocean. PV is less than twenty miles southwest of LA, but it feels like a different world.

Troy Vincent had told me he didn't have a class until eight and had agreed to meet with me at half past seven. At twenty of eight, a young man approached drinking a Coke and eating a Slim Jim sausage. He had a deep tan, and his long, wet hair had natural blond highlights from the sun. His garb was beach casual: board shorts, a T-shirt from a local surf shop, flip-flops, and white-framed, smoky-lens sunglasses.

"Sorry I'm late," he said. "I was out with the dawn patrol and the waves were awesome."

He didn't offer a hand to me but did to Sirius, saying, "How's it going, Bubba?"

Sirius casually sniffed the offered hand and then licked it, either for a taste of sea salt or Slim Jim.

"Where were you surfing?"

"Haggerty's," he said.

I nodded as if I knew the spot. In truth I had heard of it, but my awareness was limited to oldies radio. Haggerty's was part of the lyrics in the Beach Boys song "Surfin' USA."

"When we talked yesterday you were reluctant to speak ill of the dead," I said.

Troy shrugged. "Why mess with bad karma?"

"Wouldn't it be worse karma if you didn't help, and by doing that someone got away with murder?"

He took a bite of his Slim Jim, considered my words, and finally offered a shrug and noncommittal nod.

"Tell me about the lacrosse game where you and Klein went at it."

"He was a dude with a 'tude," said Troy. "He was acting like he was the big kahuna out on the field. During the match there were some infusions going on, you know? That's part of the game, so when the two of us collided he got all hot and told me I rammed his space. So I told him, 'Brah, that's not my way,' but he still had a pile of sand in his shorts and I could tell he was ready to go aggro. I didn't back down, though, and told him if he wanted to barnie, then we should do it, but he just gave me the stink eye, or that's what I thought until a little while later when I got acid-dropped."

"You were hit from behind?"

He nodded. "It was totally fubar."

Translation: fucked up beyond all recognition.

"But you didn't actually see Paul Klein hit you?"

"That's right, which is what made it so nitchen. Instead of manning up, he did a sneak attack and made sure no one was looking. And then he lied about it."

"His coach said you coldcocked him."

"That's totally bogus. That dude made up that story."

"Did your teams meet up again?"

"Not on the field. That was one of the last games of the season."

"Not on the field?" I asked. "Did something happen off the field?"

Troy turned his gaze to the Pacific and said, "I'm still not sure if I should narc on him, seeing as he's dead."

I didn't say anything; I was pretty sure Troy would spill if I was patient. He took a bite of his Slim Jim, pulled the last bit free from the wrapper, and asked, "You think Bubba wants to finish it off?"

"I have no doubt of that. But I have to share a car with Bubba."

"Sorry," Troy said to Sirius and finished the last bite, chasing it with his Coke.

How is it that surfers can eat like that, I thought, and still look so healthy? It wasn't a question I asked him; bad karma or not, Troy had decided to give up the rest of the story.

"So, a month or two after lacrosse season's over someone came to my house late at night and set a surfboard on fire on our front lawn. The board must have been really juiced, because it was flaming everywhere, and our lawn got this huge burn spot."

"You think it was Klein?"

"No doubt, man. He must have soaked some gas in the grass in order to leave me a personal message. Even though the lawn got all charred, you could still make out the letters BH."

"I assume a police report was filed?"

Troy shook his head. "Because of the black patch from the burning surfboard, it took a few days for the letters to show themselves. Before then I was sure this Torrance dude had done the burning because of a run-in we'd had at Rat."

Rat was the name of another surfing spot. A surfer friend once told me that Rat wasn't named for a rodent but was a spot designated by PV surfers as Right After Torrance. Some of the most impassioned territorial disputes in SoCal are between local surfers defending "their" waves.

"I should have known it wasn't another dankster, though," Troy said. "Not even a durfer would set a board on fire. That's too fubar."

"Yeah," I said, "that's too fubar."

* * *

As I was pulling into the parking lot at BHHS, my cell phone rang. I didn't recognize the number but I did the voice. Dottie Antonelli said, "Hey, Joe Friday, I've been doing your secretarial work all morning."

The old Michael Gideon, the one before I lost my wife and did my fire walk, had enjoyed repartee. The ghost of Gideon tried to reprise that role. "Just the facts, ma'am," I said. It either wasn't a very good Jack Webb imitation, or Dottie chose to ignore Joe's and my request.

"So, wasn't that pumpkin bread as good as I told you?"

"You're assuming I even tried it."

"I'm assuming you ate the whole thing."

She was right, but I wasn't about to tell her that. "It was very good," I admitted.

"Didn't I tell you it was *habit* forming?"

"Don't you get tired of hearing people groan when you tell them that?"

With Jersey emphasis she said, "The pot's calling the kettle black?"

"You want me to say five Hail Marys?"

"It wouldn't do any good. You might as well say five Hello Dollys."

"Let's start with a hello, Dottie. What do you got for me?"

"You're in luck is what I got. I just finished talking with Karen Santos. She's pretty sure she waited on the girl you're looking for, but you better talk with her yourself, and there's no time like the present, because Karen's got the afternoon shift and the reverend mother has agreed to see you today at four thirty. I'm thinking you'll want to kill two birds with one stone."

"You're thinking for me?"

"Somebody's got to do it."

"If I see the reverend mother carrying a ruler I'll probably have posttraumatic stress disorder."

"If she scares you silent we should be so lucky. Speaking of lucky, did the chocolates do the trick?"

"Is that the kind of question you should be asking from a monastery?"

"In case you hadn't noticed, I'm no nun."

"Well, in case you hadn't heard, a gentleman never tells."

"If I was talking to a gentleman, I wouldn't have asked the question."

"Shouldn't you be selling holy water or something?"

"You're right. I'll be putting a bag together for you, and I'll make sure to include a Saint Jude medal in your order."

Saint Jude is the patron saint of lost causes. Dottie heard me laugh before I hung up on her.

I put Sirius on a leash and let him accompany me on my walk through Beverly. The presence of the canine didn't go unnoticed, and I was sure scores of panicked texts were being sent that a drug-sniffing dog was on campus.

Once again I reported to the assistant principal. Mrs. Durand surprised me by acting as if she was glad to see me, but the presence of Sirius had something to do with that. Without my partner at my side, people don't recognize me. I am Frick without Frack.

"I kept thinking there was something about you that was familiar," she said. "You're the policeman that captured the Weatherman."

"Two officers made the arrest," I said. "Meet Sirius."

On cue the mutt wagged his tail and the assistant principal suddenly acted starstruck. Long ago I had gotten used to having third billing behind Ellis Haines and Sirius. One of the secretaries in Media Relations had once told me that there had been more than a thousand requests for "signed" pictures of Sirius, which was about a thousand more than there'd been for signed pictures of me. What the public doesn't know is that the department used some other dog's paw to ink the pictures. They better hope that news doesn't leak out. When baseball fans learned that most of Mickey Mantle's autographs were forged by the Yankees' clubhouse trainer, they were ready to riot. It was blackmail I was holding over Sirius. Say it ain't so, Joe.

"I was hoping you could send for Jason Davis," I said, "and that the two of us could chat in the conference room."

Instead of raising objections, Mrs. Durand said that would be no problem and then asked if Sirius needed a water bowl. I considered saying my partner preferred coffee but swallowed my sour grapes and told her that would be nice. What can I say? I was second fiddle but I still had my part to play.

When Jason Davis appeared five minutes later, he looked none too pleased to see either Nero or me. He sat in a chair across from me, slouched down, and waited for me to speak. I decided to get his attention.

"Jason Davis," I said, "you have the right to remain silent. Anything you say can and will be used against you in court. You have the right to consult with an attorney and to have that attorney present during questioning. If you desire, the court will appoint you an attorney at no cost. Do you understand those rights?"

My words had made Davis sit up straight. His eyes were wide, and his response was high-pitched and incredulous: "Are you arresting me?"

"That depends."

"I don't believe this."

"Believe it."

"I haven't done anything wrong."

"You've obstructed justice. You purposely didn't tell the full story of Klein's bullying. Maybe that's understandable because you were part of his gang and didn't want to look bad yourself."

He shook his head. "That's not how it is. Like I told you, we never were a gang. Our group might have said a few things to a few people, but that's all."

"You threatened violence and you committed vandalism."

"What are you talking about?"

"Do you remember your trip to Palos Verdes? What was the Agency trying to do, pay homage to a KKK cross burning?"

Davis raised both his hands and started waving them as if trying to push away my words. "It wasn't anything like that. It was a surfboard, and that was Paul's thing. If you don't believe me, ask David Popkin or Cody Schwartz. All we did was drive with Paul."

"I will ask them. Everything you say I am going to personally check out. And that's why if you don't tell me the complete truth you will have reason to regret it."

Davis started wringing his hands and nodded. For the moment at least he'd lost his teenage insouciance and looked like a scared kid.

"How long has the bullying been going on?"

He sank back down in his chair and said, "I don't know. I guess maybe since junior high."

I pushed a piece of paper his way. "I'll need you to make a list of your favorite targets over those years."

"How do you expect me to remember everybody?"

"If you want, I can put you in a cell so that you can have as much time as you need to think about it."

"Look, I'll do my best."

"You better. I don't care how long it takes you—I want a complete list."

Davis took up the pen and started writing. I sat there staring at him. It took him about fifteen minutes, but he came up with eleven names. Klein and the Agency had been busy. Seven of the names on his list looked to be Persian.

"There are a lot of Persians on your list."

"There are a lot of Persians in Beverly Hills."

"They seem to have been singled out."

"I wouldn't know about that."

"You just went along with whatever Paul wanted?"

He shrugged. "Yeah, I guess so."

"You ever heard the word 'Brownie'?"

"Look, it's not like I'm a practicing Jew."

"But you've heard the word directed at Persian Jews?"

He nodded.

"Did Paul or your group commit any hate crimes?"

"We didn't do anything besides hassle a few kids."

"We know that Paul took out Troy Vincent on the lacrosse field. Did he commit any other acts of violence?"

Davis shook his head.

"Someone murdered Paul and then crucified him. That's not a crime of passion. That's something premeditated. Who could have hated Paul that much?"

"I don't know."

I studied him, hoping he was lying, but he seemed to be telling the truth.

CHAPTER 12:

APPROVED BY THE VATICAN

The shadows were already coming home to roost when I took my leave of Gump and Martinez. The two detectives would be making calls and trying to connect dots until well into the evening. No one had said it, but our efforts were beginning to feel like busywork. The three of us had even resorted to sifting through the so-called leads called into Adam Klein's reward hotline. We needed a break—or divine intervention. Such were my thoughts as I set out for the monastery.

The sun was low on the horizon and looked ready to beat a hasty retreat to the encroaching dusk. That's the way it is in January, even in California. The Golden State doesn't have such a golden luster. It was two years ago in January that Sirius and I suffered our burns, but even before our encounter with fire I had never liked the month. Maybe it was seasonal affective disorder on my part; maybe it was creeping postholiday depression. T. S. Eliot was wrong about April being the cruelest month: it's January.

My partner whined. He was probably catching the vibe from my dark mood. "It's all right," I told him.

He didn't believe me. As we drew nearer to the Monastery of the Angels, Sirius started pacing the backseat. When his Geiger counter goes off, I'm usually sensitive to it, but this time I figured I was the cause and told him to shut up.

"You were dropped on your head as a puppy," I said.

He ignored me and continued pacing.

My cell rang, and a bit of my mood came through in my voice as I answered. The caller asked, "Detective Gideon?"

The sound of Lisbet Keane's voice dispelled my January blues. "I'd rather you called me Michael. If you do that, I can call you Lisbet."

"Deal," she said and then tried my name out for size, "Michael."

In the backseat Sirius was still making his worry noises. "Shhh," I hissed and then explained, "That wasn't directed at you but at my partner."

"I hope this isn't a bad time."

"Nope," I said, "I'm on my way to a nunnery."

"That sounded like you just said, 'nunnery.'"

"As in, 'Get thee to.' I have business at the Monastery of Angels."

"Does that have anything to do with Rose?"

"That's what I'm trying to find out."

"She's why I'm calling," Lisbet said. "I wanted to invite you to Rose's funeral. It's going to be held at four in the afternoon tomorrow, but please don't feel you have to…"

It would mean a frenetic day, starting with an early flight to the Bay Area. It would mean basically writing off the day on the high-profile Klein case. But I still said, "I'll be there."

Sirius started making noises again and ignored my hand signals to be quiet.

"Do you remember how to get to the Garden of Angels?"

I didn't want to conduct our conversation over Sirius's whines, and I didn't want our talk to be hurried or only about funeral arrangements.

"Can you do me a favor, Lisbet?" I asked. "I'm almost at the monastery, and Sirius has decided this is a good time to practice his bird calls. I would really appreciate it if you could ring me back in an hour. That way I can give you my undivided attention."

"No problem," she said. "I'll catch you in a bit."

We pulled into the monastery's parking lot, and Sirius breached his training by jumping to the front seat without an invitation. His body language showed how intent he was on accompanying me.

"No," I said and signaled for him to return to the backseat.

Sirius obeyed in slow motion, his body reluctantly inching to where I pointed. As he grudgingly returned to his place, he made a plaintive sound in his throat, begging me to reconsider.

I was surprised by his acting out, and I assumed the alpha male pose while spitting out *"Lass das sein!,"* the German for "Don't do that!" Sirius shrank a little at the rebuff and stopped his noises, but he appeared to be more sidetracked than chastened.

Before leaving the car, I made sure all the windows were opened several inches. As I walked away, Sirius pressed his muzzle as far as he could out the driver's window and whined. His persistence almost made me stop, but I knew that cloistered monasteries don't make a point of welcoming two-legged outsiders, let alone four-legged ones.

Outside the monastic enclosure were displays showing the Stations of the Cross. Each of the stations portrayed Christ on his fateful journey from Gethsemane to Golgotha. The women inside the monastery, I thought, had devoted their lives to remembering that journey.

I passed by the stations without stopping. There wasn't a soul at the deserted meditation garden—Nordstrom was probably having a sale—and I continued on to the gift shop. Standing inside the door and finishing up with a customer was a woman I assumed was Karen Santos. Karen and the woman she was talking to were both Filipinas, and as they said their good-byes they spoke a combination of Tagalog and English. I held the door as the woman made her way out. She looked to be weighed down by her package, which meant she was probably carrying a loaf of the pumpkin bread.

Karen turned to face me with a tight smile. She extended her hand and in unaccented and precise English said, "You must be Detective Gideon. I'm Karen Santos."

Second generation, I decided. Her parents would have pushed her to succeed in the new land, and her dignified bearing made me think that she had. We finished our handshake, and then Karen did a little hand wringing. "I just wish Dottie had arranged for you to call me before you made your trip here, Detective. She seems sure that I can help you with your case, but I have my doubts about that, and I am hoping this won't turn out to be a fruitless journey for you."

I tried to put her at ease: "Well, it won't be *fruitless*, because I'm picking up a loaf of pumpkin bread. Or are pumpkins a vegetable?"

"Pumpkins are a fruit, I believe, because they contain seeds."

"Then my visit will be fruitful, although I do have some non-fruit-related questions."

"I'll be glad to answer them if I can."

The fruit icebreaker had her looking more relaxed. "Dottie told me that you waited on a customer that bought some blue and pink bootees, and a loaf of pumpkin bread."

Karen nodded. "I think she was here last Friday. It was the blue and pink bootees that made me remember her visit. Most of the time people buy one color or the other, but she bought both."

"Tell me about her."

"I wish I could. I've been trying to remember anything that might help you, but I'm afraid our encounter was brief and not very memorable."

"Let's start with a description."

"I am fairly certain she was Latina, but she didn't speak with any accent. She had a dark complexion and had brown eyes and black hair. As far as I recall she was of average height, but on the heavy side. She was shy, but after we talked a little I saw that she had a beautiful smile with very white teeth."

"What did you talk about?"

"I commented on the bootees. I think I said something like, 'Are you buying for twins?' And then the girl said they were for her aunt, who wasn't sure if she was having a boy or a girl. After she told me that I said, 'You're smart to not take any chances.' And then I said that she could return one pair of the bootees if she brought the receipt back with her."

"How did she react to that?"

"I think she nodded, but she was too shy to make much eye contact."

"You said she was heavy. Do you think she could have been pregnant?"

Karen hesitated before answering. "That thought did cross my mind, but I learned long ago that you never ask a woman if she's pregnant unless you're absolutely sure she is. All you have to do is make that mistake once and you'll never do it again. As soon as she told me the bootees were for her aunt, I took her at her word."

"How old was she?"

"She could have been anywhere from fifteen to twenty-five, but now that I think about it I'm guessing she was in her late teens."

I encouraged Karen with a nod and a look that reassured her so that she continued talking.

"I think she was wearing costume jewelry, and her makeup was on the heavy side, with lots of black eyeliner."

"Can you recall the clothing she was wearing?"

Karen grimaced. "I seem to remember she had on jeans and an oversized sweatshirt with an animal logo on it. It had writing of some kind."

"You don't remember what that logo was?"

"I wish I did. It feels like an image I should know, but the more I think about it, the more it won't quite show itself, which I now know is even more frustrating than trying to pull out a word that's stuck on the tip of your tongue."

I nodded and tried to give off the impression that it was no big deal. "Don't sweat it. When you least expect it, the image will probably just pop into your head."

"That's what I have been telling myself."

"How did she pay?"

"We only take cash here."

"Maybe you should have one of those signs that say 'In God we trust, all others pay cash.'"

Karen laughed and then said sotto voce, "I don't think the sisters would approve."

"What else can you tell me about this woman?"

She thought a moment, shook her head, but then thought of something. "I don't think she had very much money."

"Why is that?"

"When she was buying the bootees, she kept sniffing the air and taking in the aroma of the pumpkin bread. I told her that over the years I'd probably gained ten pounds from inhaling pumpkin bread, or at least that was my story and I was sticking to it. That got a little smile out of her, and then she asked how much a loaf cost. When I told her the price, she thought about it, and after some deliberation she decided to buy a loaf. It wasn't an impulse purchase but one that she weighed out, as if debating whether she had enough money. I remember feeling almost guilty taking her money."

"What time of day did she come in?"

"It was in the early afternoon, probably somewhere around two o'clock."

"Was it your impression that this woman was familiar with the gift shop and monastery?"

Karen shook her head. "I am fairly certain she'd never been here before. When she walked into the gift shop she looked around the way people do when they come here for the first time."

I mulled that over. "What do you think brought her here?"

"Some people visit the monastery to reflect. It's a holy place."

I smiled, encouraging her to talk. A witness that is comfortable tends to remember more than one who is on edge.

"I thought the monastery was closed to the public," I said.

"The cells are cloistered, but there are gardens and public areas open to visitors, and on occasion there are services open to the public. They're very simple but beautiful. When I attend I usually find myself looking at the monstrance. It's shaped not only in the form of a cross, but also that of the sword of Saint Michael."

I didn't have any idea what a monstrance was, but I nodded knowingly.

"Were you named after the Archangel Michael?" she asked.

I shook my head. "I was named after my great-uncle Mike, and as far as I know he was about the opposite of an archangel. Uncle Mike had a lot of fishing poles, but I don't think he had a sword."

"I always liked the story of Saint Michael's sword. I remember when I was a girl, a demonstrative priest showed our communion class how Michael struck down a fiery dragon with his sword."

Karen offered these words while staring at my burn scar, and then she suddenly turned away in embarrassment. Her face flared red, but I pretended not to notice, just as I had pretended not to see her stare. I began circulating around the gift shop, poking at this and that.

"You manage to pack a lot into a small space," I said.

"The nuns make many of our products. They bake and knit and paint."

I paused to look at some of the paintings on the walls; most were scenes from the monastery.

"All those paintings you're looking at were drawn by the sisters," she said.

"I guess that explains why there are no nudes."

Karen laughed from behind a closed hand.

After finishing my deliberate inventory, I made my way back to where Karen was standing and suddenly asked her, "What was on the girl's sweatshirt?"

The abruptness of my question produced an immediate answer: "A bird."

Karen looked surprised but then started nodding definitively. "It was a bird."

"What color was it?"

"Gold, I think, or brown."

"Can you describe it?"

"I remember it being—feisty."

I couldn't think of any California teams with a bird, and wondered if the girl could have been a migratory NFL fan. "Could it have been an Arizona cardinal or a Seattle seahawk?"

She shook her head. "I don't think it was a bird representing a professional team. I'm of a mind that it was a school mascot."

"Do you think it was a high school mascot or college?"

Karen's face scrunched up in concentration. "I'm fairly sure it wasn't high school. I probably would have taken more notice of it if it was."

She offered me a small explanation and history: "I was a high school teacher for many years before going into school administration."

"So you think the bird was a college logo?"

Karen offered a tentative nod. The two most recognizable university mascots in the LA area are the UCLA Bruin and the USC Trojan, but there were plenty of other smaller universities in and around Los Angeles. Later, I would have to go mascot hunting.

"Can you tell me what this case is about?" she asked.

"I can only say that this woman might be a person of interest in a crime that occurred."

Karen nodded. "I'll probably close up by the time you finish your meeting with the reverend mother, so you better take your package now. Dottie wanted me to tell you that she put it together especially for you."

"Bless her," I said in tones not exactly ecclesiastical.

I pulled out my wallet, and Karen quoted a price that sounded high. "Did the price go up for pumpkin bread and chocolates?"

"No," she said. "Most of the expense is for the medals that Dottie picked out for you. She chose two of Saint Jude, and one of Saint Michael."

"Is there a patron saint for suckers?"

Karen looked innocent. "I am not aware of one."

"I suppose I should be glad Dottie didn't add gold, frankincense, and myrrh to my order." I thumbed through my wallet. "It looks as if I've got just enough cash."

"We can bend our cash-only rule for you. Your check is good with us, Detective."

"Then you must know something my bank doesn't."

I finished paying, and then Karen escorted me over to a building not far from the gift shop. As far as I could determine, I was now officially in cloistered territory. There was no one in sight, and I wondered if all the sisters were praying.

The Catholic church makes no secret of the fact that over the last half century the ranks of nuns have been in serious decline. Some believe the sisters are becoming an endangered species. I wondered if anything was being done to reverse the trend. Most vocations recruit when they experience declining numbers. I probably wouldn't have become a cop if not for a job fair I had attended at college. It was only after talking with LAPD recruiters that I began to entertain the idea of being a police officer. As I recalled, there had been no recruiting booth for sisters. Maybe it doesn't work to advertise when the job description is chastity, poverty, and obedience.

The sound of footsteps approaching along the tiled floor made me hastily stand up. The reverend mother was slightly bent from age, but her stoop didn't slow her down. She was wearing white robes and black open-toed sandals with white socks. A fringe of white hair could be seen underneath her black habit. The sister wore thick glasses, but the eyes behind them were clear and appraising.

"Thank you for seeing me," I said. "I am Michael Gideon of the Los Angeles Police Department."

With a slight rustle of robes she offered me a small hand. "I am Sister Frances."

She took a seat at the table and looked at me expectantly. Most people are nervous around cops, but she wasn't. Apparently the reverend mother had a clean conscience. Either that or she had nerves of steel.

"I believe a young woman visited the monastery last Friday," I said. "I am trying to find this girl so that I can question her about a case I am working on. I think it's possible that she approached someone inside the monastery and engaged her in conversation."

"And why do you think that?"

The prioress's voice was soft, but there was an amazing clarity to it, like one of those bells that aren't overloud but ring in such a way that they can be heard over just about anything.

"I am only guessing, but I suspect this young woman had a guilty conscience. I think she came here looking for answers and maybe a way out of her situation. It's possible she was hoping that she might escape her problems by becoming a nun at this monastery."

I waited for the reverend mother to answer, but she didn't seem to be in any hurry. One of the interview techniques every cop learns is to let the silence build. I was quickly learning that strategy doesn't work with nuns. They are old friends with silence.

"I need to know if this woman talked to anyone here."

The reverend mother's serene face regarded me. For a woman of her apparent age, it was remarkable how unwrinkled she was. Her composed expression would have been at home at a poker table: it gave away nothing.

"And how would that help your case?" she asked.

"The nun with whom she talked might be able to give me information about this girl."

Her nod showed that she understood, but it wasn't a nod of agreement. "It is not uncommon for troubled girls to make vocational inquiries. We stress to them that ours is a calling from God and not an escape from the world."

"Is there one nun in particular who talks to these girls?"

"Usually they are directed to me."

She didn't elaborate further. When silence stopped being golden, I decided to be more direct. "Did you talk to this girl?"

Instead of answering, the reverend mother said, "I refer all serious inquiries to the vocational director of our order. I am well aware that there is no one nun-size habit that fits all."

I thought I saw a little smile on her lips.

"In fact some orders don't even wear habits," she said. "There are sisters that go out in the world and there are cloistered nuns. Is the candidate looking for a community of sisters that is evangelical, monastic, or apostolic? Many of the orders require a minimum of a high school education, as well as work experience. Young women are often surprised to learn that in many orders they have to be at least twenty years old before they can take their vows."

"Did that rule out this candidate?" I asked.

Once again she chose to answer a question I didn't ask. "It is one thing to be a potential postulant, but it is quite another to arise at four forty-five every morning. That is our daily routine here."

"Did the thought of those long working hours discourage this girl?"

"What you need to understand, Detective, is that you don't become a sister merely by knocking at the door of a monastery. There is a demanding system in place."

"And you need to understand, Reverend Mother, that as far as I know the rules of the confessional don't apply here. Anything this girl might have said isn't privileged."

"I imagine you are right about that."

"Did you talk to this girl?"

A hardened criminal could have taken pointers from the reverend mother on how to avoid answering questions. "Did you know that last month I had my eighty-ninth birthday, Detective?"

"Congratulations."

"I am getting worried about my memory. I have heard when you are as old as I am your memory plays tricks on you."

"I think it's playing tricks on me."

With unruffled calm she asked, "Can I be of any other help?"

There was no threat that would make her talk. My rules and laws didn't concern her. Besides, I was keeping her from praying, and that was something the world could ill afford.

"Apparently not in this matter," I said.

"Is there another matter you wish to discuss?"

The day before, Dottie had told me the prioress experienced a miracle. Since that time I had been recollecting the media's reporting on the story of the reverend mother's miracle. At first her identity had been withheld; she had only been identified as a nun at the Monastery of Angels, but as the beatification process for Mother Serena ran its course, her name and position had been revealed by the press. According to the Vatican, the woman sitting across from me had experienced a miracle.

"My inquiry isn't a professional one, but I wanted to hear about your miracle."

With her great calm she asked, "What is it that you wish to know?"

"I seem to remember that you were diagnosed with brain cancer, and that after you and the nuns in the monastery prayed to Mother Serena, you were cured."

"Your explanation is short on many details, but on the whole it is accurate."

"How do you know your disease just didn't have some spontaneous remission?"

"The disease had ravaged my body. I was blind and incontinent, and cranial nerve palsies and seizures had left me in a state where I could not leave my bed unassisted. I remember being frustrated by my inability to do the smallest tasks. I couldn't even write a note. Muscle twitches and numbness made my handwriting completely illegible. As I understand it, most spontaneous remissions aren't really spontaneous. They don't happen all at once."

"But that's what happened to you?"

She nodded.

"How long had you been diagnosed with brain cancer?"

"For almost three years. The cancer had metastasized. All the specialists agreed on one thing: the cancer was terminal."

"And in one fell swoop you were better?"

"I would call it the opposite of a fell swoop, wouldn't you?"

"How did the other sisters happen to pray to Mother Serena?"

"She had passed away only days before."

"And you think her spirit healed you?"

"As you see."

"Were you and the sisters praying for a miracle?"

"No. We were asking for her blessing upon me."

"Tell me about the moment when you were cured."

"I felt the hand of God, and Mother Serena, wash over me."

"And it happened right after the sisters prayed for you?"

She nodded.

"Might your cure have been psychological?"

The reverend mother smiled. "It seems that everyone wants to credit my mind and not my God. My medical records were scrutinized. Every blood test and every X-ray was studied. My disease was well documented."

"I understand your miracle was approved by the Vatican."

"The beatification process for Mother Serena is still going forward," she said, "so it appears that is so."

Medical miracles approved by the Vatican had to be deemed sudden, conclusive and permanent, and inexplicable to medical authorities.

"Have you ever wondered why God thought you were worthy of a miracle?"

"I cannot pretend to be worthy; I can only think he decided my work here wasn't done."

"But why would you be singled out?" I asked, not quite able to hide the frustration in my voice. "Is God running some kind of lottery and you just happened to hit the jackpot on a certain day and at a certain time?"

With a calm I would never have, the reverend mother said, "I can't tell you why things happened as they did, but I don't think that God is running a lottery."

"I suppose He wouldn't want to compete with Friday night bingo," I said.

The reverend mother actually smiled. You take small miracles whenever you can get them.

"Thank you for your time," I told her.

"Go with God," she said.

I was grateful for her blessing but wished it came with directions.

CHAPTER 13:

DO NOT RESUSCITATE

It was dark outside when I left the world of the cloistered and set out for the parking lot. Although it wasn't even six o'clock, the night had fallen with a hard finality. The gloom seemed to extend to the heavens; the stars were hidden in murk and there wasn't even a sighting of the moon to mitigate the night.

Out of respect to the reverend mother I had set my cell phone to vibrate. I was at the far end of the meditation garden when my pocket started buzzing. As I accepted the call, I heard a whooshing sound. My hello was left hanging—much like I was. I was pulled backward by my neck, and my cell phone and bag of gift shop goodies went flying from my hand. I tried to cry "Shit!" but the tightening noose around my neck didn't even leave me enough wind to curse.

Denied air, I panicked and clawed desperately at the noose. My attackers expected that; loops closed around my wrists and took over the control of my arms. I felt like the steer in a team roping event. I was wrapped up so tight all I was missing was a bow on my head. No air was making it to my lungs. I frantically tried to reach for my gun but was pulled from so many angles I couldn't even get close to it. The more I struggled, the more the loops dug into me.

There were three of them. The working part of my mind realized I was being taken down with animal-control poles. The rudimentary part of my mind was screaming for flight or fight, but I couldn't do either. I was in the grips of three animal-control poles, the kind of devices used on a Rottweiler or a pit bull. The poles had been designed to neutralize dogs with fierce teeth and big muscles. I was short those teeth and muscles; worse, I was snared in three places and becoming oxygen deprived. Animal-control poles are made from aircraft-grade aluminum; they resist bending or breaking even under extreme conditions, and the cables are designed to not twist. No hangman could have hoped for a better noose, or three better nooses. Still, I reacted as a panicked animal would, twisting and pulling and struggling.

My attackers were on all sides of me. I tried to strike out at them, swinging with my arms and kicking with my legs, but the poles were too long for me to get to them, and they worked as a team to control me. When I lunged in one direction, they yanked me in another. Time was on their side. Every moment brought me closer to unconsciousness.

The sleeper hold is prohibited by the LAPD, but every officer on the force still knows how to apply it if needed. Get a neck in the crook of your elbow and compress the carotid arteries and jugular vein, and the flow of blood to the brain abruptly ceases. Usually it's only a few seconds until lights out. Law enforcement describes the result as the "funky chicken" because victims often flop and shake almost like they are doing dance moves.

I was getting close to the chicken dance. My ears felt like I was deep underwater with my ear drums at the point of bursting, and I wasn't seeing so much as being an unwitting witness to a stream of black dots and silver lines swimming in front of my eyes. The only question was, which would come first: my blacking out from asphyxiation, or my brain becoming so blood starved that I'd start doing the funky chicken?

The neck noose eased slightly, and the change in blood pressure almost made me black out. If I had not been snared on all sides, I would have fallen over. As it was, I dropped to my knees and tried to stay conscious while drawing labored breaths.

My assailants had on the kinds of uniforms worn by animal control: olive pants, dark shirts with badges, and protection gloves. Their animal-control poles wouldn't have looked out of place to a casual onlooker; they were the telescoping variety and would compact into a neat baton. The only thing different about their official-looking uniforms was their ski masks. It was probably an unnecessary precaution: the darkness was mask enough.

"Steady him," said the man with the noose around my neck.

The men with the animal-control poles holding my arms did as ordered. It probably looked like they were doing a dance around the maypole; I was the maypole. The animal-control poles, I realized, probably weren't just for me. They had prepared for Sirius as well. The grip around my neck loosened slightly, and I took in what air I could, sounding like someone in the midst of an asthma attack.

"Make him assume the position."

My puppet masters evidently knew what the position was. With a few twists and turns, they manipulated my hands behind my back. I wanted to tell them they were making a huge mistake but didn't have enough wind for my desperate lies.

I had to do something, so I twisted and shook, but I wasn't a fish on the line: I was a fish on several lines. My shaking wasn't even a good delay tactic, but more a gesture as impotent as shaking a furious fist at a storming sky. That was all I could do, though.

The man in charge dropped his pole and approached me. He leaned toward me, and I saw tattoos on the inside of both his arms. One looked like a red *A* and the other was circular with jagged, lightning-like lines. He ran his hands along my body and then relieved me of my Glock.

"It is time to disabuse the world of the notion that good triumphs over evil, or that the concept of good or evil even exists. The new order is Ragnarok."

The philosophy behind the words—or lack of it—sounded familiar to me.

The tattooed man continued with his rant: "It is time to lose the shackles of morality."

"Let's take the prize and get out of here," said one of the captors to my side.

"The Prophet's going to love this," said the other.

They sounded excited, like kids at a piñata party. It was a shame I was the piñata. All three of the men sounded young, probably early twenties.

The tattooed man reached into his shirt and pulled out a nasty-looking knife. From behind his mask, his eyes were scrutinizing my face.

"Hear no evil," he said. "But what if we were to leave with another trophy besides his ear?"

"You said that was how it's done in a bullfight," said one of his wingmen.

The other added, "You said that would settle the score."

"Why settle the score when we can finish the battle? What better way to announce Götterdämmerung than by taking his beating heart?"

"We can't kill a cop," said one of those holding my arm.

The man with the knife said, "Why not?"

My voice was raspy and raw and little more than a whisper: "Because you'll be executed for the crime."

The leader didn't acknowledge my words. "His death will show that no life is sacrosanct. In the twilight of the gods there are no rules. His spilt blood will avenge the Prophet."

"You don't want to do this." My voice was little more than a hiss. I directed my comments to the two men holding me. "You don't want to be a party to murder."

"Hold him tight," said the man with the knife.

The rack ratcheted up another notch, and my arms were pulled taut. As I tried to come up with a last convincing argument, I heard a scream and the tension from the pole holding my left arm grew slack. To my left, a hundred pounds of fury were tearing into a man's arm and shaking him savagely.

My partner had arrived. If I'd been left with a voice, I would have screamed my enthusiasm, but I still might not have been heard. Sirius was an avenging fury. His target was screaming like someone being torn apart. Maybe he *was* being torn apart. He tried to fend off Sirius's slashing teeth and in doing so dropped his hold on the control pole.

The pole remained attached to my left wrist because the automatic locking mechanism had already been activated, but that was fine by me. I was now holding a combination of quarterstaff and nunchucks.

I whipped the pole around and heard a satisfying crack, but the man on my right didn't loosen his grip. The tattooed man lunged for my pole, but I swept my arm to the side and he missed. Unfortunately, he got a grip on the pole he'd abandoned, and the noose around my neck tightened.

I tried swinging at him, but my range of motion was limited by the grip on my right wrist. Denied one target, I went after the other, hitting my hangman on the right once, twice, and then a third time. Cries came with every blow, but not my freedom. The SOB wouldn't drop his pole or let go of his grip on my wrist. I was operating on fumes; no air was getting to my lungs.

Starved for air, I changed tactics and instead of trying to resist, I ran in the direction I was being pulled. I slammed into the hangman, and as we fell to the ground I smashed his nose with a head butt, but the noose around my neck pulled me away from the fight and to my feet. As I tottered around, I swung the poles attached to my wrists like a drunken Edward Scissorhands.

Desperately, I tried to find a way out of my hangman's noose, seeking out the release knob of the control device that was choking me. During my time with K-9 we had worked with control poles, but never while being choked and shaken. Even as the fog grayed my mind, I recognized that my thumb was resting on a protrusion. I pulled the knob outward, my noose loosened, and I began sucking in air.

Sirius had sensed my desperation and raced to my side. He stood in front of me, hackles raised and teeth bared, ready to attack any threat that came my way. I tried to speak, tried to tell him to attack the tattooed man, but it was all I could do to breathe.

"Call him off or I'll shoot you." My own gun was aimed at me.

"*Steh noch!*" I managed to say, and Sirius did as I asked: he stood still.

Without lowering his gun, my assailant said, "We're out of here."

The hangman that Sirius had chewed on was slow to get to his feet. He was bleeding all over and wasn't able to move one of his arms.

My partner and I weren't part of the marching orders. Because I couldn't chance speaking to Sirius, I surreptitiously signaled him. Instead of immediately obeying, he looked at me, hoping for a reprieve, but I signaled once more and this time he raced off.

The tattooed man raised his gun and tried to track my partner, but he was too late. We watched as Sirius squeezed through shrubbery and was lost to sight.

"The rat leaving the ship?" he asked, not realizing I had sent Sirius off.

"He's watching you now in the darkness," I whispered. "He's waiting for his opportunity."

The gun was directed my way. "Throw us the poles."

I freed myself from the restraints. With each toss of a pole I took a step back and managed to put space between me and my assailants. The meditation garden wasn't large, but I did manage about fifteen yards of separation.

From the distance came the sound of sirens. I wasn't sure if they were coming for me, but the Klaxon calls had their desired effect. The tattooed man knew there was no time to linger. He either had to shoot me or let me get away. Even though it was dark and he had a mask on, I could still read his eyes. Bullets from a Glock travel around nine hundred feet per second. I wasn't going to out-quick a bullet. If he was going to shoot at me, I would have to make my move before he did.

I watched his eyes and waited a long moment, and then another. And then I saw his eyes signal their intent. His mind was made up, and I knew what he was going to do.

I threw myself at the only shelter that was available: the concrete foundation upon which the statuary of Saint Dominic and Mary rested. An instant later, Saint Dominic took two bullets for me, and the plaster shattered everywhere. Dominic bought me just enough time. The call of the sirens made the shooter decide they had to leave.

"Hurry!" he called to the others.

From behind Mary's fissured robes I watched the pack disappear into the darkness.

* * *

In the immediate aftermath of the attack, the impact of my near-death experience didn't feel like mine but someone else's. I felt disembodied, or at least I did until Sirius crawled up next to me and I threw my arms around him. From the ground I looked around and saw pieces of plaster all around me and made a vow to replace the statue of Saint Dominic and Mary. I took deep breaths of the suddenly sweet night air; short minutes later my brothers in blue arrived on the scene.

Cops don't like it when one of their own is attacked, and they had lots of questions for me. My injuries saved me from having to provide too many answers. Although I tried to demur, I was given no choice but to go and seek medical help. I refused the ambulance ride, though, and instead got an officer to agree to drive me in my vehicle to the nearest emergency room.

My partner also rode with me. We were going to drop him off at an animal clinic not far from the hospital. Sirius had suffered some cuts during his skirmish. Or maybe he'd incurred the wounds another way. Some escape artists have been known to dislocate their shoulders in order to get out of a straightjacket. It was possible he'd gotten hurt making his escape from the car.

"So, how did you do it?" I asked him.

The four doors of my car had been locked, and the windows had only been opened a few inches. But like any good magician, my furry escape artist wasn't explaining how he performed his trick.

Maybe Sirius's rescuing me was another miracle. Of course it was possible that he'd managed to push the glass from one of the open windows out far enough for him to wiggle out. But all of that didn't explain how Sirius had known something was wrong before we reached the monastery, and before the attack on me. Maybe my shaman was right and Sirius was my guardian spirit.

* * *

A few hours after being admitted to the hospital, I started feeling like myself again. During my stay I had been visited by Anna Nguyen, a detective assigned to my case. I told her everything I remembered about my attackers. Nguyen used her youth and good looks to draw out almost everything I knew. She was a good artist and was able to draw my attacker's tattoos almost exactly as I remembered them. The only thing I didn't give Nguyen was my suspicions: I had a pretty good idea who the "Prophet" was.

After Nguyen left, I was ready to take off myself. Among health workers it's universally acknowledged that doctors make the worst patients. Cops probably rank second on the pain-in-the-ass scale. I buttonholed my doctor as he came in to check on me.

"When can I leave?" I asked.

"You'll need to stay overnight," Dr. Fish said. My physician's name was matched only by his personality.

"I suppose that decision was made after you did a wallet biopsy and discovered the state of my health insurance?"

Dr. Fish decided to take a moment to point out the errors of my ways. Even with managed health care, doctors can still find the time to do that.

"When you arrived at this hospital," he said, "you were experiencing dizziness, had lingering issues from the compression of your air passages, showed trauma to your neck, had problems with your balance, had two cracked ribs, and you told me there was a ringing in your ears. It was clear you were suffering from a mild concussion, as well as physical trauma from being beaten."

"That was a few hours ago," I said. "Now I'm more worried about boredom doing me in."

Dr. Fish decided to study my charts rather than listen to me. He made a few notes on my paperwork. It wouldn't have surprised me if he was writing DNR in big letters. After finishing with his scribbling, Fish swam off.

I punched the call button with my finger, and it wasn't long before a nurse appeared. "I'd be grateful if you could get me some writing paper."

The nurse, a petite Asian woman, happily nodded at my request. In heavily accented English she asked, "Do you want it for a letter?"

I shook my head and said, "Last will and testament."

The nurse managed to keep a frozen smile as she beat a quick retreat. A short time later, paper and pen were delivered to me; maybe my condition was more serious than I thought. Nguyen might have been assigned to my case, but I had more than a passing interest in it myself. When I cleared my own books, I was going to find these three. I began making my own notes from the attack. I was halfway through my memoirs when I heard a whispered conversation out in the hallway and a familiar voice saying, "I'd appreciate it if you gave this to the detective."

Maybe it was the hushed words that had made me take notice; maybe I became aware of what was being said just because the speaker's voice was one I really wanted to hear.

I called out, "I would much rather that you gave it to the detective in person."

There was a little more whispering, and then I heard a throat clearing and Lisbet Keane appeared at the doorway. Blushing red, she gave me a half-wave and then took a few halting steps into the room. She didn't meet my eyes and didn't seem to know where to look.

"I didn't want to disturb you," she said.

"I am glad you came. I would have called you, but they took away my cell phone."

Lisbet's call had saved my life. She had phoned me just before I was attacked, and heard enough of my beating to call 911. Lisbet had even added the magic words "a police officer is being attacked at the Monastery of the Angels" to the emergency operator. Her call had received immediate attention.

"In fact, I'd be bounding out of my bed to shake your hand and thank you if they hadn't taken away my underwear and put me in this ridiculous gown. So please accept my apologies that you didn't hear from me, and that I don't know quite what to say to the person that saved my life other than I owe you big time."

"I only made a call," she said.

"I don't think I'd be alive if you hadn't made that call."

She wasn't comfortable being my savior and looked more ready than ever to leave. I patted the chair next to me and said, "Have a seat. Please."

Lisbet took the kind of tentative seat you do when you're playing musical chairs and expecting the music to start up again.

"Was it some kind of attempted robbery?" she asked.

I shook my head. "Some people wanted to hurt me."

Lisbet grimaced and still managed to look good. "Who and why?"

I didn't like seeing her look so uncomfortable, so I said, "I'm thinking it might be some goons sent by the Book of the Month Club. They were really pissed off when I decided to cancel my membership."

That got a smile out of her, and also made her remember the package she was holding. "Speaking of books," she said and handed me the bag. "There's a silly get-well card, and a little gift. I didn't know how long you'd have to stay here, so I tried to think of what I could get you that might help pass the time."

"Your being here helps pass the time better than anything I can think of."

I opened the bag and pulled out a copy of Michael Connelly's *The Drop*.

"I haven't read it," she said, "but I know it's about an LAPD detective."

"Maybe I should take notes when I read it so I can learn how to be a real detective."

Lisbet edged forward another inch in her chair, and looked that much closer to taking off. Embarrassed, she said, "I guess it wasn't the best choice."

"No, it's my lame sense of humor that wasn't the best choice," I said, and then I reached out and lightly touched her hand.

She relaxed enough to take up a little more of the chair's real estate, and I thought of something that might keep her there a few more minutes.

"Do you have a sweet tooth?"

"I have thirty-two of them."

"Do me a favor and get that bag over there."

Lisbet followed the direction of my finger and then brought me the bag I'd been holding when I was attacked. The cops on the scene had gathered my goodies and brought them to the hospital. Now I saw a use for them. Dottie from the gift shop had suggested I might get lucky with their chocolates. I hoped she was right.

I pulled out the box. "Here's a token of my esteem for saving my life."

Lisbet smiled and said, "If I had known saving lives involved chocolate, I might have made it my full-time vocation."

In a Forrest Gump voice I said, "Momma always said life was like a box of chocolates."

"Hand-dipped chocolates," Lisbet said, reading the box. What she read next surprised her: "'Monastery Candies—better than the best.'"

"You know the nuns wouldn't say that if it wasn't true."

"Nuns made these?"

I nodded. She studied the box once more, ran her fingernail under the slogan, and said, "I suppose we owe it to science to find out if these chocolates really are better than the best."

"Apparently, the nuns didn't have to take a vow of humility."

"It's not bragging if you can back it up," Lisbet said, opening the box and passing a chocolate my way.

As I stuffed it into my mouth, I said, "I am sure this violates the hospital's Jell-O dessert laws."

Lisbet had already bitten into her chocolate, and her rapturous sounds reminded me of how the cartoon character Snuffles reacts after eating doggy treats. She didn't quite levitate like Snuffles, but I think I saw one foot leave the ground.

"The nuns didn't lie," she said.

"There is a commandment or two that frowns upon that."

"Another?" Lisbet said, holding the box out to me.

"The rest are for you."

"You're the one that's a patient in the hospital."

"I'll let you in on a secret. If they don't release me in the next few minutes, there's going to be a prison break."

"But I thought they were holding your underwear and cell phone as ransom."

"They are, but extreme circumstances call for extreme measures."

"Doesn't knowing about your prison break make me an accessory to the crime?"

"It does. And let's not forget that you're already complicit in the receipt of a bribe."

"You led me down that slippery slope."

"I was helped by the nuns."

"I can resist everything but temptation," she said and started chewing on a second chocolate.

"It's good to know you're human."

"And not a saint?"

Lisbet's tone was playful, but there was an edge to it. The look she gave me also suggested she had some issues with her nickname.

"People respect you," I said. "That's why they call you that."

"I'm no saint. I take in abandoned newborns and see to their burials because I think it's the right thing to do. It's not as if I believe that God spoke to me and told me what to do. I know a lot of people think that what I do is strange, and that the only possible explanation is that I'm a bit touched."

"I am glad you're not a saint. I can deal with strange just fine, but I'm not very good with sanctity."

"What about you?" she said. "I've given up my halo, but you still have your pedestal."

"What pedestal is that?"

"You're a hero, a modern-day knight-errant that braved dragon fire to bring a notorious villain to justice."

"Now that you saved my life, I'll let you be the hero."

"I dialed three digits. That's all."

"And all I did was my job. The news of my heroism was greatly exaggerated. But there are perks. Did you know that this is Go to Lunch with a Hero Week?"

"That somehow escaped my notice."

"Well, it's true. That means your civic duty requires you to have lunch with me, and me with you."

"I'm not one that usually shirks her civic duty."

"Nor am I. You mind if my partner joins us? Sirius pouts a lot if he thinks he's being excluded."

"I am all for Sirius joining us, but I'm wondering if the restaurant will be as welcoming."

"We know all the restaurants in the city that are dog friendly. My partner's favorite watering hole is this microbrewery with a nice outdoor patio. I always order a burger and brew, and he has a burger along with a water bowl, and we're both happy."

"They ever mix up your orders?"

"That happens all the time."

"I think I'll order a salad to alleviate the confusion."

Suddenly I was feeling a whole lot better.

* * *

An hour after Lisbet took her leave, I announced that I was leaving the hospital and demanded my cell phone and underwear. The powers-that-be didn't think my leaving was a good idea and decided that I should have the exercise of jumping through hoops before departing. My final act of contrition was waiting on my release papers. As I watched the billing clerk work on my file, I couldn't help but be mesmerized by her long, rainbow-colored, painted fingernails. Her talons rivaled those of Manchu royalty, but somehow she was still able to clack away on the computer keyboard.

"Dr. Fish wanted you to sign this," she said.

Her index fingernail, about as long as a letter opener, tapped imperiously on the signature line. I glanced at the paper and saw the acronym AMA in several places.

"American Medical Association?" I asked.

With curt emphasis she said, "Against medical advice."

I signed where she told me, but not in my usual scrawl. With very neat handwriting, I penned in the name Mary Baker Eddy.

"You'll also need to sign this," the clerk said.

The last time I'd had that much fine print thrust under my nose was when Jenny and I bought our house. "Am I promising my firstborn?"

Bored, she said, "You're agreeing to be liable for payment if for any reason your health insurance doesn't cover treatment received during your stay."

"It's been my experience that only two professions wear masks: bank robbers and doctors."

She was not amused. I doubt whether an MRI could have found her smile. It had to be an oversight, but for some reason I wasn't offered a wheelchair ride to the curb.

I sprang Sirius ten minutes later. The clerk at the animal clinic was considerably friendlier than her counterpart at the hospital. Most kids grow up wanting to work with animals. There's a good reason for that. The alternative is to work with humans. When I signed Sirius's paperwork, there were no notations of AMA.

When Sirius was brought out for me, I took a knee, and then I went nose to nose with my friend, giving him a hug and getting in return a tongue on my face and a whipping from his tail. His eyes were shining; mine were a little wet. They'd had to shave a few patches and sew him up where he'd sustained cuts, but he didn't look too bad.

We weren't more than a dozen steps out the door when Sirius paused at a fence post and lifted his leg for a long pit stop. "Save some," I told him. "I was thinking we could do a drive-by at the hospital where I was staying."

It was an unnecessary request, of course. I have never seen my partner run out of ammunition.

I drove in the freeway's slow lane. My only goal was to get home in one piece. Earlier I'd taken some codeine with Tylenol, but the meds felt as if they'd worn off already. Any movement of my neck hurt and my ribs ached like hell. It didn't help knowing my injuries would stiffen up and get worse overnight, but I wasn't about to cancel my next day's appointments, especially after what had happened.

The shaman-mobile was in Seth's driveway. There was also another car, but that wasn't unusual. Seth is the exact opposite of a hard-body LA surfer, but that doesn't stop him from being incredibly popular with the opposite sex. I have accused him of getting into the shaman trade for the purpose of learning how to concoct aphrodisiacs. He has never denied it.

Before getting out of the car, I sent Sirius out on reconnaissance. In my old age and after almost being killed, I was getting careful. Sirius wasn't gone long and came back wagging his tail. According to him, no bad guys were anywhere near our house.

The two of us went to Seth's door. I tapped lightly and hoped I wasn't intruding at a particularly bad moment. Before opening the door, Seth turned on the front light. I had hoped he wouldn't do that.

"I'd almost given up on you," Seth said, and then he stopped talking when he got a good look at my face.

"I'm sorry I didn't bring Sirius earlier, but we ran into a little trouble."

He motioned for us to come inside, but I shook my head. "Early flight," I said, "remember?"

"I remember telling you I didn't think much of the idea of you going north, and judging by how you look, I especially don't think it's a good idea now."

Instead of commenting on what happened I said, "I appreciate your taking Sirius. As you can see, he picked up a few bumps and bruises but the vet says he's okay. I hope to pick him up in the early afternoon."

"We'll manage. Will you?"

"I'll try to keep my soul as intact as possible through tomorrow."

I don't think Seth knew whether I was joking or not. I don't think I knew either.

CHAPTER 14:

NOT SO SAINT QUENTIN AS EXPLAINED BY THE DEVIL

The whisper of his voice played off the cold, concrete walls and sought me out even before we were in sight of one another. "But the wilderness found him out early and had taken vengeance for the fantastic invasion. I think it had whispered to him things about himself which he did not know, things of which he had no conception till he took counsel with this great solitude—and the whisper had proved irresistibly fascinating. It echoed loudly within him because he was hollow at the core."

There was a momentary pause, followed by his insinuating words: "I worry about you being a hollow man, Detective Gideon."

I answered the voice before yet being able to see the face. "That's nice," I said. "Have you been rehearsing just for me?"

"You hear those whispers, don't you, Detective? Those are Conrad's words from *Heart of Darkness*."

"Thanks for the Cliffs Notes."

Ellis Haines's cell in San Quentin was in the Adjustment Center, known as the AC, the death row that housed the worst of the worst. He had been placed in one of the six so-called quiet cells, a segregated area that had the most stringent security in the Q. Others in the Adjustment Center included Richard Ramirez, the so-called Night Stalker, and Richard Allen Davis, the murderer of twelve-year-old Polly Klaas. Charlie Manson had once spent time in one of the quiet cells in AC.

We were about to meet in our usual spot, a holding cell called the Lawyer's Room. The space was bigger than the eight-by-six-foot cells at San Quentin, but not much bigger. When Haines was in the room, it always felt too small.

San Quentin sits on over four hundred acres of land, much of it bordering San Francisco Bay. The land alone is said to be worth over a billion dollars. Because it's the oldest prison in California and because the land is worth so much, lots of people would like to see San Quentin razed, with the proceeds going to the state. I doubt whether the inmates would object. Despite being the most valuable prison in the world, San Quentin is still a shit hole.

The Q's exterior belies the interior. From a distance, the town of San Quentin looks charming. The homes occupied by staff are inviting and well maintained, and the grounds inside the gate are attractive, with nicely tended lawns and rose gardens.

From certain angles, San Quentin looks like a castle, with high granite walls and ancient battlements. You can even imagine the bay as its huge moat. Put lipstick on a pig, though, and it's still a pig. The gardens and the ocean can't disguise the fact that the Q is a prison with gun towers and razor wire. If you watch any old black-and-white films that have a prison setting, you'll get a feel for what San Quentin is like.

Although I'd been making trips to San Quentin once a month for the past year, I was no more comfortable now than the first time I visited. On my calendar I always marked impending visits with a black X, and as the date drew closer the black X always seemed to get bigger and darker, mirroring my own personal gravity and mood. I always pretended the visits weren't any big deal;

Seth Mann knew that wasn't the case. I suspected Ellis Haines did as well.

His singsong voice reached out to me again, traveling along the concrete made cold from the damp grip of the bay: "This alone, I was convinced, had driven him out to the edge of the forest, to the bush, towards the gleam of fires, the throb of drums, the drone of weird incantations; this alone had beguiled his unlawful soul beyond the bounds of permitted aspirations."

I didn't answer his, and Conrad's, madness.

Ellis Haines wouldn't talk with the FBI. He didn't deign to open up to his court-ordered psychiatrist and wouldn't participate in therapy. Haines refused any interviews that weren't of his own invention. Many death row inmates solicit correspondence; Haines received ten thousand letters a year and answered very few of them. The warden had told me that in the past year more than five hundred women had expressed interest in marrying Haines.

He was the "it" serial murderer. There were websites selling Ellis Haines action figures, calendars, and playing cards. To too many, the ramblings of Haines were considered gospel, and there were many people trying to make him out as a twisted prophet. The darkness that was Haines had caught on worldwide. Other killers had tapped into humanity's collective shadow side, but no one had ever been as popular a sideshow as Haines. His public pronouncements were among the most viewed on YouTube. The world wanted more and more of him; I think one of the reasons he liked seeing me was because I wanted less.

When I turned the corner, I could see Haines's face from inside the Lawyer's Room. He smiled for me; I didn't return the smile. Haines had been an exceptionally handsome man, but the fire had scarred him. Our burns were on the opposite sides of our faces; his scarring was on the left side of his face, mine on the right. Haines's scarring gave him a leering look that he didn't seem to mind. It was ironic that both of us had a matching set of hypertrophic scarring on our faces; in truth it creeped me out.

"Detective Gideon," he said, "always a pleasure to see you."

I nodded.

"And I believe you know my posse?"

There were correctional officers inside and outside the cell. The solitary CO that had accompanied me saw me to the door but not beyond. As usual, I'd be left alone with Haines. Because his hands were shackled, Haines assumed the position for their removal, turning his back to the door and sliding his hands through an opening in the now-locked door. His body language suggested he was the one doing the correctional officers a favor by being in their company. After his handcuffs were removed, Haines momentarily rubbed his wrists before being herded to a seat.

Haines never went anywhere without at least three correctional officers accompanying him. Inmates were not allowed to approach him; nor were they supposed to speak or talk to him. The prison officials didn't want Haines dying in captivity, like Dahmer or DeSalvo. They knew that other inmates were jealous of his notoriety, and that his death would be a feather in the cap for anyone taking him out.

As I sat down at the table, I found Haines's eyes fixed on me. "Hello," he said; he wasn't addressing me so much as he was my bruising.

The correctional officers filed out. When we were alone I produced a piece of paper with typewritten questions on it.

"The last time we talked," I said, "we began to discuss your family."

His eyes continued studying my neck. He was like a wino fixated on someone else's full bottle.

"Your bruising is recent," Haines said. "It's not yet in full bloom. I would guess it happened last night."

"According to you," I said, "you had a perfectly normal childhood, with no physical or sexual abuse."

"I don't believe your bruises are consistent with manual strangulation; I see no telltale marks from prying fingers."

"Did you love your parents?"

"And what you have isn't the kind of bruising that occurs from a figure-four hold or a carotid restraint, or even a lateral vascular neck restraint. Neither is the bruising pattern consistent with the ligature marks from a tightened stocking, but it was some kind of garrote, wasn't it?"

"I'm into autoerotic asphyxiation. Is that something you practiced as well?"

I was rather proud of my transition into another question. The Feds had actually wanted me to ask him about autoerotic asphyxiation.

"If I answer that question," Haines said, "will you answer mine?"

When I finally nodded he said, "I never practiced, or was personally interested in, autoerotic asphyxiation. What caused those marks around your neck?"

"An animal-control pole."

My answer delighted Haines. "I never considered such an application. What a perfect use. As you know, I prefer the up-close-and-personal techniques, but there were those occasions when having a little distance would have made things much easier. And while I would never perform the coup de grace with such a tool, it could certainly prove useful as a prelude to a kill. Now who was it that wanted you hurt and why?"

"It was my girlfriend. She was dressed up as Little Bo Peep and I was the sheep. I'm afraid she got a little rough."

"I hope you don't think you're pulling the wool over my eyes with that story."

He wanted a smile, so I frowned. Haines's initial greeting had summed up only too well where we were: in the heart of darkness. Whenever I visit San Quentin, I have to sign a form at reception that states the prison authorities aren't responsible for me if I am taken captive and won't be bargaining for my release. The form also states they aren't liable for any injuries I sustain and that if I die it's my own tough luck.

San Quentin is the only place in the state of California where you can legally kill another human being. The prison has the dubious distinction of having the largest death row contingent in the nation. At last count, almost six hundred fifty prisoners were waiting to die. They once hung inmates at San Quentin, and then they built a gas chamber and gassed them with hydrogen cyanide, but nowadays lethal injections are used on the condemned. The gas chamber—painted in awful lime green—has not yet been retired, though. It is still the death room. The condemned inmates are strapped down on a gurney inside of the gas chamber and lethally injected.

Most of the condemned inmates live in the East Block, a five-story cage of the damned that is loud and leaky. Scott Peterson, who was convicted of murdering his pregnant wife Laci, is one of those there. The privileged killers are in North Segregation. No one would mistake North Seg for a country club, but it's relatively quiet and on a good day wouldn't be mistaken for a leper colony.

I was a visitor, but it still felt as if I was the one on death row.

"Actually," I said, "one of the reasons I came here was to question you about my attackers."

"And why would you question me?"

"Because my assailants sounded as if they were acting on your behalf. They definitely were true believers, referring to the Prophet. Isn't that what you're calling yourself these days?"

"I have never referred to myself as a prophet. It is others that have given me that title."

"These three had all swallowed your end-of-the-world drivel hook, line, and sinker. I heard them talking up your favorite buzzwords like 'Götterdämmerung,' and 'Ragnarok,' and 'the twilight of the gods.' They also said something about settling the score."

"I had nothing to do with the attack on you."

"Their leader said my death would debunk the very notion that there is such a thing as good and evil. That sounds like your blather."

"I find all of that interesting."

"That's all you have to say?"

"Do you blame Christ for his many so-called followers that have killed in his name?"

"I'd be more comfortable if you compared yourself to Adolf Hitler."

"My point is that if these want-to-be disciples were trying to act in my name, they were not directed by me. I am very selective in the followers I choose."

"What? They need to have a pulse?"

"Many are called but few are chosen."

"I am going to nail my attackers," I said. "The ringleader had some distinctive tattoos. You better hope he doesn't implicate you."

"I am guilty only of being a visionary."

"Spreading ignorance doesn't even make you a false prophet."

Haines continued to stare at the bruising on my neck. "I suppose I should be flattered that they tried to avenge me as well as pay homage to my handiwork."

"When you strangled your victims, were you playing out some kind of bondage fantasy?"

"Is that one of the questions those Quantico miscreants prepared for you?"

"Is that a yes?"

"Why do you shill for the Behavioral Science Unit?"

"Since you won't talk to the FBI, I ask questions on their behalf."

"And you think that serves a purpose?"

"You were a meteorologist."

"I *am* a meteorologist."

"You studied weather patterns. For a time your specialty was hurricanes. You worked on trying to understand what caused hurricanes to form, and when they did form you tried to predict their paths. The profilers are doing many of the same things you did. They accumulate data and try and figure out why certain individuals act as they do."

"So, I'm a hurricane, is that it?"

"Don't flatter yourself. The similarity starts and stops at a lot of hot air."

Before my partner and I captured Haines, he had been known in the media as the Santa Ana Strangler. After he was arrested a new nickname had caught on, one that was proving more popular than the original. Most people now called him the Weatherman, a nickname Haines detested. While it was true that he had been a weatherman on television for two years, he thought the title demeaning. As Haines was quick to point out, he was a trained meteorologist with many years of experience in the field.

I liked it that the nickname of the Weatherman nettled him. At his trial, he had helped bring the name upon himself. After his guilt was pronounced by the jury, Haines had stood up and sung the song "Stormy Weather." He didn't quite do the Billie Holiday version, choosing to alter the lyrics to suit his own situation, but the effect was absolutely chilling. As the judge tried to regain control of his courtroom, Haines assumed a weatherman persona, complete with hand gestures and facial emphasis. Pointing to an imaginary screen, he said, "You can see we have an intense low-pressure area forming all over the Southland, and with it you can expect *killer* winds. If I were you, I'd shut your windows and lock your doors, because the big, bad wolf is about to blow."

And then, even as the bailiff was dragging him away, Haines did his imitation of the wolf blowing down a house, which caused more screams in the courtroom.

He was always a good meteorologist, though. Later that day there were heavy winds throughout Los Angeles: Haines knew his stormy weather.

Instead of being put off by my comments, he said, "The FBI brain trust would like to establish that I was a bed wetter, started fires, and abused animals, their famous holy trinity for serial murderers. You can cross those three questions off your list, as none apply."

"When did you first start to have thoughts about killing women?"

"Why do you ask? Are you troubled by such thoughts?"

"You keep projecting onto me. We're nothing alike. You remind me of the kid who murdered his parents and then asked for mercy from the court because he was an orphan."

"Is that what passes for wit among gendarmes these days?"

"No, what really makes us laugh is seeing pictures of you behind bars."

The behaviorists at the FBI would have been aghast at my interviewing technique. They had given me courses on how to "engage" Haines. I was supposed to be stroking his ego, not putting pins into it. They had stressed how I couldn't be judgmental or challenging, and that the best way to proceed was to quietly listen. Tough shit.

"Since you're trying to get Brownie points from the FBI," Haines said, "here's a little tidbit for you. My lawyer is putting together an appeal. His claim is that I suffer from seasonal affective disorder. As has been well documented, all of my excesses occurred during Santa Ana conditions in the late fall and winter. He believes I became depressed because of the lack of light, and that this resulted in my temporary insanity."

My cough into my hands sounded amazingly like the word "bullshit."

"If my lawyer has his way, I'll be reclassified from a serial murderer to a seasonal murderer."

"I could do without that weather report."

"You don't like the forecast?"

"Not when the climate doesn't agree with me."

I looked down at my notebook and read another one of the FBI questions: "Did you suffer any physical injury, or was there a traumatic event that occurred, prior to when you first murdered?"

"Oh, that's right. You want a precipitating event that prompted my fall from grace. Why, yes, as a matter of fact something did happen. I attended my prom and some nasty girls dropped a bucket of pig's blood on me."

I deviated from the prepared questions: "Do you enjoy horror novels?"

"No, I detest stupid questions. However, I will offer an answer to your FBI handlers that might help them crack the Haines enigma: rosebud."

I gave Haines a hard look. It just made his smile grow.

"Do you wish you'd killed me?" he asked.

"No. If I had, my partner would have died."

"I was prepared for anything with two legs. It was the four legs that got me. How is my friend Sirius?"

"Do you put bullets in all of your friends?"

"Haines nodded. That happened in the heat of battle, Detective. And I still bear the scars where he put the bite on me. But none of that matters. Something happened to all of us that day. We bled together and burned together and came out on the other side together. I am convinced there was an amalgamation of beings."

"Do you hate cats now like you hate women?"

"Whatever gave you the ridiculous idea that I hate women?"

"Maybe I'm wrong, but eleven murders suggest just an itsy-bitsy bit of antipathy toward them."

Haines waved away my theory and said, "We've had enough of this charade, haven't we? Why don't you put away your prop?"

"It's called a piece of paper, not a prop, and on it are the questions I came to ask."

"It's called your excuse to come and see me. We know why you're really here, though."

"We do?"

"We've been dancing around the subject for months, but you've been afraid to bring it up. I've watched your struggles. Do you fear it's your Pandora's box?"

"I think you're confused. This isn't the confessional."

"Isn't it? We shared something in that canyon, didn't we?"

"We probably don't see eye to eye on this, but I wouldn't call being shot by you *sharing*. That's kind of like passing on an STD and referring to it as sharing love."

"Do you have your own name for what occurred?"

"In police parlance it's called an arrest."

"You know that's not what I'm talking about."

"So what is it that you think happened to us?"

"We were surrounded by fire, and the smoke was everywhere. It was so hot our flesh was burning right off, but then in a blink of an eye everything changed."

"The wind shifted."

Haines shook his head. "I have studied weather patterns for all of my adult life. What happened cannot be explained in meteorological terms."

"We got lucky."

"You decided on our route based on how to get to Neverland. And right after that the light showed us the way; a silver path opened up for us."

"It was probably a random pattern of embers falling from the fire."

"Embers?" He put his incredulity on display. "And I suppose that what we did was merely fire walk over those embers. Those were strange embers indeed. They gave off light but they didn't burn."

"I'll tell Tony Robbins he should get some of those for his next fire walk."

"We escaped death by walking on a silver pathway that went straight through the fire and allowed for a way out."

I thought of Sister Frances. She had experienced a miracle. I didn't want to think that I had. "Maybe the fire had already burned through. Maybe it blazed a trail for us."

"We were delivered from that fire."

"What happened was a fluke of nature, a confluence of unrelated events that allowed for our escape."

"I don't think you believe that."

"Suit yourself."

"We made it to Neverland together, and our triumvirate is secret sharers of what occurred."

"Are you having a jailhouse conversion? I always find it amazing how cons get that old-time religion, especially while sitting on death row. Did you have a vision from Saint Quentin himself?"

"I have not had such a conversion, and besides, this prison was not named after Saint Quentin."

"Then who was it named after?"

"A Miwok warrior named Quintin."

"How did an Indian warrior became a saint?"

"He didn't. Sainthood was added when the people of Quintin jumped on the saint bandwagon, wanting to name their city after a saint like San Francisco, San Mateo, or San Jose, I don't think Quintin would have approved of his posthumous title. While alive, he supposedly refused to convert to Christianity. I find that story much more interesting than the usual tripe attributed to the other Saint Quentin, except the accounts of his torture and beheading. Those are always interesting."

"Speaking of the usual tripe, should I be contacting your lawyer? Your finding Jesus might fly better than your seasonal affective disorder murderer ploy."

"Jesus is not what I have found, but I do believe I was delivered from death because my work here is not finished."

"What work? You are a fucking serial murderer. Oh, excuse me: seasonal murderer."

Haines only smiled. "You'll see. It's only a matter of time before I am delivered from this prison."

"That's only going to happen when they wheel you away with a body tag on your toe."

"Judging by your cuts and bruises, I think you're the one that should be more concerned about that tag hanging from your toe."

"Shall I tell the Feds that you're expecting God to deliver you out of here?"

"Who said anything about God?"

"I need a shower. You want to answer some more of my questions so I won't feel this visit was a waste of time?"

"You know it was anything but a waste. We're finally learning how to be honest with one another."

"If that's the case, I can see the merits of being dishonest."

"You're already well acquainted with such merits. Do you worry that you damned yourself to perdition by lying after you were sworn in at the trial and offered your testimony?"

"I didn't lie."

"You never read me my rights, but you said you did."

"You're wrong."

What I was saying was another lie. I knew all too well that I had neglected to inform him of his rights on the day of his capture.

"If you say so," he said.

"I say so."

Because I wanted to make sure Haines was convicted, I had told several lies on the witness stand, something I hadn't done before or since. Haines's sworn version of his capture was the truth, but the jury had thought he was the liar. They hadn't believed that I had threatened to murder him, and that I had come close to doing so more than once, because I had denied doing any such thing.

"Are we done here?"

"Not quite yet," he said. "You said the man directing your attack had tattoos. Can you describe them? Or better yet, can you draw them?"

"Why are you interested?"

"Humor me."

I thought for a few moments and then took a pen to my piece of paper. "One of the tattoos looked like a red *A*," I said, "or an inverted *V* with a line running well beyond the edges. The red figure stood out because it was surrounded by a circle of black."

The Weatherman nodded and said, "Typical poseur. That red *A* is a symbol for anarchy. But what self-respecting anarchist would advertise in such a way?"

I was busy trying to draw the other tattoo, but wasn't having the success that Detective Nguyen had. "There were a lot of squiggles in the second tattoo," I said. "They were coming out of an eye, or a circle."

Haines looked at my drawing, gave it some thought, and then extended his hand and asked, "May I?"

I gave him my pen, although that went against prison rules. He changed my design, making my lines look more like elongated *Z*s, and asked, "Did it look more like that?"

When I nodded he said, "Black sun."

"What's a black sun?"

"There are old and new meanings. In ancient times it meant one thing, but the Nazis made it something else. Today it's usually viewed as an antisun, or burned-out sun. Some think of it as a black hole."

"So it's more of your chaos?"

"Not mine; the world's chaos."

"My visits with you are always so uplifting."

"I feel the same way. Same time and same place next month? We have so much yet to talk about."

I called for the CO, and from outside our cage he put out a call on his walkie-talkie to summon the rest of Haines's escort.

While we waited Haines said, "I am glad you survived the attack. You should know that I will put the word out that you are to be unharmed."

"Don't do me any favors."

"It's not a favor. When you die, I want it to be by my hand."

"Great minds think alike. When your judgment day comes, when the death juice is flowing into your veins, I'll be the guy waving bye-bye to you."

Haines's entourage showed up. He backed up to the door and extended his hands through the slot so that his hardware could be reattached. While he was being cuffed, he faced me with a taunting smile.

"Detective?" he said.

"What?"

"Under current circumstances, it is difficult for me to practice my vocation in a professional manner. I have no access to a computer and I'm even denied such rudimentary essentials as a thermometer or barometer, not to mention a weather meter or wind speed meter, but despite all of those limitations I try and keep up with our state's weather patterns. Necessity being the mother of invention, I have managed to find ways of perpetuating my craft even from the confines of my cage."

"Is there a point to all of this?"

"If not a point, there is at least a weather forecast. Red sky at morning, sailors take warning."

"Thanks so much for that rhyme. I'll be sure to keep my yacht in the harbor tomorrow."

"A Santa Ana condition is forming in the Los Angeles area, Detective. I can feel it stirring in my gut. Strong, dry winds are coming. They'll start tomorrow, but just wait until the day after tomorrow. That's when you'll really feel those killer winds blow."

He paused, perhaps remembering his days as a television weatherman and the need for occasional dramatic effect. "That's when all hell will break loose, Detective."

CHAPTER 15:

SO SOON DONE, WHY WERE YOU BEGUN?

The Weatherman's forecast kept intruding into my thoughts on the flight back to LA. When I landed at LAX at one forty-five, it felt as if I'd been away for a week instead of a very long morning. The day promised to get a lot longer. I had an afternoon funeral to attend.

Seth is always happy to look after Sirius, but I never like imposing longer than necessary. Besides, I wanted company for the drive, so I swung by Sherman Oaks and picked Sirius up. At least I wouldn't have to change for the funeral. I was already wearing a dark blazer and gray pants.

I called Seth's cell number, but he didn't pick up. Maybe he was on a spirit quest, but it was more likely he was at a client's house. I left a message telling him not to be worried when he found his charge missing. When I opened Seth's gate to the backyard, Sirius gave me a hero's welcome.

"Just what I needed," I said, "a dog-hair coat."

Methinks I protest too much. I had welcomed him into my arms; his hairs had followed. I stopped inside my house to grab my electric razor, and then the two of us set out on our road trip.

The hoped-for smooth sailing didn't materialize, as the 134 was already tight with commuters. In LA, all roads lead to gridlock. When the 134 merged with I-210, it wasn't quite a parking lot but the traffic was moving slowly enough for me to leisurely shave. One highway patrol officer I know describes the LA morning commute as the "cosmetics interchange." MPG doesn't stand for miles per gallon, he says, but makeup per gallon. The afternoon commute isn't any better, but beautifying isn't the concern—everyone just wants to get the hell out of Dodge.

Traffic opened up once I passed Glendale, and I kept a heavy foot on the accelerator. The Eleventh Commandment among law enforcement is "Thou shalt not give a ticket to a fellow cop," which means that if you have a badge, you can speed with impunity whenever pressed for time. However, getting stopped for speeding isn't a pleasant experience even if you are a cop; you escape the ticket but not the aggrieved sighs that come with wasting another officer's time. Because of that, I was about as watchful as your average speeder and spent as much time watching out for CHP as I did the road.

I traveled along a route made famous by the *Jack Benny Program*. Benny's series aired before my time, but my father used to always laugh whenever repeating the route called out by the show's train conductor: "Anaheim, Azusa, Cuuuuu-ca-mon-gaaaa." In reality there was never such a train route, but the cities are real enough. Apparently, no matter what the situation at the depot, Cucamonga was the punch line. My father said that sometimes a whole skit would take place between conductors announcing Cuca and concluding with monga. Many years after the show last aired, my father was still laughing about Cuuuuu-ca-mon-gaaaa, and because his funny bone was tickled, so was mine.

Seeing the turnoff sign to Rancho Cucamonga, I remembered my father and said, "Cuuuuu-ca-mon-gaaaa." Sirius seemed to find that amusing and encouraged me with some tail wagging.

"Cuuuuu-ca-mon-gaaaa," I said again, stretching out the word for about half a minute.

Sirius tried working me to do another encore, but with Hollywood sincerity I said, "No, really, I can't." My father had been dead for a dozen years, but I was still getting a kick out of the punch line that had brought him such pleasure. Of course Jack Benny and my father probably wouldn't have even recognized Rancho Cucamonga in its present incarnation. It had been known for its orange groves for much of the twentieth century, but that was before the Los Angeles borders spread north, south, and east. Now I was willing to bet there wasn't a single citrus grove left in town. The former sleepy hamlet was now approaching big city status and had a population of more than a hundred sixty thousand and counting.

Thinking about my adoptive father made for a pleasant trip down memory lane. Those that didn't know better always assumed I was my father's biological son, and whenever anyone commented on our resemblance, my dad always gave me a big wink. Being raised by a loving family had helped me all but forget that I'd been abandoned by my biological mother, but today wasn't one of those days that I could forget.

The death of Rose and her impending burial made me remember the story of a grieving father who had put a philosophical epitaph on his infant daughter's tombstone: "So soon done for, what was I begun for?" I didn't have an answer to that question and doubted that I ever would, but I believed society owed a debt to Rose and it was my job to see it paid in full.

The southern California desert can be a cold, windy place in the winter, but the weather was cooperating for Rose's burial. The sun was shining when I arrived at the small town of Calimesa. The Desert Lawn Cemetery is only a short distance from I-10; the dead apparently aren't bothered by the nonstop traffic.

Most of the cemetery's expanse is out in the back, but the Garden of Angels has its own separate plot located in the front.

As I went down the driveway, I looked over at the final resting spot for so many abandoned children. There were rows of close-set crosses—about eighty in total. The proximity of the grave markers reminded me of how the headstones of some family plots are situated close together, and I couldn't help but think that these little ones abandoned at birth had finally found a family.

There were already a number of people milling around the Garden of Angels waiting for the service to begin. Through word of mouth and an obituary notice that Lisbet always put in the local papers, there was usually a good turnout at the funerals. The way these newborns were abandoned tears at the moral fabric of our world; those that come out and show they care give me hope that all is not lost.

I parked out back and reached for one of the spare leashes I keep in the car. "Let's go," I said.

We made a stop at a willow tree that was well away from any grave marker, but I still made sure the coast was clear before giving Sirius the okay to relieve himself. Afterward, the two of us walked up the driveway and then started up the rose garden path that led to the Garden of Angels. For most of the year the roses are in full bloom, but this was winter and the flowers were scarce. There were some buds, though, that offered the hope of spring.

Sirius stopped to smell the buds, and it crossed my mind that we would soon be planting a Rose.

In the front of the garden was a statue of three happy children; one of the boys was fishing. Since the last time I had visited the boy still hadn't landed a fish, but that didn't seem to diminish his happiness. We continued up the path, where we encountered more statues, figurines, memorials, and markers: a little girl holding up a basket to gather flowers, flying cherubs, biblical passages offering comfort. I paused to read the words from Jeremiah 1:5: "Before I formed you in the womb, I knew you; before you were born, I set you apart."

I moved on to the memorial bricks. Some of the bricks displayed engraved names of companies, colleges, and hospitals, but most bore the names of individuals. There were inscribed messages on some of the bricks; one said "Lullaby & Goodnight." On the ride over I had thought of my father, but now I remembered my mother and Brahms. I wondered how many others heard the voice of their mother when hearing the music of Brahms's "Lullaby." Mental note to self: Call Mom.

Usually I don't spend my time looking back. Like most men, I think that introspection is a luxury I can't—or I'm afraid to—allow myself. For whatever reasons, Rose's funeral had opened lots of windows to the past. My parents had thought themselves blessed to finally have a child. There were other people out there waiting for a baby like Rose to come into their lives.

Blinking hard at the past and present, I moved on to another brick. The inscribed message was a plea to the dead: "Babies Forgive Us." I almost commented to Sirius that I was glad I wasn't in the forgiveness business, but other people were now in hearing range.

Footsteps approached and a familiar-looking couple greeted me. The man extended his hand and offered his name, and I remembered that we had met at baby Moses's funeral. No one forgets you when you come and pay respects with your dog. The couple did their best to not stare at my face. This time it wasn't my scar drawing interest as much as the bruises and cuts from the night before. They were too polite to inquire but too curious not to look.

"Good to see you again, Detective," he said.

The man's wife didn't forget Sirius, offering her hand for him to sniff. "And good to see you, too," she said.

More people followed behind the couple, and it felt as if Sirius and I were suddenly the objects of a reception line. A lot of eyes studiously ignored the state of my face and neck. The regulars felt the need to make friendly reintroductions, and Sirius wagged his tail as if he remembered each and every mourner; maybe he did.

In the midst of all the shaking and wagging, I caught sight of Lisbet. She flashed me a smile before returning to more last-minute demands on her time. Lisbet was wearing a dark outfit, but pinned to her blouse was a bright red rose.

The notes from a flute called all of us to gather, the music playing over the freeway noise. The same flutist had also played at the last funeral. Sirius and I took up positions on the outskirts of the garden, and my eyes drifted over to all of the gravestone crosses that were already in place. A number of items had been left atop and around the crosses. There were religious objects to be sure—crucifixes and Saint Christopher medals—but most of the remembrances were kid things like toy cars, superhero necklaces, stuffed animals, and dolls.

I studied the names on the crosses. There appeared to be about an equal number of boys and girls buried. In the middle of the plot was a large tree; the last funeral I'd attended had occurred on a hot desert day and I remembered how that tree had provided needed shelter. The shade wasn't necessary today, but the shadows of the tree seemed to be reaching out to offer a group hug.

A clergywoman stepped forward to give the eulogy. You wouldn't think there would be much to say about Rose. There wasn't much entered in her murder book other than pictures from the crime scene, my notes, and the coroner's identification card, which showed two baby feet and ten perfect little toes. A coroner's ID card isn't the kind of memento that should be in a baby's scrapbook. Luckily, I wasn't giving the eulogy. My emphasis would have been on the death of baby Rose, but the clergywoman was somehow able to make it about her life. She built on the scant hours that Rose had lived, and personalized her. The death of an innocent, we heard, was a sacrifice from which all of us should learn. The clergywoman quoted from Matthew, saying how we had to become like little children in order to enter the kingdom of heaven. According to her, that was where Rose already was. I hoped she was right. In the meantime, I'd be working the case on planet earth.

When the minister finished talking, a man stepped forward and opened a birdcage. It took a little prompting for the three white doves inside to realize that the prison doors were open. When the birds flew out, they circled above the garden and for a few moments appeared unsure of which way to go, but then all three of them set off east in the direction of distant mountains. The doves had the good sense to be flying away from LA.

The flute music started up again, and I recognized the tune to "Rock of Ages." There were a lot of wet eyes in the crowd, but more smiles. Normally, I would have hurried away while the music was still playing, but this time I felt the need to socialize. I wasn't alone. Fellowship seemed to be on the docket of all. I wanted to talk to Lisbet, but she was surrounded by those who also wanted a little of her time. Our eyes met over the crowd, and I signaled for her to meet me over at the punch bowl. She nodded but managed to convey that I would need to wait for her to disentangle herself.

Sirius and I slowly made our way over to the refreshments. We were stopped by a few people that had missed us on the first go-around. Once we passed through that gauntlet, I poured Sirius a cup of water and me some punch.

The sun was setting and the Garden of Angels was bathed in golden light. The sun's rays seemed to spotlight one grave marker in particular. Beneath the name Amanda were the words "Deserved to be loved."

Sirius's happy sounds alerted me to Lisbet's approach. "Hello you," she said, talking to the dog and then leaning down to scratch him.

"If I make those sounds," I asked, "will you scratch me?"

"Only if you roll over and beg first."

She smiled at me and made me feel good inside. I had planned on nothing more than a short conversation with Lisbet, but suddenly that wasn't enough.

"I hope this doesn't sound inappropriate," I said, "and it probably is, and if it is I apologize, but are you doing anything afterward?"

It took Lisbet a moment to make sense of my meandering question.

"I have to stay here for another half hour or so," she said, "but I'm free after that."

My head started bobbing up and down, but the bobblehead imitation didn't help me with my speaking skills, and once more I found myself babbling. "Good. I mean, that will work for me. We are talking about dinner, aren't we? Because I know we discussed having lunch, but this way we can kill two birds with one stone."

I finally took a breath and then said, "Sorry, that didn't come out quite right."

Lisbet lightly touched my burning left cheek and delivered me from feeling felony stupid with a smile. "Dinner sounds great."

"Good," I said. "Okay, then. I guess I'll take Sirius for a walk while you finish up here."

"Enjoy your walk."

Waving seemed like a better option than talking. I needed to study those tapes of the old me again, I thought, so that I could remember who I was supposed to be and how I used to act. I wanted to be that self-confident man again and not some blithering idiot.

There wasn't much in the way of scenery near the cemetery, and I didn't think it appropriate to go look at headstones with Sirius, so we set off up the long driveway. After the fact, I started giving some thought as to where I'd be taking Lisbet to eat. I wanted a quiet spot that was comfortable and not stuffy. Usually my only concern is if the restaurant has a patio and allows me to bring my partner. Tonight my date was going to be much less hairy and only have two legs.

I used my phone to check out dining options in Palm Springs. Usually I only care if the food is good. This time I also checked on comments that spoke to ambience. The Europa Restaurant received high marks in both. I called for reservations and then asked the hostess for directions. She provided them and then said, "You can't miss it."

I thanked her, and hung up, but was sure she had jinxed me and said as much to Sirius.

"Whenever anyone says, 'You can't miss it,' you always do," I said. "When 'Wrong-Way' Corrigan took off from New York, he didn't end up in California. No, he ended up in Ireland. I am sure someone said to him, 'You can't miss it.'"

Sirius didn't look interested.

"Cucamonga," I said, and my partner responded with a little dance.

We began walking back to the Garden of Angels. From a distance the cemetery appeared to be deserted, but as we drew closer I could see that Lisbet had one final task awaiting her. Two cemetery workers were lowering a small pink casket into the ground.

Sirius and I didn't encroach. With a bowed head, Lisbet waited for the casket to be positioned and the hole filled. Her vigil continued even after the workers finished with the burial. It was dark when Lisbet finally took her leave of Rose. I was feeling a bit uncomfortable by then and wondered if suggesting dinner had been a good idea, but Lisbet quickly dispelled any doubts.

"Sorry to keep you waiting," she said, "but I don't like to leave the children until I have this sense that they're settled. It's always a huge relief for me when they're buried and, well, when they're home. I know that probably sounds crazy."

"What's crazy is that they're here in the first place. Are you still okay for dinner?"

"Okay? You hear my stomach grumbling? I'm afraid if you listen closely you might hear it growling the words 'Donner Party.'"

"Barring any blizzards, we should get to the restaurant in about half an hour."

"I hope you're right, otherwise it might cost you an arm and a leg."

Once we were in the car and on the road, I pointed to the glove compartment. "Inside you'll find your choice of appetizers, madam."

Lisbet flipped it open and started pulling out odds and ends that I'd taken away from restaurants. There were several packages of saltines, oyster crackers, sugar packets, dinner mints, and some hot sauce.

"You really know how to spoil a girl."

"If you're still hungry, there's also a box of dog biscuits under your seat."

Lisbet rummaged around and came up with the box. Sirius's ears perked up at the sound and she asked, "Can I give him one?"

"He's sort of particular and won't take food from someone he doesn't know well."

Sirius put his muzzle on Lisbet's shoulder and took a dog biscuit from her without any hesitation. He was already munching when I told him, "It's okay to eat, boy."

He nudged Lisbet for another, and I nodded. The second one also disappeared without any demur.

"Why are dog biscuits colored if dogs are color blind?" Lisbet asked.

Instead of telling her that dogs aren't completely color blind I said, "That sounds like a Stephen Wright observation." And then imitating Wright's deadpan voice, I added, "I have an inferiority complex, but it's not a very good one."

Lisbet was busy tearing at a saltines package with her teeth, but stopped her shredding for long enough to laugh. After devouring those, she also finished the oyster crackers and then picked up the box of dog biscuits and started looking at the ingredients.

"These don't look that bad. The primary ingredients are wheat flour and wheat bran, and they also have wheat germ and brewers' yeast."

"Go for it."

She turned her head to me, made eye contact and regarded my smile—well, sneer.

"I double dog dare you. Come to think of it, I double dog biscuit dare you."

"One of these is supposed to be peanut butter flavor," she said and pulled some of the biscuits out of the box and started doing a sniff test.

The hairy beggar in the backseat took her inspection as an invitation to plead his case and was rewarded with another treat.

"This one is the peanut butter," Lisbet said, brandishing it at me.

"*Bone* appetit," I said.

She didn't hesitate but bit into it and started eating. After swallowing she said, "It's possible that was the bacon flavor."

Her poker face didn't tell me anything else. "I hope you're not looking for a second opinion."

"You think I would share with you?"

Lisbet opened one of the hot sauce packets and lathered the remaining half of the dog treat in it. She popped it in her mouth and started chewing. The more I laughed, the more she looked at me as if to say, "What's so funny?" That, of course, made it all the funnier.

Despite the presence of dog biscuit crumbs on the side of her mouth, I wanted to lean over and kiss her. I didn't want to rush it, though, so instead of reaching with my lips I used my index finger to lightly brush the side of her mouth and said, "You might consider having a few of those dinner mints now."

She hit my arm and I pretended to be in pain. It was great to feel like I was in second grade again.

For a time, Palm Springs was known as a place for the newly wed and the nearly dead, but nowadays the oasis in the desert is home to a diverse population. As we entered the city I followed the directions I had been given and surprised myself by not getting lost.

Before decamping from the car, I opened some windows and poured some water. "I hope you don't mind," I said to Lisbet, taking the box of dog biscuits from her and pulling out two more to give to Sirius.

"Are you planning on holding that over me?"

"For a long, long time," I said.

Instead of objecting, she smiled.

The Europa Restaurant was located in the middle of the Villa Royale Inn. Fountains gurgled and planters spilled over with flowers. Trellised bougainvillea was everywhere. Overhead, the night sky was thick with stars that looked almost close enough to touch, and in the distance the shadow of Mount San Jacinto appeared as an impressive backdrop to the property. As we walked by a pool with glimmering lights, it almost felt as if we were in some villa in the Mediterranean.

At our approach the hostess looked up from her stand, and for just an instant her welcoming smile faltered at the double whammy of my scarred and bruised face before regaining its full wattage. She asked whether we had reservations, and I said, "Yes, Donner, party of two."

Lisbet nudged me, and I gave my real name. The hostess rewarded my honesty by seating us near a glowing fireplace. For once, I didn't worry about fire. The heat from the fire offered comforting warmth, and in Lisbet's company I could forget all the bad things that had happened to me in the past twenty-four hours.

I ordered the rack of lamb with the tapenade of dates, and Lisbet had the salmon in parchment with wild mushrooms drizzled with crème fraîche and sprinkled with dill. The food was wonderful, but even if I'd been served MRE rations, I would have been mightily pleased. This wasn't a date where I was going through the motions and was out with someone because I was supposed to be getting on with my life; I was where I wanted to be and Lisbet seemed to be enjoying my company as much as I was hers.

Our server came around, and although there wasn't much left on our plates, both of us asked for a doggy bag. "I told Sirius that he'd be getting a treat tonight. That usually means a stop at In-N-Out Burger and a Flying Dutchman cooked rare."

"I'm no stranger to In-N-Out," she said, "but I'm not familiar with a Flying Dutchman."

"It's two meat patties and two slices of cheese with no bun, but you won't find it on the In-N-Out menu. They have a secret menu, even though I think half of southern California is in on the secret. All the employees know the code words. They never blink when I order my burgers *animal style*, which means I want the patties cooked in mustard."

"How come I don't know about this secret menu?"

"You haven't been hanging around with the right people."

"Or the wrong people?"

"I resemble that remark."

The warmth from the fire made me too comfortable; my grin turned into a yawn. "Excuse me," I said.

"After what happened to you last night, you probably shouldn't even be out."

"After what happened to me last night, this is the best medicine I can think of."

"Any leads on those men that attacked you?"

I opened my mouth to tell her about my morning in the Bay Area but then decided not to talk about it. Ellis Haines wasn't going to spoil my evening. I shook my head.

"What is it?"

"Nothing," I said.

Her face told me she knew I was being evasive. "Someone once told me that when you're in the presence of a real friend, you can think aloud."

"It's hard enough for me to think in silence."

Lisbet offered only a hint of a smile, prompting me to say, "I think there's a lot of truth in that saying. I used to think aloud with my wife."

"What was her name?"

"I never settled on just one. In the course of a minute I could call her Jenny, Jen, or Jennifer."

"Do you mind my asking how she died?"

"I don't mind, even though most people think the answer is anticlimactic. She died of the flu."

In a voice that was little more than a whisper, I repeated an old rhyme: "I had a little bird and its name was Enza, I opened the window and in flew Enza." In a normal voice I continued, "Out of the mouths of babes, you know. That rhyme was popular with children during the Spanish influenza pandemic. There was a ghoulish quality to those words, because around the world forty million people were dying from the flu, and they weren't mostly the old and young but healthy adults between the ages of twenty and forty.

"We've forgotten that, of course. People usually do a double take when I tell them my wife died of complications from the flu. Nowadays, the flu isn't supposed to be fatal to a healthy and athletic twenty-nine-year-old woman. It was probably that thinking which killed Jen. Even though she was sick, she kept pushing herself. Instead of bed rest and fluids, she dragged herself into work. She downplayed her symptoms. What she called a chest cold was actually pneumonia; what she described as a little fever turned out to be a dangerously high temperature. I shouldn't have let her keep reassuring me that she was all right when I knew she was sick, and I shouldn't have let her keep working. By the time I talked her into going to the hospital, her system was already in meltdown."

"I am sorry."

There was a moment of contemplative silence, but it was broken by the server who swooped in to ask, "Can I interest the two of you in some dessert tonight?"

Lisbet was about to decline the offer, but I said, "When it comes to dessert, my mom always quotes Erma Bombeck: 'Seize the moment. Remember all those women on the *Titanic* that waved off the dessert cart.'"

Because Lisbet didn't look quite won over, I added, "What happened to those thirty-two sweet teeth you told me about?"

"I suppose it is only right to remember the *Titanic*," Lisbet said. She turned to the waitress and asked, "What do you suggest?"

"The chocolate mousse is heavenly."

There was a meeting of raised eyebrows, and then I said, "Heaven can't wait. We'll take two mice."

Later, as the two of us were searching with our spoons for any speck of mousse that we might have missed, I said, "I'm doing this for Sirius, you know. Chocolate is not good for dogs, so the mousse can't be part of his doggy bag."

"No sacrifice too big," Lisbet said, patting her hips. "But I am thinking that you really should get him that Flying Dutchman."

"I might even get him a three by three."

"Is that more secret menu talk?"

I nodded. "Three meat patties, three slices of cheese."

"Do you order with some kind of Masonic handshake?"

"That's not necessary, but they'll give you free fries if you drive up to the takeout window in a Shriners car and shake your fez in the prescribed manner."

"Who could resist a man in a fez?"

"It's the tassel."

"Be still my heart."

The waitress brought the check and our doggy bags. Lisbet said, "Can I...," and I raised a hand.

"You cannot."

"Next time is my treat, then."

I liked the sound of the words "next time."

She asked, "If I give you my doggy bag, can you be trusted to pass on the salmon to Sirius?"

"Scout's honor," I said, holding up my index and middle fingers in a *V* sign, "but I should mention that I was never a Scout."

"Sirius will tell me whether you made good on your promise or not."

"The salmon's a bribe, I think. You're trying to get him to forgive you for eating his dog biscuits."

"It was *one* dog biscuit."

"That's how it innocently starts. The next thing that happens is you're hitting the kibble pretty hard, and then you begin experimenting with rawhide chews. Before you know it, you're out on the corner doing Liv-A-Snaps and Snausages. I've seen it before and it's not pretty."

"I'm so ashamed."

I paid the bill and the two of us took the long way to the car. By the time we reached the first of the inn's two pools, we were walking hand in hand. The bright lights of LA make it easy to overlook the stars, but out in the desert the stars can't be ignored. One bright flickering star stood out more than the others.

"Sirius," I said, pointing, and then added, "the Dog Star."

"After his heroics I'm thinking that Sirius should join Lassie and Rin Tin Tin with his own star on the Hollywood Walk of Fame."

"Not a chance," I said. "He thought it was a travesty that Benji never got a star, so he's made it clear that if Hollywood comes knocking, he's not interested."

We paused in our walk to take in the stars. Lisbet leaned a little into me and I liked that. She said, "I used to go camping in the desert with this friend who would bring out his huge telescope and spend most of the night hunting down stars and planets and moons. He taught me to look up at the sky and see the constellations. Orion was easy: pick out the three stars that make up Orion's belt and work from there. And finding Sirius always made it easy for me to work out Canis Major."

I was feeling a little jealous of another man's being Lisbet's guide to the stars, so I decided to sound like I knew something about the subject. "You ever hear the story about how Orion and Sirius got up there?"

Lisbet shook her head, which allowed me to show off the lone piece of star trivia that I knew. "According to Greek mythology, Apollo tricked Artemis into killing Orion by challenging her to shoot an arrow at a faraway speck in the ocean. Artemis didn't know that the object Apollo targeted was Orion, who was out for a swim. Because she was overcome with grief at what she had done, Artemis decided to place Orion in the heavens as a constellation. But Artemis wasn't the only one grieving. Sirius was Orion's faithful hunting dog, and when his master disappeared, he tirelessly searched for him. Because of that, Artemis decided that Sirius's place was in the heavens right at Orion's heel."

With one hand I was pointing to Sirius; the other hand had found its way around Lisbet's shoulder. Our heads moved from the stars to each other, and we kissed.

CHAPTER 16:

LIAR, LIAR, PANTS ON FIRE

Gravity didn't seem to have quite the same hold on either one of us after the kiss. It had been a long time since I'd felt good like that, and that feeling of exhilaration kept bubbling up and going to my brain. Lisbet's smiles and animated conversation told me she was feeling the same thing, which made the return drive to the Garden of Angels and Lisbet's car seem all too short. As I came to a stop in the cemetery's parking lot, Lisbet surprised me by asking, "Where are you sleeping tonight?"

"I imagine the same place where I've slept for the last eight years."

"Someone wants you hurt or dead. Maybe you should find another place to stay the night."

"Sirius is the best guard dog in the world—no, the universe."

Sirius heard his name spoken and thought that meant it was time to socialize. He settled in for some serious scratching, acting more like a lapdog than a guard dog.

"I do have a comfortable sofa bed," she said.

"You don't need to spoil Sirius. He can sleep on the floor."

"He can sleep with you on the sofa bed."

"I thought your apartment didn't allow dogs."

"As you've mentioned a time or two, Sirius isn't a dog but an LAPD officer."

"You really don't need to worry about me. I'm pretty sure those bad guys are either holed up or on the run. No one is coming after me tonight, Lisbet."

She didn't look completely satisfied but didn't push it further. I extended my hand, and we twined fingers.

"I am not ready for the night to end yet. If you're not too tired, you're welcome to come to my place for a nightcap."

"I'd like that. But I will need to attend to bowser burger business on the way."

"Then I'll not get in the way of your alliteration or Sirius's dinner."

Sirius must have been eavesdropping—either that or his burger radar, which worked better than Pavlov's bell, went off. The slap, slap, slap of his tail made it clear that he knew dinner was imminent.

Lisbet lived in a multicolored apartment in West LA not far away from Loyola Marymount University. The apartment's color scheme looked as if it had been inspired by the choreography of *Miami Vice*, with the exterior stucco painted in pastels of peach, pink, and lime. At least there were no plastic pink flamingos in front.

She was waiting in her car out front, and per her hand gestures I followed her down to the garage and took a space in visitor parking. Then Sirius and I crammed into Lisbet's Civic and all of us drove over to her assigned parking spot.

"You better stay in the car while I make sure the coast is clear," she said. "I don't want to run into the apartment manager."

While Lisbet was doing her scouting, I broke Sirius's three by three into pieces and fed it to him. He was already sniffing at the restaurant's doggy bags when Lisbet came back and signaled for us to join her. We took the elevator up to the second floor and

made our way across a walkway to her unit. Lisbet had personalized the exterior of the apartment with an entry mat that actually said "Welcome." Her particular patch of stucco was the color
of peach. The entryway was festooned with several ridiculously
healthy hanging plants overhead. Decorative stained glass lined
her windows. There was a wooden planter next to her door that
held several succulents with eye-catching geometric shapes. I
wasn't the only one sizing up the plant life, but I was pretty sure
Sirius wasn't doing it for aesthetic reasons. Since I had taken him
for a walk at the In-N-Out, I knew his need wasn't to pee but to
advertise.

"Don't even think about it."

The circling leg stilled.

Lisbet finished working keys to locks and opened the door.
"Be it ever so humble," she said.

If I'd had the same living area, it would have remained insti-
tutional, but in a glance I could see that Lisbet had tailored her
apartment into a warm nest.

"Would you like the grand tour?"

"Lead on."

The kitchen was small, but a rolling butcher block evidently
served as an island when needed. There were two framed prints in
the kitchen, Van Gogh's *Café Terrace at Night* and a black-and-white
picture of an old Earl Grey tea box. A ristra of red peppers hung
down from one of the cabinets. Over the sink was a wooden over-
hang for wine glasses; above it were flavored oils and vinegars with
sprigs and stalks that appeared to be as much for use as decoration.

"Are you in the mood for a glass of wine?"

"Only if it's red or white."

She checked the refrigerator and found an opened bottle of
sauvignon blanc. Before pouring, she twisted out the cork, sniffed
the vino and decided the wine was still drinkable. We clicked
glasses and she led me into the living room. There was one picture
on the wall, a large black and white of trees shrouded in fog.

"I love the fog," she said, "except when I'm driving in it."

We continued down the hallway. As I entered the room I felt eyes tracking me: there was a Felix the Cat clock with moving eyes on one wall. The bedroom was set up as an office, with a light table, art supplies, two computers each with a different printer, and a photo workshop. One wall of the office was set up for cubby holes, with markers, pens, brushes, papers of all sizes and colors, proofs, and work supplies. I reached for a red Swingline stapler.

"Don't touch my stapler," Lisbet said, using Milton's voice from the movie *Office Space*.

"Where are your TPS reports?" I asked, and we exchanged grins at being in synch with movie shorthand humor.

I moved to the next wall and looked at two different René Magritte prints. Lisbet must have interpreted my nod as meaning something and asked, "Do you have any art at your house?"

"I don't, but Sirius does: *Dogs Playing Poker*. It's not as bad as it sounds, though. It's on velvet."

There was one other piece of wall art in the office, a reproduction of an old map of the world. It bore some resemblance to the present-day world maps, but there were the notable omissions of a continent or two.

I pointed to the words "Here there be dragons" and said, "The cartographer got it right."

"How is that?"

"Where he wrote those words is right where LA is."

The master bedroom was filled with mission-style furniture. Along the longest wall were shelves that held books, CDs, and an assortment of keepsakes. In the corners of the room were sconces for soft lighting. Lisbet's green thumb was evidenced in a number of houseplants, and a variety of fresh and dried flowers filled half a dozen vases. One of the walls was devoted to a display of framed familial pictures, and among them were a number of smiling faces that resembled Lisbet.

"Four sisters," she said, "three nieces, two nephews, and one brother."

"*And a partridge in a pear tree*," I sang.

In the air was the scent of potpourri, the balsam of pine sachets, the sandalwood of scented candles, and the fragrant gummy smell of eucalyptus leaves. It was a feminine room, because few men would take the time to make a space so appealing to the senses, but it was a room that would be easy to leave your boots in.

Her apartment couldn't have been more than eight hundred square feet, but she'd managed to pack a lot in. Mirrors, recessed lighting, and Lisbet's good taste made the space feel much larger than it was. She left exploration of the loft—or what she called "my meditation space"—for last.

The loft was a fusion of East and West. There were definite shrine elements to it: a tatami mat, a shoji door, and a small rock garden with trickling water. The space was set off by wall dividers of shadowed ravens and cranes. There was no altar but a table that seemed to be a memorial of sorts. Laid out on it were items Lisbet must have deemed significant: a piece of amber with a fossilized insect; some sea shells; a few interesting-looking stones; a tiny pink baby blanket that held an ostrich egg; a cameo locket; a feather; a snow globe; a well-thumbed Bible; a book-sized container filled with white sand and a tiny rake; a small music box; and a framed black-and-white picture of the Garden of Angels.

I picked up the picture and studied it for a moment. It wasn't one of those views of a cemetery with creeping fog and shrouded images, but neither was it an inspirational shot of the sun rising. The picture showed the youthful reminders without the youths. It was sort of like seeing a deserted playground; you knew what was missing and what should have been there in place of the grave markers.

"You've made a special place on this planet," I said, carefully returning the photo to its place.

"A lot of people have made it a special place. Today you saw how many are involved. I always like to quote from one of the memorial bricks: 'Our share of night to bear.'"

"Sometimes it seems like a long way to dawn."

"Sometimes it does, but not tonight."

"No, not tonight."

I took her in my arms and we held one another. The moment seemed to stir a lot of memories and feelings in me: the burial of Rose, Sister Frances's miracle, the pleasure of holding Lisbet, and the thought that I wouldn't be alive if she hadn't saved me with a fortuitous phone call.

"If you're ever up for sainthood, I wonder if you saving my life would qualify as a miracle."

"I already told you that I don't want to be a saint."

As if to emphasis this, she offered up a long and passionate kiss. When our lips finally disengaged I said, "I'm beginning to believe you."

She felt along the right side of my face, gently touching the scar tissue there. "Do you mind?"

"Do you?"

"I want to feel free to touch you."

"I hereby give you permission to ravage me wherever you want."

"Are you sensitive here?"

"I can show you a few spots where I'm a lot more sensitive."

"I'm being serious, Michael. If touching you here isn't pleasurable for you, I'll stop."

"Don't stop. What's prickly is my personality, not my skin. The scarring makes that area not as sensitive to the touch as other parts of my face, but your warm hand still feels good to me."

"I'm glad."

"You're actually feeling my buttocks, you know."

"You could have fooled me."

"That's where they took that particular skin graft from."

"So you're speaking out of your ass?"

"You really have forever dispelled your saint image."

"Good," she said, still stroking my face. "You know, the first time we met I asked around about you. That's when I learned that you were the officer that was burned while bringing in the Strangler."

"That explains why you were nice to me. You felt sorry for Quasimodo."

"You mean I heard bells ringing?"

I used the pretense of stretching to move my face away from her hand. I don't like being self-conscious, but I am.

"No, that's not what I meant," I said, changing the light tone of our conversation to something more serious.

Lisbet took a read of my eyes and then a more pointed read of my scarred face. "I hope you're not implying that this is some kind of mercy date. Yes, the first time we met I couldn't help but notice the scarring on your face, but I stopped seeing it after that."

"You're doing better than me, then. Sometimes I'm still startled when I see myself in the mirror."

"Sounds like me when I have a bad hair day."

I didn't have to force my smile. "I'm getting used to the new me, but I was really self-conscious when I first started going out in public and noticed all the surreptitious staring directed my way."

"I'll bet not as many people were staring at your scars as you thought."

"You'd lose that bet."

"I'm not saying that people weren't staring, but not all of them were looking at your scars. They were staring at a hero. Your capturing the Strangler was a huge story. I still remember all those breaking news reports on how you and Sirius were doing."

"I guess I missed all the hoopla being in the burn unit. Everything was sort of a blur the first few days. There was a TV in my room, but I couldn't watch it because the fire had burned my eyelids and corneas, and my face was swaddled in bandages."

"That must have been awful."

Her sympathetic voice kept me talking. "I don't think I've ever felt so isolated. What made it even worse was that my doctors told me I might lose my sight. So there I was in my personal darkness with nothing to do but worry, except on those too frequent occasions when I was being tortured."

Thinking that I'd offered up too much poor, poor, pitiful me, I finished with, "Aside from that, Mrs. Lincoln, how'd you enjoy the play?"

Lisbet had the good sense to groan.

I said, "You'd think all of that would put a few scars in perspective, wouldn't you?"

"Didn't it?"

I shrugged. "I wasn't only worried about my life or my sight. I was afraid that without a full recovery I wouldn't have a job on the force."

"If I was fighting for my life, the last thing I'd think about was my work."

"When Jen died, work took on a new importance for me. It gave me a reason to keep going. So even when the doctors told me I was out of the woods, I kept worrying about the department finding some medical reason that would prevent me from returning to the force. That's why I memorized eye charts and prepared for how to best answer questions about my physical and mental health. To tell the truth, I'm still paranoid."

"Is there a reason to be?"

Instead of answering, I did a De Niro parody straight out of *Taxi Driver*: "You talkin' to me?"

Her smile afforded me the opportunity to echo the same bad impersonation, and the second time around it even got a laugh. That spared me from having to provide Lisbet with a real answer.

We made our way back downstairs and settled on her sofa. I asked Lisbet about her work, and afterward she asked me about mine, and I told her a little bit about the Special Cases Unit.

"I am glad the LAPD considered Moses and Rose special cases," she said. "It wasn't that way in the past."

I didn't tell her the department hadn't had a change of heart. "I guess Moses and Rose are a little more personal to me than they would be to most other cops."

She waited for me to elaborate. Anyone but Lisbet would have had to wait for a long time.

"I was abandoned as a newborn. It's likely my mother was a druggie, but I don't know for sure. The police never found out who she was, but it's not like they looked very hard either for her or for answers."

"I am sorry."

"Don't be. I had two great adoptive parents. And I've found some unexpected bonuses to not knowing my background."

"And what might those be?"

"I get to celebrate every ethnic and religious holiday like it's my very own. On Saint Patrick's Day I'm an Irishman, on Cinco de Mayo I'm Mexican, and on Chinese New Year's I'm Chinese."

Lisbet looked at me skeptically. "Chinese?"

"*Gong xi fa cai*," I said, establishing my Chinese credentials. "What's your ancestry?"

"I'm a mongrel. I'm part English, French, German, and Italian."

"That's perfect. The two of us can celebrate Guy Fawkes Day, Bastille Day, Oktoberfest, and Ferragosto."

"What? No Druid holiday?"

"It's not December twenty-first without a winter solstice pagan ritual."

"Do you sacrifice a virgin?"

"Druids don't appreciate that stereotype. Solstice Day finds me and my brethren imbibing in potent Druid fluid and dancing around oak trees."

"It sounds like you have a full dance card. Is there any holiday you don't celebrate?"

"I haven't celebrated Valentine's Day in a long time."

My announcement made for a prelude to a kiss. It was a long time before we came up for air.

"Valentine's Day is still three weeks off," Lisbet said.

"I believe in precelebrations." We kissed again.

"That's why I never did one of those DNA ancestry searches," I said. "I prefer being an international man of mystery."

"If you can't beat 'em, join 'em," Lisbet said. She raised her wine glass and said, "L'chaim."

We clinked and drank.

"Were you really considering doing one of those DNA tests?" she asked.

I nodded. "I think what stopped me is that I was afraid of opening Pandora's box."

"It's better to not know some things?"

"Something like that."

"Did you ever consider trying to track down your birth mother?"

I was already shaking my head halfway into her question. "In my book my birth mother is guilty of a lot more than child abandonment. It was only by luck that I didn't end up like Rose. Even if she is still alive, why would I want to establish a relationship with a woman that discarded me and left me to die?"

"You have good reason to be angry with her, but you don't know the circumstances of her life."

"And I don't want to know. There are some crimes that aren't forgivable."

"You are sounding like judge, jury, and executioner."

"I wouldn't mind being all three."

"Have you considered there might have been extenuating conditions? What if your mother was mentally ill, like Moses's mother?"

"Being sick in the head doesn't give you a free pass to kill your child. Moses's mother went off her meds. That was her choice, and her son died because of it."

"So you think she should have gone to jail?"

"Damned right," I said. Because of her schizophrenia, Moses's mother had skated on any jail time, and that still rankled.

"You don't see any circumstances where you could forgive these mothers?"

"I'm a cop, Lisbet, and my job is to enforce the laws of our fair city."

"Enforcement is one thing but exacting vengeance is another."

"And just how am I exacting vengeance?"

"It sounds as if your own abandonment comes into play."

"If that's part of my motivation, why is it a bad thing? You don't want to see justice handed out to these women?"

"I don't think all these cases are the same, and I don't think there is any one punishment that fits the crime."

"I guess we don't see eye to eye then."

"Or eye for an eye?"

"There's that, too."

We sipped our wine. With anyone else I probably could have been assured of my self-righteousness, but not with Lisbet. She might not have been abandoned herself, but she dealt with the consequences of abandoned babies, making her more than entitled to her opinion. Besides, she didn't let me pout for long. My high dander was interrupted by her stretching out her bare foot and tickling me in the ribs.

I grabbed said foot while taking note of its shapely toes and high arch, and began tickling it in turn. After our squirming and laughing was done we were in each other's arms again, where the only thing we were tickling was each other's fancy. Our touching became more urgent until Lisbet gave herself some space from my hands.

"You and the wine are making me dizzy."

"Clear thinking is overrated."

"You really should spend the night so I don't have to worry about you."

"I think you'd have more to worry about if I spent the night."

"The sofa bed really is comfortable."

"If that's the extent of my options, I should probably hit the road."

Lisbet bit her lip and then opened her mouth to say something, but I interrupted her before she could speak. "I have to be leaving anyway. The last twenty-four hours have been a roller coaster, and tomorrow I have a ton of work waiting for me."

She nodded, and I was glad to see that Lisbet looked disappointed, or at least that's how I wanted to interpret it. "Promise me you'll be careful tonight."

"I promise."

We sealed the promise with a kiss.

Lisbet walked me to the door, where we did a little more canoodling, and where I told her, "I could canoodle with you all night."

That made her laugh and ask, "Are you sure you have to go?"

Her eyes made their offer to me, and it was one I wanted to take up, but I said, "I think I better."

I took my leave with a last kiss. What Lisbet didn't know was that what stopped me from staying more than anything else was the prospect of my dreams. It was too late to explain about them and me. I didn't want to venture into her bed and then wake up screaming and burning. I was more afraid of that than the two of us sharing our bodies for the very first time.

I should have told her, I thought. It's not good to start a relationship with a lie, and that's what it felt like I had done.

"Liar, liar, pants on fire," I said, the echo reverberating around the parking garage. It seemed an appropriate rhyme, and I remembered the next line: "Hanging from a telephone wire."

Ever since the fire I had been hanging. My burning had never stopped, and I hadn't yet found a way to get beyond that.

"You got a stupid partner," I told Sirius.

He didn't argue.

CHAPTER 17:

THE EAGLE HAS LANDED

It had been a hell of a day. I was hoping it wouldn't be a hell of a night. My burning dreams had been working overtime lately. When they occur two or three times a week, I try to tell myself that's manageable. Of late, though, it had been a nightly event. My cases seemed to be stirring up my subconscious and the end result was me burning.

The next day was Sunday, I told myself. I could sleep in.

I remembered when Jen had shared my bed. We always held one another before turning in. If Jenny kissed me on the lips, that meant she wasn't ready for sleep. A kiss on the nose was another matter. That meant it was time to snooze. That kiss on my nose always brought a smile to my lips, and the next thing I knew it was morning.

I touched my nose for luck. Within seconds I fell asleep. You'd think I would have been too exhausted to have had one of my dreams. My subconscious begged to differ. As usual, hell broke loose in the middle of the night. Most people drool if they're sleeping deeply. I am into combustion.

The fiery blast furnace, pushed by the swirling winds, blew into my face. I recoiled from it, but too late. The fire was being blown every which way and there was no escaping it. We staggered away from the worst of the heat and paused to catch our breath. With so much smoke in the air, there seemed to be a great divide between me and the Strangler, but there was only the length of a dying dog that separated us.

The light from the burning fires allowed me to see his face. His features were almost totally black from all the smoke and soot. The Strangler's eyebrows had been singed away along with much of his hair, and I knew the flames had exacted the same toll on me. His eyes were red and enflamed, and they were so deep within his sockets they looked like burning embers. But he could still see well enough to plot.

I watched him take a quick peek over his head and sensed he was ready to make a run for it. The Strangler knew how hobbled I was, knew that every step hurt like hell.

"You can't outrun a bullet," I croaked. "Before you get two steps away I'll empty my gun into you."

He reconsidered his flight, if not his plight. "The dog's dead," he said. "We have to think of ourselves."

I forced myself to look at Sirius. If the Strangler was right, I knew what I'd have to do. "Put him down," I said, "carefully."

We lowered Sirius to the ground. As I dropped to one knee I kept my gun pointed at the Strangler.

"See," the Strangler said. "He's not breathing."

Earlier Sirius had been panting wildly, but now he was still. My heart started pounding, and the static inside my head made it impossible for me to hear anything other than my surging blood pressure. With my free hand I reached out and touched Sirius's chest.

Nothing.

The Strangler looked hopeful. He wanted Sirius to be dead. He thought that not having to carry a heavy dog around would be a good thing for him. He was wrong. My trigger finger tightened, but at that moment Sirius's paw moved and then his chest rose.

"He's alive," I said.

"We can't..."

I moved my Glock no more than half an inch; I wasn't going to miss. The way I was feeling, it didn't really matter to me whether the Strangler cooperated or not.

"We'll lift him on three," I said.

"We have a chance to live if we leave him. We're dead if we don't."

"One."

"If we find a way out of here we can send help for him."

"Two."

The Strangler's head jerked in my direction. He could hear the intent in my voice and he suddenly realized that there were two counts going on, and that one of those counts was going to end very badly for him. He dropped down and placed his hands underneath Sirius, and it took me a moment to realize what I was feeling: disappointment. Now I would have to keep going.

"Three," I whispered, but instead of my shooting the Strangler, we lifted Sirius up and started walking. It was up to me to lead, even though I didn't know how to lead anymore and hadn't for some time.

Fire blew our way again, and the pain made me cry out. It surprised me that I was still alive enough to feel.

Something dug into my arm, and I felt pressure on my chest. I opened my eyes to see my shepherd hovering over me. One of his front paws was on my arm, and the other was on my chest.

"I'm all right," I said, patting him.

Once again I had done my Lazarus act and returned from the dead, but this time, more than any other of my resurrections, I recognized that being alive was a good thing. It hadn't always been that way. When you're severely burned it takes a long time to get better, but that had been the easier recovery for me. After Jen's death I tried to hide from everyone how bad off I was. Few people had any idea I was a basket case, and my severe burning had helped to mask my other symptoms.

My dreams were now forcing me to look back. There was no longer any hiding from what I'd been. Part of me had wanted to die in the fire. Jen's death had left me a hollow man, a shell ripe for going up in flames. Being responsible for my partner was the only reason I hadn't let myself become a human flare. As bad as reliving the burning was, facing up to the old emotions was worse. It was a hell of a lesson to keep on burning night after night.

My moment after stripped away my veneer. I had gone out into that fire wanting to die. Ironically, getting burned probably saved my life. I had been contemplating suicide, but I hadn't wanted it to look like a suicide. That was my own personal insight. I had a feeling my vision somehow applied to the Klein case, but I didn't know how.

Inspiration might strike, I told myself, if I got more sleep. Later, I told myself, I would think about it. And then, knowing I wouldn't burn anymore that night, I fell asleep again and awakened much later than usual.

Every PTSD burning takes its toll. Satchell Paige once posed the question, "How old would you be if you didn't know how old you are?" In the morning following a burning I usually awaken feeling as old as Methuselah. When I got up, I was parched and drained and achy. I downed an Advil with two glasses of water and then started thinking about my moment after.

My visions—for want of a better word—are not always straightforward, but unlike dreams I always remember every detail of them. I would like to believe that the after-fire message comes from my subconscious, but I don't know if that's an adequate explanation. Before my walk through fire I was never prescient, but now some strange door seems to have opened up for me. My oracle demands a high price, though. It needs its pound of burning flesh.

I made myself a breakfast of Cheerios and coffee. While I sipped my coffee, I thought briefly about my moment after but didn't stay with it for long. It was too personal. I didn't like remembering the suicidal thoughts that I'd had and was glad that darkness was no longer with me.

During my talk with Karen Santos, she had recalled seeing a "feisty" bird on the sweatshirt of the young woman that had bought the baby bootees at the monastery's gift shop. Her impression was that the bird was gold or brown and belonged to a college. It was time to find that bird. I started entering information into my laptop.

"*Road Runner*," I hummed as I typed, "*the coyote's after you.*"

The search engine told me there were more than twenty four-year colleges in Los Angeles, Orange, and San Fernando Counties. The mascots were varied: there were lions and tigers and bears (oh my!), as well as an anteater, a beaver and, yes, a roadrunner. There were mascot characters such as Prospector Pete, Matty the Matador, and Johnny Poet (which makes sense only if your school is named after the poet John Whittier), and nonanimal mascots in the forms of titans, Trojans, and waves.

There were also two eagle mascots. One belonged to Biola University, and the other to Cal State, Los Angeles.

I went to the website for each school. Both of their eagles looked feisty, but the CSULA golden eagle looked more like the bird that Santos had described. It was golden brown and black, and had an attitude. The demographics and location of the school also made it a more likely choice. Biola University was located in La Mirada, about a forty-minute drive from the Monastery of the Angels, whereas Cal State, LA was only about five miles from the monastery, with the same Interstate 10 passing by both of them. The more I read about CSULA, the more it fit the profile of the young woman Karen Santos had seen in the gift shop. Sixty per-cent of the Cal State, LA undergrads are women, and almost half of those are Hispanic. The vast majority of the university's twenty-one thousand students lived off campus. Assuming Rose's mother was a typical commuter student, it wouldn't have been hard for her to maintain a low profile while attending classes. No one might have even noticed she was pregnant.

Sorting through my notes, I tried to find Karen Santos's telephone number. Some of my notes had gotten scattered after the attack on me, and the only home number I could find was that of Dottie Antonelli.

When I dialed her up I said, "I'd like to return a barely used Saint Jude's medal."

Dottie didn't sound surprised to be hearing from me. "It's about time that you called to say thank you."

"And what am I thanking you for?"

"I'm thinking those Saint Jude and Saint Michael medals saved your life."

"I'm surprised you're not crediting the pumpkin bread as well."

"Who says I'm not?"

"Is there a patron saint for pumpkin bread?"

"There's a patron saint for farmers: Saint Isidore the Farmer."

"Thanks for distinguishing. Like there would be another saint named Isidore."

"For your information there's at least one other saint named Isidore."

"You're kidding?"

"I am not."

"But there is only one Saint Isidore the Farmer?"

"That's right."

"With a patron saint named Isidore the Farmer, it's no wonder that there are so many jokes about farmers' daughters."

"I hope you're not calling to tell me one of those jokes."

"It didn't start out that way, but maybe you'll get lucky. I called for Karen Santos's number."

"I'm afraid that puts me in a bit of a dilemma, Detective. We're not supposed to give out the phone numbers of our volunteers."

"She already gave me her number. I misplaced it."

Heavy on the mock skepticism, Dottie said, "Is that so?"

It took me a moment to interpret what was going on. "You're shaking me down again, aren't you?"

"Did you know that Saint Michael is the patron saint of law enforcement? We just got in a shipment with some new Saint Michael medals. I'd be glad to put one aside for you, along with a few other choice items."

"How much is all that going to set me back?"

"Your donation of a hundred dollars will be greatly appreciated."

"Who's the patron saint of extortionists?"

"I don't believe there is one."

"In that case, you want me to write a recommendation letter for you to the pope?"

"If you do, don't forgot to mention our statue fund. You do remember what our beautiful statue of Saint Dominic and Our Lady looked like, don't you?"

I remembered only too well. "That concrete foundation saved my life."

In a tone suddenly as serious as mine, Dottie said, "God saved your life."

Even though we both knew that insurance was going to cover the repair of the statue, I said, "Forget the Benjamin and put me down for two fifty. But that donation comes with strings. Does the gift shop ship items?"

"That can be arranged."

"In that case I want a monthly monastery candy-gram."

Sounding all too pleased, Dottie said, "You want a box of our chocolates sent to you every month?"

"That's what I said."

"It worked, didn't it? Talk about a miracle. You found a woman through that box of chocolates."

"It wasn't the chocolates."

She offered up a noise that sounded suspiciously like a snort and said, "Yeah, right."

"The real miracle will be you giving me Karen Santos's number."

"Temperance is one of the seven heavenly virtues."

"Right now it's feeling a lot more like one of the seven deadly sins."

She gave me the number.

* * *

Luck was with me—Karen Santos was home and said she would be glad to help me with my bird hunt. I waited while she turned on her computer and then directed her first to the Biola University site. As she studied their eagle she made a lot of uncertain sounds before finally saying, "It's possible that's the bird I saw, but I can't be sure."

From there she went to the Cal State, Los Angeles site, navigating from the athletic department, to a picture of the school's mascot, to the T-shirt and sweatshirt offerings at the bookstore. With each jump of a webpage she became increasingly more enthusiastic. "The CSULA lettering looks very familiar," she said, "and I am all but sure that's the right eagle."

I thanked Mrs. Santos. The eagle had landed.

Assuming Rose's mother was a student at CSULA, I needed to find the best way to leave her a message. Since CSULA was mostly a commuter school, students would be dependent on getting their news online or from a school newspaper. I did another computer search and found the school had a student newspaper that came out every Friday called the *University Times*.

I started writing entries in my notepad. If I could get the student newspaper to run a story, Rose's mother might take notice. I blocked out the story as I wanted to see it in print, omitting information I didn't want to disclose, and embellishing on that which I wanted to play up. A cynical reporter might have said I was playing fast and loose with the facts. If I was lucky, the fledgling journalists working at the *University Times* weren't old enough to be cynical.

Because Rose's story needed a human interest angle, I decided Lisbet would fill that bill perfectly. Of course I didn't bother to inform Lisbet of that.

I called the *University Times* in the hopes that some eager beaver was up against a deadline and working on a Sunday. Sylvia Espinosa, the news editor of the paper, was that eager beaver. By the sounds of it, she was the only person working the offices. When I told her I was calling about a murder with a potential tie-in to the campus, she sounded positively ecstatic.

"The only off-campus calls I usually get are from press agents trying to publicize some concert or speaker," she said. "And this week's on-campus stuff isn't much more exciting. Our lead story is on a potential misuse of one hundred dollars in funds by the ASI—that's our student government."

"That's not exactly grand larceny."

"It was either that or a story on a rally attended by eight students for a history professor that was denied tenure."

"I can see that would make for a tough choice."

"Manna from heaven is a murder with a campus tie-in. Tell me about it."

With her appetite whetted for some banner headline, I laid out the story for her. When I finished, I learned that Sylvia was old enough to be cynical.

"The connection with our school sounds iffy," she said.

"There was a positive ID regarding the CSULA sweatshirt."

"I've seen winos walking around wearing Cal State clothing, Detective Gideon, but that doesn't mean they're students here."

"The profile of our person of interest fits the average student profile at your school."

"It also fits me and half a million women in the LA area."

"As you might imagine, this is a sensitive case and I'm limited in what I can tell you, but I can say that we have several significant leads that suggest Rose's mother is, or has been, a student at CSULA."

"And your eyewitness saw this woman carrying a covered basket near the Angels Flight landing?"

Because I didn't want the monastery connection revealed, I had intimated that the sighting had taken place at Angels Flight, without actually saying it. Cops and the media have a strange symbiotic relationship: they use us to try and get a good story, and we try to use them to get the story we want.

"The sighting didn't take place there, but we have a witness that offered a description of a young, heavy Hispanic woman in her late teens or early twenties. Our witness talked with this woman and said she was well spoken and didn't have any discernible accent."

I could hear Sylvia scratching away. "So you have more than one witness?"

"We're talking to several people now that are assisting us in this case."

By the sounds of it, Sylvia was continuing to scribble down all of my double-talk, but I wasn't sure if she was buying it or was even planning on using it.

"Has your newspaper ever done a piece on the Safely Surrendered Baby Law? It's what most people call the California Safe Haven Law."

"Not that I remember. What is it?"

"It's a law that allows any newborn to be dropped off at a hospital or a fire station with no questions asked. The mother doesn't have to give her name or be fearful of any kind of punishment."

I told her about Lisbet and her work to get the law on the books. I also mentioned her tie-in with Rose, and the Garden of Angels. That was the hook Sylvia needed. Having the makings of a human interest piece, as well as a public service feature, made her much more enthusiastic about the story. We talked for fifteen minutes, and I played up the bullet points I'd written down on my notepad, trying to spin the story of Rose and her mother as I wanted it written.

"I'd like to run this as our lead story this Friday," Sylvia said, "but I can't do that without pictures. I am going to need a close-up shot of Rose's grave, and a big background shot of the Garden of Angels."

"That would be just the thing for the story."

"I know it would, which is why the story will have to wait. I have a hard enough time getting one of our staff photographers to do a shoot in downtown LA. No way will I be able to get one of them to agree to go out to the desert without at least a week's notice."

I found myself saying, "What if I was able to get you some pictures? I'll be going to the cemetery today on police business and I am pretty good with a digital camera."

"That sounds perfect!"

"I can probably even e-mail them to you tonight. Will that work?"

"That sounds great."

"Will I need to do the shoot in black and white?"

"No, color is fine. Our photo editor has software that converts color shots into black and white."

Now that she had a new lead story for the next edition, Sylvia went back to asking me questions. After grilling me for another ten minutes, she finally seemed satisfied.

"Friday's issue is sounding a whole lot better," she said. "I think I'll make the safe haven story a sidebar to the death of Rose."

"I'm sure Ms. Keane will like that," I said and then gave her Lisbet's numbers.

Sylvia asked for my cell number in case she had more questions. "Looks like we'll both be working late," she said.

"There's no rest for the wicked."

She seemed to think that was funny.

* * *

Because of my wanting to get the story planted, I had to pay the piper and drive out to the desert. The change in my plans prompted a call to Gump and Martinez. I told them something had come up with my other homicide, and that I wouldn't be meeting with them that morning as planned. Both men were fine with that; to their thinking I was the third wheel, and a necessary evil at that. We talked for a few minutes about the Klein murder. The case was stalled, but both detectives were following up on potential leads in the investigation, although neither sounded hopeful. I told them I would call later that afternoon.

Moments after we finished up, the phone started ringing. "Gideon," I said.

"You sound busy," Lisbet said. "Should I call back later?"

"No, now is fine."

"I'm not sure if it is."

I didn't like the sound of that, or the obvious strain in her voice. "What's wrong?"

"I'm upset and I don't want to be, but I am. I just got off the phone with Sylvia Espinosa."

"I'm sorry. I shouldn't have given out your number without your permission. I just assumed…"

"I'm not upset about you giving out my number. I am about the only person I know who doesn't have an unlisted number. What I don't like is being used. You sold me as part of your story."

"Wait a second. I gave out your name so you could talk about the Safe Haven law."

"And you wrapped it in Rose's body."

Even to my own ears my answer sounded hard and angry: "I didn't do that. Rose's mother did that."

"Sylvia said you were driving out to the cemetery today to take pictures."

"That's right. I'm working the case."

"Are you working it for Rose or for yourself?"

"I'm working it to bring a murderer to justice."

"You played that reporter. You didn't want a story about Rose so much as you wanted one about her mother."

"And what's wrong with that?"

"I don't remember being deputized as part of your posse."

"You're not part of my posse. You're the Good Samaritan in an awful story, because without you Rose wouldn't exist for most people. They would just look away. No one wants to deal with throwaway babies. That kind of death is just too ugly."

"And I don't want to make it any less so."

"My job is to find Rose's mother. I am sorry you don't like that."

"I respect your job. I understand the need for it. I just don't understand you getting any joy from it."

"Putting bad people behind bars is one of the great perks of being a cop."

"Do you really think Rose's mother is a bad person?"

"I do."

"On a cold night, she covered her newborn with a warm blanket and put bootees on her daughter's feet."

"And then she abandoned her to die."

"I used to be angry like you. The first few times I buried my children—and yes, I think of every one of them as a child of mine—I thought no punishment could be harsh enough for the monsters that abandoned them. I wanted those creatures found and sentenced to death, but not before being tortured. But then I happened to meet one of those monsters and then another, and suddenly they weren't monsters anymore. They were mostly young women overwhelmed by a situation that they didn't know how to deal with, and in a panic they made the worst decision of their life. I am not excusing what they did, but I have not yet heard of a mother that was in her right mind when she abandoned her baby."

"I don't believe in diminished capacity. What I do believe in is jailhouse conversions brought on by defense lawyers."

"I can understand why cases like these hit home for you."

"Don't make this about me. It's about Rose and other newborns like her."

"And weren't you a newborn like her?"

"I didn't die."

"And you haven't forgiven."

"Why the hell should I?"

"Hate is a heavy burden to carry."

"I hadn't noticed."

"I am certain that Rose's mother is suffering more than we can even imagine for what she did."

"Then she shouldn't mind doing that suffering in prison."

"Having her wear a scarlet *M* won't make anything better."

"I don't agree. Society needs its pound of flesh."

"I believe Rose already paid that price."

"So you think her birth mother should just get away with what she did?"

Lisbet's voice softened. "No," she said. "But when you find her, and I know you will, I wonder if you'll be as certain about what justice is or isn't as you lead her away in handcuffs. I think what you'll find is a young woman living in a hell of her own making, a hell that she'll have to live with until the day she dies."

"What I find too often are crocodile tears passing for the real thing. I am not good with the idea of supposed remorse paying for a crime. What works for me is punishment."

"I can understand why you would want that. I hope you can also understand why in the future I don't want to be used to further your investigations."

"No problem."

Both of us fell silent. Wounded pride kept me from saying anything else.

After a few seconds, and an eternity, Lisbet said, "Before I talked to Sylvia I had planned to call you to say what a wonderful time I had last night."

"It's still the same number."

"But will anybody be home?"

It was a good question. Had I already checked out of our relationship even before it had begun? I might have been able to smooth things over then, but I didn't. I put the ball back in her court—or maybe it was just the gauntlet.

"I guess you'll have to call to find out."

"Good-bye, Michael."

"Adios," I said.

* * *

I did a lot of muttering during the drive out to the desert. I was in a foul mood, and my partner had to listen to me vent.

"She doesn't understand that it's my job. And when you do the job right it's not tea and crumpets. If I dangled her as bait in front of that reporter, and I'm not exactly saying that's what happened, I did it because this is a homicide investigation."

I took my partner's silence as tacit agreement.

"I am looking for a murderer, dammit. My job is police work, not social work. I have to do whatever it takes to make an arrest."

What I was saying sounded right to me, but it felt wrong. My motives had been anything but pure. Lisbet had seen through my ploy.

"Besides, shouldn't she want to help me? I mean if something was there between the two of us—if it was real, that is—shouldn't she want to stand by me?"

I sighed.

The drive east was relatively free of traffic, but the ride home promised to be a bear. Every weekend Las Vegas gets in the neighborhood of a hundred thousand visitors from LA. We would be part of Sunday's return caravan.

The winds were kicking up, which made my foul mood that much worse. I hate it when Ellis Haines is right. The weather pattern had Santa Ana written all over it.

"Like my dad once told me, 'If she's stupid enough to leave, then you have to be smart enough to let her go.'"

My father had said that back when my high school girlfriend broke up with me. His words hadn't made the event any less painful then, and they didn't help now. Someone was bowling in my gut and using my ribs as pins.

"This too shall pass," I said.

Words don't impress dogs. They're a foreign language to them. My partner knew what lay behind the facade, and he tried to reassure me by nuzzling my neck with his muzzle. I reached back with my hand, gave him a pat, and decided not to bullshit him anymore. We rode in silence. He stayed close to me, and every so often one of us touched the other.

With every minute that passed I knew that the divide between Lisbet and me was growing. I knew I should call her back. I thought about what I would say. But that was as far as I could bring myself to go.

Arriving at the cemetery was almost a relief. Men don't like to address their feelings. Emotions make us feel helpless. My job gave me something to do, a task to perform, a reason to move. I needed that.

There was no one around, so I let Sirius walk the grounds with me. The desert winds can be fierce, and nothing stirs them like a Santa Ana condition. Swirling winds pelted my face with granules of sand and dirt. I knew it was only going to get worse.

Camera in hand, I went and joined the waiting waifs at the Garden of Angels, but at first I couldn't bring myself to click away.

I stood for a minute, and I wasn't sure if I wanted to pray or wanted to apologize. I felt the hurt in my throat and swallowed hard.

Damn feelings again.

I started taking pictures. When you look at the world through a viewfinder, it doesn't hurt as much.

Most of my shots were of Rose's cross. That was why I was here. I wanted a poignant reminder of her life on the front page of the *University Times*. That might make them wonder about Rose's mother and remember something. Lisbet had been right. I hadn't wanted the readers to think about the dead baby so much as I wanted them to think about her mother. I wasn't asking them to behold the rose so much as I wanted them to think about the thorn.

Of course the oversized CSULA sweatshirt might just be my wild goose chase. The sweatshirt could have belonged to a sibling, or a friend, or maybe Rose's mom had bought it at a thrift shop for a buck in order to hide her burgeoning belly.

I kept clicking anyway. Occasionally, my lens wandered, and I found myself looking at another name on another cross. Or I focused on a gravesite with a toy car, or a doll.

Leaning against Rose's grave marker was a white feather, a small offering left by one of the doves. The swirling winds had driven the feather to this spot, where it looked as if it had found refuge. I wanted to believe it was a sign and took several close-up shots. I knew the feather wouldn't be able to hold out long against the wind, so I picked it up and placed it in my pocket. Maybe I was hoping the feather would bring me peace in much the way a four-leaf clover is supposed to bring luck. Or maybe I'd contract avian flu.

When you take something, you should give something back. Head lowered to the wind, I trudged back to the car and went through the change drawer. As luck would have it, I found a shiny, newly minted penny. Maybe it wasn't as good as finding a penny from heaven, but it was the best I could do.

There was something else I needed to leave as well. I took some tape from the glove compartment and walked back to Rose's grave. I hoped that what I planned on doing wasn't some kind of sacrilege.

Rose's death had resulted in very little publicity. There had been no coverage of her funeral, and no mention anywhere of where she was buried. If Lisbet was right, Rose's mother would care about her buried daughter. I was betting on Lisbet's judgment more than mine. I was hoping Rose's mother would read the newspaper article and find out where her daughter was buried. Maybe that would spur her to visit Rose's grave.

On the stone cross I placed the penny on the west crossbeam. The skies didn't open and Bing Crosby didn't sing about pennies from heaven. And then I took a step over and on its east crossbeam I taped my business card. I didn't leave a message. The person I was leaving it for would know why it was there.

"I am sorry," I said.

My business card had no place being on the cross. My only defense was that Rose had no business being dead.

CHAPTER 18:

SCARECROW'S CONFIDENTIAL

The drive back from the Garden of Angels was stop and go, and by the time Sirius and I made it home, my mind was about as tired as my brake foot. During the drive I kept hoping that Lisbet would call my cell, but that never happened. I had tried to multi-task during my trip and spent half an hour on a conference call with Gump and Martinez, but it was more of a gripe session than anything else. Everyone was getting increasingly frustrated with the stalled Klein case.

"As of tomorrow Paul Klein will have been up on his cross seven nights," said Gump, "and us there with him."

He was overstating the pressure associated with our working the case, but not by much. All of us had agreed to meet at head-quarters early. Maybe the new day would bring us something.

I had promised Sirius a walk when we got home, and as soon as we pulled into the driveway, it was clear he was more than ready to collect on that promise. As we set out I said, "Let's make this short. It's not a night fit for man or beast."

My partner didn't seem to be of the same mind. His credo is pretty much the same as that of a postal carrier when it comes to his walks. Neither snow nor rain nor heat nor gloom of night deters him, and although it wasn't rainy or even particularly cold, the winds were kicking up and pushing dust and microscopic debris everywhere. Those same desert winds had also sucked the air dry, and the lack of humidity was making my skin feel like sandpaper.

We were headed for our usual destination, a park three blocks away. As we walked, a headwind pushed at us, but it was a wind that kept starting up and then stopping, and it seemed like whenever I lowered my head and pressed my shoulder into it, the air currents died down. This rising and falling of the wind kept me off balance and made me feel like I was taking Frankenstein steps. The uneven walk made the park seem farther away than usual, and I tried to negotiate an early out.

"Are the smells really that much better in the park?" I asked. "I mean, look at this pine tree. Doesn't it make you want to stop and sniff?"

Sirius wagged his tail but continued forward. The pine tree didn't interest him, and I remembered how John Steinbeck had brought his dog Charley to the giant redwoods with the expectation of the poodle's being beside himself at the prospect of watering at the altar of one of the biggest trees on the planet. Charley didn't respond as expected, and it was all Steinbeck could do to make his dog lift his leg.

As we passed by the tree I said, "I'm not sure if you're telling me to piss off, or that I just don't know shit."

Because the LA Basin is near sea level, it's particularly vulnerable to weather conditions happening hundreds and even thousands of miles away. When high pressure builds over the Great Basin, the clockwise flow of air pushes toward the sea, and as those winds come into LA from the northeast and the east, they are compressed and warmed. There is also a funneling effect from the winds being pushed through the county's canyons and passes that increases their speed. I had apparently heard Ellis Haines lecture on Santa Ana conditions too many times. He liked to call the Santa Ana winds the "devil's breath."

At that moment, the devil's breath was blowing down my neck. Haines was probably the only person in California that liked that feeling. When he was on trial, he had volunteered the fact that he'd worn a trench coat on most of the occasions when he'd strangled his victims, saying that he'd gone out "looking like a flasher." He'd talked about the exhilaration of the winds whipping his coat open and closed, and I remembered how he'd emphasized this while on the stand by raising his hands and saying, "Look, Ma, no hands." And then he'd laughed.

I could use an exorcism, I thought, to rid myself of my demon. I suspected that Haines would continue to plague my thoughts until the Santa Ana condition departed, and according to weather reports that was at least a day off. Maybe then he'd stop playing on my mind.

We made it to the park without seeing a soul. When the winds blow hard, LA likes to hibernate. I let Sirius off his leash and he was immediately onto the scent of something he liked. I thought about Charley again and the big redwoods. Even though Sequoia National Park is only about a hundred fifty miles away from Sherman Oaks, I had never taken Sirius to see the giant trees. It would be a good trip for us, I thought, although I suspected Sirius would react like Charley had. I doubted his taking aim at one of nature's skyscrapers would make Sirius any happier than his daily sprinkling at his little patch of park with its weeds, mulch, and spindly shrubs.

As Sirius deliberated over his exact "Kilroy was here" spot, I said, "I can't see the attraction of this place over the pine tree we passed."

Sirius didn't explain his choice but merely kept sniffing. Finally, he made up his mind. As he finished with his business I asked him, "Plastic or paper?" Since he didn't express a preference, I bagged with plastic and made the deposit into one of the park's anchored trash containers.

With our mission accomplished, we hurried back toward home. The streets were deserted except for a passing car or two. There was a light in the windstorm, though. Seth Mann's Jaguar was parked in the driveway, and his porch light was on. The shaman was in.

When Seth has company he usually parks in the garage and leaves the driveway for his date's car. Tonight it looked as if he wasn't entertaining. Normally I don't barge in on him without warning, but tonight I found myself walking up his drive.

The door opened just as we stepped onto the porch. "I felt my radar going off," Seth said.

"Is that a nice term for shit detector?"

"As it so happens, five minutes ago I called your house to see if you and Sirius wanted to come over for a visit."

Sirius was already inside the doorway looking back at me and wagging his tail. He looked like a happy child saying, "Can we, Dad, can we please?"

"I'm surprised you don't have a date tonight."

"I'm surprised *you* don't," he said, giving me a knowing smile.

"I am afraid that's yesterday's news. We hit a stumbling block today. She came to her senses."

"Stumbling blocks can be surmounted."

"So can Mount Everest, but not by me."

As I followed Sirius into his home, Seth asked, "What's your poison?"

"I need a comfort drink, preferably some sour mash from either the great state of Kentucky or Tennessee."

"Tall glass?"

"Make it as high as an elephant's eye."

A minute later Seth brought out the drinks. We clicked glasses and I said, "Cheers."

We tilted glasses in each other's direction, and in the upward movement of Seth's glass I saw a dark shadow floating in the midst of his amber-colored drink.

I craned my head for a closer look and said, "Don't tell me that's a worm in your glass."

"You have your comfort drink and I have mine. I prefer my mescal *con gusano*."

Seth is one of those Anglos that insist upon pronouncing Spanish words as if he was born to the language. "No one really prefers a drink with a worm in it, except for drunken college students on spring break."

"In Mexico the maguey worm is considered a delicacy."

"In France they love snails, but I don't see the French floating escargots in their cognac."

"That might be so, but mescal aficionados believe the maguey worm enhances the taste. Besides, it's nostalgic for me."

"You're nostalgic for worms?"

He responded to my sarcasm with a shrug. "As you know, I have spent some time living with native peoples. Because they don't have access to the kind of proteins we do, they happily eat certain ants, grasshoppers, grubs, and termites, as well as the larvae of bees, wasps, and beetles."

"And let's not forget worms."

"Mostly the worms are used as bait for fishing, but there are some that are served as snacks."

"Worms and alcohol," I said. "What a wonderful combination."

"Perhaps you'd prefer manioc beer?"

"Is that another one of your native specials?"

Seth nodded. "What's unique about it is the brewing process."

"I'm almost afraid to ask how it's done."

"It's basic science. In all brewing you need a fermenting agent. In the tribes I've spent time with, the maniocs—or other starchy roots—are cut up and boiled, and afterward the roots are chewed up by the young women of the tribe and then spat into a barrel. Add a little water, boil it all up, bottle it and let it ferment for several days, and you have beer."

"You drank spit beer?"

"The chewing and the saliva are what split up the starches and start the fermentation process."

"That takes backwash to a whole new level."

"I always considered it an honor to be offered manioc beer, knowing the work that goes into the making of it."

"I don't think I could be phlegmatic like you." I emphasized the word "phlegm."

"I suppose I could say it all comes out in the wash."

"If I'm going to swap spit, I want to do it the old-fashioned way."

"And what—to use your words—stumbling block occurred that's preventing you from doing that?"

I took a swallow of my drink and considered what to say. "She—Lisbet—wasn't happy that I involved her in a newspaper article I wanted done."

"Was there a reason for Lisbet being unhappy?"

"She knew I was hoping to flush out a suspect through the article and didn't approve of my tactics."

"And let me guess: you thought the end justified the means."

"I am trying to catch a murderer."

"You're talking about the mother of the abandoned baby?"

I nodded.

"Was she right about your using her for your own purposes?"

"The article would have served her purposes as well."

"In retrospect, do you wish you had consulted with Lisbet before giving her name to the reporter?"

"I was doing my job."

"Inspector Javert thought he was doing his job."

"Who is Inspector Javert?"

"He is a man who understood the letter of the law but not the spirit of it."

"Understanding the spirit of the law is above my pay grade."

"How did you and Lisbet leave matters between the two of you?"

"I'd say we finished our last conversation on a strained note."

"And how do you feel about that?"

"Right now I'd rather not think about it. With everything that's going on, I don't have time for a personal life anyway."

Even to my ears that sounded lame, but Seth didn't push me. Instead he spent a few moments studying me. "You look even worse than you did on Friday night. Since that time your bruising has truly blossomed. I don't think I've ever seen that shade of purple."

"I am just a canvas for art."

"You didn't tell me what happened."

I hadn't wanted to, but now I did. I described the attack and my strange assailants and their mumbo jumbo, and how Sirius had saved my bacon.

"Right now that's all I can tell you," I said. "Another detective is working the case and is trying to track down my attackers based on their tattoos. It's possible they're not in any police database, though."

"Do you think Ellis Haines sent them to attack you?"

"They seem to have bought into Haines's gibberish and wanted to do something for their guru. I wouldn't be surprised if Haines was somehow acquainted with them, but I don't think he put out an order for a hit on me."

"Manson might not have ordered the Tate-LaBianca murders, but even if he didn't say the words, he was found to be guilty. It sounds as if Haines's followers were trying to please him in much the same way. In a messianic situation there exists an environment of *proba te dignum*—prove yourself worthy."

"When they're caught they can prove themselves worthy with a long stretch in the pen."

"Is that imminent?"

"The tattoos were distinctive—symbols for end-of-the-world stuff. And Sirius did some serious chewing on one of them. We'll get them, but I am not sure if it will be sooner or later."

A sudden gust of wind shook the windowpanes and made me start. "Damn Santa Ana," I said.

"There's a big fire in the Angeles National Forest. The winds are making it impossible to fight."

"I'd hate to be a firefighter. I'd hate to be told to go take on an inferno in seventy-mile-per-hour winds."

"It's not a job I'd want either, but neither would I want to do your work. You've had to confront two very difficult homicides this week. That has to have taken its toll."

"They get their hooks in you," I admitted. "I purposely skipped Rose's autopsy. Unfortunately, I had to spend a lot more time with Paul Klein's body. He is going to be my ghost for as long as the case goes unsolved, and probably for a long time after that. Seeing him nailed to the tree is a sight I'd just as soon never have seen. I can't get the image of his body out of my head, even though for the sake of the case I need to."

"What do you mean?"

"I need to get beyond his crucifixion. I need to see as the killer saw. I have to look at the staging that was done, and I have to understand the hate. When the killer staged Klein's body, it was almost like he was saying, 'Look, everyone, here's a false prophet.' Klein was crucified because the killer needed him exposed. I have to ignore the violence of the image to read the message there. The killer wanted to show what a bad guy Klein was."

"You said Klein was a bully. Was he a terrible human being?"

"He was arrogant and full of himself, but it's hard to imagine that he deserved to die like he did. That's why I need to understand the killer's hate. What makes someone hate with such virulence?"

"Hate is arguably the strongest of all the emotions. It is nourished in the darkness of the human soul. Hate is fueled by anger, whether it is rational or not."

"The killer's hate was personal."

"If that's the case, then there might have been pathology involved."

"Meaning what?"

"The perversion of love is hate. One of Newton's Laws of Motion is that for every reaction there is always an equal and opposite reaction."

"There's something to that, but I still can't put my finger on it."

"Did you ever hate anyone?"

"I hated myself."

"And why was that?"

"I could have saved Jenny's life. I could have insisted that she go see a doctor earlier than she did. I could have been less absorbed in my own work and seen how sick she was."

"You blamed yourself for her death?"

"Sometimes I still do."

"You punished yourself. I know that. Did you ever think about killing yourself?"

"I tried to do it indirectly."

Seth nodded. He had been there and knew that I had. Sirius stirred and sat up, and then put his head in my lap. My guardian spirit wasn't going to let me brood.

We sat in companionable silence. Outside, the wind was gusting and swirling. I did my best not to listen to its echoes. I reached the bottom of my glass and Seth went and got us both refills. When he came back, there was a fresh worm in his drink. We began talking about less weighty subjects, and our conversation and the drinks took the edge off of the night even while the Santa Ana winds howled.

Seth noticed my wince as he consumed another gooey maguey. "It's just a worm," he said.

"You remind me of a character from the original Dracula film with Bela Lugosi," I said. "Ever see it?"

"I *vant* to suck your blood," Seth said in a bad Hungarian/Transylvanian accent.

Instead of telling him that Lugosi never uttered that line I said, "Anyway, this poor guy Renfield is bitten by Dracula, which causes him to lose his mind and get locked up in an insane asylum. And because he was bitten by a vampire, Renfield starts getting some strange cravings, so when he's in the asylum he takes to eating creepy-crawlies."

"And I'm supposed to be this Renfield?"

"If the insect fits," I said. "One of the film's classic scenes is when the guard at the asylum stops him from eating a fly and Renfield indignantly says, 'Who wants to eat flies?' And the guard says, 'You do, you loony.' Then Renfield tells him, 'Not when I can get nice, fat spiders.'"

"You actually memorized that dialogue?"

"I'm surprised you didn't, what with Renfield being your role model."

"I wasn't the one bitten by a vampire."

I ignored the Ellis Haines reference. I didn't want to talk about him anymore.

Outside the wind howled.

"It's playing my song," I whispered.

"What song is that?"

"It's the song of the Scarecrow."

"Scarecrow?" Seth asked.

"Dorothy's Scarecrow," I said. I tried to make light of my statement by attempting the Wicked Witch of the West's cackle and saying, "How about a little fire, Scarecrow?"

Seth wasn't sidetracked. "The Scarecrow was afraid of fire. Is that what you're hearing—and fearing—with the Santa Ana winds?"

"You sound more like a shrink than a shaman."

"The two disciplines are closer than you might think."

"That's nothing I'd brag about."

"You haven't answered the question."

"I've already done my obligatory therapy, Dr. Freud."

"And what did you get out of it?"

"I got exactly what I needed. A slew of mental health professionals agreed that I was fit to return to duty."

"Did you lie to all of them?"

"I told them what they wanted to hear."

"You haven't told me what I want to hear. I know how you suffer. I've just been waiting for the time when you were ready to talk about it."

Attempting sarcasm, I said, "And what is it that you think you know?"

"I know that you still burn."

His words made me burn again—in shame—and in that instant any and all anesthesia from the alcohol disappeared.

"I often hear you scream in the middle of the night," he said. "The way you scream and some of the things you shout make it clear you are reliving what happened the night you were burned."

"Shit. If I'd known I was being the town crier, I would have gotten my room soundproofed."

"That's not the answer."

"Neither is my being the village idiot."

"Is it always the same dream?"

"It's never exactly the same. I keep reliving different moments of our fire walk, but everything is so vivid it's like I'm back there again. And in every dream I find myself burning up."

"You feel the heat?"

"I am fucking on fire. That's how much heat I feel. My mind and body so believe what is happening that there have been times I've awakened with blisters on my skin."

"You are afraid of the fire?"

I reached for my scarred face. "That's an understatement."

"Fire isn't always about destruction, you know. Many famous fire stories are about revelation, rebirth, and even resurrection."

"The burn victims I know aren't phoenix stories. None of us rose out of the ashes that way."

"Are you sure?"

"I'm very sure."

"Fire has often been a messenger. It was out of a burning bush that Moses heard an angel speak. And despite the fire spouting from the bush, it was not consumed."

"I saw lots of burning bushes. All of them were consumed and I never heard an angel talk to me."

"Many of our myths are built on fire stories. Prometheus stole fire from the gods so that humans could become like gods."

"And didn't he get chained to some rock where he had his liver pecked out by a vulture every day?"

"That's one version of the myth."

"He paid quite the price."

"So did you."

"I know that. Once was more than enough. I'm tired of burning and burning and burning."

"Maybe you haven't allowed yourself to accept everything that happened to you."

"You're not going to start talking about how that fire caused part of my soul to escape and now it can't find its way home, are you?"

"Not if you don't want me to."

"I don't."

"I'll talk about fire then, and how you need to make your peace with it. I've been asked to put on a program at this year's Burning Man event. Why don't you go with me? The atmosphere might be therapeutic for you."

I had heard of the annual event. Every year, thousands of people gathered at a remote desert spot in Nevada and burned a huge wooden effigy of a man. It sounded about as appealing as an STD.

"Send me a postcard from there, would you?"

"Fire isn't your enemy. It's one of the revelatory elements."

"If that's the case, then maybe we should go out to your backyard and make a campfire and tell ghost stories."

"I don't think tonight's a good night for that."

"Damn, I was looking forward to s'mores."

"Tell me about your fire dream."

"I already told you: it's not a dream. It's a reliving of what happened."

"And in that reliving have you ever made it to safety?"

I shook my head. "Not yet. It's always the horror show but never the relief. In every dream the situation feels helpless. Sirius is always dying, and I can't do anything to prevent that. The only thing I can do is burn to death with him."

"That must be a horrible feeling."

I nodded. "I feel responsible for his dying because I'm the one that put him in that position. And my only consolation is that Ellis Haines is going to die with us, but even that is anticlimactic."

"Why do you think that is?"

"The idea of killing Haines doesn't make me feel better. I know I have to stop him from hurting anyone else, but for me it's just one last duty, like shooting a rabid dog. Feel free to call me Atticus Finch."

"You suffered a trauma," Seth said, "and the fire still has a grip on you because part of you remained behind in that place."

"Yeah, I left behind about a pound of flesh."

"You must accept the flames if you would gain enlightenment. You won't be able to go forward unless you go back."

"Thank you, Obi-Wan Kenobi."

"Instead of shrinking from the fire, use it for the purpose of illumination."

"That's easy for you to say. You're not the one that's burning up."

Both of us sat looking in our drinks for a minute. Seth didn't see the world as I did. He believed as much in the invisible as he did the visible and saw dreams as journeys. I didn't want to hear about befriending spirits or gaining empowerment through my travels, or at least I didn't think I did. Still, when he'd spoken about enlightenment, I couldn't help but dwell on what my fire dreams kept bringing to me.

"Each time that I awaken from the nightmare," I said, "when I realize that the fire happened in the past and that Sirius and I are now safe, this strange thing happens."

I stopped talking for a moment, trying to get a handle on how to explain the ineffable.

"I always think of what occurs as being the moment after. It's the instant when the horror is behind me, and this kind of window opens and I get this clarity. I can't really describe it any better than that. It's like getting a glimpse into my world from the heights of Olympus. It almost feels like I've suffered in order to be able to see what I otherwise wouldn't. Sometimes I call it my boon from the gods."

"What kind of things do you see?"

"Lots of times they are just little things, but they always help me make sense of situations. Sometimes I remember something, and it gives me this insight I didn't have before, or I'm able to apply it to some situation that's been puzzling me. Lately the images have been more elaborate, though."

"And you've been experiencing these Images and insights with every fire dream?"

I nodded.

"Medicine for your burns. It is your armor for battling the dragon."

"I'm tired of battling the dragon."

"Then you must vanquish it."

"I think you've mistaken me for Saint George."

"All heroes resemble one another and are forced to travel a perilous path."

"You've had too many worms tonight. They've gone to your head."

"The Ojibwa called alcohol 'firewater.' It won't stop the burning."

I nodded and downed my glass of firewater. Then I thanked Seth for his hospitality, and Sirius and I headed home.

CHAPTER 19:

MAKE-UP SECTS

Usually when I don't have a fire dream I awaken feeling renewed, but not this time. I awoke with a sense of loss. Lisbet Keane was the first woman that had made me feel alive in years. For a long time I had just been going through the motions of living, an actor playing the role of the old me. I didn't want to go back to that tired role.

I went online and did a search. I had thought what I wanted would only entail the use of my credit card, but it quickly became apparent that I was out of my league and needed help. After doing a search of florists and determining that none of the twenty-four-hour cookie-cutter sites could help me, one particular florist and his claim caught my eye: "Whatever flower it is, no matter how rare, I will find it for you." The floral shop making this promise was located in Connecticut.

It was a little before nine on the East Coast. The male voice that answered my call already sounded aggrieved, maybe because it was early in the morning, or it was Monday, or he just enjoyed acting put-upon.

"I'm calling from Los Angeles," I said.

"My condolences," he said in a condescending tone.

"I didn't call for sympathy. I am looking for a particular flower. According to your ad, you can find it for me."

"Oh, dear boy, some copywriter came up with that phrase. I am not the floral Mountie. I don't always get either my man or my flower, but Lord knows I try."

"Forget-me-nots," I said.

"What was that you said? I forget."

"I'd like a bouquet of forget-me-nots."

"No, you really don't."

"Excuse me?"

"Have you ever seen a forget-me-not?"

"I'm looking at a picture of one on my computer right now."

"The picture you are looking at was taken with an oversized lens," he said, somehow managing to infuse a prurient edge into his words. "Forget-me-nots have small flowers that are difficult to appreciate without magnification."

"I want to send the thought more than I do the flower."

"Oh, no," he said. "I think I hear the wailing of disco past."

"I don't know what you're talking about." I wasn't exactly being truthful. I did know what he was talking about.

"Do you want to sing it for me?"

"Sing what?"

"Are you afraid of your voice, or is it sentiment in general?"

"Both," I admitted.

"Forget-me-nots," he sang, actually hitting the high notes.

I interrupted before he could sing any more. "Okay, maybe I was inspired by the song 'Forget-Me-Nots.'"

"Who recorded it?"

I played his trivia game: "Patrice Rushen."

"She should have sung about pink hydrangeas. I can get you some beautiful pink hydrangeas."

"Can you get me the forget-me-nots?"

"I don't know."

"Today?"

"You must be kidding."

"I am afraid not."

"All women love roses. I can definitely get those delivered today."

I thought of baby Rose. Roses wouldn't do. "My mind is set on forget-me-nots."

"Do you understand that a bouquet of forget-me-nots is out of the question? They're not flowering this time of year, and even if they were flowering, their flowers would be too small for a bouquet. My advice for you is to forget forget-me-nots."

"What about a forget-me-not plant?"

"What kind of statement are you trying to make? That plant would have the appeal of Charlie Brown's Christmas tree. Even the Almighty overlooked forget-me-nots, or so the story goes. That's how the plant got its name."

"I don't know that story."

"And you think I'm Hans Christian Andersen?" He mock-sighed and then said, "Supposedly God had named all the plants in the world except for one. He had overlooked a small flowering plant, and it cried out, 'Oh, Lord, you have forgotten to give me a name.' And so He called it 'forget-me-not.'"

"That's a good story."

"It's a legend. A good story is what I will need to take on this mission."

"I don't understand."

"Before proceeding on this fool's errand, you'll need to tell me a good story about why I should spend my morning hunting down a weed that's probably not even flowering this time of year."

"I'm not rich. I'm a cop. But I'll pay you for your time."

"That's not a good story unless I somehow missed a part about handcuffs. That's like me telling you I am a florist and then asking you to fix a parking ticket for me for a fee. I'll need a story from you to work on."

"What the hell kind of florist shop do you run?"

"As you might have imagined, it's a quirky one. But it's also quite popular and customers are already waiting for me to open my doors. I chose my line of work because I like to be surrounded by beauty. And I like to be inspired in my work."

"I called to get flowers, not psychotherapy."

"I throw the therapy in for free."

I considered hanging up, but then found myself talking. "My wife died three years ago. Two years ago I was burned in a fire. In some ways being burned was a relief because it gave me an excuse to not get on with my life. I could tell myself it was just enough to survive. But this week I asked a woman out, and for the first time since my wife died I began imagining a future with someone else. Yesterday, though, we had a spat. I don't want us to be over before we've even begun. And that's why I want forget-me-nots."

"Now that's a good story. And because it is, I will try and do the impossible to get you your forget-me-nots and have them delivered today."

"I really appreciate that."

"I'll include some poem or lyrics with the plant so that she realizes the uninspiring potted plant you've sent her is a token of much more."

"She'll know the song. She'll know what I was trying to say."

"Yes, about that song. You do realize that for the rest of the day it will be cycling through my brain?"

"It could have been worse. It could have been 'Disco Duck.'"

For the first time since our argument, I felt better. The condemned man had a pulse. Maybe my relationship with Lisbet still had a chance. It would be up to her to forgive or not, and to forget or not.

I picked up a large coffee at a drive-through and finished it over the course of my commute. There was no one in Robbery-Homicide, and I felt a bit like an interloper. I had a right to be there, but I didn't feel as if I belonged. I commandeered a con-ference room and spread out some papers. Gump and Martinez arrived a few minutes after I did, and we started comparing notes and divvying work.

"I've been going through the bully list," Martinez said, "and checked out eight of the eleven names. Three of the names I wasn't able to cross-index with school records."

"That doesn't surprise me," I said. "Jason Davis only knew Dinah Hakimi by the nickname the Agency gave her: Bugs."

"What an embezzle," Gump said in a Bugs Bunny Bronx accent. "What an ultramaroon."

"Who do you still need to run down?" I asked.

Martinez handed me the list with Travis's writing. Three of the names were circled: Sophie Gabor, Danny Marxmiller, and Laura Barrel.

"I'll go back to Davis," I said, "and tell him to do better with those three names."

Martinez said, "I've talked to the other eight kids. They said that Klein and his group were annoying assholes."

"What a news flash," Gump said.

"I asked them for an accounting of their time from Monday afternoon to Monday evening. It seems as if they all have wit-nesses and alibis. I haven't checked out their stories, but I'll be doing that today."

"While you work on your bully list, I'll work on my bucket list," Gump said. "How do you spell 'ménage à trois'?"

"Even the Make a Wish Foundation couldn't pull that one off," Martinez said.

* * *

One of the Robbery-Homicide detectives was out on leave, so I commandeered her desk. I worked the phones all morning. Three of my calls were to Jason Davis's cell phone. When it was apparent he was ignoring my messages, I called a fourth time and said, "If I don't hear from you within fifteen minutes, I'll be contacting your parents so that they can arrange for a lawyer for you, and then I'll be visiting you in one of your classrooms at Beverly to pick you up."

He called back within five minutes.

"Some of the names on your victim list we haven't been able to identify. I'm going to need you to get them right."

"It's not like I really know any of those people," he said.

"You knew them well enough to hassle them."

"That list goes back years. I haven't seen some of those kids since forever. People have moved and graduated and stuff."

"We've already identified most of the names but need clarification on three of them. We couldn't find anything on Sophie Gabor, Danny Marxmiller, and Laura Barrel. I need you to get back to me on those three."

"Isn't that your job?"

"You really want me to acquaint you with my job?"

Davis sighed and then said, "I'll work on it."

"I need to hear from you by the end of the school day. And make sure you spell the names right this time."

"Maybe if you don't call every five minutes, I might be able to do that."

He ended the call, and I found myself glowering at my cell phone. The best of teens are adept at pushing adult buttons, and Davis and his spoiled brat pack were not the best of teens. Just as I was about to officially turn into a curmudgeon, my phone rang. At first I didn't recognize the name of Dearly Departed on the readout, but then I made the connection with the business that ran the online obituary service and remembered their tribute wall to Paul Klein.

"Is this Detective Gideon?"

I confirmed my identity, but that wasn't good enough for Mary Ann Wiggins. "Our counsel gave me permission to talk to you,

Detective," she said, "but I'd be more comfortable going through an official switchboard instead of calling your cell phone directly."

I gave her the LAPD number and the extension where I could be reached and then waited for her return call. Finally, the phone at my temporary cubicle rang.

"I am sorry I had to do that," she said, "but my work has made me suspicious."

"Identity theft is the new bubonic plague," I said. "You can't be too suspicious. But in my case, I yam what I yam."

"I see," Wiggins said, apparently not as impressed as Olive Oyl. "When we talked last week you asked if we could flag any negative comments or poison-pen letters directed at Paul Klein. Are you still interested in those things?"

"By all means."

"In the last four days there have been seven attempted postings that we deemed inappropriate."

"Can you forward those e-mails to me?"

Wiggins hesitated a moment before I added, "If you want, I can send you an e-mail with my official LAPD e-mail address, and then you can forward those letters to me."

"I'll respond directly after hearing from you. And when you receive the forwarded letters, don't be fooled by the two notes with biblical quotes. You'll find they are disingenuous."

"In what way?"

"The same writer wrote both. He pretended sympathy for the victim and cited what you would imagine were inspirational biblical passages, but anyone referencing those chapters and verses would be in for a surprise. They are anything but sympathetic."

"Clever."

"We're used to that. What is harder to pick out is a note like the one we received today on a matter unrelated to your case. The remembrance was written by a daughter to a father. That seemed well and good until we realized the deceased only had two sons."

"Daddy, we hardly knew thee."

I thanked her, took down her e-mail address, and then said I'd appreciate it if she could forward the letters as soon as possible. I sent off my e-mail information to her while Wiggins was promising that she would do just that.

"I might have something here," I announced to Gump and Martinez.

The detectives walked back to my desk, and I told them about the toxic notes that had been written for Klein's memorial wall.

"A high-profile murder always brings the crazies out," a skeptical Martinez said.

"Yeah," Gump added, "we've already had at least a dozen false confessions."

"Maybe the memorial wall brought out someone besides the crazies," I said. "Anyone that hated Klein enough to kill him would hate the idea of him getting what would be perceived as false praise."

"Computer Crimes Unit can help us get the real names and addresses of the writers," Gump said. "It's been my experience that most killers don't have helpful websites like www-dot-I-am-a-murderer-dot-com."

I pulled up my e-mail, but there was nothing new in my inbox. A minute later I tried again, with the same result. It was like watching a pot waiting for water to boil. The two detectives continued to hover right behind me.

"Did you tell your contact that sometime this century would be nice, Gideon?" Martinez asked.

I didn't answer but instead tried my mailbox again—still nothing.

"Pony Express would be faster," Gump said.

I checked the time. Only ten minutes had passed since I'd talked with Wiggins. Once more I went to the e-mail well.

"Bingo," I said and hit print.

We took the printouts to the conference room, and Gump and Martinez quickly leafed through the lot.

Gump didn't hide his disappointment at what was there. "I don't feel the hate," he said. "And two of these are God-is-good notes that don't even belong."

"Hold that thought," I said, writing down the biblical passages and then exiting the conference room. A minute later I returned with two more printouts.

One of the notes read, "Take solace in God's plan: Isaiah 13:16." As far as I could see, there wasn't much solace to be gained from the cited biblical passage, which I showed to the two detectives: "Their children also shall be dashed to pieces before their eyes; their houses shall be spoiled, and their wives ravished."

"What the hell?" Gump was suddenly interested.

The other note read, "Embrace the ways of the Lord: Ezekiel 9:6." In this case, judging by that particular chapter and verse, the ways of the Lord included murder: "'Kill them all—old and young, girls and women and little children. But do not touch anyone with the mark. Begin right here at the Temple.' So they began by killing the seventy leaders."

"I got dibs on God's avenging angel," Gump said. "You got to believe this is a guy that would love to carry out a crucifixion."

We went through the other "tributes." Even Gump seemed taken aback.

"These guys won't be working at the Comedy Store any time soon," he said.

We studied the words on the first note: "In this day and age it is hard to imagine someone being crucified. Paul Klein died in the City of Angels. When he was nailed to the tree, Klein looked down below and said, 'Hey, I can see my house from here.'"

The second attempt at humor wasn't any better: "This young man's death was a tragedy. My condolences go out to his friends and family. When I heard how he died, I was quite cross."

At first read, the third note seemed legitimate: "What a terrible, senseless death! My thoughts and prayers go out to those that knew and loved Paul. As most of you probably know, the family has asked that all donations should go to the Arbor Day Foundation."

The last attempt at comedy was a double entendre: "In the midst of the mourning woods, Paul Klein died. Last night I wept with the willows; at daybreak I contemplated my own morning wood."

Not everyone was a comedian. Some writers were purely spiteful. One wrote, "Maybe his daddy will make a film on his son's murder and call it *Jesus and Paul*." Another tried to remember him with "All of Richie Rich's money didn't do him any good, did it?"

The poison-pen e-mail that interested me the most read, "Some say Paul Klein's death was tragic. Those that knew him would say it is karma." Unfortunately, I didn't claim the note fast enough. Martinez grabbed it and said, "I want to talk with this guy."

We divided up the work, and then Gump gathered all the printouts. Even though our case was a priority, it helped that he knew someone in Computer Crimes that he claimed owed him a favor. If we were lucky, by day's end we would have the names, addresses, and telephone numbers of the writers.

I was talking on another line when Jason Davis rang my cell. Ten minutes later I listened to his message.

"This is Jason," he said. "I'm assuming you still want those names so I went to the office. It wasn't Sophie Gabor but Soshi Gabay, which is spelled g-a-b-a-y. If that's not right, don't blame me. I got it from the office secretary, so call her.

"And it's not Laura Barrel, but Helena Beral. Her last name is b-e-r-a-l. And Danny wasn't Marxmiller's first name. The lady at the office said it was his middle name. His real first name was David."

There was a pause, as if Jason was thinking of saying something else, but he chose not to. Instead he closed his message by saying, "I hope we're done here."

I saved his message and muttered to myself, "I wouldn't count on it."

I wrote the corrected names down and brought the amended list over to Martinez. "You want help running down these names?" I asked.

"I might as well just finish it up," he said.

As I started back to my desk, my cell phone rang. When I saw who was calling, I made for the hallway where I answered the phone. My heart was pounding, making it hard to hear.

"Thank you," Lisbet said.

"You're welcome." I tried to think of something to fill the silence. "I am sure it's an ugly-looking plant. The florist wasn't sure he could find one, and said if he did it would look like a weed."

"Someone once defined a weed as a plant whose virtues have not yet been discovered."

"I think they said the same thing about me."

"I want you to know I love my plant, and I love the poem that came with it."

"I can't take credit for the poem," I said. "The florist told me he'd find something nice."

"Everything was perfect. You didn't need to send me anything, but I am glad you did because it gives me the opportunity to say I am sorry. Since yesterday I've been trying to figure out how to tell you that without sounding pathetic."

"You're not the one that needed to apologize. I am. And in case you hadn't figured it out, that weed I sent was my way of an apology."

"It is not a weed. You'll need to see it in person. It has the most delicate blue flowers."

"The florist was afraid it wouldn't even be flowering. That's why he tried to direct me to a different selection. But I went with music over his floral aesthetics. That was my inspiration for sending you the forget-me-nots."

"I've always loved that song. Now I love it even more."

"Look, I'm tied up for a bit, but what are your plans tonight?"

"Now that I no longer have to keep vigil by my phone, I have no plans."

"How does dinner out sound? And is eight too late?"

"Eight is not too late, but dinner in at your place sounds better to me than going out. Do you know a good pizza delivery?"

"I have three on speed dial. How is that for a confession?"

"You have me beat by one."

"What do you like?"

"Just about anything as long as it doesn't have anchovies, olives, or green peppers."

"Great minds think alike."

"What's your address?"

I gave her my address and heard her repeat it. After a few seconds of clicking in information, Lisbet said, "Okay, it's programmed in my GPS."

"If the satellite breaks down, call me."

And then I told her that my house would have the porch light on and that I'd be waiting for her.

* * *

At six thirty I was glad to see Gump getting ready to call it a day. I hadn't wanted to be the first to leave, but there was a lot I needed to do before Lisbet came calling. Computer Crimes had come through with the names and addresses of the poison-pen writers, but so far nothing had panned out. Martinez wasn't yet ready to give up the hunt, though.

"I have a few calls in," he said, "and I might as well get the case notes in order while I wait to see if they call back."

"Ka-ching, ka-ching," Gump said. "That's the sound of Martinez collecting overtime pay."

"Not all of us are ready for early retirement," he said.

I didn't let Gump or Martinez know I was in a rush, or even the reason for my need to hurry. Unless you enjoy constant speculation about your love life, you don't let other cops know you have a date. When I was safely out of sight, I began running to my car. Even if the traffic wasn't bad, by my calculations I'd have six months of cleaning to do in sixty minutes.

Sirius was waiting for me in the car. Usually I don't leave him there for more than an hour, but dogs aren't welcome in the Police Administration Building. As I tell him, it's just as well, because I wouldn't want Sirius to get fleas.

He gave me my usual hero's welcome, the same welcome he'd given me three times that day when I'd visited to give him walks.

"Strap in," I told him. "We got to get home pronto."

The traffic gods apparently disagreed. It was a stop-and-go ride almost all the way home, which gave me even less time to clean.

My partner watched my mad dash around the house. I vacuumed, mopped and swept. I took on dust, dog hair, and clutter. There were bed sheets to change—it didn't hurt to hope—and bathrooms to be cleaned. There was calcified toothpaste that had to be scraped away that must have dated back to Jen's death. Her hand had been sorely missed in the cleaning of the house; her arms around me had been missed much more.

"A lot of this mess is yours," I told Sirius. "The least you could do is offer a paw."

My partner apparently didn't do windows, but judging from his wagging tail he was pleased by my efforts, or at least my running around.

There had been no fire in the fireplace for years. Jennifer's death had something to do with that, as well as my not wanting to build a fire for just one, but the biggest factor for the cold hearth was my night of fire walking with Ellis Haines. Sitting in front of a roaring fire no longer comforted me. Once burned, twice shy. Still, the night was chilly and Lisbet would likely welcome a fire. Besides, a little smoke in the house might help with the lingering scent of eau de dog. I tentatively gathered the makings of a fire and found a pack of wooden matches to ignite the kindling. The fire was just starting to burn nicely when the doorbell rang.

Although my house wasn't looking even borderline presentable, its grooming had superseded my own. I hadn't had time to brush my teeth or run a comb through my hair. I did my limited preening between the fireplace and the front door. It was a good thing I looked out the peephole before opening the door. I don't think the pizza delivery kid would have appreciated the overly friendly greeting I had in mind.

After stowing the pizza, I hurriedly showered, shaved, changed my clothes, and swigged some mouthwash. That took five minutes. I considered breaking open a bottle of old cologne but didn't. The cologne still looked new, even though Jenny had given me the bottle early in our relationship. Either she hadn't known I wasn't a cologne kind of guy, or maybe she hoped that I might occasionally start applying a dab or two. I never had and probably never would. But the bottle was safe. It would always have a place in my medicine cabinet.

Sirius barked—a sound I knew to be his happy greeting—even before the doorbell rang. He knew who was walking up the front path and that it wasn't the pizza guy.

There wasn't the awkward moment between us that I had feared. Once the door was open, we were in each other's arms. Sirius added his welcome, joining us by leaning on our legs.

"Group hug," I said.

I motioned for Lisbet to come inside. "*Mi casa es su casa.*"

Sirius ran inside and then hurried back outside, as if he was also waving her inside. "What he's telling you is that I should have said *nuestra casa es su casa.*"

"The two of you had me at *hola*," Lisbet said.

"Before I exhaust my bilingual skills, I can offer you some *vino* or *cerveza*. The wine has only been in the refrigerator for thirty minutes, so it might need to age another half hour. The beer is cold."

"You can't improve on the combination of beer and pizza," she said.

"You're a girl after my own heart. Do you want to eat at the table or dine in the living room?"

"Let's enjoy the fire," Lisbet said.

"Get comfortable while I get the fixings. You have four choices of pizza: pepperoni, tomato, mushroom, or sausage."

"How many pizzas did you order?"

"Two half-and-half," I said. "I wanted to make sure you had a variety to choose from."

"In that case I'll take one slice of each kind."

"And I'll make imitation the sincerest form of flattery."

I went out to the kitchen and plated our pizza. "Glass for your beer?"

"That would spoil the ambience of the meal."

"I think that's the first time the word 'ambience' has ever been used to refer to one of my meals. I feel so inspired I'm going to remove the cap to your beer."

"Who says that chivalry is dead?"

I brought her the pizza and beer—sans cap. She was sitting in the sofa nearest the fire. After delivering her plate, I went for my own and then joined her on the sofa. She extended her bottle my way, and I tapped glass to glass. The contact sent the foam up and over the lid of her bottle, and though Lisbet raised it to her lips, she wasn't quite in time and some of the beer spilled on her sweater and jeans.

"What a waste of good beer," I said, handing her my napkin.

"You're not offering me your shirt?"

"If it worked that way, I'd be spilling all over myself."

I went out to the kitchen to get more napkins and also brought back a wet dish towel.

"Thanks," she said, taking the dishcloth. "Luckily, it was just a little foam, but I better keep this towel handy. For my next trick I'll probably spill some pizza on my blouse."

"I don't think I have any club soda. How does beer work as a stain remover?"

"I think beer is more likely to get you into than out of trouble."

Raising my bottle, I asked, "Can we toast that?"

"No, we can't," she said, moving her bottle away from me. "And besides, I notice you still haven't removed the cap to your own beer."

"Really? I hadn't noticed that."

I popped the lid and then took a long pull on the beer as a preventative spilling measure. Half-empty bottles don't go Vesuvius very easily.

Both of us started in on the pizza. Lisbet hadn't just put in her order for show. She took a bite or two from each of the four pieces of pizza, savoring the flavor of each. After that she attacked the pieces indiscriminately, probably in an attempt to match me bite for bite. In that contest I prevailed and even went for an extra piece, choosing the tomato.

"There goes my diet," Lisbet said. "Next time do me a favor and order an anchovy, olive, and green pepper pizza. That way I can pretend I subsist on small green salads and tepid tap water."

"Hold the anorexia," I said. "I prefer your healthy appetite. I just wish I had some of those nuns' chocolates to offer you for dessert."

It was easy talking with her, and we talked about everything and nothing. Slowly but surely the space between us closed. One of us would say something and touch the other; one of us would shift and our legs would press up together; then there came the moment when both of us moved in unison and we were holding each other and kissing.

The moment lasted a minute, and another, and then we lost track of time. There was no doubt what we both wanted and where we eventually would be headed. I think both of us were grateful we'd weathered our first fight. Jen had used to say there was a great reason for our fighting: make-up sex.

When you lose a spouse, it's easy to look back upon your marriage with rose-colored glasses, something I was certainly guilty of, but that's not to say that Jenny and I didn't ever fight. Even when we argued, though, the spat seemed to serve the purpose of allowing us to reconnect and renew. After whatever raw emotions of our disagreement were stripped away, it was always that much easier to remember how exciting our love was. One moment we would be angry and posturing, and the next our clothes would be off and we'd be saying how much we loved each other. Nothing brought out our heightened passion like make-up sex.

Once or twice I thought of extending my hand and leading Lisbet to my bedroom, but I didn't feel the need to rush. Besides, we were enjoying our time on the sofa entirely too much.

What I hadn't counted on was my cell phone ringing. It was bad timing and then some. I wanted to ignore it, but I was as trained as Sirius to respond to certain commands. "Excuse me," I said, checking to see who was calling. The readout said it was Anna Nguyen. "I have to take this call," I said, and with some untangling and readjusting of partially unbuttoned and opened garments, I managed to rise.

Detective Nguyen said, "We think we've found all three of your attackers."

I was about to say that was good news when she added, "They're all dead."

"Shit."

"Each of them was done execution style, with a bullet to the head. They were dropped at the arboretum. I'm told the dumping spot is near Australia, if that means anything to you."

"It does." The arboretum is set up by continents with flora native to each.

As the kookaburra flew, the arboretum was about twenty-five miles east of Sherman Oaks in the city of Arcadia.

"Traffic willing, I'll be there in about forty-five minutes," I said.

I pocketed my phone and turned around to face Lisbet. "It's work. I am really sorry."

She smiled to show me that she was good with duty calling and said, "Do you want me to wait here for you?"

I thought about it and shook my head. "It will be late before I get back. That wouldn't be fair to you."

"I wouldn't have made the offer if I didn't want to."

"And I appreciate that offer, and I'll hold you to a rain check for another time, but not this time. Do you have plans for tomorrow night?"

"Yes, I'm cooking dinner for you and Sirius."

"I can make it, but I'm not sure about him. He has quite the social life."

"What about it, Sirius?" Lisbet asked.

At the mention of his name, Sirius came over to her and put his head in her lap, prompting me to say, "Hey, that's my gal."

"He tells me he likes roast beef," Lisbet said.

"I do, too, in case you were wondering."

She stood up. "Seven o'clock?"

"Count us in."

We sealed that deal with a long kiss. And then I walked Lisbet to her car, where we kissed again.

* * *

I hadn't been to the arboretum in close to a decade. Naturally, it was Jen that had arranged our first and only visit. I hadn't wanted to go, but she told me it would be fun, and she was right. There had been waterfalls, I remembered, and a turtle pond, and trees and plants indigenous to the featured continents ("What? No

Antarctica?" I'd asked Jen). During our visit, one particular pea-cock had acted as if he was in love with Jenny and had kept fol-lowing her around while displaying his plumage and trumpeting his unearthly call. For years afterward she had laughed whenever I attempted my peacock imitation.

That had been a long time ago.

There were police barricades up on Baldwin Avenue, and I had to flash my wallet badge to several officers while I made my way to Australia. Lights had been set up to illuminate a spot not far from Colorado Street. There were police cars on both sides of the street. I found a parking spot and, like a good moth, followed the brightest lights.

It wasn't cold, but the wind was whipping around, and I hugged my jacket close to me. The arboretum trees and plants were being stirred up by the wind, and the shaking branches sounded like a thousand threatening rattlesnakes. The high grass just off the road whipped at me as I made my way forward. Fronds moved in front of the light and offered the illusion that the dead were dancing. The three bodies had been dumped in a spot not far from the road, one right next to the other. Their legs and hands were still bound with duct tape.

Nguyen moved away from the lights and came up to me. She was holding her blazer with both her hands. "Welcome to the land down under," she said.

My guess was that the attractive detective was first-generation American, but that hadn't stopped her from picking up on cop humor. Her parents were probably still in mourning that she had chosen law enforcement for a career.

"Down under the earth is where these guys are going," I said, looking at the bodies.

Nguyen raised the crime scene tape and I did the limbo to get under it. We walked over to the bodies. Nguyen shone her flash-light on the man nearest us.

"Even though his hands are bound, you can still see most of his tattoo," she said. "If you want, I can have the duct tape cut."

"That's not necessary." I could see the red *A* on the one arm, and the jagged lines on the other. "This one's the ringleader. I recognize the tattoos."

Nguyen turned her beam on the other victims. I could see where all the men had been shot in the head. One of the victims showed extensive bruising to his face and neck; the other had visible bite marks.

"That bruising is consistent with where I was striking one of my attackers with an animal-control pole. And I'm sure those bites were delivered by my big, bad wolf. He's in the car if you want to take his DNA."

"I don't think that will be necessary," Nguyen said.

"I suppose you haven't had time to ID the victims."

"Actually, we have. The killer was cooperative. All three of them had their wallets and licenses."

"Do you know anything about them?"

"The preliminary information I have is that all of them lived together in some kind of ranch in Antelope Valley. It sounds like it's some kind of commune or sect."

"Sect?"

She nodded. "The person I contacted said they had some strange beliefs. We have a team that will be going out there tonight to check them out."

I was certain they wouldn't find anything. If Ellis Haines was behind the murders, he would make sure of that.

I offered up the punch line to the joke about the visitor to the monastery who grew tired of all the monks' shop talk and voiced his disgust by saying, "Sects, sects, sects, is that all you talk about?"

Nguyen didn't know the joke, and I didn't bother to explain.

CHAPTER 20:

NOT EVEN GOD CAN FIND ME

I fought against the gusting wind. It was resisting my efforts to open the front door to my house. If I'd been superstitious, I might have imagined something was trying to prevent me from getting inside, but I was too tired to be paranoid.

The three men that had attacked me were now dead. I suspected Ellis Haines had somehow reached out from San Quentin and had the men killed. What I didn't know was if Haines had acted to protect himself, or whether he had been looking out for me.

A blinking message light was casting its red glow on the living room wall. I walked over to the machine and hit Play.

"Hey, Mighty Dog," Martinez said. He sounded upbeat, a tone that had been noticeably absent for days. "I heard about your triple at the arboretum, so that's why I'm not calling your cell. Anyway, we might have something on one of the poison-pen writers, a kid Computer Crimes identified as Jeremy Levitt. He's the joker that tried to post on Paul Klein's memorial wall that Klein's death was karma. As it turns out, Levitt's a senior at good old Beverly Hills High School. What do you want to bet he's the one that's also guilty of leaving that other bad-mouthing note at Klein's wailing wall? Anyway, I didn't get to talk with Levitt for long—his parents made sure of that—but he and his mouthpiece are coming in for questioning tomorrow. Levitt tried to justify his attempt at memorial wall backstabbing by saying that Klein didn't deserve this outpouring of adoration. He said Klein was anything but a good kid.

"And then Levitt started telling me about his being friends with an older boy that overdosed two years ago. He said his friend was harassed by Klein and his wolf pack. Levitt didn't come right out and say it, but I got the feeling he and this other guy had a thing going on between them, and Klein and his friends caught wind of it and weren't exactly supportive of the gay lifestyle. Tomorrow Levitt is set to come in at ten o'clock. Gump and I are meeting at seven to prepare for the interview. If you can make it then, we'll all brainstorm."

I played the message back several times. If it hadn't been after midnight, I would have called Martinez back, but I'd be seeing him soon enough anyway. It was also too late to call Assistant Principal Durand. I wanted to know more about this kid that had overdosed.

A handful of empty beer bottles were on the kitchen counter. I was glad that I'd told Lisbet not to wait for me. The last week—no, the last three years—seemed to have caught up with me, and I was dead on my feet. I gathered the empties and put them in the recycle bin and then decided to add one more to their number. I flipped a cap, grabbed a piece of cold pizza, and planted myself in the easy chair. Sirius took his place on a throw rug next to me.

I bit into the pizza, felt eyes following my movements, and tore off a chunk for Sirius. I tossed, he caught, and we chewed. We were like an old married couple. Outside, the banshees were screaming. I thought about SID still working the crime scene at the arboretum. The conditions had been bad all the while I was there; now they would be even worse. That fucking Ellis Haines was right. It sounded like all hell was breaking loose.

I took a pull on the beer and with a backhand toss sent another piece of pizza flying. Sirius didn't disappoint. He caught and then inhaled.

By the sound of Martinez's voice, it was clear he thought this Levitt kid might have had something to do with Klein's death. My gut told me differently. All the words Levitt had offered up were passive. In the note left at the tower he'd written "What goes around, comes around." And the note he'd tried to post on the Klein memorial wall page wasn't about retribution but fate: "Some say Paul Klein's death was tragic. Those that knew him would say it's karma." If you cause someone to die, Levitt was saying, you should expect to die yourself. That wasn't the voice of a killer.

I thought about the visions I'd had while working the Klein case. I'd paid the price for those insights; I should have listened to them more closely.

"That's the problem with me being my own oracle," I told Sirius. "It's hard to interpret my own visions."

My moment after had told me that this was a revenge killing: an eye for an eye. Maybe it had also somehow told me about the kid that had overdosed, although I didn't know how that was possible. In one of my visions, Dinah had been lip-synching "A Little Help from My Friends." Ringo hadn't only gotten by with a little help from his friends, he'd gotten high.

There had been that other vision also, the one where I'd had to face up to my own suicidal thoughts. In law enforcement, one of the most dangerous situations an officer can encounter is when he's up against someone that wants to die. When a suicidal individual is unwilling or unable to take his or her life, he or she often employs the services of the police. That's why they call it suicide by cop. But just because you want to die doesn't mean you're not a danger to those responding to the situation.

There had been a part of me, I knew, that had wanted suicide by cop, me being the cop. I had wanted to die on the job. But was it possible my vision wasn't only about me? I had inquired about suicides at Beverly but not drug overdoses. Sometimes it's difficult to distinguish one from the other. The death of Jeremy Levitt's friend had been labeled as a drug overdose, but what if it was a suicide guised in needles or pills?

I fought to stay awake. Some kind of answer felt as if it was within reach, but I had reached the point where even toothpicks would have had a hard time keeping my lids up. I didn't have the strength or inclination to leave my easy chair and fell asleep sitting. I was in one of those deep REM sleeps when I awakened groggy and confused. This time I wasn't having my fire dream, but it was something just as horrifying. Nearby I could hear Ellis Haines talking. He was in my house. My heart hammered in my chest.

"How you are sleeping? Do you hear the wind blowing outside? Is it keeping you up?"

My hand was still clenched around the half-filled beer bottle. I hadn't yet gotten a replacement for my Glock, but there was a spare handgun in my bedroom. Get the gun, I thought. My body was shaking, which made it hard to get to my feet. And that's when I noticed Sirius standing at my side. My partner was watching over me, but he wasn't on alert. He knew the Weatherman wasn't in the next room. The voice I was hearing was coming from my answering machine.

"The wind always invigorates me. It almost makes me feel like I'm flying. Isn't it nice to be a leaf in the wind? Everything is out of control and direction means nothing. It is the ultimate freedom."

My heart continued to pound, but now I wasn't scared so much as I was angry. Out of my message machine Haines continued to talk.

"You looked so fragile when you visited me, Detective. I was concerned for your welfare. I didn't like the idea of others trying to interfere in our unfinished business. I wouldn't have others do my own work, Detective. That wouldn't be right.

"Naturally, I've been concerned about the state of your health. You, Sirius, and I are secret sharers. If something should happen to you, I hope you have made provisions for Sirius. Is he watching over you now?"

My partner's ears were up and his head was slightly tilted. He'd heard his name spoken, and he seemed to recognize the speaker's voice.

"When you visited, you looked like someone at death's door, Detective. I was afraid the right wind would push you over into the abyss. Are you looking into that darkness right now?"

My job forces me to deal with people experiencing times of crisis. When someone is attacked or has his property stolen, he invariably feels a sense of violation and helplessness. All of us have boundaries, and we suffer if they're breached. Haines had violated both my person and my property. That son of a bitch had found a way into my house. He had invaded my world. And there wasn't a goddamn thing I could do about it.

Sotto voce, Haines continued talking. "I love it when the Santa Ana winds begin to blow. Have you ever noticed how the wind feels like warm breath down your neck? When that happens I always feel compelled to return the favor and do my own heavy breathing over a special neck of my choosing. I become one with the wind. Take a moment to listen, Detective. Can you hear the wind calling for you?"

The asshole stopped talking long enough for the silence to fill the room. I didn't want to listen, but I couldn't help it. Outside, the wind was howling and its cries filled my house.

"It's just warming up for an even bigger show this night, as am I. As I have been wont to say, never leave your audience hanging."

I thought he was finished but he wasn't. My home invasion became surreal when he started singing. What made it even worse was the bastard had a good voice, hitting every note. Maybe it was his audition tape for *American Idol*. I knew the song: "They Call the Wind Mariah."

The last line of the lyrics was particularly plaintive, and he put everything into it. It felt as if he was singing it just for me, and that he knew how lost I had been for so long, and how "not even God may find me."

The song came to a merciful end, but the intimacy of it shook me. It didn't strike close to home. It was in my home and in my head.

"That's our song," Haines whispered. "Have a good night, Detective."

In the silence I could still hear his voice. It felt as if Haines were stepping on my grave.

The easy chair no longer felt comfortable. For a moment I considered taking a shower to cleanse myself from the toxic ramblings of Haines, but instead I just decided to crawl into bed.

I didn't replay the message. It could wait until the morning, when I would listen to it in the light of day. And maybe in that light I wouldn't feel so lost, and maybe God would find me.

Unfortunately, that light never came. An hour later I was once again burning.

The Strangler screamed for help, but his words were swallowed by the fire. I watched his mouth moving and his face contort, but as close as I was to him, I couldn't hear what he was saying. I had never heard the voice of fire—of inferno—until now. It was a terrible thing—a raging, roaring, deafening howl—and in it there was hunger and madness and worst of all, laughter. It was the sound of a demon unleashed.

The flames were whirling all around us. The wind kept blowing, the bellows kept churning, and we kept running.

The fire made us move to the rhythm of its churning jaws. It came at us from one direction and then another. And then the fire was everywhere, and our dance became wild and out of control.

I'd once seen footage of a male tarantula attempting to mate. As it performed for the female, all eight of its legs were moving. We—the Strangler, and me, and Sirius—were eight legs. My partner was grievously hurt, but sometimes his legs twitched and moved as if I was scratching him in his sweet spot.

In Italy, the tarantula inspired a dance known as the tarantella. Folklore says that when bitten by a tarantula, the only cure is doing the tarantella. It is believed that by frenziedly whirling about, you sweat the poison out.

The flames were making us dance the tarantella. There was madness in our steps; we were out-of-control dervishes. I was the one with the badge and gun. I was supposed to have answers, but I was as lost as lost could be. In the flaming wilderness, I went a little mad.

"We must sweat the poison out!" I shouted.

The Strangler still thought me sane. "What?"

"The poison," I said.

We continued the dance of the dead.

The shrieking woke me up. It took me a second to realize I was the one doing the shrieking. Sirius was nudging me and whimpering.

"It's all right," I said.

But it wasn't all right. My life was out of control. Every day I was dancing some version of the tarantella.

My racing heart began to slow, and my sweat started to cool. In the blessed relief, my after-fire moment came. It started with music, the strains of *Scheherazade*, and in my mind I saw a montage of familiar entertainers and sports figures.

Then the music stopped and I heard a familiar male voice say, "Denial, anger, bargaining, depression, and acceptance. And then murder."

I knew the voice; I was sure of that. But I couldn't quite place it. I thought about my vision. The whole thing—from music, to the images, to the voice—had probably taken no more than fifteen seconds.

Normally I sleep after a fire dream, but not this time. I grabbed my laptop and called up a search engine. I typed in "denial" and was partway through typing "anger" when the suggested entry of "Elisabeth Kübler-Ross Grief Cycle Model" came up. I clicked on that and began reading. According to Kübler-Ross, those facing death went through five stages of grief: denial, anger, bargaining, depression, and acceptance. In my vision there had been a sixth word: murder. That wasn't on Kübler-Ross's list.

It wasn't as if I had divined the words on her list out of thin air. In college, one of my psych courses had the assigned reading of Kübler-Ross's *On Death and Dying*. Still, I wasn't sure where in the course of my investigation her grief cycle model fit in.

I thought about the disparate figures in my vision. Kareem Abdul-Jabbar had been shooting a sky hook. Then I'd seen that actress from the *Seinfeld* series. It took me a moment to remember her name: Julia Louis-Dreyfus. My vision had also featured Olivia Newton-John. I think I'd conjured up a memory of her from *Grease*. Daniel Day-Lewis, who had acted in one of my favorite films, *The Last of the Mohicans*, had also been in my lineup.

Everyone I had envisioned, I realized, had a hyphenated name. Even the audio connection of my vision had hyphenated names: Rimsky-Korsakov and Kübler-Ross.

There was something there, something I knew I should be picking up on. There was a current going off in my mind, a humming. Sometimes Seth and his groups chant in his backyard, and the vigor of their sounds and vibrations always amazes me. Their voices combine into this primal force. When their chanting is in full throat, it almost feels as if I can reach out and touch a live wire.

Om…

My neck suddenly prickled. I connected the familiar voice that I'd heard reciting the Kübler-Ross grief cycle with a name.

Double om…

"You want to go for a drive?" I asked Sirius.

It was two thirty a.m., the wind was howling, and we had an hour's drive ahead of us. My partner thought it was a great idea.

CHAPTER 21:

GONE WITH THE WIND

Two minutes after I confirmed Dave Miller's address, the power went off. I didn't know whether only Sherman Oaks was affected, or if most of LA County was also in the dark.

The so-called civilized world gets a lot scarier in the absence of light, especially on a night with the wind unleashed. In the darkness I debated my options. I had planned on calling Gump and Martinez, but with the power off I wasn't able to call out with either my cell phone or house phone.

I moved toward the front of the house, hoping that if I opened the curtains, the moonlight would help me to see. After all the years I'd lived in my house, you would think I'd know my way around in the dark, but that wasn't the case. I played blindman's bluff, tapping my way over to the front window. The curtain pulling didn't do much good; there was only a sliver moon and it provided minimal illumination. What I could see wasn't encouraging: trees were being pushed to their limits, and over the wind I listened to their groaning and cracking.

Waiting would be the smart thing to do—for light, for backup, for the proper paperwork—but I have never been good at either waiting or doing the smart thing.

I could still hear Dave Miller's voice in my head talking about denial, anger, bargaining, depression, acceptance, and murder. After the fact, everything was beginning to make sense. Miller's son *had been* on Jason Davis's bully list, but as Danny Marxmiller and not Danny Miller. What had thrown us off was Danny's last name, which I was now certain should have been hyphenated as Marx-Miller.

Dave Miller had killed the individual he thought was responsible for his son's death. He had gotten his eye for an eye. Although Danny Marx-Miller had died from a drug overdose, his father must have learned there was more to that story. That's why Miller had planted drugs on Klein. His son's reputation had been sullied, and he wanted the same thing to happen to the young man he believed was his son's murderer.

There was a lot of supposition and guesswork in my theory, and yet in my gut I knew I was right. My subconscious—my visions—backed me up.

"We can call Gump and Martinez from the road," I told Sirius. "Between here and Temecula there will be plenty of cell towers still standing."

Sirius followed me while I stumbled around the house and seemed to think it was a great game. I played too much of that game until I found a flashlight with working batteries. Under its illumination I dressed. Before leaving, I holstered my backup gun.

Almost ten million people live in Los Angeles County. Walking out into the darkness, it felt as if I was in one of those end-of-the-world movies. There was no sign of anyone. I could have been the last person on earth, except for the zombies that had to be lurking out there somewhere.

I was wearing a windbreaker, which only seemed to encourage the wind. The fabric whipped and snapped and made me feel like the Michelin Man. There was a lot of static electricity in the air; maybe that was why I could feel the hair rising on my arms. Or maybe I was just afraid of the Santa Ana condition. I sniffed the air. Faintly, I could detect the smell of something burning. It wasn't nearby, but the fire was out there and on the move.

The right thing to do would have been to report to police headquarters. When the lights go out, the LAPD puts out a call for all the bodies it can muster. The brass would be worried about looting, or any appearance of lawlessness. It would want to send out as many squad cars as possible so as to give the appearance of a police presence. Tonight, though, they'd have to do that without me.

In the absence of streetlights, my neighborhood seemed to have mostly disappeared. I backed out of the driveway and began driving. My headlights, even on bright, didn't make much headway against the darkness. The strong winds were stirring everything around, and the shifting reflections played out on my windshield, making me feel as if I was taking in a black-and-white movie at a drive-in.

I tuned in to KNX and was glad to hear the blackout hadn't stopped it from broadcasting. A serious-sounding newscaster was talking about all the calamities affecting the Southland that had been caused by the Santa Ana winds.

"It's a mess out there," he said. "Power lines are down all over the county and fallen trees are causing numerous road closures. Firefighters are currently battling multiple brushfires that are raging in Whittier, Covina, and Brentwood. If you don't have to be out on the road, you are advised to stay home."

It was good advice, but I didn't heed it.

The freeways were still open. Usually a parade of big rigs travels the Los Angeles arteries at night, but not this night. The trucks were sitting it out. In all my years of LA driving, I'd never seen the highways so deserted. That should have made driving easy, except for the wind. I was driving like a drunk, unable to navigate a straight line. The wind kept blowing my sedan from one lane to another. The gusting increased as I traveled inland. I found myself leaning forward in my seat while keeping a tight grip on the wheel.

There were patches of darkness and light that showed those areas with power and those without. Whenever I had cell service, I tried calling Gump and Martinez, but the calls didn't go through, which probably meant the power was out where they lived. I could have gone through the LAPD switchboard to get a message to them, but it wasn't a good night to ask for messenger service. Judging by what KNX was telling me, all city services were being stretched to the max.

I tried not to think about the last time I'd braved the elements during a bad Santa Ana, but Ellis Haines kept invading my thoughts. Like it or not, our Santa Ana dance with death had intertwined our paths forever. I wanted out of our chain gang, but Haines wasn't making that easy. The bastard had predicted this Santa Ana; he'd reveled in it. Killer winds, he'd told me. I knew it wasn't by chance that he'd called me earlier. He had known my three attackers were dead. Later, when I was in the right frame of mind, I'd play back his message. I wasn't sure whether Haines had called me directly or made a tape and managed to get it smuggled out of prison. If he'd made a tape, that meant in his own way Haines had managed to escape his cell, and that on his orders his confederate or confederates had obtained my unlisted number. It was possible they had my address and were monitoring me. At his trial and afterward, I had seen Haines's freak show followers. The master was creepy enough; his disciples were almost as scary.

It was more likely, though, that Haines had called me directly. Cell phones are contraband in prisons, but they can be had for a price even if you're housed in San Quentin's Adjustment Center. The FBI would be able to tell me if that was the case. Thinking about his call made me remember a line from an old AT&T ad campaign: "Reach out, reach out and touch someone." That's what Haines had done. He had reached out with his toxic touch. But now of all times I couldn't let Haines get into my head. That was exactly what he wanted, of course, but I couldn't waste any more psychic energy on a bogeyman.

Aloud, I said, "I thought I saw a puddy cat."

Sirius's ears popped up at the c-word.

"But I didn't, I didn't," I added.

Sirius settled down. I tried calling Martinez and then Gump but still had no luck reaching them. I was drawing ever closer to Miller's home. My cop training told me to not proceed; my cop instinct said to keep going. Since being burned, I had come to rely more and more on that instinct. Something was about to happen, I knew, and I felt this need to get to Miller's place without any delays. My fire walk had apparently burned away my common sense.

The signs told me I was nearing the city of Temecula. The location of Temecula—roughly equidistant from LA, San Diego, and Orange County—had made it a popular bedroom community for all three when land and gas were cheap. There were still some references in the signage and billboards to the city's not-too-distant ranching past, but nowadays the cowboys have forsaken the area. Not so the Indians, who according to several billboards were running a large casino in town.

I exited the interstate and turned west on Rancho California Road. De Luz was above Temecula. I drove slowly, not because I wanted to but because conditions demanded that. My window was down and my head was out. Visibility was bad. It appeared as if the area was having a partial blackout, but it was hard to tell because the houses were spread out, with most of them sitting on so-called gentleman ranches, groves with acreage of avocado and citrus. Some of the area was undeveloped, and I passed by stretches of chaparral, coastal sage brush, and one of California's big imports—eucalyptus trees.

The ubiquitous eucs are an Australian import that date back to the nineteenth century. Gold rush settlers to California hadn't liked the treeless nature of the land and had started planting seed-lings of this "wonder tree" over 150 years ago. The Central Pacific Railroad had also gotten into the act, planting a million seedlings. Like so many other immigrants, eucalyptuses flourished in the Golden State.

I am not a fan of eucalyptus, a prejudice borne from my fire walk. Many of my facial burns had come from flaming eucs. There's a reason the trees are nicknamed nuke-alyptus. Few trees have as much oil in them as eucalyptuses. They're highly flam-mable, so much so that during fires they sometimes explode. In every big Southern California fire, news crews invariably film dramatic footage of stands of eucalyptus trees torching upward like giant flamethrowers.

The trees don't do well in windstorms. Evidence of that could be seen in the leaves, bark, and branches that littered the road. As the wind pushed at a stand of eucalyptus, the susurration of dry branches sounded like fingernails on a chalkboard. Then a gust came up, and the sound changed to that of bones rattling.

The wind brought with it a scent I didn't like, and I felt my chest tighten: there was smoke in the air. I looked around for any sign of fire, but it wasn't showing itself, at least not yet. The area was probably a firefighter's nightmare. Many of the estates were situated between the canyon hills. The wind was already whipping through those canyons. The wrong spark could mean a conflagration. According to my nose, that conflagration might already have started.

I could turn around and in twenty minutes be in Temecula. From there I could get a squad car or two, and maybe even a fire engine, to accompany me to Miller's avocado grove.

There was no time, my little voice told me. I wanted to tell my little voice to shut up and that haste makes waste. I kept driving. It was my nose and not my little voice that told me I was driving toward a fire.

I turned onto a cul-de-sac. Miller's spread was supposed to be at the end of the street. The darkness and the smoke grew worse as I drove forward; the reason for the darkness quickly became apparent. A power line was down. It was acting like a snake with its head cut off but unaware that it was dead. The line arced and moved, and I had to carefully inch my car by it.

Wetting my lips, I started whistling an off-key rendition of "Wichita Lineman." I *was* whistling in the dark, while the wind was pushing hard and making all sorts of shadows jump. It struck me that maybe I should have packed a crucifix and a silver bullet.

Sirius whined. He always senses when my moods turn dark. Or maybe he didn't like the plaintive tune I was whistling. I was no Glen Campbell, but the wire he sang of was out there. I could hear its rattled threats.

We reached the end of the cul-de-sac. There was a gated entry to Miller's driveway and house. From what I could see, a chain-link fence stretched along the perimeter of the property.

"End of the road," I said to Sirius.

My partner's ears went up and he eagerly made circles in the backseat. He was ready to get moving. I didn't quite share his enthusiasm. All around us was the beginning of a bad horror story: it was a dark and stormy night, or at least a blustery night. The gusts were hitting my parked car with such force it felt as if I had a case of delirium tremens.

"Curiosity killed the cat," I told Sirius. "It's a good thing you're a dog."

We got out of the car. As we started our walk toward the fence I was greeted by the smell and sight of smoke. I still couldn't see or hear the fire, but its presence couldn't be ignored, and I had to fight the instinct to flee. The entry to the house was set back about seventy-five yards from a wrought-iron fence. From inside the house I could just make out a tiny, flickering orange glow.

It was possible the house was on fire, but it was more likely that I was seeing the reflection of a candle. Still, I took the light as an invitation to proceed. If questioned, I would say it was probable cause for me to enter Miller's property. Someone had to play the role of Smokey the Bear.

I eyed the wrought-iron fence, and the best point of entry, and thought about leaving Sirius behind. He must have read my mind, because he started pacing and whining.

"It's better if you stay," I said. "You smell what's in the air? There's a fire and I think it's getting closer."

Sirius positioned himself between me and the fence. He was determined not to be left behind.

"Anyone ever tell you how stubborn you are?" I muttered.

My partner knew I was posing. I was glad he was with me, and the two of us went in search of a way to get him inside. The wrought-iron fence extended all along the front of the house, but the rest of the property line was set off by chain-link fencing. We looked for a chink in the chain link, and along the south side of the house found some give in a section passing over a small gully. I lifted up the fence from the bottom, clearing enough space for Sirius to shimmy under. He took the low road and I took the high, climbing up the six-foot fence and then hoisting myself over. The wind was blowing from the north to the east and played havoc with my dismount, dropping me to the ground like a winged bird. Luckily, I didn't hit one of the many landmines—cacti that made up most of the front landscaping. With the flashlight and moon-light, I avoided the cacti. Sirius used his dog radar, moving in and out of the needled obstacles. We made it to the pathway and walked toward the house. I still wasn't sure how to best approach Miller. My little voice was no longer talking to me.

At the front of the house was the window where I'd seen the glowing reflection from inside. I put my hands up to the window and looked in. A single candle was lit at the dining room table. Sitting at that table in a low chair was Dave Miller. I wasn't sure if he could see me in the shadows, but he seemed to be looking my way. Because I saw no point in hiding, I raised my hand and rapped on the window. Miller didn't respond. It was possible he thought the sound was only the wind, so I tapped the pane even harder. Still he didn't rise or motion but just continued to sit.

Drawing my gun, I walked to the front door and knocked hard enough to be heard even over the noise of the wind. I took cover at the side of the house, waiting to see if Miller responded to my knocks. Paul Klein had died from a gunshot wound to the eye, and I had to assume Miller was still armed.

When Miller didn't come to the door, I retraced my steps to the front window and again looked inside. He hadn't moved, so I once more waved and knocked to get his attention, but he ignored me. I was forced to again return to the front door. I expected it to be locked, but the handle turned and I swung the door open.

I shouted so as to be heard over the wind: "Mr. Miller? I'm Detective Gideon. We talked the other day."

He didn't respond. A heavy scent of paint fumes pervaded the house, and I wondered if those fumes had gone to Miller's head.

"May I come in, Mr. Miller? We need to talk."

Miller still didn't answer. I entered the house, doing the kind of peek-a-boo with my head and gun that you see fake cops do on television, but without their panache. Miller wasn't waiting for me with a gun. In fact, when I stepped into his sight, he barely gave me a glance.

By that time my eyes were watering. It wasn't only paint fumes in the air. There were multiple scents of varnish, solvents, and cleaners. There was just enough light that I could make out several drop cloths in the living room. A ladder was in the middle of the room and next to it was a work bench with paint.

Miller broke his silence. "You and your dog need to leave," he said. His words were slow and slightly slurred. An opened vodka bottle sitting at the table might have had something to do with that.

"We'll do that, but we'll need you to come with us. There are some questions I have to ask you."

He shook his head. "I'm not going anywhere."

I didn't like the vibe I was getting. I didn't like the fumes in the air.

"I am not asking. Mr. Miller, you are under arrest."

He interrupted me before I could finish and read him his Miranda rights. His hand was poised near the candle. "There's furniture stripper on the table. You really don't want this candle to fall over."

I could see—and smell—the puddle of furniture stripper on the table. Miller's eyes were glassy, but his hand was uncomfortably close to the candle. There was no way I could get to him without his knocking the candle over first.

"I don't want to have to use force, Mr. Miller."

"If you shoot me," he said, slurring his words, "you'll set off the fumes. You shoot me, you shoot yourself."

I edged forward as I continued talking. "I'm putting away my gun. See? Why don't you let me open a window and then we can talk."

"No," he said, running his finger just above the flickering candle. "You and your dog get out."

"Is it all right if I sit down? All I want to do is talk to you."

I moved toward the table, not waiting for his answer. Even though he was impaired, Miller was still watchful.

"That's close enough," he said. "And keep your dog back."

I made a hand gesture to Sirius, and he backed off several steps while I took a seat at the far end of the table.

Through blurry eyes, Miller regarded me. "Why couldn't you have waited for just a few more minutes?"

"What happens then?"

"You have eyes, don't you?"

He motioned with his head to the window behind him. The fire was no longer hiding from me. A long line of flames was now lighting the sky. My heart started pounding and I had to control my voice.

"We all need to get out of here," I said. "With the way the wind's blowing, that fire will be on us any minute now."

"I'm here for the show."

My eyes went from Miller to what was coming our way. My throat tightened. The fire was still a ways off, but it wasn't far enough away. The flames were being pushed by gusting winds. The inferno was growing.

"Fire isn't something you want to mess with," I said. "Believe me, I know."

"That's why you and Fido should take off."

"That's why we all should. My dog and I were caught in a fire a few years ago. We got burned up, and it was as bad as anything I ever want to experience. You don't want that."

The window behind Miller was now a vivid orange. If I hadn't known better, I would have thought the sun was rising. I wiped my suddenly wet brow. My body seemed to have forgotten that I don't sweat as much as normal people.

Miller took note of the growing fireball behind him. "The flames were hot on my feet when I took off. It took longer to get here than I thought it would."

"You started the fire?"

"I drove my ATV to the end of my property line and then walked into the canyon. I knew once the fire started the winds would drive it over the crest and move it in this direction. I wouldn't have gone to all that effort if I'd known you were going to show up. I just would have set the damn house on fire."

"Maybe I was meant to show up. Maybe you should take it as a sign that you weren't meant to die."

Miller didn't seem to be listening to what I was saying. "I had to get the fire going good," he said. "Avocado and citrus are more fire resistant than most trees. But I made sure to put a lot of dry mulch in my groves. It's making for good tinder."

His eyes strayed to the fire, and he nodded, but then his head swung back toward me. Despite the booze and whatever else he might have taken, Miller was still very much aware.

"You don't want to die in a fire. I can't think of a worse way to die."

"I can," he said, "lethal injection."

"Once a jury hears how your son was bullied, they'll be sympathetic to your position. They'll understand you were in pain."

"My son wasn't just bullied. He was murdered. He couldn't take the suffering anymore. I only saw him weekends, you know. My wife and I divorced ten years ago. I knew my son was unhappy, but I didn't know why. I learned too late how they killed him."

Orange light now filled the dining room. The fire was announcing itself.

"What do you mean when you say they killed him?"

"Dinah opened my eyes. When she first called the crisis line everything she said had this terrible déjà vu quality. So I did a little digging, and I found out about my son and his friend. Someone saw them hugging one another. That really brought out Klein and his jackals. They never gave him any peace after that."

"Was his friend Jeremy Levitt?"

Miller sighed and nodded. "I don't know if my son was gay, but I do know how special he was, and how sensitive. Those animals played on his sensitivity."

"He died of a drug overdose," I said.

"That's what he wanted it to look like. It was an accident, just like this fire was an accident. Like son, like father."

An orange light was now reaching out for my body; I was in its light and heat. The fire was descending on the house. There was no time for stories, but I continued to listen.

"My son didn't want my ex-wife and me to feel responsible for his death, so he made it look like he was taking drugs and had an overdose."

"Jeremy told you this?"

"Jeremy told me he never saw my son take drugs and never heard him mention using them."

"There was a report that your son went to raves, and that he was seen taking drugs."

"He went to one rave. That's where he bought the drugs that he used two weeks later to kill himself. That's why he made a show of taking them at the rave."

"Let's say you're right about all of this. In the end, it was Danny that took his own life. Why did you murder Paul Klein?"

"'Suicide Is Painless.'"

"I don't agree."

"I'm talking about the title to a song. You've probably heard it a million times but don't even know it. It's the opening music to the show M*A*S*H*. I learned that Klein liked to hum that tune when he bullied my son. He'd phone my son and play that tune. He wanted Danny to think about suicide. He pushed him into the abyss."

"How do you know all of that?"

"I asked the right people. It was Dinah that made me ask the questions, because he was doing the same thing to her. Whenever he got the chance, whenever others weren't around, Klein hummed his dirge around Dinah."

There was another scent now in addition to the fumes in the air. Smoke was filling the house.

"We have to leave."

He shook his head. I wanted to flee, but curiosity kept me there a few moments longer, trumping my fear. "Why did you crucify Klein?"

"Why did he crucify me?"

The room was heating up rapidly, which could only mean one thing: the house was on fire. Miller was a dead man, and if I didn't leave, I'd join him. But at that moment Miller decided to satisfy my curiosity.

"I am not sure when the idea first came to me to crucify him," he said. "I had already decided to kill him, but that wasn't punishment enough. I wanted his death to be a spectacle. I wanted to mock him in death as he had mocked my son in life."

The window behind Miller began to crack. He turned his head, but out of the corner of his eye saw me move toward him. Miller grabbed the candle. There was no way to reach him without his sending the house up in flames.

"No," he said, brandishing the candle.

It was his last chance, and mine. I couldn't afford to try and rescue him. "Let's go!" I yelled to Sirius.

The two of us raced for the front door. I reached for the handle, and then recoiled. It was hot to the touch. I looked through the window and saw flames enveloping the front porch.

We sprinted toward the back of the house. As we passed by the dining room the window broke. Shards flew as the fumes and whatever had been poured on the table ignited, and Miller was encased in flames. His screams trailed behind us.

Suicide wasn't painless.

We ran out the back door. Most of the house was already in flames. There was no choice where to run. While we'd been talking, flames had swept over the grove. The fire had leapfrogged into outlying areas; the chaparral on the south side of the fence was already torching, and offered no escape. The only area not yet overrun by flames was to the west.

I kept low, trying to swallow as little smoke as possible, trying to find a way out. The fire seemed to have outflanked us and was attacking on all sides. I cursed myself for having stayed in the house too long, for once again putting our lives on the line. Of all people, I should have known the perils of a wildfire. As we ran I tried to figure out how we were going to survive. Was there an answer? If you believed Bob Dylan, it was blowing in the wind.

Hard as it was to do, I stopped my mad dash. We couldn't outrun the fire for long. If we were to survive, I had to outthink it. The way the wind was gusting, there was no safe spot. You had to assume the fire was going to burn everything and everywhere.

I patted down my pockets. That's what people do when they're desperate to find something they know isn't there; they search anyway because they don't know what else to do. This time I found what I was looking for and pulled free the matches I'd used to start a fire the night before.

The wind kicked up around us. It was a warm wind, but I still felt chilled. I knew what I had to do: I needed to fight fire with fire, and I was Scarecrow afraid.

I needed to create a firebreak. With a big enough dead zone of consumed tinder, we might survive the flames. Firefighters are good at setting back burns, but then they know what they're doing. They burn an area of vegetation, working to create a fire break that doesn't add to the main fire. There is an art to back burns. Firefighters set their flames near enough to the primary fire so that it sucks the backfire inward. With no fuel to burn, the fire's approach is often stopped.

There was a channel running through the grove that was crisscrossed by other smaller conduits. At one time the land might have been irrigated. I made for an area ahead of the fire and then gathered anything that might be combustible, clearing a ten-foot-by-ten-foot area of all its mulch, dried grass, twigs, and branches. Then I spread my gathered tinder along a line and lit a match. Either the wind, or my shaking hand, extinguished the flame.

I opened the matchbox again, and several of the matches spilled to the ground. It took me three attempts to successfully strike a match, but the sparking and glow lasted only a moment, and once more the flame died out.

The fire was coming at me, reaching out with its heat and smoke and roar. I chafed at the irony of not being able to start my own fire. In Catholic grade school, I remembered Sister Bernadette reading the class "The Little Match Girl." I was nine years old, and I don't think I'd ever heard such a sad story. When Sister Bernadette finished reading, I did my best to hide my tears from my classmates. I didn't buy Sister Bernadette's explanation that by striking her matches the girl had been able to illuminate an unseen God, and she was helped to go to a better place. I just remembered the image of a bareheaded and barefoot girl freezing to death on the last day of the year.

I struck another match and failed again. Now I was getting angry. I'd already gone through half the matches. I tried again, and this time the grass lit. I blew gently, added some kindling, and the fire caught. It wanted to be fed, so I added more twigs. When the line of tinder started to burn, I pulled down a dead avocado branch and held it out to the fire. It took maybe half a minute for my makeshift torch to catch, and then I started walking around the space and igniting all the material I'd gathered.

The big fire was drawing close. I threw down my torch and ran to a denuded spot along the channel and began to dig. I wondered if I was digging our grave. We would need a bunker to survive the fire. Sirius took a spot next to me. I didn't know the command for "dig," but he worked without being told, and the dirt began to fly. I clawed and he dug in a desperate race against the licking fire. Smoke clawed at our noses and lungs, but we kept digging. And then the fire was too close. There was too much smoke to effectively see if my backfire had worked. If enough vegetation had burned, maybe we'd have haven enough from the nightmare around us.

I called Sirius to get into the hole we'd dug, and then I piled dirt all around its top, trying to make a barricade to ward off the blaze. The fire kept coming, getting nearer and nearer until I was forced to jump into our foxhole, where I held Sirius close and tried to shield him from the flames.

CHAPTER 22:

GRAVE CONFESSIONS

The locomotive didn't kill us.

That's how I described it to Seth when he visited us in the hospital. I said as the fire passed over, it felt like I was lying between railroad tracks with a locomotive sweeping by overhead, and nothing separating me from death. All I could do was to wait it out. The sound almost drove me from our hole; the voice of fire is a terrible thing. It raged and roared, and all the while the wind blew dirt and debris and embers at us. I held on to Sirius as the flames swept past us and took their toll. I don't know how long our torment lasted, but the locomotive finally passed us by.

It left burns all over my back, neck, and arms, but I was alive.

Later, I was told how lucky we were. My backfire might, or might not, have helped us survive. More than anything else, the location of our foxhole probably saved us. It was down low and far enough away from the trees that we were spared from the fire. William Cummings was right: there are no atheists in foxholes.

For three days we'd been at the burn unit. Strings had been pulled from above, and Sirius and I were allowed to share the same hospital room. Officially, Sirius was my Seeing Eye dog. My burns were much worse than his, as they should have been. It was my fault for putting both of us in the middle of a fire. Still, we came out of our second fire walk in much better condition than we had our first. Our burns weren't life threatening, and it looked as if I'd avoid adding any new scarring to the old. But then the old were bad enough and didn't need the help.

Gump had stopped by the hospital a few times, so I wasn't surprised when he appeared unannounced once again.

"I was thinking of bringing you a plant," he said, "but they didn't have any poison ivy."

"Don't worry. Your presence is toxic enough."

Gump took a seat next to me and looked around to make sure the coast was clear. "You want a drink? I smuggled in a hip flask."

"I better not. Nurse Ratched checks in on me frequently."

We talked, and Gump got around to his purpose for being there. I answered more questions about the case, and then I must have drifted off. I'd been doing that for a few days. When I awakened, Gump was gone, but I traded up. Lisbet was there.

In all her visits to the hospital she had never arrived empty-handed, despite my telling her that she was all I needed. This time the aroma gave away the secret of what she had brought.

"Pumpkin bread," I said.

"It was fresh out of the oven when I picked up a loaf."

"It would be a sacrilege if we didn't eat some now."

"I figured you might say that," Lisbet said and pulled some paper plates and plastic cutlery from her bag. She cut each of us a generous slice, and we munched happily while holding hands. Sirius gave her a plaintive look and got rewarded with his own piece.

"I also brought us dessert."

"Let me guess: penguin chocolates?"

"Close but no cigar."

"I didn't guess a cigar."

"Do you like peanut brittle?"

"There are those that might argue that sugar, peanuts, and butter are as holy a trinity as barley, hops, and wheat."

"Let's eat to that," she said, opening up the box and handing me a piece of brittle.

When we had our fill, I noticed that Lisbet had left a few crumbs on her fingers. I decided to lick them off. She returned the favor. And then the two of us started kissing. We kissed for a long time and would have kissed for even longer except for a strange thump-thump sound that forced us to investigate.

Sirius was watching us and wagging his tail.

"Quit being a voyeur," I said.

We had another piece of brittle and then did some more kissing. It really was a great combination. There wasn't much of a view from my hospital room, but the two of us sat contentedly watching the afternoon shadows give way to evening.

When all vestiges of the day were gone, Lisbet sighed and said, "I wish I could stay longer, but I took on a new job and that's going to force me to burn the midnight oil."

"As soon as you finish this project, I call dibs on you and the midnight oil, as well as the massage oil."

"I look forward to that."

"That's two of us."

Something in my voice must have made Sirius decide to start thumping again. I looked at him and said, "I said the two of us, which means that two is company, and three is a crowd. The next time I have the pleasure of this woman's company, you're going to be doing your thumping from another room."

"Don't worry, Sirius," Lisbet said, "his bark is worse than his bite."

She patted him but kissed me and then stood up to leave. "You don't have to walk me out," Lisbet said. "I'll see you tomorrow."

"I do have to walk you out. It's a good excuse to get out of bed, and besides, when we meet up tomorrow, it won't be here. I intend on checking myself out in the morning."

"I thought your doctor wanted you to stay through the weekend and then evaluate your condition on Monday."

"That was before my miraculous recovery."

"You haven't told him you're checking out, have you?"

"It might have slipped my mind."

"I hope you're not pushing it."

The concern was in her words and her face. It had been a long time since someone had cared for me like that.

"I'm not. And FYI, the only reason I didn't check out this morning was that I didn't want you to freak out."

"FYI, I like that."

We smiled for one another, and then Lisbet picked up the bag in which she'd brought my presents. She seemed surprised that it wasn't quite empty but then remembered what was inside.

"I almost forgot," she said. "Sylvia Espinosa called and wanted to know if I'd like her to send me a copy of today's *University Times*. I told her that since I was going to be driving by the campus, I'd stop and pick up a few copies."

She handed me a paper. Instead of looking at it, I casually put the paper aside. "Thanks for thinking of me."

Lisbet and I had fought over the article, and I wanted her to know she was more important than any case. Instead of holding the paper, I held her.

"I'll let you play nurse tomorrow if you come to my place for an early dinner."

"I'll let you play doctor if you order Thai food."

"That's what you call a no-brainer. If you're lucky, I might even share my pad Thai with you."

"Panang curry with shrimp on the spicy side," she said, "a seven or eight, and an appetizer of spring rolls. And don't count on my sharing with you without some creative begging on your part."

"I don't mean to brag, but I do look sexy in a sandwich board soliciting handouts."

"You found my kryptonite."

The two of us walked to the elevator, and we made good use of our wait time for the car. Our kiss was long and leisurely and when we finished, Lisbet said, "You seem to be coming along in your physical therapy."

"I've been practicing on all the nurses."

She feigned umbrage and we kissed and made up. When Lisbet had first visited me in the hospital and seen my burned face and damaged lips, I told her that my physical therapist was insisting that I do a lot of kissing to assist my lip recovery. That had made her laugh and gotten me a kiss. Even though my lips were still raw and cracked from the fire, they were on the mend, and I was convinced Lisbet's lips were working miracles.

As the elevator door opened, I started to loudly hum "The Shoop Shoop Song," which got the desired effect of Lisbet's laugh. I loved it that she got all of my references without explanations. I didn't need to sing the words; she already knew the lyrics, and she already knew the meaning behind my kisses. As the door closed, she blew me a kiss. I felt good but maybe just the tiniest bit guilty. There had been no lie in my kiss, but there might have been a little dissembling. The truth is, I couldn't wait to read the newspaper article that Lisbet had brought. Cops can fall in love, but they're still cops.

I hurried back to my room and then tore into the article. When I finished reading, I decided that I wasn't going to wait until morning to check myself out of the hospital.

* * *

Both my doctor and Sirius's vet wouldn't have approved of our doing stakeout duty, but the two of us were doing just that.

When we'd arrived at the cemetery, I'd scouted the best viewing area for the Garden of Angels. I'd brought binoculars, which allowed us to park outside the grounds and still be able to have a good vantage spot. Before settling in I'd checked Rose's grave marker. My business card, with work, cell, and home numbers on it, was still taped to her cross.

Sirius doesn't mind stakeout duty as much as I do because he invariably sleeps through it. Any cop will tell you there's nothing as tedious as working a stakeout. Einstein once explained his Theory of Relativity by saying, "When you are courting a nice girl an hour seems like a second. When you sit on a red-hot cinder a second seems like an hour. That's relativity." Einstein's explanation of relativity makes sense to me. When you're doing a stakeout, time slows. It's watching and waiting, but mostly it's just waiting.

Maybe Rose's mother hadn't had classes that day. Or it was possible she never looked at the student newspaper. There was no guarantee she was even a student at Cal State, Los Angeles, and even if she was, the idea of her showing up was probably just wishful thinking on my part. She had left Rose in a cardboard box at night to fend for herself. That didn't make her mother-of-the-year material. Why would anything in the way of maternal responsibility kick in now? Her baby had been dead for almost two weeks, and any grieving she might have done was likely to have played out by now. And anyway, self-preservation would probably keep her away. The farther she kept from Rose, the less chance she'd have of ever being discovered.

There were those reasons and dozens more for Rose's mother to not show up. There was only one thing that made me think she might appear at her baby's grave: Rose's pink bootees. I wanted to hate the woman, and I felt the need to arrest her, but she hadn't abandoned her child in the way my mother had me. I was left to die, while Rose was left to live. My survival was a fluke; Rose's death was a terrible accident. But it was still a crime. And it was my job to redress it.

I checked the time: half past nine. We'd been in the car for more than an hour. Even Einstein probably would have agreed it felt like at least eight hours. I kept rubbing my hands. I had forgotten how cold the desert can be on a cloudless January night. It felt more like Siberia than Southern California. The cold wasn't playing well with my body, in particular those parts of my flesh that had burned. It felt like I was on fire again.

That wasn't something I wanted to be thinking. I didn't want to jinx myself. During my stay in the hospital I hadn't awakened on fire, hadn't been tortured by my old nightmare. It seemed almost too good to be true, but maybe I wasn't the burning man anymore. Or it could have just been the heavy-duty pain meds I was taking.

Sleep—especially sleep without my pyre—was sounding better and better.

More time passed. In my two hours at the cemetery there had been no visitors to the grounds. That made sense, of course. The cemetery was closed. Besides, no one in their right mind would visit on such a chilly, dark evening.

My hand kept reaching for the ignition key, but each time I pulled it back. I tried to check the time no more than once every five minutes, but kept falling short of that mark. It was that damn relativity again.

I'll leave at 9:45, I promised myself.

A few minutes later that time came and passed, but I still didn't leave. It was easier for me to make a new promised departure time. I'll take off at 10:00, I told myself. At 10:05 I pretended that I'd meant 10:15.

At 10:08 I noticed the headlights. The car was an old American sedan, a Buick, but the light wasn't good enough to make out its driver. The car slowed at the driveway leading to the cemetery and then passed by it. I let out a lot of air at the false alarm.

Four minutes later the car was back. This time it pulled into the driveway. Instead of parking out back, the car came to a stop in the shadows about halfway down the drive.

Sylvia Espinosa's article had been very specific about the location of the Garden of Angels. The car was parked near the pathway that led to it. The driver turned off the ignition.

I raised the binoculars. The driver was sitting in the dark, and the night prevented me from being able to see much. The shadow in the driver's seat didn't move for a long time. There wasn't a second shadow, and there were no steamed-up windows, so the driver hadn't pulled in for a make-out session.

In my gut I knew it was Rose's mother sitting in the car. She was ready to be spooked. Most people are freaked out by visiting cemeteries at night. Don't be afraid, I thought. All is well. I tried to breathe normally and keep my racing heart in check. I didn't want to put the vibe out there, didn't want to scare her away. I'm superstitious that way. I kept thinking soothing, calming thoughts.

The door finally opened, and as she stepped out I snapped off a few pictures. I was working without a flash and operating the camera in its night mode. After clicking, the shutter exposure was so slow it seemed to be on a time delay.

She began walking toward the Garden of Angels. Her face was obscured in shadows, but she looked young. She was wearing jeans and a black jacket. I wondered if she'd already burned her CSULA eagle sweatshirt.

Halfway down the walkway, she stopped and raised her hand to her heart. She looked like she was scared, or uncertain, or both.

If she got cold feet, I'd have to be prepared to intercept her. I eased out of the car, moving as quietly as I could. Sirius was awake now, but I whispered to him to be quiet and stay behind. I crept forward, keeping to the shadows, drawing closer to the woman. Along the way I stopped to take some shots of her car and its license plate.

I turned my attention back to the garden, but it took me a few moments to make out where she was standing. She had come to a stop among the crosses and was standing so still she could have passed for a statue.

And then the statue started crying.

Being a witness to anguish is a part of every cop's job. During my career I've seen too much suffering, but this was emotion at its rawest. Some people need to emote to an audience; it's almost like their pain can only register if seen by others. Rose's mother wasn't like that, and her misery seemed all the more profound because she thought she was alone.

Her body shook as she cried, and each wail was worse than the last, even though I didn't know how that could be. As I heard her talk to her dead baby, as all her despair poured out, I silently backed away. Her confession was too painful to hear; her pain was too painful to bear.

I made it back to what I thought would be the safety buffer of my car, but even though I couldn't hear I could still see, and that was bad enough. I was forced to watch as Rose's mother beat on her own head without mercy, and just when I thought I'd have to intervene for her own safety, she fell exhausted to the cold ground, done in by her own hands. But even then she wasn't through hurting herself. I saw her hand rise and fall, and I realized she was pulling out clumps of her own hair.

Finally, her hands full of hair, she crawled over to Rose's grave, and there on bent knees she prayed. Her prayer took a long time. Most of the time she was shaking so hard it was a wonder that she managed to keep from falling over.

I was clothed in rectitude, and I tried to tell myself that her sorrow did not change the situation, but her misery hollowed out my beliefs and made them feel brittle.

At last she stood up. Through binoculars I watched as she touched her daughter's memorial cross and then saw her fingers pause on my card. She brought her head closer to read the writing and see what was there. Then she freed my card from the gravestone.

As she made her way back to the car, she passed several spots that were well enough illuminated for me to get a good look at her. It was a face I wouldn't ever forget, even if I wanted to. My face bears the scars from fire, and it has turned many an eye away. The hurt that showed on her face, the pain that registered there, was much harder to look at than my scars.

It was time to intercept her before she reached her car. It was time to make the arrest.

Maybe I'd be doing her a favor. It was clear that she needed to pay for her sins. That's what I told myself the whole time she was walking to her car.

Wasn't I the one who said the law was the law? It wasn't my job to judge. I was supposed to uphold the law, and that meant processing this woman through the system.

She reached her car, and I didn't stop her. I watched as she drove away.

CHAPTER 23:

SURELY THERE IS A FUTURE

By the time I got home my body was hurting, and that gave me an excuse to take my pain and sleeping meds. I didn't want to think about what I had seen and what I had done, or not done, and what I would do.

The horns of a dilemma were deep into me, and no solution seemed right. I was afraid what I'd seen was going to bring on my burning dreams, but that didn't happen. I slept through the night and woke up at a quarter to six. Without my dreams I had no second sight, and the new day did not bring me any resolution to my problem.

I had witnessed how distraught Rose's mother was, but in this world, tears don't count.

My cell phone started ringing. The display said, "Caller unknown." Whoever was calling me didn't have caller ID.

I answered the phone, and a second later the caller clicked off. It could have been a wrong number, I knew, but I was betting that Rose's mother had been on the other line.

I decided to take my own bet. If the mother came to me and didn't force me to go to her, I would take that as my sign. If she gave herself up, she had to know she was looking at jail time. Her coming forward also meant that she was willing to accept the rest of the consequences. She would be a pariah, shunned by friends and family. The community would look upon her as a monster.

Most people would do anything to avoid that.

She had taken my card from Rose's grave marker, though. And she had come to the grave. I had seen her suffering. The responsibility for her actions weighed heavily upon her. But would she call the cop? Would she confess her sins?

My cell phone was mute.

Fear usually trumps any and all motives. Everyone professes to want to do the right thing; doing it is another matter. It is the rare murderer that offers up a confession that hasn't been coerced one way or another.

My cell phone rang again. "Detective Gideon," I said.

No one said anything back, and just as I was convinced the caller had clicked off she said, "This is Inez Vargas. I'm calling about..."

She started crying, and the harder she tried to talk the more she failed. Her speech was high pitched and unintelligible if you didn't know what was behind it. I knew what was behind it.

"I know what you're calling about, Inez," I said, "and we need to talk. Is there a place we can meet? How about a coffee shop near to where you live?"

It took her a few seconds to clear her throat and be able to speak. In a little voice she was finally able to say, "Do you know the Twelfth Street Coffee Shop?"

"I'll be there in forty-five minutes," I promised.

Inez was sitting at a table in the corner. She wasn't looking up, and made no motion in my direction. An untouched cup of coffee sat on the table in front of her. Only when I sat down did she look up. Her face was pale and drawn, and dark circles dominated her features. She wasn't wearing makeup and had on the same clothes she'd been wearing the night before.

"I'm Detective Gideon."

She nodded but said nothing. My appearance didn't frighten her or interest her. She was already in prison.

A server came along, and I ordered coffee and toast. When the server left, Inez's eyes briefly met mine. "I think I should kill myself," she said, "even though it's a sin, but that will be just another sin, and maybe it will make up for what I did."

"Don't say anything else to me. Let me talk."

Inez was on the heavy side but had a pretty face—or it would have been pretty had the murder of her daughter not weighed upon her. At that moment, she appeared as if she was nineteen going on ninety.

"There's a story you need to hear."

I had no right to be doing what I was doing, but I did it anyway. It was the only way Inez was ever going to have a normal life.

"I know you called to give me information about the newborn that was named Rose found at the Angel's Flight landing."

Tears filled her eyes and she nodded.

"Yesterday I got back the coroner's report with the results from Rose's autopsy. The coroner originally thought she died of suffocation, but as it turned out, Rose was born with a heart defect. I don't know all the fancy medical terms, but the doctor said that Rose had a congenital condition that couldn't have been treated. He told me that even had Rose been born in a hospital with all the best neonatal facilities, she would have died by morning."

The permafrost that was Inez's face began to thaw. Something resembling relief, or at least something short of complete despair, showed in her features.

"She would have died?"

"Nothing could have prevented that."

"But she didn't get the right vitamins, or the right care. If she had…"

"Even if she'd had the best prenatal care in the world, she would have died. That's what the doctor told me."

Her eyes took in mine. She made my glance a lifeline, and I had to support the burdens weighing so heavily on her. I didn't blink.

"Yes?" she begged.

"Yes," I said.

"She was so beautiful."

My coffee and toast arrived, and the two of us stopped talking for a minute.

"Jail won't be so bad now," she said.

I surprised myself by saying, "I am not going to arrest you."

Inez shook her head. That didn't sound right, even to her. "I should be punished for what I did."

"Normally you would be, but Rose's heart condition changed things."

Inez started to silently cry. I handed her some napkins. We didn't talk for a few minutes while she tried to control her emotions. Our server came over to make sure everything was all right, and I nodded to thank her for her concern, and with my eyes tell her the situation was under control.

"I didn't know I was pregnant until a few weeks ago," she said. "I've always been heavy. When I realized what was happening to me, I kept thinking it wasn't possible. You see, there was only the one time."

I nodded, encouraging her to keep talking.

"I couldn't tell my family. The shame would have killed them. And I didn't know what to do, or who to talk to. I did a lot of praying. I kept hoping my problem would just somehow disappear."

She reached for another napkin and wiped away some more tears.

"I didn't know I could turn in the baby like the paper said you could. I thought if I gave the baby up, I'd have to answer all kinds of questions."

For once, I hadn't come to ask questions. I was there to listen and occasionally nod.

"I even thought about becoming a nun," she said. "It made sense at the time."

Inez dabbed her eyes. The tears weren't falling as fast anymore. "When I left her there, I made sure she was warm. I thought it was a good spot for her to be found quickly. And I always liked the name of that spot: Angels Flight."

A glimmer of a smile appeared on her face.

"Do I need to go with you?" she asked. "Will I have to talk to other people?"

I shook my head. "But I do need you to promise me something. You can never talk about this with anyone else."

Her eyebrows furrowed. "Why?"

"Even though Rose died of natural causes, you abandoned her, and that's against the law. I don't want to have to arrest you, and the DA doesn't want to have to prosecute you, because it's a case we can't win. It would be easier for us if you just said nothing. Do you think you can do that?"

Inez nodded.

The waitress came to the table with the check and asked if we needed anything else. I told her we didn't, then handed her a Jackson and said no change was needed.

"So, what do I do now?" Inez asked.

When Father Pat had baptized me for the first time and hadn't known if I would live, he'd offered to my ears only his Whispered Verse of Assurance. Not all priests include such a verse in their ceremonies. When the baptized child is old enough, the verse is revealed. It's supposed to be a biblical verse that's easy to memorize, and one that reassures. Father Pat hadn't known I would live. Maybe that's why he'd chosen Proverbs 23:18 for me. I passed on his words to this girl that was so in need of them.

I reached for a package of sweetener, emptied it on my plate and in small lettering wrote down the following on the paper: "Psalm 23:18."

"That's your psalm now," I said. "It was given to me once, and now I am giving it to you. Remember these words always: 'Surely there is a future, and your hope will not be cut off.'"

I said the same words to her that Father Pat had whispered in my ears when I was a newborn. Then I handed her the paper where I'd noted the psalm number and walked away.

CHAPTER 24:

JUST ANOTHER BRICK IN THE WALL

It was a warm, sunny day when the three of us took a drive to the Garden of Angels. For most of the drive, Sirius kept his head out the window. Lisbet thought it was funny the way the wind sometimes blew his lips back, and Sirius seemed to be happy to accommodate her laughter.

Right after I met with Inez Vargas, I told Lisbet everything that had happened. Everyone needs a confessor. And in her arms she absolved me of my cop sins of omission. We talked about Rose and justice, and I told Lisbet I wanted to get a memorial brick for her.

"What do you want your brick to say?" she asked.

"I'm not sure," I told her. "I've been trying to think of some poetic line involving a Rose, but nothing seems right."

"It will come to you," she promised.

For a few days we went back and forth before I settled on a quote from *The Little Prince*. Because of his Rose, the Little Prince had gone on a great journey. The Little Prince said his Rose had "cast her fragrance and radiance over me." My Rose had done the same, and I was better off for her. Rose had brought many unexpected blessings into my life. That doesn't happen with most homicides.

Lisbet and I made our way to the brick memorial. Sirius stayed in the car. He needed a nap from all his wind wrestling.

In my hands was another brick for the collection. Maybe the band Pink Floyd was wrong. Maybe this wouldn't be just another brick in the wall. Maybe one day soon there wouldn't be any need for more bricks in this garden.

Lisbet prepared the spot for me; I played the mason, working the brick into its place in the ground. There was no attribution on the brick, just Antoine de Saint-Exupéry's words: "The Stars are beautiful, because of a flower that cannot be seen."

We stood there silently for a minute until I said, "Ready to go?"

"Are you?" Lisbet asked.

I nodded, and she offered her hand, and together we found our way out.

EPILOGUE:

"867-5309/JENNY"

Finally, I called the number. For days I had been holding on to it, deliberating the pros and cons of making contact. It was late when I called, well after midnight, but he was expecting my call.

"Dr. Livingstone, I presume?"

"If the DOC catches you with a phone, they'll throw you in the hole."

"After our conversation, this phone will be in a thousand pieces."

"Too bad you couldn't be in a thousand pieces."

"Is that any way to thank me for your gifts?"

During my stay in the hospital, Sirius and I had received a number of presents. The chief had sent me a fruit basket and Sirius a bone. Central Community Police Station sent us a dozen doughnuts. No one ever said cop humor was a good thing. There were plants and flowers and lots of get-well cards.

I also received an overnight mailer with two CDs inside. The package had been addressed to me care of the hospital, with no return address. The only identification had been an LA postmark.

The first CD featured the music of Robert Goulet. If Haines had wanted to insult my taste in music, I suppose he could have sent me the Disney rendition from the movie *Pocahontas*. According to the song's credits, the lyrics were by Alan J. Lerner, and the music by Frederick Loewe. They had written it for the musical *Paint Your Wagon*.

Sending me the song was Haines's idea of a little joke: "They Call the Wind Mariah."

The second CD had struck even closer to home. I didn't want Haines to know that, though, for fear he might decide to belt it out on his next late night call. He had sent me a rerelease from 2003 that featured Tommy Tutone performing "867-5309/Jenny."

"I tossed your gifts in the trash," I said. "I should have tossed your number as well."

He laughed, knowing I was lying. It bothered me that Haines had reached out and dirtied that which should have remained unsullied. "Jenny" might not have been our song, but it was a special song—special because it was my wife's name—and he had tarnished that magic. I had frequently gone around whistling the tune just to make Jenny smile. It's a catchy song—and number—that people remember. When Tommy Tutone released "867-5309/Jenny" in 1982, it drove the phone company crazy from all the complaints caused by young men calling the number and asking for Jenny.

Haines sensed my resentment, or he read my thoughts. "I used your sentiment to get your attention," he said. "You wouldn't have noticed the number if it hadn't been written in behind your deceased wife's name. It was for your eyes only and a precaution in the event your mail was being monitored."

When I'd looked at Jenny's name on the CD packaging, I had noticed some discoloration. After pulling out the CD sleeve I'd found the number written on the opposite side of "867-5309/Jenny" and had known it was the handiwork of Haines. I had debated whether to call him or turn him in.

"Am I supposed to tell you how clever you are?"

"The true realization would be how predictable you are."

"You're clever and I'm predictable. Anything else?"

"I am glad you are well. How is Sirius?"

"Why do you ask?"

"There is a connection between us."

"You drink out of the toilet too?"

"That night forever changed all of us. It forged a kinship."

"That's all in the past."

"Is it? I understand you dream as I do, and have the dream that isn't a dream. Both of us continue along in our fire walk. But where are we going?"

"I don't know what you're talking about."

"The only difference between us is that I embrace the fire, whereas you resist it."

"If you like fire so much, you've got hell to look forward to."

"Do you get the same wonderful insights that I do from our fiery walks? I call them the gift of the phoenix."

"What I want now is the gift of silence."

"I hope that one day you will be able to be honest with me. I know you are afraid, but you shouldn't be."

"You're the one who has a date with the needle, not me."

"Give Sirius a hug from me."

"I'd be afraid he might get rabies."

"I am glad you have found love again. It provides you with a vigor you were missing."

I didn't say anything. I would never whisper Lisbet's name to Haines. She was off the table.

"Don't call me in the middle of the night again," I told him. "If you feel the urge to sing, wake up one of your neighbors."

"I will respect your wishes. Good night, Michael Gideon."

"Do let the bed bugs bite," I said.

I listened to the dial tone for a dozen seconds or more but couldn't shake the feeling that he was still on the line.

ALSO BY ALAN RUSSELL

Other novels by Alan Russell:

NO SIGN OF MURDER

THE FOREST PRIME EVIL

THE HOTEL DETECTIVE

THE FAT INNKEEPER

MULTIPLE WOUNDS

SHAME

EXPOSURE

POLITICAL SUICIDE

ABOUT THE AUTHOR

Critical acclaim has greeted Alan Russell's novels from coast to coast. *Publishers Weekly* calls him "one of the best writers in the mystery field today." *The New York Times* says, "He has a gift for dialogue," while the *Los Angeles Times* calls him "a crime fiction rara avis." Russell's ten novels have ranged from whodunits to comedic capers to suspense, and his works have been nominated for most of the major awards in crime fiction. His novels have garnered him a Critics' Choice Award, the Lefty (awarded to the best humorous mystery of the year), and two San Diego Book Awards. A native and longtime resident of California, Alan Russell is a former college basketball player who these days barely can touch the rim. A proud father of three children, Russell is an avid gardener and cook, and fortunately is blessed with a spouse who doesn't mind weeding or washing dishes.